THE SWEET HILLS OF FLORENCE

Jan Wallace Dickinson has lived and worked in both Italy and Australia for more than twenty-five years. She has a wide range of commercial and academic experience at all levels, in both countries. Her particular interest is Italian literature and history, and she has worked as an editor, translator and bookseller.

Ai partigiani

For Alice and Tom

THE SWEET HILLS OF FLORENCE

Jan Wallace Dickinson

HYBRID
PUBLISHERS

Published by Hybrid Publishers

Melbourne Victoria Australia

First published 2018

ISBN 9781925272840 paperback
ISBN 9781925282542 ebook

Cover design by Art on Order

 A catalogue record for this
book is available from the
National Library of Australia

LIST OF CHARACTERS

Anna Maria: elderly servant, husband Sesto

Annabelle Albizzi: youngest child of Achille (Papà) and Eleanora (Mamma)

Benito Mussolini (Ben, Il Duce): leader of National Fascist Party, Prime Minister

Bruno: Ben's son who died

Carla (Elena) Capponi: works for underground, loves Paolo

Clara (Claretta) Petacci: Mussolini's lover, daughter of Dr Francesco and Giuseppina Petacci

Delia (Dellie): youngest child of Umberto (Bert) and Madeleine Morton (Maddie), sister of Frank and Tom, granddaughter of Achille

Edda (Countess Ciano) and Galeazzo Ciano: daughter and son-in-law of Mussolini

Elena: Mussolini's daughter from mistress Angela Curti Cucciati, works in his office

Elsa Albizzi: Annabelle's aunt, mother of Enrico

Enrico: Francesco and Elsa's only son, Achille's nephew, first cousin to Annabelle and Delia

Francesco Albizzi: Achille's older brother, Annabelle's uncle, father of Enrico

Giacomo: Annabelle's brother

'little' Anna Maria: Ben's daughter who is not normal

Lorenzo (Enzo): Annabelle's second cousin; son of Michele and Elisabetta

Marcello (Marc): Clara's brother

Myriam (Mimi): Clara's sister

Nonna Annabelle: Annabelle Drummond, Australian, mother of Achille & Francesco, grandmother of Annabelle, for whom she was named

Nonna Lucrezia: Annabelle's great-grandmother

Rachele Guidi: Mussolini's wife

Roberto: second cousin to Annabelle and Enrico

Romano: Ben's son

Rosario (Paolo) Bentivegna: works for underground

Umberto (Bert), Annabelle's brother

Vittorio: Ben's eldest son

PART ONE

CHAPTER 1

Florence 1941
The Day of the Dead

Mussolini did not feel the rain. Straining tall in the open tourer beside his great friend, the Führer, his exaltation would have overcome a blizzard. The Official State Visit. All the pomp of the preceding visits had paved the way for this. It was a long way from Predappio. He would suffer now with his usual cold – could feel it coming on, but just this once he did not care. He clenched his teeth, praying his nose would not drip. He clenched his hands too, arms rigid at his sides, legs wide apart to maintain his balance in the lurching vehicle. Chest puffed to bursting point, he managed to maintain his stony expression, only with great effort. A certain dignity was required, and really, the difference in height between him and Hitler was barely a few centimetres.

'We passed like two gods over the clouds,' he boasted to Clara that evening.

The streets glistened. The wheels of the cavalcade sucked and slobbered at the paving stones and tram tracks, spraying grubby water onto the shoes and trousers of the welcoming citizens. *Duce! Duce! Duce! Heil Hitler! Heil Hitler!*

Standing beside her father, Annabelle could smell his rage, more pungent than sweat.

'*Pagliaccio! Fantoccio! Vigliacco!*' Quietly. The time for shouting was past. A clown, a puppet, a coward. Achille would rather be dead than see this day – he said it over and over – but he had Annabélle and her mother to think about. Hysteria, he said. Hysteria. His long, narrow face was more lugubrious than ever. The chanting and salutes soared on the frosty air. A brass band played.

In sunshine, the colours of Florence were golden: ochre, sienna, umber. In today's rain, the colours seeped and ran together into grey and greyer. Achille averted his eyes from the sodden swastikas drooping from the buildings, their scarlet and black piercing the drear of the day – the only colour anywhere. His muttering was in monotone too – he wondered they hadn't put them on the Duomo as well ... his own father saw that icing-sugar facade go up after so many centuries ... thank God he was dead and couldn't see this, not that he, Achille, believed in God ... only an expression. And so on and so on.

November, the worst weather of the year. Annabelle's nose and eyes were streaming, her lacy handkerchief a soggy mess. Her father handed her his own sensible, monogrammed one. She blew and wiped and sniffled, facing the procession. Her eyes flicked back and forth like a small animal in a forest, searching the crowd for Enrico. *Please let him have stayed away, or if he came, please let him not do anything stupid, or if he did, please let him get away.*

'The imbecile,' said Achille. 'The country is broke, the army is a shambles, Italians are dying like flies in Russia, they've already surrendered in Africa and he still thinks he can ingratiate himself with that bastard. March on Rome! He did not march on Rome. He caught an overnight sleeper from Milan!'

Mumbling, grumbling, rumbling to himself – Annabelle had heard it all before. For the first time she thought of her father as old. His words formed bubbles of condensation like word-bubbles in cartoons. She prayed they could not be read here. Even in the house now, they had to whisper. The servants in town could no longer be trusted and neither could the *contadini* on the farm. It was appropriate tomorrow was All Souls Day, her father continued. The Day of the Dead. There were already too many dead in Mussolini's wake.

Now, as the cavalcade swept by, Achille sighed deeply. 'Let us hope it is over quickly.'

Did he mean the visit or the war? Annabelle shivered and pulled her coat tighter. Only last year they had stood here beneath a blue,

4

blue June sky, listening to Mussolini's voice booming from the loud-speakers: 'An hour marked by Destiny is striking in the sky of our country.' They were officially at war. Today, the sky was pewter, steel, lead.

'Let's go,' said Achille, taking her arm to steer her against the surging tide. His nose was also running, but he did not have another handkerchief. With the back of his glove, he wiped at tiny droplets on the hairs of his nostrils and moustache. His greatcoat was wet through. He was only there because, like her, he was frightened for Enrico. As the motorcade and its roaring motorcycles neared Piazza Signoria, the crowd congealed to a solid mass, a single entity, a heaving and tossing restive animal. The cheering rolled in waves. Annabelle was not cheering. Many around her were not cheering. The tannoys on every corner spewed recorded cheering for them. Over the top of it, the trumpets from the balcony of Palazzo Vecchio heralded Hitler's arrival at the Town Hall. Annabelle plodded beside her father, eyes raking the swirl of people, ears straining for the sound of shots or confusion. Nothing. Deep in the pockets of her coat she curled her fingers tight. Her chest was tight too, but it seemed Enrico and his friends had done nothing stupid, for today.

'Are you going back out or staying in town, Papà?' she asked.

'No, I have an appointment with Aldo,' Achille replied. 'Do you want to go back to the country? It will be hard to get there today with all this confusion.'

'No. I'll stay with you.' That way she could search for Enrico.

Achille nodded. 'Talk some sense into your cousin.'

The saturated wool of her stockings pooled in heavy rings at her ankles. She hated the itch and smell of wet wool. Her plaited hair, normally so fair, was dark with rain and her head itched as much her stockings. Her father's hat was soaked. It would be ruined – the brim dripped like his nose. They turned down via Roma. At least here, he rambled, via Roma really did once lead to Rome ... via Roma ... via Roma ... Annabelle's mind strayed. As they stepped from the kerb, her father put out a restraining arm to stop her walking into the path of a sleek grey and black Lancia. In the rain, the powerful car purred and gleamed like a wet panther. As it slowed to turn, Annabelle saw a driver in peaked cap and uniform, and in the back, a young woman in a dark fur coat, soft and high about her throat. Long, pearl drop-earrings bobbed against the fur. Glossy dark curls, a pale, oval face. As she leaned forward to speak to the driver, one gloved hand on the back of the seat, she glanced out the window into Annabelle's eyes and away again. Annabelle's gaze followed the car as it glided off in a spray of dirty water. Her father gave a soft *hrmmph* and took her firmly by the elbow, turning her towards home. In answer to her unasked question, he muttered to her to get a move on because he did not have all day.

Annabelle squelched from foot to foot on the carpet before the fire-place in her father's study.

Achille put his head around the door. 'I shall be back for dinner. It will be better if you stay in today, *Tesoro*. The streets are no place to be. Take off those wet shoes.'

He said nothing about the soggy patches on his Persian rug.

Annabelle nodded. She was not going anywhere. She waved her father off. The streets were never any place to be. Certainly not in her lifetime. Right from the Renaissance, really, and before. Florence, City of Strife. Her father had taught Classics at the university until he took early retirement rather than wear a Fascist Party badge. He had not worked since Annabelle was seven or eight. She had little memory of him working. Neither had *Zio* Francesco ever held a job that she knew of. He devoted himself to the oversight of the family investments and factories in the north.

Things would not be the same after the war. Enrico said so. Fear of Communism and the Bolsheviks and their land and labour reforms had made the upper classes wilfully blind to the excesses of the Black Shirts these last twenty years. They despised the fascists but were willing to allow them to do the dirty work. Enrico said so. The world has to change, he said, often. And not 'so that all could remain the same'. Nothing would be the same. Enrico said so. Annabelle was permanently afraid. Everyone of her age had grown up afraid. She was tired of being treated as a child, ready to revolt, to take a hand in changing things, like Enrico – whatever he was doing.

Rain tinkled at the mullioned windows. She loved her father's study with its burnished bronzes and gleaming walnut furniture. The patina of age and permanence mantled everything in a glow of safety, but there was no comfort for her there today. In the mirror above the marble fireplace the air trembled with the rising steam of her damp clothes, but she did not want to go upstairs to change. Enrico really was too difficult! He was thoughtless and completely irresponsible. Her father said so and it was true. She ached to look for him but she did not know where to start. She waited with a clutch in her stomach for what seemed like hours – and then he was there, face flushed, eyes burning. His clothes and hair were soaked.

'Where were you?'

His breathing galloped wildly. 'I was there. I saw you and *Zio* but I had to go to a meeting as soon as the cavalcade passed. Did you see those two arrogant crazy bastards!' It was not a question. 'Papà says that's what you get when you put two teetotallers together.'

He did not laugh and neither did Annabelle.

'The crowd was so thick I could hardly move.' Her hands balled into fists by her sides. 'I was afraid for you.'

His hair was wet too. A darker blond than hers, more light brown really, it was fine and very thick, even if the high forehead and sharp widow's peak did not bode well for his hairline in the future.

Enrico's breath settled but he was still taut with excitement. 'Italians! There they are, the heroes, on their way to sign away more lives for Hitler's war. Italian lives are cheap to Benito anyway.'

They had taken to calling him Benito between themselves but the irreverence failed to lessen the fear.

Now Enrico was safe, however, Annabelle had other things on her mind. 'Is it true you went with Clarice?'

Her chin jutted and her voice wobbled. The daughter of friends, Clarice was seventeen, the same age as Enrico. Annabelle overheard him getting a dressing-down from his father last night, for an escapade with Clarice.

'*Ficanaso*. Stickybeak.' Enrico smiled. He flicked the tip of her reddened nose with her damp plait. 'Went with! Mind your own business, *Ciccia*. You have been spying on Papà and *Zio* again. Listening behind doors. My little worry wart.' His indulgent grin made her want to spit at him.

He too smelled of steaming wool. She could smell his sweat, a sugary-smell. Caramel.

At fifteen, Annabelle was already tall but Enrico towered over her by a full head and he was still growing. It was their Australian blood on the distaff side. Their Australian grandmother, Nonna Annabelle, Annabelle Drummond from Orange, was tall for a woman of those times and she came from a long line of males much taller. All that sunshine and food. Annabelle was named for her but her grandmother died when Annabelle was three. Orange, what a beautiful name for a town.

Australia was a ridiculous shape on the map, a whole country in a single continent. Imagine having a whole continent, all to yourself! A continent at the bottom of the known world. Further than the moon. The Gumnut babies lived there. Her mother read stories of Snugglepot and Cuddlepie from an old book with magical images of cherub babies with fat little bottoms, who lived in exquisite flowers, the *putti* of her Renaissance ceilings transposed to the New World. In another book, exotic creatures ate from a pudding that never got smaller. Antipodean fables were so much lighter and sunnier than the European myths and legends of vengeful Gods and poor children. She listened to all the stories – all of them, the old ones and the new ones, and she melted into them and tried on the lives she found there. What else did she have to do?

Annabelle had never seen Australia but when a distant cousin was executed by the fascists, Papà sent her brothers there, to relatives, to save them from being drafted into Mussolini's army, or shot. It had been more than two years. Enrico was to have gone but now it was too late. He would never have gone anyway. She missed Giacomo and Umberto, and the whispers in the house frightened her. What *was* internment?

In Annabelle's family there were more cousins than she could count. No-one of her age except Enrico, and Lorenzo, a little younger. Annabelle and Enrico had shared every story and every secret since they could talk. Now, most conversations between his father and hers about Enrico – half-heard, overheard and misheard – began with

'*Quel ragazzo* …' Annabelle had grown used to eavesdropping in a society where it was commonplace.

'That boy …' too had lived his whole life under the shadow of Il Duce, in a family that did not belong to the Party. At seventeen, he was in great danger. Soon, they feared, he would be conscripted for Mussolini's war, or – more frightening and more likely – be arrested for some act of rebellion and disappear into the maw of *Le Murate*.

Seen from above, in the newsreel Annabelle watched at the cinema afterwards, the crowd on the day of Hitler's state visit was a living organism, a brain-coral: a collective brain given over to a single function. Fascist propaganda newsreels were obligatory in cinemas before the screening of a film. In her short life, Annabelle had known no politics but that of Mussolini.

They had no contact with the main branch of the family and had long since parted ways with many friends and family as fascism drew a dividing line right through the middle of personal relations. Although she officially lived in the Kingdom of Italy, the flag of the National Fascist Party, with its gold Fasces and Axes, swamped the King's Tricolour. Fascist posters loomed everywhere and on everything. D'Annunzio extolled the Duce in poetry and Marinetti shaped the art world to his visions. Mussolini's thrusting jaw and bellicose oratory formed the backdrop to the daily events of her life. His bellowing voice bombarded every home with a wireless radio. It was only two years before Annabelle's birth that the first radio broadcast in Italy went to air, but the Regime took to it immediately and radios in bars, schools and fascist headquarters and buildings pumped out propaganda, day and night. Florence was a city of military uniforms, marching feet and blaring loudspeakers …

When she was small, Annabelle had pined to be allowed to join the Sons of the She Wolf. She watched with envy as girls between eight and eleven participated in the *Piccole Italiane*, with all their sports and games, or the *Balilla Giovani Italiani* physical education programs, with exercises such as 'farmers hoeing' and 'sailors rowing'. She gazed with wonder at their splendid uniforms with the 'M' on the buckle. She yearned to grow up to be part of the fascist *dopolavoro* circle, with all its sporting grounds and clubhouses and cinemas. What fun. But she was never permitted to take part in Mussolini's 'indoctrination program', as her father called it. The cover of her school notebook in fifth grade carried a striking image of a child in uniform at attention, a rifle with bayonet over his right shoulder and the words *Giovinezza in Marcia* – 'Youth on the March' – across the top. Her *pagella*, her school report, was adorned with the word *Vincere*. Win. Conquer. 'War,' said Il Duce, 'is to man what maternity is to women.' It was too much. That was Annabelle's last year of school. From then on, she was tutored at home.

London 2008
Memento mori

Delia checked the flashing screen. Her mother. There goes another half hour, she thought, watching her Blackberry jig across the wooden table beside *The Guardian*. Outside the window, Saturday people in Burberry and cashmere thronged Kensington High Street. She debated letting it go to message bank. Her mother was losing it a bit. Her father was worried too, but Bert was not given to confronting things before he had to. Her brother Tom was as hearty as ever: 'Come on, Dellie, Mum's always been vague.' Alzheimer's. No-one wanted to say the word aloud … Delia sighed and answered the phone brightly. 'Hi, Mum.'

Today, Maddie's voice was youthful and firm, though it must have been late in Sydney. 'Hello, darling. Your uncle Enrico died last night.'

'Shit!' Delia closed the newspaper and fished out her address book. 'I'll go over straight away. What happened?' … Whatever that means, she thought. Nothing had to happen. Enrico must be eighty-five, and hadn't been well for a while, but he always behaved as if death did not apply to him.

'Have you spoken to Belle?'

'No. I'm about to telephone her now, but I wanted you to know first.' Maddie had forgotten to reprimand her for swearing.

Delia rang off, found the number for British Airways and booked a flight to Florence for later that day. She ordered another coffee. Not that piss-weak French stuff this time, but a double-shot espresso. *And* an almond croissant. Why not! No matter how many almond croissants she denied herself, she never got any thinner … Enrico was not her uncle. He was her father's cousin and Annabelle's cousin, her second cousin. She had always called him *Zio* because he seemed too old to be a cousin. She sent a text to Annabelle who *was* her aunt, saying simply, 'I'm on my way. There this afternoon.' Between them, no more was necessary.

Florence

'Eight o'clock is too early to kill yourself.' Delia's tone was light but her heart was not in it. Beside her, Annabelle faced the television, hunched into her high-backed armchair, chin resting on her drawn-up knees.

'And nine o'clock will be too late,' she replied. 'I would like to kill somebody. Anybody will do.' The 8 pm *telegiornale* was only ten minutes in but it was all bad news. The polls had just closed and counting had barely begun, but it was already clear that Silvio Berlusconi would be catapulted back into power. A leap year, 2008. Delia loved that expression. Leap Year. It carried a sense of vitality, hope, joy even. For superstitious Italians though, an *anno bisestile* brought bad luck and it looked like they were right this time. It had turned out to be a leap back into the past, with little joy and no vitality. All day, the terms 'crushing victory' and 'greatest post-war majority' boomed from the media, and not only from Berlusconi's own TV channels.

Annabelle's hands were splayed into her hair on either side of her face, reminding Delia of the way, when she was a small child afraid of monsters, she used to peek at the cinema screen through her fingers. On the low table before them, the pizza from the Neapolitan place in the street below congealed, untouched, into what looked like vomit. No-one was going to eat that tonight. Delia gathered the plates, walked to the kitchen door where she tipped the triangles into the bin from on high, threw the box onto the bench and picked up another bottle of wine. It was going to be a long night. She should have cooked something. At the best of times neither Delia nor Annabelle was very interested in cooking, and this was not the best of times. It was not yet the worst of times but it was shaping up that way.

Delia followed Italian politics closely but they did not affect her except as an onlooker. She was resolutely Australian. She loved the orderly nature of Australian politics and civic life. She loved the way her Australian history was so close to her: so recent, newly formed, still evolving. White settlement was concurrent with the French Revolution; Achille, her grandfather, was born only fourteen years after Ned Kelly's trial in Beechworth. Although a Republican, she loved the ceremony of the old ways. The Queen and her aunt Annabelle came to Australia for her, the year she was born, she told a school friend in first grade ...

In the bluish flickering from the screen, Delia observed, almost as if she had not noticed before, the knotted joints of Annabelle's slender fingers and the vertical crevices at the sides of her face – suddenly she looked every one of her eighty-three years. It hurt Delia in her heart to see it, made her afraid. In Italy, Delia often found herself feeling like an indulged only child, in that country of only children. Annabelle was her rock, her mentor, her image of everything strong and dependable. She did not want to see fragility and vulnerability in her adored aunt. The ravages of time. Where on earth did that expression came from? Shakespeare? She wasn't strong on Shakespeare.

In the half-light, Delia spread her own hands before her, examining the slender, slightly squared fingers with deep, regular nails. A little on the large side for a woman but nice, capable hands all the same. The scarlet polish was not the only difference between her hands and Annabelle's. No sign of the inflammation and swelling at the joints that plagued Annabelle. Or not yet. Perhaps sixty was the turning point. Oh well, she still had a few years. Had to watch those kilos too. A kilo or two didn't matter now, but ... Delia was a bit apprehensive about sixty – it could hardly still be called middle age. The other milestone birthdays had come and gone without a blip on the graph but sixty ... Shouldn't you have more to show for sixty? A few books about dead Italians suddenly did not seem like all that much.

No husband? No children? Old ladies always asked that. The long and colourful procession of men had not turned up one who would have made husband material, or perhaps she was just not wife material. Certainly Marcus could not have been a father. As for children, she could have had them all the same; people did. Only it had never occurred to her. She saw a greeting card once with a woman, hand to mouth, saying, 'Oops, I forgot to have children'. Most of her friends did not have children. Were they friends though, or more colleagues, acquaintances? Annabelle regarded most of the people she knew as acquaintances. She seemed perfectly happy with that situation but she was much more self-contained than Delia. Her cousins, Enrico's daughters, Clare and Diana, were good company, but she could not recall ever having an intimate conversation with either of them.

Delia leaned to her father's side, sharing her emphatic nose and the deepening horizontal lines of her forehead with all her Italian family. The Albizzi strain was geometric – spare, angular. Delia and Annabelle had Bert's square jaw, thank God. It held things up well. Maddie tended to the curved and portly, her outline gently diffused as she aged, as if softly backlit, her waistline drowned in the ebbing tide of oestrogen. Maddie still looked like an hourglass, Bert joked, only with more hours in it. Delia worried about her weight and whether she should stop colouring her hair, but she could not be bothered worrying too much.

Bert radiated goodwill, though not given to conversation of any sort unless it was the price of sheep and wool. Maddie's chatter turned largely on the doings of the Royal family and their own circle. They were happiest now at the homestead, pottering arm in arm, admiring the camellias. In a recent photo, they reminded her of Malcolm and Tammie Fraser. Or the Queen and Prince Phillip. They drank cups of tea with their dinner, ignoring Delia's eye-rolling. They only occasionally went to Sydney these days and every couple of years, to London. They still loved London. Delia was born in London in the days when Bert and Maddie travelled by sea and stayed a year. They did not stay so long now and went less, as age overtook them. Maddie and Bert were fond, indulgent parents and she knew they loved her and were proud of her, even if she was a mystery to them, a bit of a cuckoo at times.

The boys, Tom and Frank, were made of the same prosaic stuff as their father. Both married girls from the country, settled on the family properties, wore RM Williams boots and lived exemplary lives. Neither of them had ever seen the need to learn Italian and their only overseas travel was to London. A bit suspicious of 'The Continent', they were. They were fond of Aunt Annabelle, but were amused and bemused by Delia's deep attachment to Italy. Their sons attended Knox, where they played Rugby and cricket. Their friends were from their own schooldays, as if they had all set in aspic in that formative period of their lives and lived there ever since. Decency and convention dictated that they avoided any form of thought or conversation deeper than the weather, sport and the local news.

Delia was very fond of all of them ... Fond, odd word. Was fond enough? she wondered. The word was used a lot in the family, as if they were afraid of anything deeper, wilder. The only person she was passionately attached to was Annabelle. How dare she show signs of mortality. The thought of Annabelle dying was like looking over the edge of an ice crevasse, into the endless blue depths of nothingness. It caused a pain in her chest: indigestion, heartburn. A burning of the heart.

Annabelle uncoiled from her chair and turned on two more lamps at the back of the study. At once the buttery light dispelled the ghostly pallor of the TV. Tensed and leaning forward to the screen, her thumbnail in the corner of her mouth, Annabelle was once again the fit, vibrant woman of daytime. She was still tall, straight, spare, and there was still as much goldish chestnut in her thick unruly hair as there was grey – testimony, as she put it, to the advantages of red wine and HRT. But Delia was unsettled. She had seen the skull at the bottom of the painting and the image was indelible. She could not unsee it.

Outside, beyond the milky glass of the ancient windows, Florence settled into evening. The Leap Year Florence of today. Florence, the modern city within the caul of a medieval one. Modern bars and restaurants vied with the Renaissance on every corner. Experimental art flourished alongside Botticelli, Brunelleschi and Masaccio. It was a city of jazz and modernity, where the past and the present and the future existed at once, within each other, like Calvino's *Invisible Cities*. At her gym, Delia endured the drudgery of the electronic treadmill beneath the pale blue and gold of vaulted, frescoed ceilings from the sixteenth century and voluptuous Venuses who certainly did not need to bother with gymnastics.

On the screen, the news ground to a conclusion. Throughout the election campaign Berlusconi had adopted fascist symbolism, attacked democracy as outdated, derided the Euro and EU and even claimed 'Mussolini never killed anyone, he just sent them on holiday'. Now, as his victorious leer filled the screen, both women stilled. Delia's jaw actually dropped and Annabelle's hand flew to her mouth. Wearing a black shirt and a hand-knitted hairline, his surgically reinvented face bulging with hubris, Silvio Berlusconi raised his arm to the nation in the fascist salute. *Viva l'Italia!*

'Noooo! This is too much!' Annabelle flung the remote control to the floor where it skidded across the tiles and shattered against the wall. The back flew off and the batteries rolled under the sofa. She launched herself across the room and gave a vicious jab to the off button of the TV. In the stillness, the batteries rocked back and forth, a metronome … The crisp April air carried the waft of shades passing. Delia shivered. Stop it, she told herself. It's because Enrico has died. It has spooked all of us. The End of an Era – historians could not help thinking in epochs and eras.

Annabelle collected the pieces of the remote and clattered them onto the side table. 'He did not have to see this. I cannot stay in this country any longer.'

Dealing with the past was much easier for Delia than for her aunt. Delia could simply decide not to revisit scenes of past pains or sadnesses, or indiscretions. She was good at moving on, leaving behind the past and all its accoutrements when it had outlived its usefulness, without a backward glance. Here in this old, old country, it was not so easy. For Annabelle, every day was lived on the same earth, beneath the same sky, on the same streets as the moments of her past, with all its tragedy and plangent memory. For Annabelle, Enrico, and all Italians, life had to be lived in all its quotidian mundaneness within the caul of a history of blood, passion, loss, love and hatred.

How do they bear it? she wondered. Does the power of the past leach slowly away when you walk its path every day? She could see that for Annabelle, the past existed in a dimension other than the physical and geographical, in a part of the mind and heart and memory having nothing to do with the external world. This, Delia realised, was yet another of the endless differences between Australians who roam the world and feel at home anywhere, and Italians with their visceral, atavistic attachment to soil and place. Much harder to escape the past here. It could very easily strangle you.

Annabelle's brothers, Giacomo and Umberto, arrived in Australia by ship in 1938. Giacomo hated it from the first moment. He would have refused to disembark if he'd had any choice. Umberto, on the other hand, felt the weight of centuries lift from his shoulders and rise into that illimitable sky. He had never actually had a job, after doing a half-hearted degree in architecture. He knew all about Palladian form and nothing about how to actually build a house. He knew immediately though, he wrote, that here he could be anything he wished. He could breathe here; the air was lighter. Umberto loved Sydney Harbour and he loved the lack of history. He loved the way Australians simply turned their faces to the sea and their backs to the vast, rust-coloured emptiness behind them. He loved New South Wales and he loved the broad vowels of his Australian neighbours and the clipped English ones of his relatives. He did not even mind the urine stench of the roast mutton all Australians seemed to eat for Sunday lunch, which they called dinner.

When Italy joined the war, they were interned. His brother took it as a personal affront but Umberto could see perfectly why Italians and Germans would be viewed with mistrust, and he knew from news from home that English and Australians were being treated in the same way in Italy. He also knew, though, that many other 'enemy aliens' in Australia suffered much more than they had. On their release at war's end, Giacomo took ship immediately for Italy and died on the voyage, of influenza. Giacomo had never been sturdy. Umberto happily worked out his time of internment as a labourer on the elegant property, Blackheath, belonging to the old grazing family, the Mortons. He married Madeleine Morton and within a few years, they had three children in rapid succession, of whom Delia was the last.

When Delia was born, he became Bert and renounced his Italian citizenship. He was naturalised. Neutralised, Delia called it as a child. She was reared mainly in English and she only spoke Italian on visits to Italy, or during her adored aunt Annabelle's many visits. Once she was able to travel to Florence without her parents, Delia grew used to her Italian life with her aunt, between worlds, in the ancient building in Borgo Pinti with its five floors of relatives. Her father rarely used his apartment there, and she and her mother preferred to stay with Annabelle when they visited. After a time the room she used became her room, reserved from other guests. It seemed natural that she would gravitate to Florence for her university studies and even more natural that those studies would revolve around the families who had made Florence and her forbears. While their history stifled Bert, Delia carried it lightly, it not having been forced upon her.

Delia came to terms early with her mixed heritage. Tom and Frank always found their Italian name a bit of a worry, happy for it to be Australianised. Delia insisted on the correct pronunciation. She had romantic pretensions and enjoyed her exotic image. Albizzi was a mouthful, certainly, but Australia was full of stranger names than that in those days – Poles with waxed moustaches, Lithuanians with sad eyes, Estonians, whatever that meant, Serbs and Croats who carried knives, and lots of other Italians, but Italians much smaller and darker than any she had seen. Most of them were there to build the Snowy River dam. Most of them did not speak English. Many of the Italians did not speak Italian. Neither did Tom and Frank. For the boys, Albo was the obvious nickname and it stuck. Albo and Albi – boys' schools were like that. St Catherine's was not. Delia was Dellie only at home.

Bert's was not the only title among his fellow internees, including one, he said, who claimed to be a prince: dime a dozen, Italian counts and barons. Always someone ready to take the piss – Bert learned a lot of his English from the shearers and jackaroos on the property. The King's English that Bert learned as a boy was a different language from the gnarly vowels and the sly, wry humour of the shearing shed. That was the 1950s. In the 1960s, in Sydney and especially in 'Swinging London', it was quite fashionable to have a Florentine connection.

When Delia made her laconic way to Sydney University in 1972, with not much idea of what she wanted to do apart from meet boys who were not friends of her brothers, it seemed logical she would jump at the chance for a ready-made subject and Italian history did not seem too hard. Nothing seemed hard in Australia then – the fizzy optimism of Gough Whitlam's ascension to the throne at home and the tempered hope of Nixon's visits to China and Russia, coursed through the veins at social gatherings, together with cask wine. By then, she had become used to travelling back and forth between Sydney and Florence. Completely smitten with her exotic aunt, she would have done anything to please her, but following her into medicine was not an option because Delia had not exactly distinguished herself in the sciences at school, so, history it was. She thought history might be useful, though at the time she could not have imagined falling beneath the spell of all the early Medici. She fell in love at first sight with the Laurentian library: the arched cloisters full of potted orange trees around the central well, honey-coloured stones full of secrets, the great church of San Lorenzo with its rough unclad façade and porphyry and marble tombs. The moment she saw the sensuous sweep of Michelangelo's majestic staircase and breathed in the heady scent of ancient books and young Italian professors, she realised history could also be sexy.

November 1, 1941

Our famous Duce could barely keep the grin off his face today. How I hate that man. I could kill him but I'm so afraid Enrico will. Papà is afraid. We are all afraid. I am tired of being afraid. I have been living with fear for as long as I remember of my life. All the fault of Il Duce. Enrico says it is the fault of Papà and Zio too and all of those who thought him a fool and did not oppose him.

'So you found them.' Delia leaned against the doorjamb, lanky, a little tense, with a nod at the diary in her aunt's hand. 'I could never keep a diary. I could not,' she said, 'even imagine committing to paper my innermost thoughts, let alone my secrets and indiscretions.' She snorted. 'Of which, I might add, there have been far too many.'

Delia had wanted to read Annabelle's wartime diaries ages ago, wanted to write something about her aunt's part in the rescuing of the art treasures looted by the Nazis. She had suggested Annabelle get the diaries out and go through them.

Annabelle had been resistant. No, she said. No. She had kept a diary since she was six years old. 'I never read them. I never look back. I have no desire to go back. If the past is another country, then I no longer speak the language there. Anyway, diaries should be burned. I'm not even sure where they are.'

Yet, here they were, piled precariously on the desk. Annabelle turned, trailing her finger across the brittle page. She closed the notebook on her finger, marking the place, and regarded the tottering pile of diaries. Some were in worse condition than others, but most were still pretty good really.

'I always ... I ... knew where they were. I haven't had any desire to get them out until now.'

Delia nodded at the newspaper clipping in her other hand. 'Is that it? Somehow it seems more official in the hard copy.'

Annabelle held it out to her. 'It came in today's post. The only time he did not have the last word!'

The piece of newsprint was much more real. So dry. Is that a life? Annabelle felt tremors from very deep within, which made her think of ground resonance. She once read that a helicopter, on landing badly, could shake itself to pieces if care were not taken. She took great care.

Delia crossed to her, put a hand on her back in a gentle caress and took the clipping. Backing up a couple of steps until she felt the sofa behind her knees, she sat, reading the *Sydney Morning Herald* obituary.

Enrico Francesco Albizzi 1925–2008

'Home is the sailor, home from the sea/and the hunter home from the hill.'

So he wished to be remembered, the distinguished Classicist, Professor Enrico Albizzi, who died this week in Sydney after a short illness. He was eighty-five. He leaves two daughters, the violinist Clare Morgan, and Dr Diana Croyden, whose work on tropical diseases is well known. Professor Albizzi immigrated to Australia in 1952 after completing his studies in Bologna. His translations of the early Roman poets are still used in schools today, and his recent translation of Marcus Aurelius from the Greek is credited with bringing the Stoic Emperor to a whole new generation. His fiery temperament added an edge to the Classics, said a fellow academic. He fought as a partisan in the Civil War in Italy, between 1943–45. He made a significant contribution to the nascent wine industry in Australia and was a well-known identity in the sailing fraternity, having participated in his first Sydney to Hobart yacht race in the year of his arrival. He only missed one race in the intervening years. His ashes will be scattered outside the Heads in a private family ceremony.

'Are you all right?'

Annabelle smiled at the question. So Australian. 'Am I all right? Yes, I suppose I am, my dear. We are all quite used to obituaries by now.' She stood very straight and bit her bottom lip hard.

'This isn't just any old obit though, is it?' said Delia.

Annabelle wandered to the window. Not just any old obituary. In the distance, thunder rolled.

It was nearly three years since Annabelle had seen Enrico and they did not part on good terms. He had been in Florence for something to do with the byzantine terms of his father's will and the trust. It was Annabelle's eightieth birthday and he'd insisted on taking her to lunch. He had something on his mind. We must talk, he said. Yes, she said. We must talk.

Always thin, Enrico was gaunt. His abundant white hair, still worn longish and brushed back, gave him the look of an aged lion. It had lasted him surprisingly well, given the high widow's peak and his father's early baldness. His eyes were unnaturally huge in the light refracted through the thick glass of his round spectacles. He was fading, like the Cheshire Cat. Soon there would be nothing left but his smile. It hurt her heart. Although he and Roberto had just completed a long walk in the Dolomites. He was actually as dogmatic and energetic as ever, despite being, surely, one of the last smokers in Australia – he had already been outside four times for a cigarette, cursing the recent laws that had finally arrived even in Italy. He was, as always, elegant and dashing in a soft linen jacket and open-neck shirt.

Too much wine loosened tongues. Too much talk. Too many words. Once words break free they cannot be reined in. Words traded, bartered, lying like stones on the table. For hours, they sat at the vast expanse of glass at the back of Omero's. Annabelle gazed out over the Tuscan countryside, which looked as if peace had reigned there forever. Rolling green hills, bosomy folds etched with the darker green of Cypress pines; improbable, a child's drawing of trees and hills. *Le dolci colline.* The sweet hills of Florence. Sweet now, gentle now, but fertilised for aeons with real blood and real bone. It was only since the 1970s that Tuscany had suddenly become the must-see tourist destination. Until then it had been just one more of the poorest regions in Italy, the glory days of the Grand Duchy a long way in the past. It was as if Tuscany had been reinvented with mass travel. In a sense, she supposed, that was true. She couldn't remember using the word much: Firenze, Florence, you said. Or San Casciano. Or Impruneta. Chianti, never, unless you were going to drink it.

She played with her unsalted bread, picking bits from the dry centre and rolling it into doughy balls on the tablecloth.

'Tuscany, nowadays, is a sort of construct,' she said, turning back to Enrico.

He took a deep swig of his grappa and refilled the small glass.

'Spare me the philosophical meandering, *Stella*,' he said. 'You always overthink everything. You and your fucking secrets. Where do we go from here? Are you or are you not going to come back with me? You cannot be worried about incest by our age. You worry too much.'

'And you do not worry nearly enough.' The tremor of Annabelle's hand rippled the surface of her wine.

Neither had touched the artful dishes that had come and gone across the table. The second wine bottle was empty. For a long time she stared at his hands, spread on the stiff white cloth. He had her father's hands – large, capable, smooth and very brown, with short practical nails. Workman's hands, not the hands of an academic. Ernest Hemingway once said Mussolini had feminine hands. Enrico was missing two fingers of his left hand at the first joint, from when the grenade exploded while he was priming it. He remained intractably left-handed. His hands were still beautiful. 'When I die, I will have loved you all my life,' he had once told her and, in his own way, he had. In his own way.

'We are too old to begin again.' She looked up from the table, directly into his eyes. She could see herself reflected in the heavy lenses. *'Acqua passata.* Too much water under our bridge.'

'Well, fuck you,' he said and walked out. Leaving her to pay the bill.

Her throat ached. Nothing changes.

Rome 1943
The gilded cage

Clara was ready before her mother's knock at the door. She gave a last check in the full-length mirror, pleased by the fall of the soft wool of her navy pleated skirt. She squirted one more spray of Arpège between her breasts – not too much. She replaced the tasselled, crystal perfume bottle, gathered her bags and descended the curve of the staircase to the foyer, where her driver, cap in hand, chatted with her mother. The keys to her beloved Alfa hung forlornly among the keys on a board by the front door. Ben had bought it for her and she loved it. The car sat, shrouded and on blocks, in the garage. Rationing. No petrol, no tyres. She nodded graciously, at the *'Buon giorno, Signora'* from the driver, who followed her to the gravel drive where the taxi waited.

Surely, it would not be long before she would drive herself again. Still, she had to admit she did not mind the extra attention, the cloak-and-dagger ride from the family villa to Palazzo Venezia. The police escort, the clandestine messages at each checkpoint, the changes from taxi to motorcycle sidecar and back to a taxi, exhilarated her. The furtive entry from via Astalli through the courtyard and up to the Cybo apartment in a private lift had an air of the cinematic about it and she did love the cinema. It was an exciting punctuation to what could otherwise be endless hours of boredom. Please let Ben be in a good humour, she thought. Today, she was not feeling up to dealing with his behaviour if he was out of sorts. Which was more and more often lately.

Entering the wide double doors of the Zodiac Room, she sagged beneath a wave of fatigue. She had not fully recovered from the last miscarriage. Hormones, her father said, hormones were the cause of the debilitating blood loss. Whatever hormones were. In the reflection in one of the many tall gilt mirrors, her stomach was completely flat. That was something. Ben hated her to be fat, but he did not like thin women either so she had better be careful. She cupped her breasts in her hands; they were still nicely full. To her left on the sideboard were three dressmaker's boxes. She wandered over, lifted the lid of the top one, flicked the pale blue tissue paper aside, let the lid drop. Not even new frocks could hold her interest today. Perhaps she was coming down with something. She massaged her temples. She fingered the pearl rosary in the pocket of her skirt but did not feel like starting a rosary either ... one decade perhaps ... but even that seemed too long today. At the small side table, she stood on one leg and flipped through Ben's copies of Plato and Socrates. The books were much-thumbed, the pages dog-eared and covered in Ben's annotations. Socrates was in Greek so she could not read that and though the copy of Plato was in Italian, it may as well have been Greek – it gave her a headache. Ben was so clever.

Careful not to smudge her make-up, she put her fingers to her temples again and massaged them gently. Ben hated her to wear make-up. Dirtying your face, he called it. It was the same with perfume. He liked the hair of her armpits and between her thighs to smell just a little. Not too much. To smell natural, but Claretta had her wiles and her ways. You had to be careful to look as if it were all natural. Really, it took much longer to look natural. She clicked her tongue: *tsk tsk*.

Clara regarded her reflection again. Apart from the minor distortions of such old glass, she was happy with what she saw. No grey hair yet. That was a relief because when her mother was her age, nearly thirty, she already had fine filaments of silver in her black hair. That could look very elegant … but not yet. She was glad her face was oval – wasn't that supposed to be the perfect shape? She wandered across the room to the high step at the windows giving onto the lush garden of the internal courtyard. Her world began and ended these days with this room and that view. Last summer and the secret trips to the seaside seemed a lifetime away. Outside, the light had changed. Autumn, already mornings were chilly, dark. The leaves were turning too. She shivered. Behind her, the door opened but the footsteps were not Ben's. Quinto Navarra entered, carrying the tea tray. He smiled at her, inclining his head in a small bow.

'Will he be joining me?' There were two cups on the tray.

He shook his head. 'Who knows? Today has not gone well.' His face said he felt sad for her. He waited.

'Would you like a cup then?' she asked.

Her loneliness filled the room.

Quinto Navarra was used to standing in for his boss and it seemed to happen more and more often. He smiled at her, poured himself a cup of tea and sat on the long sofa opposite *la signora*. Tea. He hated tea but they both affected to like it and he was never offered coffee these days. Ever since the gastric ulcer, coffee had disappeared from the menu of Il Duce. Like so much else, the days of extra strong espresso were long past. The March on Rome had been fuelled by coffee as black as pitch. Now the Regime ran on camomile, he thought glumly. Quinto had habituated himself to it. It was the least of the things he had learned to get used to.

In twenty years, his boss had never once asked his opinion on politics but he sought it on everything else. The only other person as close to Il Duce was Clara. Until she came into his life, Mussolini had been a lonely man. He had never had a friend that Quinto knew of. He regarded the woman seated before him, thinking that nowadays being Mussolini's lover was not all that much fun. She was very pale today. Getting very thin. So was the boss. This stupid dieting of his was killing them both. He had always been a picky eater but it was becoming obsessional. With every month, the boss's dietary restrictions got harder and harder to understand. He must have lost twenty kilos. Every week he had a new complaint but if you said anything, you got your head bitten off. If anyone else mentioned the health of Il Duce, it was almost regarded as treason.

'Tell me who he has seen today,' said Clara.

She could not, he knew, abide silence. She was always on the lookout for information, about the people around Ben and especially about her competitors. Quinto leaned back in his chair and recounted the morning's discussion about the progress of the secret shelter being built for the Duce, deep beneath Palazzo Venezia. Then he related the amusing story of a visitor who had been thrown out for wearing a beard – could there be anyone left in the country who did not know of the Duce's aversion to beards? He moved on to the details of the gruelling meeting with the Foreign Minister; the Duce's son-in-law, Count Ciano, had left the meeting an unhappy man. Ciano had lost faith in the war and was urging the Duce to find a way to bring it to a conclusion. He argued ever more openly with the Duce's policies and was ever more critical of the Germans. The Count was becoming careless, thought Quinto. Nevertheless, the Duce had noted with satisfaction that Ciano's diaries were being kept up to date. The diaries were their insurance against carrying the blame for Hitler's excesses, though it was important the Germans never saw them, as Count Ciano was well known to be no great friend of theirs. The Red Cross notebooks, filled with Ciano's cramped script, lived in a small safe in the Count's office.

Quinto knew, however, that Clara wanted to know about the others – the women. Her jealousy was legendary – the shouting and weeping and scenes of recrimination regularly leaked out beneath the heavy doors and washed over Quinto and the rest of the entourage. Il Duce's habit of fathering children by his mistresses meant many of them remained in his life. The list was a long one. Angela Curti Cucciati – the mother of his favourite daughter, Elena – was a permanent thorn in Clara's side, and Quinto was relieved to be able to say with impunity that she had not visited today. In fact there had been no female visitors, no 'fascist visitors', recorded in the usual slot in the log of Palazzo Venezia today.

There had certainly been the full complement of fervid letters from crazed female admirers. Some of them were quite disgusting, but the boss loved it all and always read their letters aloud to his staff and to Clara. He fucked more than the odd one or two as well. Said it was good for his health. Sometimes as many as four in a day and he even boasted to her about it. *La Signora* Clara seemed to take it as his due. Quinto shook his head. Doesn't seem natural to me, he thought.

The camomile finished, he rose. 'I will take this away and bring a fresh one when he comes.'

She had not touched the delicate *biscotti*.

Clara glanced at the cards and could not be bothered with Patience. Her nails – she could paint her nails, but then, Ben might come early and they would not be dry. She rummaged in the bottom of her bag for her *cloisonné* pillbox and extracted one small pill. Just one would not hurt. Well, perhaps two. She threw her head back, swallowed the pills without water and stood an instant, as if awaiting their effect. Gently she lifted the gramophone needle onto her favourite recording of Chopin's *Nocturnes*, fished out her stitching and stretched on the sofa in the cavernous centre of the room, beneath the lapis and gold of the Zodiac. Her gilded cage.

Another long evening yawned in her face. She yawned back, tossed aside the stitching, took out her diary and flicked back through the pages of cramped handwriting. *We passed like two gods over the clouds.* Ben's words to her after one of Hitler's visits. She uncapped her pen. Writing their life had become her great consolation. She had written constantly to Ben since their first meeting, letters mostly, which she kept meticulously, along with his to her. The diaries she began in earnest the year after their love affair started, recording everything: every telephone call, every conversation. God knows she had enough time for it and for reflecting upon Ben and his mysteries. Sometimes she thought her life was actually lived more between the pages of her diaries than in reality.

By the time the sentries in the corridor stamped to attention for Ben's arrival, the shadows had lengthened to become the dark. Clara jumped to attention herself, turned on the lamps and rushed to recline casually upon the sofa in what she hoped was an enticing pose, her skirt draped a little high. One look at his face told her she might as well not bother. Quinto Navarra followed him with a fresh tray of tea, which he placed on the table with the small dish of Ben's medicines, then withdrawing without a word.

'Would you bring some fruit as well?' Clara asked as he neared the door.

'I don't want fruit. I'm not hungry.' Ben did not sit but strode to the darkened windows where he planted himself, hands on hips, feet apart.

His jowls quivered, his neck now too scrawny for his collar. Why hadn't Rachele ordered him new collars? It was the least she could do.

She suppressed a sigh. She could feel her shoulders going up. Don't start, my love, she thought. Do not start. Tonight I cannot take it.

But she smiled and said, 'Come and sit with me, *amore*. Has it been hard today?'

Time, Clara had learned, was a mutable thing. Some days it whirled and swirled and curled and left her dizzy. Other days it stalled and crawled. 'Time is not linear', Ben once said, in his schoolteacher voice. She was not sure what he meant but she certainly knew that time was heavy, that it weighed upon her and often pressed inexorably on her chest. Today it was suffocating her.

'I am not feeling well at all.' He paced and postured. 'My head aches and my bowels are playing up again. I did not sleep at all last night.'

Nonsense, Clara thought, though her face did not say so. Ben affected to sleep little and his loyal subjects believed him to be always alert and working on their behalf, but she knew her Lion slept like a cub and could sleep through a war. In fact, he often slept through this one. *I'm the one who doesn't sleep for worry*, she sniffed silently. Most afternoons while Ben slept on the sofa, she sat awake beside him, watching his face in repose, covering page after page of the heavy blue notepaper she used for her letters, notes and diaries. Navarra knew to awaken him only in the most extreme circumstances.

'My son-in-law has been at it again. And I've been locked up with Achille for most of the afternoon,' Ben continued. 'He has some thoughts on a new national holiday. It might have merit.'

Achille Starace. She hated him. The feeling was mutual. 'I'll bet he has some thoughts. He has thoughts on everything,' she said.

Ben's brow lowered. 'Don't be stupid. Just because you have an irrational dislike of the man does not mean he is not a genius.'

She did not like the way Ben slapped the back of one hand into the palm of the other, rising up and down on the balls of his feet. It was not a good sign, but today Clara was not heeding signs.

Starace. That man and his manias. He had gradually altered the whole way Italians lived their daily lives. True, some of his ideas were good but Clara liked the way people used to shake hands. Now it was no longer allowed. Too English, Starace said. So everyone had to give the Roman salute. It was all right for men perhaps, but it was ridiculous for women. Now anyone who shook hands was designated a bad fascist, of dubious character. It did not stop Ben shaking hands with his dear friend the Führer though, she noticed. On the other hand, the way Ben's title must be entirely written in capitals pleased her. DUCE. It definitely carried more weight. It had been Starace's idea to have the lights of Palazzo Venezia burning all night so the citizens would think their DUCE worked all night for them, and it was a good idea too, though Ben had enough sense to have the lights turned off after midnight. Let us not exaggerate, he said.

'You are obsessed with Achille,' Ben said.

'No,' she said, her voice rising dangerously, '*you* are obsessed with him. You listen to him more than me.'

'Well, at least he is loyal to me. He will be loyal to the end.' He hiked the needle off her Chopin record, scraping it across the shellac, and dropped it roughly in its cradle.

'Loyal!' She heard her voice crack but there was no turning back. It was going to go that way tonight; she could see it. 'I am the only one who is loyal to you, who is here by your side day and night, who truly loves you. And how dare you call me stupid.'

Most of the time Clara tried to placate him: diffuse the bomb, soothe her Lion, turn away the wrath – but when Ben wanted a fight, nothing on God's earth would deflect him. Try as she might, the dam would burst and the blows would rain. Sometimes she did not care, and this was one of those times.

CHAPTER 2

Florence 1942
The Day of the Dead

November again. All Souls Day again. Again and again. A whole year since Hitler's state visit. Annabelle opened her eyes reluctantly and wiggled deeper beneath the heavy blanket. The rough wool itched her chin, but at least it was not that awful synthetic stuff people were using since wool became unavailable. Lanital – her father said it was made from milk. How disgusting. To think Florence was once the city of cloth.

She sighed and forced herself out of bed. A great lassitude assailed her; the shadow of a monster loomed at her shoulder. The war was going badly. America had been in the war for nearly a year but still it dragged on. For months, photographs of captured Italian soldiers in Egypt had been circulating. El Alamein. Wasn't that where their cousin Roberto was fighting? Italian troops were in Russia too – Stalingrad. A new name. The whole world was at war: countries Annabelle had never heard of were fighting with each other in places she could not even find on a globe. Thailand! Where on earth was that? Terrifying stories of what Hitler was doing to the Jews were no longer in doubt. She had never given much thought to whether people were Jews. Now there were Jews in hiding all over the city, many from the north, running from the Germans.

It was not Il Duce's fault, people said. Everything, they whispered, was the fault of 'that woman', Clara Petacci, who governed the country from his bedroom. *Le voci corrono*, word has it … Annabelle heard these conversations between Anna Maria and her husband in the kitchen, at the vegetable stall in Sant'Ambrogio market, between elderly ladies at the butcher and, in a slightly different register, in her own drawing room. It was open conversation now, as Annabelle's parents had given up any pretence of keeping her inured to the goings-on in the nation. The city was full of gossip and fear, of plot and counterplot. It must be the fault of the woman beside the leader. To blame him would be, her father said, to lose the last shred of faith holding the whole shambles together. *Se lo sapesse Il Duce*, they said. 'If only Il Duce knew about it ...' He would do something. Put a stop to the things done in his name. The saying had been in currency for as long as she could remember, had become a matter of derision, though all mirth was gallows humour now. Mussolini did know and did not care.

Annabelle was both horrified and titillated by the stories of Mussolini and his lover. Claretta, she was called, and the walls of her parents' Roman villa were, almost daily now, covered in graffiti: *puttana, troia*, whore. The *Carabinieri* guarded the house on Mussolini's orders. Clara's father was a Vatican doctor, the Pope's doctor. Wealthy and once well-respected, they had behaved for many years as the in-laws of Il Duce. The newspapers revelled in stories of their doings. Lately, the role had less cachet. People were looking for someone to carry the blame and shame and fear of a failing war, and they did not have to look far. According to Enrico, Mussolini had become a syphilitic megalomaniac who was afraid to go out. He must hear these things at his secret meetings, Annabelle supposed. Meetings Enrico refused to take her to.

Up at Piazzale Michelangelo – last year it would have been – she recalled seeing several stylishly foreign women in elegant suits and high heels, wearing jaunty hats a bit like the shape of the *Alpini* brigades, some with a feather. They posed for a photograph, self-consciously ranged down the steep slope of the stone parapet, the Duomo behind them, a chattering, cheerful flock of migratory birds. German. She could hear the guttural consonants. Behind her, two elderly gardeners muttered to each other:

'Hitler's lover,' said one, with a nod at the women.

'Which one?' asked the other.

'That one,' he replied, with a thumb in the direction of a woman with light brown hair and a rather plain face, wearing one of the feathered hats.

'Hrrumph,' his companion grunted, '*la nostra è piu bella!*'

They sniggered and sauntered off. Ours is better looking. Annabelle pondered the joke but it made no sense. Then.

A short while ago she furtively cut out a photograph of *La Signora* Clara Petacci from a newspaper. The dress had a deep, crossover V-neck. Black hair thickly curled in satiny bunches swept back from a high forehead, in a pose reminiscent of images of the women of ancient Rome. The lips were deeply etched, with what would certainly have been scarlet if it were in colour. Clara gazed off to her left with longing. Annabelle was certain she was gazing at her lover. In the V of her neckline, a heavy ball pendant on a long chain rested between full breasts, and in her ears were large pearls.

Annabelle curled her toes as they hit the icy *cotto* floor. Sliding her feet into her *ciabatte*, she tied her dressing-gown and made her bed, taking care with the corners. Her mother worried greatly about properly made beds and such matters now. Eleanora spent long periods reorganising the cutlery drawers and linen press and giving minute directions in the kitchen. It soothed her 'nerves', gave her a sense of control in a world gone mad, a world where her sons had disappeared. Annabelle understood and tried not to be irritated.

She dragged a comb through her hair – the bone one with the wide teeth that Nonna Lucrezia had given her. Her hair, once so fine and fair, had darkened to a deep golden blonde and was too thick for the fine combs and gilt-backed brushes on her dressing table. She paused before the mirror, one hand raised to her hair, as her dressing-gown fell open. Beneath her nightdress, the swell of her breasts was satisfying; they too had grown. Not as much as she would like, but still … She unbuttoned the childish floral nightdress, running her hands softly over pale nipples and then in gentle circles around each breast, shivering from her scalp down. She closed her eyes, thinking of the soft white skin at the base of Enrico's throat, the downy hair of his forearms as it caught the sunlight. What if he kissed her? What if he put his full lips on hers, his tongue in her mouth? She knew people really kissed like that. It made her feel a little queasy, set off great surges, convulsions, waves rising and breaking. She pinched her nipples until they hurt and an electric current zigzagged through her centre to somewhere deep, deeper. She threw back her head, arched her spine and let the waves crest and the wetness flow down her thighs. Sinking to the cold tiles, she stifled a moan – sound carried in the vast spaces of the upper floor.

Did Claretta feel this? What did they do together? What would it be like to defy all conventions for love? Would she, Annabelle, do it for Enrico? No reading of Boccaccio or Petrarch or the letters of Heloise could answer these questions. The only naked men she had ever seen were statues: the tortured body of Christ in all its agony, or the images of impaled saints on constant display in every church and museum. Repulsive. There was the gigantic member of Neptune in Piazza Signoria – surely no-one could really look like that? She sighed, shivered, got unsteadily to her feet and picked up her brush again, observed from the mirror by a serious girl in a sensible floral nightgown. A clammy nightgown – damp and sticky.

She dropped the brush with a clatter as her father passed her door, giving it a hearty morning thump on his way downstairs. The rich basso of the Duomo's bells reverberated through the walls, mimicked by the tinnier ones of the Badia. Annabelle tied her dressing-gown tightly, picked up her chamber pot and headed down the long cold hallway to the bathroom. Unsteadily.

In the breakfast room, Enrico was already seated at the far end of the table, deep in conversation with her father, whose large bowl of *caffe latte* was almost empty. Enrico had lately taken to drinking only strong black espresso, which made Annabelle shiver. The ground barley they called coffee was only bearable with milk. *La Nazione* was open before them. That was sure to inflame outrage. They were in accord in their disdain for the editor, a loyal functionary of the Regime. One of the first acts of the fascists was to abolish a free press, so the English newspapers, which were all Annabelle had known, were no longer available. She missed them.

She longed for once-upon-a-time mornings when conversations turned on matters such as whether the inventor of chamber music was Haydn or Sammartini. Goethe described chamber music as 'four rational people conversing'. Would that ever happen again? Nevertheless, they took *La Nazione* to know what the day's line in propaganda would be. This morning their outrage centred upon news that important pieces of Renaissance art had been transferred to Germany for protection. Protection! Theft, plain and simple! Nazi opportunism! They were both taking affront with their coffee.

'Good morning.' Annabelle poured some warm milk into her bowl, her voice a little loud, guilty, as if Enrico could somehow know of the performance before the mirror. Most mornings she prayed he would be there at the table. Most mornings, her prayers were answered. Her mother was always prepared, the big blue and white bowls of *caffe latte* and the *brioche* ready. Aunt Elsa did not rise early. They all spent most of their time in the palazzo in town now. Annabelle had not been out to Impruneta for months. Her parents went for the *vendemmia* – the grapes had to be gathered, but she remained in town with the excuse of her hated schoolbooks. The *raccolta* was due but they could press the oil without her.

She dropped a casual kiss on the top of her father's head, and then on Enrico's in the same manner. The effort nearly killed her. He greeted her absently with a pat on her hip as she passed. She twitched away; *who does he think he is?* Her father? He was ever more taken up with his clandestine activities. He would not tell her anything, supposedly on the grounds of her safety. Her safety! She was so tired of being a treated as a child.

Annabelle had been an introverted child in a darkening world: a non-believer in a Catholic country and a non-fascist in a fascist country. The fascist hierarchy was often manned by members of the aristocracy and many were relatives. She had more cousins than she could count but most were estranged, living on the other side of the political divide. She had no school friends because she had no school. She knew no life but that of a stranger to her caste and her country and her city. Now, she was still anxious … no longer a child, but not yet free to be an adult either, in this world turned upside down. Florence had become a city of shadows and running footsteps and sudden pounding on doors and marching boots and the clash of metal arms and explosions. She thought she might explode too.

Giacomo and Umberto had been interned in Australia. Papà had explained they were better off interned far away in safety and relative comfort than here in this vile morass. He only wished he had sent all the children. As for internment, he said, every country did it. The day war was announced here in Florence, the police turned up at the door of Villa La Pietra to arrest Hortense Acton and all the other foreign residents of the city. The venerable Lady Acton was tossed into jail wearing only her summer dress and without so much as a toothbrush or an apology. The great difference, he said, was that here, many people were able to bribe their way out.

The declaration of war changed everything. Florence became a fortified city, not so much for its residents, but for its art. Florentines lived in a city of ghostly statues whose wrapping and padding made it seem they had grown fat while real people had grown thin. Glass was removed from doorways and barriers built. Walls were bare, with only the faded outlines of pictures taken down and packed for safekeeping. Blackout material gave the city an air of mourning. Most churches and major galleries were emptied, their contents stored in country villas and castles, like Castello Montegufoni, sequestered by the government from Sir George Sitwell. The Germans were shipping art treasures to Germany 'to protect them'. By now, the hiding of art was not only for protection against possible bombing by the enemy Allies, but, said Achille, more against the depredation of our so-called friends. Annabelle was not interested; she just wanted to know what Enrico was doing and be doing it with him.

Rome 1943

Du-ce! Du-ce! Du-ce!

Clara was tired of being in bed, but she was still not well enough to get up. Ben would be here soon, loving and solicitous again now, after she had nearly died. Ectopic pregnancy. She had never heard of such a thing. It was nearly fatal, her father said.

She sighed, shifting her weight in the bed to ease the pain. Time was passing. Was thirty too old to have children? She said a quick prayer to Saint Rita. She had so wanted to have the baby.

'Women are born for babies and blows,' Ben once said, and God knows she had had enough blows. All his other women had borne him endless children. Why could she not give him that joy? She really had thought he was going to leave her the last time. If only she were the mother of his child, she would be guaranteed the place in his life of Rachele, or Alice and Rospilda and Angela Cucciati. Eleven children that she knew of. Ben did love children. He had even passed a law forbidding childless bachelors a place in the civil service.

He was being so nice to her now in the face of this terrible loss. He would never marry her; she knew that. Ben did not believe in marriage. He denied ever having married Ida Dalser, even though everyone knew he did and the courts decided the boy was his. He only married Rachele under protest before the second child was born – Edda was born out of wedlock. Even when he gave in to Rachele's pressure, he refused to consider a church wedding, but married her in a civil ceremony. He said he was too ill at the time to argue, bedridden with typhus during the war. Ben cared nothing for religion or for convention, but then, neither did she really. There had been talk of bigamy but he assured her it was his political enemies spreading lies. No, Claretta would not want to be his wife. He'd had Ida Dalser locked up in the madhouse and her son too. Rachele, the harridan, might rule in Ben's home but she had a terrible life, really. His mistresses fared much better. Clara would happily bear his child if only things went better the next time.

Doors, draughts, footsteps, voices: the fuss of arrival downstairs. 'Richard' was due at 4 pm, the usual message said, and Ben was always punctual. Clara sank back onto the pillows, studying the effect in the corner mirror, pleased to note that she was still quite pallid. She admired the impressive solitaire diamond glittering on her left hand. Ben would be a while, because her illness had brought him even closer to her family and he would stop to talk to her mother and to her sister Myriam – he was helping to further her acting career. Her father would be back from the Vatican soon and Ben would be pleased to see him. When he was actually here, she was happy – at least he was not out making love to other women. Though he found it boring for *her* to be the invalid.

She heard him mount the stairs with the energetic gait he used for outsiders, but once in the room, he deflated onto the chair at her side.

She held out a limp hand to him. '*Amore*'. She smiled wanly.

Ben took her hand, held it to his cheek then kissed her palm. 'How is my angel today?' He leaned towards her with concern. 'I need to speak to your father. He has not come in from the hospital yet. My cold is not improving and the doctor has prescribed some new pills for me.'

More pills. Their life was a sea of pills. Sometimes she wondered if all these medicinals were really helping.

Ben was on the balcony and beneath him, the crowd roared. *Du-ce! Du-ce! Du-ce!* The twenty-first of April, the anniversary of the founding of Rome. From where she stood, it was obvious to Clara that the crowd was much smaller, but he seemed happy and that made her happy. She massaged her left shoulder where she had fallen against the table the other night. It was three days ago but the bruise was still tender. It was her own fault. She should not have provoked him. He would be nice this afternoon. They could have a peaceful time together, like earlier times when she used to stand here in the shadows, Ben performing for her, before the horde of adulators below. Afterwards they would make love like wild creatures – then her bruises were a pleasure. Or when, in the early throes of his infatuation, he would ensure she was seated at an angle to him at public events, so he could fix her with his eyes like a falcon.

'See. They love me. A ring of the bell and everyone rushes under the balcony to hear me,' he exulted as he turned back inside 'These boots are too tight. Get Navarra to bring me the others.'

She sighed and turned to ring for Quinto.

'Why are you sighing? You don't agree with me? You don't think they adore me as always?'

He was not happy, then. He had another cold too. She tried to deflect his ire, indicating the new painting Quinto had delivered, a gift from Ottone Rosai. Years before, Ben commissioned Rosai to paint two huge landscapes for the railway station of Santa Maria Novella. How many railway stations, he boasted, are adorned with original art? In private though, Ben was bored by paintings. He barely flicked the new picture a glance. Even on a state tour of the Uffizi with Hitler, who was obsessed with art, showing intense interest and curiosity about the Botticelli and the other famous paintings, Ben could barely suppress a yawn. Clara would need to come up with something else to distract him.

'Have you had bad news from Africa, my pet?' she soothed. The war was going badly – and not just in Africa, but Ben no longer seemed to care.

'This war is not for the Italian people,' he replied. For the looming humiliation of defeat in Tunisia, he blamed Rodolfo Graziani. He should have known better than to put Graziani in charge of the African campaign. 'The Italian people do not have the maturity or the consistency for such a tremendous and decisive test.'

Ben had lost faith in Italians and in the war. His voice had the edge it got when losing his temper. Was he taking more pills she did not know about? Sometimes he took too many and sometimes new pills upset him. He was puffed with rage.

Ben rose on the balls of his feet, his body turned away from her. 'The Grand Council met today.'

The Grand Council could only be convened by the Prime Minister, that is, by Ben. Clara had known nothing of a meeting today and she prided herself on knowing these things. She knew Ben did not mean the full Council – that had not met formally since the war began. He meant Starace, Pavolini, Farinacci … that lot! Still, his use of the term was sinister.

She was alert. 'What was it about?'

'It was about you!' Ben whirled to her, his face contorted. His collar was too tight, choking him. 'You! Always you! This cannot go on. It makes me look a fool. I have decided to end it.'

Again! Each time was worse. The last time, it was that swine, Ciano, who wrote to his father-in-law that her family was interfering in politics. She had copied the letter into her diary: *The whole family interferes on the left and protects on the right and threatens above and intrigues below.* Ben's sister Edvige was in league with the Count, accusing Clara and her family of profiteering and causing scandal. Marc's activities certainly did not help, but it was so unfair. People even blamed her for the way the war was going.

It was the fault of the English, who broadcast constant lies about her. They said Ben was bewitched and she was an evil force. If only

37

they knew. Ben could not function without her. Twice recently, she had arrived at the gates of Palazzo Venezia only to be refused admittance. She begged and pleaded and sobbed and wailed and he shouted and stamped and raged and capitulated. That was the way things went these days.

'How dare they! How dare you!' she cried. 'They all want me dead. One day they will have me killed. Is that want you want? You want to be rid of me! You want me killed!'

Her voice climbed to a screech, hurting her throat. She grasped the heavy silver teapot with both hands and pitched it across the room. It landed with a spray of tea-leaves and tile slivers, leaving an ugly crater in the antique majolica of the floor, and bounced against the wall. For a moment after the racket, there was silence.

'It is no use.' He was calm now. His eyes were empty, in the way that should have warned her. 'I have decided. The cycle is closed.'

Clara had no life outside their life. She had formed no friendships; how could she? She was the target of envy and hate. She had no education, no career. She had nothing but Ben and her family. All of this she gladly suffered for him, for love. Was he blind? She knew her Lion would be nothing without her and she knew that without him, she would be eaten alive. She grasped the fruit knife, holding the tip at her throat.

'It is better if I die now, then.'

The slap echoed in the vast chamber. Ben hit her with his open hand and the force snapped her head to the left. She thought for a moment her head might swivel right around, but then the back of his hand took her from the other side. She saw the blood spray from her nose onto his cuff. Then the palm of his hand swung back. She flailed at him, scratching, clawing, hissing. The teacups crashed across the room and the small glass table shattered against the window step. Shards of her life cut them both. Ben was no longer calm. The punch felled her. So you really do see stars, she thought. The dark descended.

Clara opened her eyes to the ornate blue and gold Zodiac on the ceiling far above her. Her father was talking quietly to Ben, whose eyes were red and puffy. Quinto hovered at the foot of the chaise where she lay. On a table beside her was an array of bottles and ampoules. She felt wonderful, infused with peace. She wanted to raise her hand but it was too difficult. She smiled. Quinto smiled back at her and touched Ben on the arm. He turned, throwing himself to the floor beside her.

'*Amore mio*. My love. My love. Thank God you are all right.' He kissed the palm of her hand over and over and stroked her cheek.

Was that blood on his sleeve?

'Your father has given you some special medicine. You will be better soon.'

Clara smiled again and closed her eyes. She felt as if she was back at school with the nuns. She might say a prayer, or perhaps later. She was very tired. There was a pain somewhere but it was not hers. The storm had passed.

CHAPTER 3

Rome 1943

Et tu, Brute

The doctor was gone and the injection was beginning to work. Ben was quiet now, stretched out on the sofa, almost asleep, his breathing raspy but regular. He was not at all well. The strain of things was wearing him down. Clara smoothed his forehead but he brushed her hand aside. His ulcer was playing up – his breath smelled of vinegar. She had told him not to go to Libya and the ulcer was the result. This heat was not helping. July was all very well and fine when you could go to the seaside but it was hell when you were confined to the city. She opened the doors to the courtyard a little wider and closed the external shutters to keep out the sun. The bars of light through the shutters set sunbeams dancing off the colours of the marble flooring. They had not made love for days. How she wished they could, just once, lie together in a bed, naked, and fall into sleep afterwards. It would be so good for Ben. It was the only position they had not tried – that of husband and wife. Ben was often in a hurry and at times he liked to leave his boots on. He liked fast, violent sex and she was adroit at exciting him to exhaustion, but sometimes she wished for a calmer, quieter moment.

She longed to be free. Memories of the summers, of last summer, had faded to sepia. They swam openly at Castelporzione, surrounded by a swarm of security men like a school of jellyfish. Her favourite two-piece swimming costume with the tie between her breasts had not been out of her bureau drawer once this summer. A shiver ran right through her. Perhaps she was unwell too? They would not be going to the seaside this month. Ben's constipation was getting worse and he was not good at bearing pain. Women were much better with pain. Look at the pain she herself had borne – menstrual pain, miscarriages, and yes, the pain Ben inflicted at times. He was always sorry afterwards.

He was gloomier each day and was losing confidence in himself. In recent times, requests for his photographs had dropped off sharply. Where once, every classroom and home had a photograph of Il Duce on the wall, people seemed less interested in their leader now. That hurt Ben. What, he said, are things coming to? The more fearful and apprehensive he felt, the louder he shouted and the angrier he got. Or the quieter and more withdrawn he became. Depression, her father said. The more pain he suffered, the more often his doctor gave him the injections and the more injections he had, the more timid and distressed he became. Claretta said a whole rosary for him last week – not that he knew. He had no patience with such things. She was worried silly about him, and about herself.

She crossed to the gramophone but did not lift the needle – unfriendly silence echoed about the room. Mounting the steps to the windows, she gazed into the internal courtyard as if hoping to see open fields. From a box with gold paper, she popped a chocolate into her mouth and then regretted it. She poured a lemonade from the tall crystal jug on the sideboard, watching the beads of condensation turn to prisms of light. She opened and closed one of the pile of unread books and threw it down. She made three paces through the room. The clock in the corner tick-tocked the minutes by, then the hours.

There was to be a meeting of the Grand Council this evening. The full Council. Clara's sources had reported rumours the army was conspiring against Ben – perhaps it was about that. How dare they. Even the members of the Grand Council of Fascism treated him in a manner they would once not have dared. Clara's network, developed with great application over much time, was usually reliable. There was even a whisper the King had lost faith in his Prime Minister. The King! Without Ben, that Frenchman would not even be in power. Ben said he had called the meeting himself, but would not discuss it any further, despite her inveigling. He must be about to put a stop to all this nonsense. The war was lost, but they could not blame Ben for that. The whole city heaved with unrest.

41

Clara had urged Ben to act, to quench the rumours and plots and counterplots, but he seemed at one moment decisive and the next, completely indifferent. A fortnight ago, when the Allies landed in Sicily, his only comment was, 'The situation is delicate but not worrying.' She was doing the worrying. She was on alert all day and all night. She did not know from day to day, whether her Lion would roar or plead. One day he was utterly dependent upon her and the next there would be more talk of the closed cycle and rejection. She knew much of this was owed to pain and anxiety and, perhaps, to the treatment for syphilis when he was young, though he denied that. At times he hardly knew what he was saying and Clara knew she had to be strong for him – the worse he got the more she loved him.

What about her own health? Her pulse raced at the slightest word, the slightest frown from Ben. She lay awake at night, unable to get enough air into her lungs. She was very tired. Only this morning she found three grey hairs at her temple and she was certain there were deeper lines around her eyes, lines that had not been there before. If only this dreadful war would end and they could have babies and be happy. Perhaps somewhere quiet, somewhere in the countryside. Well, perhaps not, Ben hated the country. He loved to talk about his country origins and his peasant ancestors but he could not wait to get back to the city whenever he was forced to visit the country.

There were no visits to the country now. For long periods they did not leave the room, and the world outside was becoming a fading memory. Clara left Ben snoring gently and went home to her family.

At precisely fifteen minutes after five in the afternoon, Mussolini arrived at the Quirinale, atop the highest of Rome's seven hills. The graceful building was backlit by the sapphire sky of early evening, the lamps glowing against the warm sandstone of its walls. He arrived deliberately late for the meeting he had called for 5 pm. His chin jutted and he took the stairs with a violent stamp. The Grand Council of Fascism was his own creation and only he could call a meeting. Yet, here he was, summoned to attend as if he were no longer the one who governed. It was an outrage and they would pay dearly, those traitors who thought they could undermine his authority. Clara was right. He should have listened, but he would attend to them now. There would be no more of this insubordination. It was not to be tolerated.

At least he had had the presence of mind to take control once a meeting was inevitable. He was wearing his formal militia uniform and had ordered them all to wear full black ceremonial dress. He puffed his chest out, thrusting his jaw forward like his old self, but he knew he was too thin now. Rage was not good for his ulcer, which was clawing his guts, but he could not control it.

At the door to the chamber, he turned to his aide. 'Are we walking into a trap?'

Inside the chamber, he strode to the front, carrying his heavy file. Frowning sternly, he thumped down the file, placed his fists on the table on either side of the document and began his oration. This would bring them to heel.

Mussolini's voice rose and he made good use of all the quotations he had prepared. Many of the men in the room tensed forward in their seats, holding their breath. As he expounded his version of the war and the quandary of the present, they glanced from one to the other, eyebrows raised, at first surprised, then incredulous. Then, one by one, they exhaled loudly and relaxed into their seats, realising that the Duce of old was no more and that Mussolini had absolutely no idea what he was talking about, no grasp of the war. They had never heard, one said later, such woolly, rambling and inconsequential nonsense. They knew then they had made the right decision. Even those like Ciano, who had been difficult to persuade into this dethroning, were now convinced.

Mussolini droned endlessly in the late afternoon heat, at last concluding lamely, 'The dilemma now is, war or peace? Surrender now or resistance to the last?'

He dribbled to a halt. A blowfly buzzed itself against the window until it fell dead. The air congealed and settled upon the listeners, who awoke from their torpor and, avoiding each other's eyes, shuffled papers in embarrassment, shook heads. Whispered conversations sputtered back and forth, then Dino Grandi, Count of Mordano and President of the Chamber, rose to deliver the resolution he had drafted. In a long and ardent speech, lasting an hour and replete with every accusation, every sin committed or omitted, he put the motion that Mussolini resign forthwith and hand authority to the King, the Government and the Parliament.

The others waited, not even shame-faced: Farinacci, Bottai, Federzoni, and yes, even his son-in-law, the ingrate – though Count Ciano did look mortified, his face the colour of suet. For more than twenty years these men had done his bidding, shared his victories, been the beneficiaries of his largesse. There had been grumbling and complaining and muttering behind the scenes from time to time, but they had always obeyed him implicitly and not once had one of them ever dared to openly question his authority. They seemed as surprised as he to find themselves here this evening, and for a few minutes the atmosphere was strained. The chamber was mute. Then a spate of accusations spewed over him. Sharpened questions flew at him from every direction, assertions shouted, aspersions cast, all inhibition tossed aside. He thought of Caesar.

No longer did they cower before his great desk in the vast Mappamondo salon of Palazzo Venezia. Once, they would have had to walk the long, long length of that salon, from the door at the far end to his desk, before which no-one was ever asked to be seated, but was left to stand for the whole of the interview. Now it was as if Mussolini were the defendant in the dock.

'You have imposed a dictatorship on Italy that is historically immoral!'

Did Grandi have froth at the corners of his mouth? His sweaty face was that of a stranger. It seemed a long time ago, that Grandi had written to him, 'My life, my faith, my soul, are yours.'

Mussolini thought he might faint. It must be the heat. He tugged at his collar – his face felt florid and sweaty and his breathing was ragged. It was important, however, to speak with authority. 'I think we will take an adjournment until tomorrow. As you know, my health is poor and I am feeling unwell.'

An exchange of astonished glances arced around the room. Grandi stood. 'We have been kept here on many occasions until five in the morning to discuss some trifle you thought was important.'

He made it plain that they would be here all night, if that was what was required. They would allow a short adjournment and then recommence.

They *were* there all night. Exhaustion, reaction and fear had set in by the time Mussolini, still nominally chairing the meeting, put the motion to the vote. It was carried by a majority. The reign of Il Duce was over.

His voice feeble and tremulous, Mussolini leaned on the desk as he rose to speak. 'We can go. You have provoked the crisis of the Regime. The meeting is over.'

It was two o'clock in the morning. Most left hurriedly, guilty and shaken by what they had set in motion. A few stalwarts remained for a desultory discussion of retribution against the rebels. Mussolini's heart was not in it. He was too tired to care.

Clara woke early to the summery Roman morning, anxiety weighing upon her like a winter eiderdown. Kicking herself free of the damp sheet, she lay wondering what terrible thing had happened – she had faith in her instincts in these matters. She rang for her maid and ordered a cup of tea. Kneeling quickly, she crossed herself and muttered a plea to Saint Rita. Then she slipped an arm into her organza negligee, hesitated, pulled it off and tossed it onto the back of a spindly chair where the pale green gossamer fluttered softly in the breeze from the open window, a butterfly settling. Better to dress immediately and face whatever had occurred at the meeting.

More meticulous than ever in the choice of her ensemble, she chose a light cream cotton suit with short cap sleeves, a narrow peplum and a lace collar. She loved that skirt for the way it hugged her bottom and thighs and flared at the knee – though not too showy. High-heeled, tan summer shoes with open toes and a handbag to match, she put aside with the clothes, on a chair.

Her maid arrived with the tea and a tall pitcher of water. Clara poured the cool water into a washbasin, wrung out a soft cloth, wiped her face and neck, and then, sprinkling some perfumed lotion onto the cloth, she carefully washed under her arms and between her legs.

It was going to be a very hot day. In the swivel-mirror, she checked the back view and decided her hair would be better pinned up. Holding six bobby pins in her mouth, she picked up her comb – it would take another ten minutes but was worth it.

Her parents were stirring in the villa but she avoided the breakfast room, going straight to her father's office where she lifted the brass handset of the telephone and asked to be put through to Ben. She did not normally telephone him at home – across the way in Villa Torlonia – she made him call her. Let it not be Rachele's rough voice on the other end. She did not want to have to argue with her this morning. The housekeeper was up and put her straight through to Ben, who was not encouraging.

'*Amore mio*, are you all right?' said Clara. 'Come to the window. I have a bad feeling.' She scribbled tighter and tighter circles on the pad on her father's desk.

Ben was terse. He was anxious, certainly, he said, but no more than he ever was. Nothing has happened, he said. Your imagination is getting the better of you. No, she said. You must listen. This is what I think you must do. Don't tell me what to do, he said. Tell me what happened at the meeting, she said. Don't worry he said. You worry too much, and rang off. He did not come to the window.

So, she thought, it is as bad as that.

In the normal course of a day, Clara would call Ben or have him call her at least twelve times, often more. Yesterday was wrong – she knew it. All wrong. And today was worse. When she had not heard from him again by two o'clock and Quinto had taken all her calls, each more frantic than the last, she decided to go to Palazzo Venezia. She told Quinto to send the driver to fetch her directly. He arrived promptly and things seemed calm and normal but she was not placated. No, said the driver, the boss had been busy all day, working from home. No more than that. On arrival at the via degli Astalli gate the attendant waved her through with a deferential nod. Normal there too.

Quinto awaited her at the lift, smiling reassurance as he escorted her to the first-floor apartment where she went straight through to the Zodiac Room.

'Shall I bring tea?'

'No. Yes. Yes, tea, but where is Ben? Where is he? Why has he not called me?' She bit her lower lip and was even tempted to chew the edge of a fingernail. She stopped herself just in time.

'He has been busy all day. He came in for a short while but left again at two o'clock. He said he was going to visit the area of last night's bombing. I will send the tea.'

Quinto turned to leave. 'He should be back soon. I am going down to wait for him at the lift.'

She heard the anxiety he too was only barely keeping under control. The portents were not good. The air was heavy.

Hours limped past; Clara had given up trying to find Ben. Her mind skittered between fear for him and anxiety for herself, and she could not concentrate on anything. One finger tapped incessantly on the magazine she tried to read. In the shadows of the silent apartment, monsters lurked. Without Ben, Palazzo Venezia was the enemy.

When Quinto returned, his frown was deep and he ran his hand through his hair, usually so carefully combed and oiled.

'He is not back. But it is all right. I have received a policeman from the Presidential Division, sent to tell me the Duce has gone to Villa Savoia. He has an appointment with the King.'

'Gone to the King!' Claretta's voice rose an octave and her throat hurt. She too wanted to run her hands through her hair but was careful not to.

'I knew it. I told him not to go, but would he listen to me? No good will come of this.'

She lunged for her handbag from the sofa and rushed from the room as if Quinto had said Ben had been in an accident.

Quinto Navarra remained standing for some time, at the open double doors to the apartment, uncertain what to do next. On the one hand, he thought, things certainly did not seem right somehow. On the other, *La Signora* Clara was given to histrionics, and a routine visit to the King was hardly anything to become hysterical about. Was it? Quinto took a deep breath and cleared the tea tray, which was untouched. There will be an explanation, he said to himself. He would have to wait until the boss got back and by the look of things, it would be late. Another long night ahead.

By morning, Mussolini had recovered and was in fighting spirits. He had visited the site of the bombing on his way home after the meeting and been encouraged by the enthusiasm of the few locals about at that late hour. He spent the night writing a rebuttal of the motion, a motion that could not stand. He telephoned his office and in a firm voice, instructed his private secretary to ring the palace and make an appointment with the King. He lunched at home – Rachele made him the only meal he really cared for these days: spaghetti with butter and cheese and a glass of orange juice.

Rachele hovered, fretting. 'Don't go to the King, Benito,' she said. 'I do not trust him.'

'Women,' he said. 'What is wrong with you?' Rachele suffered from the deeply suspicious nature of her peasant background, but only yesterday, Clara too was saying the same thing to him. He would wear his uniform, damn them all! No, he went twice a week to the King without fail and he had always been careful to wear civilian clothing. He would do so today. He undid the uniform jacket in haste and fumbled the cursed buttons, tearing the bottom one away as he ripped the jacket off and tossed it to the bed.

He stood for a moment, did some deep breathing. His legs were hard to keep still. What was wrong with him? The worst that could happen would be that the King might take back command of the armed services. Really, he had so much on his mind that the King might be useful in that role. He might as well do something useful, the idiot, instead of playing with his coin collection.

Mussolini ordered his car and arrived at Villa Savoia punctually, a little before 5 pm. His bodyguards followed in various vehicles, careful to maintain the 500-metre distance Il Duce insisted upon. They knew he could fly into a rage if they followed too closely. They parked outside the villa as he swept into the courtyard, to be greeted by the

King who was waiting for him at the door, his hand extended.

See, thought Mussolini, I knew I could rely on the King. He maintained a sober expression but was exultant. He would soon have the traitors back under his thumb.

The King seemed more subdued than usual but that was to be expected. He was seventy-three, but had changed little in appearance as he aged. His close-cropped hair was now white. His moustache was also white and, being shorter and thinner than the bristly thatch of earlier times, it failed to conceal the weak set of his mouth.

He led the way to his office, where he turned to Mussolini and said, 'We cannot go on like this.'

'No, Your Majesty. I agree.' He opened his file from last night's meeting, ready to explicate the many errors rendering the motion illegal.

The King cut him short, both hands raised. 'No! You know they are singing songs saying "Down with Mussolini"? The country cannot continue like this. I think we must accept that the right man for this delicate moment is Marshall Badoglio.'

The King's face was wan and taut. His voice wobbled and he stared off into the corner of the room. Making momentous decisions did not sit comfortably with Victor Emmanuel III.

'But, but, a crisis at this moment ...' This could not be happening. Mussolini tugged at his collar.

'My dear Duce! My soldiers don't want to fight anymore.' The King's voice cracked slightly. 'At this moment you are the most hated man in Italy. We must accept the vote of the Grand Council as the will of the people. I have instructed Marshall Badoglio to prepare to take over immediately.'

Mussolini seemed to hear the words as if from a great distance. His face burned.

'Then it is all over. All over. All over.' His voice had a peevish edge and he swayed. He put out a hand to steady himself against the mantle. In the mirror, a livid stain mottled his neck. 'What will happen to me? To my family? What will happen to us?'

His eyes, the King said later, reminded him of the horse he had put down when it was injured. King Victor Emmanuel III, by contrast, was wooden. It was only twenty past five but the meeting was over.

The King walked him to the door where he shook his hand.

'We will talk tomorrow,' Mussolini said faintly, nodding, as if the King had said it.

On the gravel drive, he looked for his car but it was parked at the far side of the quadrangle. With a sigh, he began to walk to it, too drained even to be offended that it was not brought to him. Instead, he was confronted by an officer of the *Carabinieri*.

'His Majesty the King has commanded me to accompany you,' he said, 'to protect you from the mob.'

'Oh, very well, come on then,' Mussolini replied. 'There is no need.' He made towards the car again, shaking his head. 'No need to exaggerate,' he said; the people would always love him.

'No, this way,' said the officer, turning him towards an ambulance parked off to the side. 'It is safer.'

He took the elbow of the ex-leader and, as if offering help, propelled him up into the back of the vehicle, where two armed guards waited. Mussolini was seated on a stretcher, the doors slammed and the ambulance sped out of the palace.

The evening was glorious. The heat of the day had waned and a gentle breeze wafted about the nodding heads of the flowers in the garden as the King and his ADC walked back and forth.

The King shook his head. 'The Queen is very upset about him being arrested here. It is true. She is right. Here he was our guest. The rules of royal hospitality have been violated. It is not good.' The King shook his head again and the two men turned indoors.

Not too far away from the palace, Marshall Pietro Badoglio, 1st Duke of Addis Ababa and 1st Marquess of Sabotino, had received a messenger. He was in a jovial humour. He had waited a long time for this moment.

'You're all under arrest,' he called boisterously to his family. 'No-one leave the house! Bring up the *Veuve Clicquot* and put it on the ice!' He bounded up the stairs to change into his military uniform.

Back in Palazzo Venezia, Quinto Navarra paced and fretted.

Outside Villa Savoia, Mussolini's bodyguards kept watch, forgotten by all.

It was still too warm to eat. Clara's plate was untouched – the deep green of the spinach bled onto the white flesh of the fish. She pushed it away with a pouty sigh, almost overturning her wineglass – why did her mother always set a wineglass when she knew Clara only ever drank water? She had changed into a floral cotton dress without sleeves, but under the wide red belt her bodice was soaked with perspiration.

Evening sounds drifted up to the terrace on the soft air, as if it were a day like any other. The debris of the meal was scattered across the table. The cork and golden foil from a bottle of Spumante lay beside a crystal salt dish and the terrace lanterns refracted amber light through the Frascati in the tall glasses. Beside her father's elbow, the bottle of Sangiovese left a magenta ring on the starched tablecloth. Claretta played with the drawn thread design of its border until she poked a hole in the fine work. Her mother glared at her but said nothing and she let the fabric drop. Strawberries glistened in a crystal bowl set in ice.

Dr Francesco Petacci was not hungry either. His forehead glistened with perspiration, all the way back to where the last of his hair still clung on. He was in his shirt-sleeves despite his wife's disapproval – it was too hot to dress for dinner when there was only the family present. He refilled his wine glass for the third time. His wife would disapprove of that too. He could see from the state Claretta was in that things were grave. Ben had disappeared, she said. He cannot have disappeared, thought Francesco, but if there was another woman involved, it could be a while before he showed up and he knew what that would be like, dealing with his daughter. More likely affairs of state, he said aloud. No, his daughter shouted, he has gone to the King and I cannot find him. Unrest was in the air and everyone except his wife, it seemed, was anxious.

Clara's mother, Giuseppina, had no difficulty at all eating her supper, despite the heat. She frowned at Francesco as he poured more wine, while she slid the strawberries towards her and helped herself to a large spoonful, which she sprinkled with icing sugar. She fanned herself lightly with an embroidered napkin and sighed as loudly as Claretta. Her daughter's distracted air irritated her and spoiled the nice evening, but Claretta always over-dramatised. They all knew Ben could be difficult – not that she called him Ben to his face – but God knows Claretta did provoke him at times. Going to see the King was hardly the end of the world. Giuseppina was certain he would turn up tomorrow and resolve the problem. She did hope so, because it was too trying to have Claretta in this mood. She mopped the corners of her mouth, patted gently at the light perspiration on her throat and pushed back her chair, the iron legs grating across the tiles.

'Shall we go in for the bulletin?' she asked.

They drifted into the salon through the open French doors. Giuseppina surveyed the room with a pleasure undiminished by familiarity – gracious, it was, despite the modernity. She was not as certain as Francesco about all those stark lines, but it seemed to work pleasingly. She pressed the button for the housekeeper and ordered coffee.

Francesco turned on the wireless to warm it up for the 11 pm news broadcast. He settled into his chair with his pipe, tamping the tobacco with his thumb in pleasurable anticipation of the first puff. Claretta perched distractedly on the rolled wooden arm of an antique sofa, one of the few old pieces in the room.

'Don't sit on the arm. You will break it,' her mother said with the tedium of habit.

With a shake of her head, Claretta slid into a lolling position, gazing out through the doors to the starry night and the last fading light. She chewed the inside of her cheek. Her mother turned the volume knob of the wireless and sat opposite as the clock chimed eleven.

> *His Majesty the King-Emperor has accepted the resignation from the Office of Head of the Government and Chief Secretary of State, of His Excellency Cavaliere Benito Mussolini ...*

Claretta's scream was more of panic than surprise. She struck her forehead repeatedly with the heel of her hand. 'What have they done to him? They will kill him. Oh, *amore mio*, I should never have left.' She slid from the sofa to the floor, keening and rocking.

Her parents were astounded – as much by their daughter's histrionics as the shocking announcement.

'Too much American cinema,' Giuseppina muttered. She glared at Francesco as if to say, this is your fault, the girl is uncontrollable. Neither went to her aid but watched her as if she were dangerous.

The bulletin droned to the end and still no-one moved. Francesco held his unlit pipe halfway to his mouth. After a moment, he rose and turned off the radio.

'I ... I must telephone someone. I ...' He waved his pipe.

Giuseppina sprang at him. 'It's the King. He has always been useless. We have a coward and a fool as our King. As for Badoglio, that cretin has always hated the Duce. I'll bet he put the King up to this. He just wants ... he wants ...' She sputtered to a halt.

Her hands flew to the pearls at her throat, fingers telling the smooth pale orbs like a rosary. '*Oddio*! What will happen to us? We are not safe. Francesco, call the police at once. At once!' Her eyebrows disappeared into her fringe. 'At once!'

She tugged at her husband's arm, sending the pipe spinning from his hand in a spray of tobacco.

Claretta was on her feet now. Like a flock of starlings in the Rome night sky they wheeled in unison, swooping from the room and across the terrace to gaze down at the outer walls to the courtyard, where their police guard was always positioned. There was no-one there. From the high terrace, they heard the raucous sounds of celebration and rejoicing. Fires burned in dancing orange points across the city.

Florence 1943
The fall

The stars glittered, no light anywhere to dilute their intensity. Annabelle was not asleep. She had gone to bed too early. The hated blackout curtains trapped the summer night, suffocating her. Drawing back the heavy fabric, she sat in her window, dreaming, drifting, imagining another life ... She was Heloise at university, disguised as a boy, having a passionate love affair with Abelard.

A commotion downstairs fractured her reverie. The very timbre of the house changed. What now? It was more than two weeks since the Allied landing in Sicily. She raced down the stairs, wearing only her voile nightgown. From her father's study came a clatter of raised voices, with the wireless on in the background. It was nearly eleven. As she rushed through the door, she was shushed from every side. No-one chided her for being half-dressed. The air was fuggy with cigar-smoke. Enrico pushed her to the front with a wave to remain silent and the evening news broadcast began. There was no usual introduction to the events of the day, the twenty-fifth of July in the twentieth year of the Fascist Era.

> *His Majesty the King-Emperor has accepted the resignation from the Office of Head of the Government and Chief Secretary of State, of His Excellency Cavaliere Benito Mussolini, and has nominated as Head of the Government and Chief Secretary of State, Cavaliere Marshal of Italy Pietro Badoglio. End of the transmission.*

For long moments, the silence beat like a human heart. Annabelle thought it was her own heart. Enrico nodded, but did not speak. His lips were white and compressed. Finally, Achille rose to turn off the wireless.

'You were right,' he said, turning to Enrico. 'What will it mean?'

Enrico had brought this news. She might have guessed. Annabelle was dulled with dread. 'I am going back to bed,' she said loudly. No-one answered.

Florentines awoke to a glorious summer morning filled with light and the call of the cuckoo. Outside the windows the air was already heavy with humidity and presentiment. Nothing was real. It was as if a play were suspended, midway through rehearsal, for a lost script. Stunned incomprehension stamped the faces of citizens. After a night of riotous carousing, the streets were quiet – littered with party badges torn from coats and trampled underfoot, smashed glass, frames from portraits of Il Duce ripped from the walls of homes and offices. The air smelt of ash and cinders. In the stillness, the ghostly covered cars on their blocks seemed like so many draped corpses. A quarter of a century of Mussolini was over. Was this good news or bad news?

No-one knew. Utter confusion washed through the city. Rumours swirled like the capes of phantoms and facts were invisible. Stories wisped, drifted, disappeared. True and real had lost their currency. Many thought the war was over, having missed Marshall Badoglio's confirmation that 'Italy remains true to the word she has given'.

'You will see, he will be back,' said others, more cautious. By afternoon, a dangerous state of euphoria wafted about, a deadly miasma replacing caution. The streets were again clotted with citizens – many kissing complete strangers, some throwing pictures of Il Duce onto bonfires, others swapping the latest wild theories, while rampaging youths defaced fascist emblems. A slate statue of Mussolini was pulled from its marble plinth and crashed to the ground – a cascading Colossus. Tricolours appeared in several windows, tentatively. The evening news bulletin carried stories of bacchanalian orgies in Milan, the cradle of fascism, where rejoicing was unrestrained. Homes and offices of prominent fascists were raided, wrecked and looted. *Viva Badoglio!* echoed from the streets and belltowers and loggias across the city. Groups of young people swaggered arm-in-arm, swigging from wine bottles and dancing around bonfires. A fascist official was forced to eat his badge. The scenes of mindless elation were distasteful and unsettling to those with a more measured outlook.

'Pandemonium in its literal sense,' Achille said, shaking his head. 'And these are the same people who were screaming *Duce! Duce! Duce!* only last week.'

Then as quickly as the ecstasy appeared, it evaporated with the confirmation from Marshall Badoglio that Italy was still at war.

For the following weeks, the sun came up each day on clocks that seemed broken. Time ceased to have meaning and each day brought new stories. In the bars and piazzas and bakeries and butcheries and grocery shops, the butcher, the baker, the candlestick maker all knew for certain that ... The sludge of rumour clogged the arteries of the whole country. Mussolini had gone mad. Hitler was dead. No, Mussolini was dead and Hitler had gone mad. The German presence increased and the talk was constantly of what Hitler might do: Hitler intended to kill the King. Hitler was going to kidnap the Pope. Hitler had kidnapped Mussolini. Where *was* Mussolini? He had not been seen since the afternoon of the twenty-fifth when he left an audience with the King. Life centred on the wireless news broadcasts but nothing was ever clear.

Annabelle drifted through each day, shoulders hunched, awaiting the news that increasingly came from Enrico. A subtle shift had occurred within the family. They seemed to have agreed to appoint him their minister of information and he was absent all day and much of the night. The people he spent his time with, such as Professor La Pira from the university and other opponents of the Regime, began to meet openly and talk about a new order. Suddenly Enrico was one of the grown-ups and Annabelle was the only child left. She had given up even the pretence of study and Enrico had not opened a book, she knew, for months. What was the point of it all? They would probably all be dead soon anyway. Hitler would kill them all. Mussolini was missing and she wondered what had become of Claretta? Her throat hurt and she cried herself to sleep at night, fat tears dribbling slowly down her cheeks onto the damp patches from the night before. She never allowed anyone to see tears in the daytime – Enrico would think she was a baby. No-one noticed.

CHAPTER 4

Florence 1943

Into thin air

Most people listened to *Radio Londra*. The real news, however, came with Enrico every evening. Pavolini had escaped ahead of a mob intent on hanging him. Senator Morgagni had shot himself, leaving a note saying: 'The Duce has resigned. My life is finished. Long live Mussolini.' Few were the men who took that recourse. Many were those who might never have been fascists. Where was Mussolini? The answer was different every day: he was at home in Rocca delle Caminate; no, he was on the island of Ponza; no, he was on La Maddalena. After more than two weeks, Enrico learned from a spy in the *Carabinieri* that Il Duce was a prisoner at Gran Sasso, high on a peak in the Apennines. A prisoner of the Italians.

'We think they will use him to bargain with the Allies. There are negotiations going on to end the war,' he said.

But where was Claretta, Annabelle wondered. There was no news of her whereabouts, only scurrilous newspaper stories of her excesses and voracious appetites. The day after Mussolini's arrest, crowds converged on the Petacci villa, scrawling obscenities across the walls, but there had been graffiti every day for years now and apart from an increase in the insults, they had come to no harm. The family too had disappeared. Though she harped on it to Enrico, he had no interest in the fate of Claretta or her family.

Then one evening he arrived with news. 'It looks like Badoglio has had them arrested. The whole family.' He was not sympathetic.

'Serves them right. She is nothing but a *puttana* and the family has profited from that.'

'How can you!' They were all used to Enrico's swearing and brutal language, but how could he call Claretta a whore when he himself would sleep with any girl he could? Men! Could he not see that it was all for love? There was no use protesting though – he treated her as a silly child. She could not flounce from the room, for fear of missing something.

'There are more important things to consider than the fate of that *troia*,' he said. 'We are being bombed off the face of the earth. And no-one is in charge here.'

It was true. Not a day passed without news of bombs pelting down upon the cities. Naples obliterated. Genoa in ruins. One of the constant bombing raids on Milan nearly destroyed Leonardo's *Last Supper. Il Cenacolo* barely survived and three of the surrounding walls were destroyed. Fascist rhetoric was at a crescendo. *The Allies are destroying our cities!* LUCE newsreels shouted about the effects of the barbarous English aggressors. Ezra Pound's radio broadcasts spewed hysterical anti-Semitic and anti-American propaganda. '*Radio Londra* knew of the bombing,' Pound raged, 'was involved in it, make no mistake, the English want to wipe you from the face of the earth.'

Lies, lies and more lies from the British radio and the Anglo-Americans. The newspapers screamed it in gigantic headlines, lamenting the philistine approach of the Anglosphere to the art treasures of Italy. Look what they have done to La Scala, seat of more than a century of glorious music. But art was not then at the top of the Allies' concerns. It was industry and communication that had to be demolished. Turin and Milan and their factories were being bombed out of existence as refugees fled the north in terror. Not far from Florence in the Val d'Orcia, her mother's friend, the Marchesa Origo, had taken in hordes of children whose parents sent them away, to save them. Food was scarce because the south was devastated and crops were destroyed. In Palermo people were starving. Thousands were dead and there was no sign of a let-up in the Allied ferocity. Everywhere was bombed except, it seemed so far, Florence. Because Hitler loved Florence, said Florentines. Hitler loves our art, they said.

To Annabelle it was all news from afar. She had shifted a small table nearer to the French doors to the garden, in a vain attempt to get more of the syrupy air. Although the sun was long since set, the sultry August night brought no relief. Thunder rolled about the hills but no storm came to save them. The heavy rugs and tapestries of her father's study oppressed her in the summer, mouldering in the humid Florence basin. The thought of all those children sent far away from their homes, to complete strangers, gave Annabelle a squirmy feeling in her stomach. It was better than being bombed, but then, how did being bombed feel anyhow? She had lived her whole life between Impruneta and the palazzo in Borgo Pinti – summer trips to the seaside at Riccione did not count. There had been trips to London, and once to Paris, but that was another world and so long ago, she was too small to remember it – a world when people travelled for pleasure.

Annabelle had no interest in her geometry homework. The problem with not going to school was that there were no school holiday and no school friends. The geometry of her world was as remote to her as the flat Mollweide Projection in its giant frame, on the wall to the left of the doors. Her world and her sky grew smaller and flatter by the day.

She sat back in her chair and stuck both feet straight out in front of her, flapping them back and forth. Childish, they looked in the brown buckled sandals. The exposed summer skin between the straps was bronzed, her tidily clipped toenails perfectly suited the sensible sandals. Her mother's toenails used to be painted scarlet. She would bet Claretta's were too. Poor Claretta. Annabelle no longer envied her, but she was still anxious to know what had become of her – was she even alive? She blew damp wisps of hair from her forehead. Her parents were out for the evening and the house lay stunned in the heat. The only sounds were the drifting voices and footfalls from the narrow medieval streets where heels struck flint from the stone and voices racketed from wall to wall, but the outside world was muted by heavy doors and metre-thick walls.

Annabelle followed the thought of scarlet nail polish upstairs to her parents' bedroom, where the door was ajar. She rarely entered their room; her heartbeat accelerated a little and her breath fluttered as she pushed the door a sliver further and edged in. The expanse of pale blue silk – coverlet and cushions, upholstery and rugs – was more her mother's domain than her father's. He often slept in the dressing-room, to the side. Annabelle had never seen her parents in bed together. Did they do that, she wondered? Do that. Do what? Her hazy ideas of what *that* might be were formed from books and from Enrico's offhand tales of his conquests.

On a high shelf of her father's library was a leather-bound volume of the *Kama Sutra of Vatsyayana* by Sir Richard Burton. Rainy afternoons during their parents' rest-times, it used to provide the perfect pastime for two adolescents. But many of the illustrations, while fascinating to Enrico, were terrifying to Annabelle. Surely real people could not do that? Beside it stood a very old book called *Justine or The Misfortunes of Virtue* by the Marquis de Sade, but, said Enrico, it was better if she did not see that. There was another, a Latin text by Marcantonio Raimondi, with sixteen sonnets by Aretino. Enrico did not know she had climbed the rickety library ladder alone one recent afternoon and nearly fallen off in shock at the explicit engravings, which looked like battle scenes more than anything. It was not possible to imagine her coolly elegant parents engaged in any form of sexual activity and certainly nothing of the sort contained in those books.

In the silence of the bedroom with its high ornate bed, Annabelle's face scalded and her heart skittered, as much at her intrusion as at the very idea of her parents in bed. Making love, she called it, preferring the romantic poets and their veiled, allusive love. She took a deep, deep breath and exhaled very slowly. Much calmer, she drifted to the triple-mirrored dressing table in the window bay and sat on an embroidered piano stool her mother used for her toilette, turning in circles until it wobbled and almost collapsed. She screwed it back in the other direction and examined the glass-topped dressing table.

Two cut-glass perfume bottles with tasselled spray-pumps; a stemmed majolica dish spilling jewellery – pearls, an emerald locket from South America, a gold chain with a watch attached to it, and dangly amethyst earrings Annabelle had never seen her mother wearing; crystal pots of creams with etched silver lids; an enamelled powder compact and several lipstick cases. A pair of tweezers rested on top of one of the compacts and Annabelle imagined herself with her eyebrows plucked to the thin arcs favoured by the women of the

Trio Lescano, whose voices dominated the airwaves. She rolled her fringe tightly in imitation of their hairstyle then let it spring back and tidied it into her headband again.

Leaning forward, she plucked a hair from between her brows – it stung. She would not do that again! She brushed the single hair from the tweezers and placed them back. Everything had a fine film of face power from a large lambswool puff thrown down carelessly. With her finger, she traced the outline of the intricate design of the inlaid timber and mother-of-pearl beneath the glass. This craftsmanship came from Sorrento. Would she ever go to Sorrento? Or Capri? Or anywhere? From the mirrors, three Annabelles observed her sulkily.

Her parents rarely went out – tonight had been an exception, because an old friend was conducting at La Pergola. How odd it was that their world was being smashed to pieces, her own world was so confined, yet out there, a caricature of normal life continued. Many men were not at war: some too young or too old, some with medical conditions or in protected industries. Then there were those of an age where they should be in the war and yet strangely, were not in uniform, sinister reminders that all was not normal at all.

There were bodies in the streets; horses and carts were the mode of transport again and the smell of horse dung and fear was everywhere, seeping and creeping through cracks. Yet people flocked to concerts, the theatre and the galleries. At her age her parents had attended coming-out parties. Even now, people held birthday parties, weddings, engagements, eating and drinking as if bombs were not belting down all over the country. As if rationing did not exist.

Some people. Not in her family. The Black Market was the only way to indulge those extravagances and the Black Market was not tolerated there. Their table was a spartan affair, laid with only the food available under rationing and what came from the farm. No wonder Anna Maria and Sesto were happy to be sent out to the farm – at least there they could eat a little better than in town. Hunger was a constant topic everywhere.

According to Anna Maria, Sesto's Neapolitan brother-in-law told them that in Naples people were eating each other and girls as young as twelve prostituted themselves to the Allied soldiers for as little as a warm blanket. In the streets, prostitutes were sprayed with delousing solution as if they were cattle. Cannibalism and prostitution. Well, they are *Napolitani*, after all, Anna Maria said, with callous disdain for the south and its sins. She crossed herself.

'It's probably true,' Enrico had told Annabelle. 'They are starving. Many of them are living in caves with no food and no water and certainly no sanitation. Naples has always been a special case and now it is in ruins.'

She shivered and turned away from the mirrors. She did not want red toenails anyway. Enrico hated painted nails. She picked up the powder puff and let it fall from a great height, watching the starburst of powder settle more thickly. Then she left, closing the door at exactly the angle she had found it. She ignored her geometry and instead went to bed with Leopardi's poetry. Leopardi seemed appropriate; they were both prisoners of their own life.

Novara 1943
Follow the leader

Clara too was a prisoner, but she had no mind to read Leopardi. Her father telephoned the police immediately on the night of Ben's disappearance and their guard was restored at once. The night was calm and, apart from more vile things scrawled on the walls of the villa, nothing had changed by morning. They left Rome that day, and with their bodyguards travelled to the villa of Myriam and her husband at Meina. Surely there on Lake Maggiore they would be safe. Less than three weeks had passed – three weeks of a nightmare for Clara who could get no word of Ben and was terrified he was dead. It was odd how few of her old sources wished to speak to her. Quinto was unavailable. First, she was told Ben had gone back to Rocca delle Caminate for his own protection. How ridiculous. Was Rachele there? Next, she heard he was under arrest somewhere else, but she did not believe any of it. They could have killed him. She might be next. Anything was possible. Badoglio was in charge and he was their enemy. No-one was safe.

The days were endless and the nights much longer. Eating made her nauseous and her mother's sullen fretting and threatened heart attacks cast a pall over all of them. Her father barely spoke and no-one from the Vatican had been in contact with offers of help. So much for your Pope, said Giuseppina. It would soon be *Ferragosto*.

Then one clear sunny morning, when more athletic citizens were already swimming in the lake, Claretta and her mother and father and sister had barely awoken when a *Carabinieri* officer arrived with his men and courteously informed them they were under arrest, on the orders of Marshall Badoglio. It was almost a relief. They were bundled off to Castello Visconti in Novara.

'Well, it could be worse,' sniffed Giuseppina. 'At least Novara is a decent town.'

She was right though, it could be worse and it was. It turned out they had been arrested because Marcello had been up to his old tricks again. Giuseppina would hear no ill of her son but Francesco put it more bluntly. 'That imbecile of a brother of yours has caused this,' he told Clara.

Marc too was under arrest, it seemed. Ben was no longer there to rescue them. There was still no word of his whereabouts. It was as if he had never existed. His name was never mentioned. Though the director of the prison ensured they were well cared for by the nuns, the circumstances were not easy: rough straw beds crawling with vermin, insolent guards, dreadful food. The other prisoners never missed an opportunity to deride and persecute them and the city suffered air raid after air raid, the disaster being attributed to their presence, though everyone knew the Allies were bombing the country to pieces and had better things to do than search for them.

After one of the raids, the water was cut off and in the suppurating heat of high summer, prisoners and keepers suffered alike. Francesco paced and muttered and tried to avoid his wife. Giuseppina fanned herself, sighed and passed her time carping to the nuns about the inefficiencies all around her and the lack of regard for her station. The nuns saw little point in advising *la signora* to offer up her tribulations to the Saviour. Mimi – or Myriam as she now insisted on being called – sniffled and snuffled and clung to her mother. Clara clung only to her hope that Ben was alive and that he would survive, his health was so poor. Her own health had deteriorated and she was weak and lethargic. She retreated into her diaries, scribbling obsessively all day, closing off the world. If he was alive, he would come for her. If he was dead, she had no further desire to live.

The Inspector-General of Police was mystified by his prisoner's compliance. Could this be the feared figure of Il Duce, so long known for his belligerence? He had never been this close to his leader, whose voice he knew well from balconies and parade-grounds and whose portrait adorned his office. This frail little man was a great disappointment. Still, he thought, he himself was only forty-two and Il Duce was old now – we all get old. His duty was a delicate one and he did his best.

After two days in the police barracks, Mussolini had shown little interest in his fate. He asked what the reaction had been to his arrest and when told of the rejoicing in the streets and that his own militia did nothing, he nodded silently and did not mention it again. He quietly allowed himself to be bustled from place to place and eventually to the Gran Sasso. No-one seemed to know what to do with him and he offered no opinion on it.

On one of the stops, at the island of Ponza, Mussolini became overwrought on disembarking the ship, mortified at facing people. He disliked the sea and was clearly loath to leave the reclusion and safety of the vessel. It took his captors ages to persuade him, wheedling as with a child, to go ashore. Eventually he sulked his way down the gangplank with collar turned up and hat pulled down.

Once ashore, he retreated into reading and complaining about minor daily irritations, boring his captors with monologues on anything that came to mind. He did not enquire about the fate of his family or his friends or Clara. In answer to his idle questions about the constant changes of detention, he was told there was concern about him being captured by the Allies or even the Germans. He was in vehement agreement that he would not want the humiliation of being returned to power 'at the point of Hitler's bayonets'. In fact, he did not want to be returned to power at all. He was resigned to being in retirement, playing cards with his sheepish guards and haranguing them with his thoughts on Nietzsche. He lived in another world, said the *Carabinieri* with a shake of their heads. In the real world – the one where the war continued – bombs fell and people died, and for those who did not, life somehow went on.

The Führer's face was puce. Rage made him incoherent. Livid and incoherent was a constant state for him lately, his adjutant later said. Because Hitler would not permit spying on his great friend Il Duce, the Germans had no idea at first where Mussolini was held. Hitler knew the Italians would not remain loyal to the Axis agreement without their leader. He feared for his friend. He shouted, screamed, raged, banged his fist on tables, issued orders.

He wanted the King found and killed. The Vatican too had certainly been involved in Mussolini's demise and he wanted the Pope killed – he had always hated the Vatican. He would send crack troops to invade Rome, have the Pope killed, secure the art treasures of the Eternal City for removal to Munich, and occupy the whole country immediately. Or have the Pope kidnapped and taken to Munich.

The British Legate in Rome, hearing these whispers, burned all documents in preparation for the invasion. Goebbels, however, dissuaded Hitler from the assassination plan for the Pope and advised that they should instead find and rescue Mussolini and have him reinstated. Mussolini was essential to the Axis. It was Mussolini, after all, he reminded the Führer, who coined the term 'The Rome-Berlin Axis', proudly defining both countries as 'anti-Democratic, anti-Bolshevik and anti-Semitic'. The world had turned on its axis and now all allegiances were realigned.

Hitler loved Mussolini. His one true friend. They had so much in common – both were vegetarian, both plagued by ill-health, both abhorred alcohol and eschewed coffee, both obsessed with fitness, with fad diets. Both were given to fits of uncontrollable rage and obsessive behaviour. Both despised religion, yet fostered the Vatican while it suited them. In fact this Pope, Pacelli, had been Mussolini's man inside the Vatican throughout his whole tenure. One of their few differences was Hitler's deep devotion to art and Mussolini's complete indifference to it. The other more important difference was Hitler's implacable philosophical commitment to his programs. When

Mussolini styled himself Il Duce, Hitler thought it a stroke of genius and adopted it himself: Führer. The Leader. From the very beginning of his rise in 1933, Hitler had modelled himself on Mussolini. He wanted his friend back.

PART TWO

CHAPTER 5

Florence 1943

La resa

September 9, 1943

Last night we listened to the radio in disbelief. The wireless is our lifeline now. The rumours were true then. Nearly six weeks since Marshall Badoglio took over. The war goes on, he said. Now we have surrendered. We did not know whether to laugh or cry. Was it good news or bad? Even today, no-one knows. Hiatus. I have learnt a new word.

The household was unnaturally silent, counterpoint to the confusion on the streets. *Che vergogna.* What shame, people said. *Meno male. Grazie al Dio.* Thank God, people said. People said this and people said that, more and more and more. For days now, tongues wagged: a whispered whirlpool of rumour and supposition and perhaps and maybe and what if. If a drunkard or a madman stood screaming incoherently on a corner, people stopped and listened, searching for meaning in his rambling. Omens were espied, entrails examined, auguries invoked, portents flickered. They were saying the King had signed an Armistice with the Allies. Now it was true. The war was over. Or was it? Would it still be true tomorrow?

It seemed to Annabelle the entire house had undergone a strange haunting and she was a wraith. Enrico flitted back and forth at all hours, with no time for her. He smoked cigarettes openly and no-one remarked. Her mother spent longer and longer inspecting bed linen and laundry and supervising poor Anna Maria in the kitchen, with excruciating directions for even the simplest of meals. Sesto pushed the lawnmower around the borders of the parched herb garden, chopped the wood, sat on the woodblock rolling cigarettes and smoking in silence. He no longer hung around the kitchen for a chat. Chatting had dried up everywhere.

The cinnamon perfume of her father's pipe-tobacco filled the house – he smoked incessantly despite her mother's warnings about its effects, and found any excuse to get out of the house to the farm. Annabelle would love to have gone out to Impruneta with him but he said the roads were too dangerous – and she was reluctant to leave town because of Enrico. *Zia* Elsa had almost disappeared, perhaps frightened into keeping to her rooms. Her husband kept to his study upstairs except for the evenings when they all gathered in the down-stairs study for the Radio London news and Enrico's report. No news of Claretta.

Outside, the muddy stink of the Arno, low and turgid, vied with the smell of drains and bodies. Annabelle was not allowed out on her bicycle. The heat simmered, turning the walls and roofs, the bell-towers and chimneys, into shimmering mirages. Running footsteps evoked fear. Florence held her breath. Oh for some rain, they all said. Storm clouds gathered but skirted around the city and the only things falling from the skies were bombs. There was an air raid on Florence yesterday but though they all heard it, the damage was not close to the centre. Shots spat out at random and a shout was enough to make Annabelle's stomach drop out of her body.

She had constipation one day and diarrhoea the next. No-one mentioned homework or even registered her existence. Meals appeared and were cleared away, but she had no memory of eating them. Gatherings at the dining table were rare. She too retreated. At times, she climbed to the loggia from where she could see out over the rooftops to the Belvedere, where red poppies dotted the slopes around the fort. At others, she sat in her window seat with her legs tucked beneath her, chin resting on her hand, and gazed for hours on end into the street, or immersed herself in her books and her diary. Writing in her diary was the only thing that reminded her she was real – that and the itch of prickly heat. She had taken to biting her fingernails and her mother did not even scold her.

For weeks, Enrico had reported that the King and Badoglio were in negotiations with the Allies and now there was an Armistice signed. They had been, said Enrico, 'screwed over by the Allies' who had announced the unconditional surrender early to circumvent any wavering. The King and Badoglio fled to the south. Smoke hung over the city in the scramble to burn documents. Who was in charge? Would the Germans withdraw? What would the army do? There were no radio transmissions, no news. Government offices were deserted, phones dead, gunfire rattled about the city from the north – whose guns were they?

Rumours swirled, largely retailed by elderly men and women who could have no idea. Mussolini was dead. My cousin told me for a fact, said Anna Maria. The Allies were set to invade Florence from the south and would be here next week. It's a known fact, said the crippled man who came to sharpen their knives. They had been in Sicily now for two months and Enrico said they had landed at Salerno two nights ago, but that was not yet a 'known fact'. Salerno was a long way from Florence. Truckloads of Italian soldiers raced through the city, going where? To fight the Germans? Many questions, no answers. Soon a stream of those same soldiers, ragged, stunned and aimless, began drifting back from the north. In the sultry heat, tempers spilled and the pus of reprisal poisoned the city. Fascists, and possible fascists and sympathisers with fascists or anyone resembling a fascist, were hunted out and beaten or humiliated or killed. Professor Ottone Rosai had been beaten nearly to death.

'What will happen to Roberto?' Annabelle wondered.

Their cousin, a captain in the army, had been wounded in Africa, evacuated back to Italy just ahead of the surrender, and placed in charge of another division.

'Never mind about Roberto,' said Enrico, 'it's what the Germans will do that we should be worried about.'

The answer came two days later. As the German forces under Himmler's right-hand man, SS General Karl Wolff, rolled through the country, the Italian Army had no idea whatsoever what to do – no orders from their King or Badoglio, no directives from the command. Nothing. As the Germans advanced there was practically no army left, and those who remained did not feel enthusiastic about Badoglio's parting exhortation to oppose the Nazis.

Civilians were terrified and exhausted and could oppose no-one. On 11 September the Germans invaded Florence, arrested all Italian soldiers, and set up their barracks and headquarters in Piazza San Marco. The Germans took prisoners by the thousands, then tens of thousands, then people stopped counting. Most of the prisoners were shipped to Germany to labour camps. The rattle of machine-gun fire was a signal that an escaping prisoner had not made it, and the body lay where it fell until nightfall, when parents or wives came to take it away. The only mitigation came the in the form of the long-time German Consul, Gerhard Wolf, who did his best to help the citizens, warn the Jews, and head off the wholesale pillage of the city's art treasures by Goering. Otherwise, German contempt for the defeated Italians seared the population like battery acid.

Under German command, the fascists were given untrammelled power to conduct their own affairs and counter-reprisals began in earnest. Major Mario Carità was given headquarters in via Benedetto Varchi and put in charge of the Office of Political Investigation with enough men to conduct torture and murder on a scale sufficient to please both the fascists and the Germans.

'We are caught between two wolves. Carità is an animal. We have more to fear from our own people than from the Germans,' said Enrico.

As the Major's activities escalated, he was given more villas for detention of his victims. They were scattered throughout the city, and he set up in via Bolognese in what quickly became known as the *Villa Triste* – villa of sadness. Enrico and his friends were driven underground again. The Tuscan Committee of National Liberation was formed, and a concerted effort to get Jews out of the city and to plan a resistance began.

Gran Sasso 1943

High up in the clear mountain air of Campo Imperatore atop the Gran Sasso, Mussolini was not enjoying himself. The modernist circular architecture of the luxury ski resort glowered like a gun-emplacement on the bare plain, which was normally covered in snow. *Carabinieri* patrolled on all sides – at least two hundred of them. What did they think he was going to do? Try to escape? He had been dragged about the country like unwanted baggage and he was tired of it. For his own good, they said. To keep him safe. One of the *Carabinieri* who played cards with him at night, told him the Germans had been flying reconnaissance missions over their positions, looking for him, which was why he had had to be shifted about. Well, they would not find him here. The only way up was by cable car from the valley floor below.

He did not care. Tired and dispirited, he was uninterested in the war or the outside world. Food did not interest him. Neither did the gramophone they had offered, and he had not touched the violin. He had his books. At least up here was the silence he craved. The exclusion zone around Palazzo Venezia where he had forbidden car horns and traffic noise was all that had made Rome bearable, until he banned private vehicles and got some peace. Sipping his camomile, he picked at a sliced apple on a plate. Dressed in his blue and white striped pyjama top over his trousers, he was expecting his barber. He had not shaved for three days and it was probably time he tidied up. It was a little brisk – some snow had already fallen. Perhaps he should have the heat turned on. Wandering to the window to check the sky, he stopped dead, mid-stride.

Out of the sky, a squadron of German gliders appeared soundlessly, settling like blue cranes on the grassy slopes. One of the gliders landed heavily, tipping sideways. Soldiers spilled from them all and suddenly German paratroopers were everywhere. An Italian officer accompanied them. The *Carabinieri* were overwhelmed within minutes, without a single shot. Told in Italian to stand down or be executed, they willingly took the former offer.

Mussolini stood too, transfixed, at the window, until an officer entered. He introduced himself as SS-*Obersturmbannführer* Otto Skorzeny, snapped to attention, gave the Nazi salute and said, 'Duce, the Führer has sent me to rescue you.'

Mussolini nodded, replying flatly, 'I knew my friend would not abandon me.'

Behind the gliders, a Storch aeroplane taxied to a halt on the tufty grass. Mussolini found himself dressed in his heavy dark coat and fedora and, and along with Skorzeny, crammed into the Storch, almost between the feet of the pilot. The overloaded little plane staggered beneath the weight of the three men but, assisted by the downhill slope and the skill of the pilot, *Hauptmann* Heinrich Gerlach, they reached into the air and stayed there. They had intended, said Gerlach, to rescue him with one of the Drache helicopters used for rescuing downed pilots, but the machine had broken down and the decision was made to use the Storch. A helicopter! Only Germany had helicopters.

Roused from his torpor, Mussolini was thrilled. He and Hitler were obsessed by flight. Mussolini and both his sons were pilots. Italo Balbo was his great friend and Marshal of the Italian Air Force which, in the 1920s, Balbo built from the ground up under Mussolini's patronage. Through the twenties, Mussolini animatedly informed his rescuers, he financed aviators to fly all over the world, and Balbo flew two transatlantic flights. It was only ten years ago, he raved, that an Australian aviator crashed his plane and died on the slopes of a Casentino mountain. Il Duce had his body retrieved and gave him a State funeral in Florence. We are living in the age of flight, he enthused.

The enthusiasm was brief. He was unshaven, ill and spent. After the initial excitement he sank into silence, gloom and apathy, shrinking into the carapace of his dark hat and overcoat.

When asked where he would like to go, he replied, 'Take me home to Caminate. Where else? I am already dead and buried.'

When he found he was on his way to Munich instead, he simply shrugged, hunched himself deeper into his coat and went to sleep.

On arrival in Munich, Mussolini found his family waiting, but still could not manage enthusiasm. He was crumpled, tired, sunken-eyed, wanting to sleep forever. He was glad they were safe but the sight of Rachele was certainly not enough to rouse him – being back under her thumb was not a prospect he relished. She would be sure to begin issuing orders and instructions and harangue him about what was to happen – and he did not care what was to happen. He was glad enough to see his eldest son Vittorio, though; his hug, if tepid, was genuine. The next day, he was no more vital – at his meeting with

Hitler, he rambled and mumbled that he wanted to retire and go home. To avoid the fear of civil war in Italy, he claimed.

Hitler was having none of it. 'Utter rubbish,' he replied. 'Here is what you will do.'

Mussolini must either return as the leader of the Italians and continue the fight alongside Germany, or Hitler would take over Italy himself. If Mussolini agreed to return as leader, he must undertake to have all the traitors who had voted against him executed, including his son-in-law, Count Ciano. To Hitler, his old friend appeared smaller, shrunken and diminished, and though he found it hard to regain the old adulation, he loved him still and he needed him.

Two weeks later, with SS General Karl Wolff, 'Supreme Leader of all SS Troops and Police in Italy', Mussolini was flown to Gargnano on the shores of Lake Garda as head of the newly formed Italian Socialist Republic. The Republic of Salò.

Back in Novara, Clara was even more tired and almost as resigned – she was convinced by then that Ben was dead and that she soon would be. Her mother carped at her to take a little more trouble with her appearance, but it was not easy to maintain standards in the convent, and really, who cared? She would write a letter for every one of the days of her imprisonment. At least she could do that.

> *Neither distances, nor walls nor bars, nor jailers, can keep me from you. I love you. I love you. I think of you night and day.*

And then, out of the lowering sky, like a bolt of lightning came the news of the Armistice and of Mussolini's rescue. She fell to her knees and drew out her rosary. She should have known Saint Rita would look after him, with all the prayers she had offered up. Claretta's sobs of relief ricocheted throughout the corridors but did not generate much rejoicing for her. Now he will have us set free and send for us, she knew. She took up her pen.

> *Suddenly, they tell us you will speak on the radio tonight at 9.30 from Germany. I have a shock to the heart. I begin*

to tremble ... and in the profound silence, the radio sends
me your voice, your voice, your voice. My Ben, my Ben.
A convulsion, a shudder, a burst of unstoppable crying,
sudden violent sobs that I try to suffocate in the arms of
Mimi. I cannot, I cannot stop myself, it is all my soul that
overflows, I hear you, I hear you, you speak, you are love,
I live still to hear you, it is you.

Some time later, one of the prisoners told her that Il Duce was now on Lake Garda and that he was back in charge of the government – what could it all mean? Never mind, as soon as he got them out, she would know everything. The days passed and the nights did not and no news came from Ben. It was not possible that he had forgotten them! Or was it all lies and he was really dead?

Giuseppina complained to her daily. 'Find a way to contact him. It is impossible to think,' she huffed, 'that he is free and we are still here, locked up with these common felons.'

Then one day, after a lifetime had passed, one of the elderly nuns, looking furtive, produced the local newspaper for Clara – the girl might be a sinner, she said to her sisters, but she was suffering, *poverina*. Greedy for news of any sort, Clara rushed to her cell to read it, only to learn that Rachele and the family had joined Ben on the lake. So it was true. The words tumbled over each other on the page as if the ink had run – the heat of her rage almost set her clothes on fire. Her breathing escalated to danger point and she began to hyperventilate. Knowing what would follow, her mother called for help – she was smaller than her daughter and could not hold the weight as Clara collapsed forward over her. The nuns ran back and forth carrying damp cloths and water. They too would be relieved when that fractious family was released. The sooner the better, they muttered.

At last, Clara managed to get a letter smuggled out through the nuns, who sent it to the German headquarters in Novara, and the very next day, a German staff car arrived with an SS escort and collected the whole family. They were taken, not to Ben, but to Merano.

'At least it is not prison,' said Giuseppina, 'and Merano has always been a very nice town.'

CHAPTER 6

Florence

Resurrection

September 23, 1943

*I will never forget the sound of his voice today. It was like
hearing a ghost. No, a monster. A monster you thought
was dead who then came back to life. People were terrified.
How I have come to hate the wireless.*

They had lived through more than twenty years of fascism, called
il ventennio, then Mussolini's dismissal, the defection by the King
and Badoglio, weeks of uncertainty, the surrender and the German
invasion. For nearly two months, Mussolini's absence glowered over
them. Then suddenly he was there: a little reedier, a faint tremor, but
indisputably Il Duce.

*After a long silence you can hear my voice again. Unless
you present yourself immediately you will be considered
rebels, ribelli ...*

It was Annabelle's seventeenth birthday. In the kitchen, her
mother and Anna Maria were making a celebration lunch, with
whatever ingredients they could assemble. They had sugar and they
had eggs – a *torta*, they said. A cake. Hearing his voice issuing from
the cathedral arch of the Philco radio, Annabelle imagined a zombie
rising from the grave like the story in an old book called *The Magic
Island*. Why did we not drive a stake through his heart? Isn't that
what they did to vampires? Her mind twitched with more static than
the radio. It made a lie of everything they thought they knew. We

thought we were at war, said her uncle, but that was nothing; for us, the real war begins now.

The familiar voice on the wireless was a sharp blade rending the already tattered fabric of daily life. The heart went out of the birthday festivities.

September 24, 1943

We have heard through Enrico's sources that Marshall Badoglio has officially surrendered and signed the full Armistice with the American President. His name is Roosevelt. Is that a Jewish name? It was on a ship called HMV Nelson off Malta. I looked up Malta on the map. It looks so small, so unimportant.

Sept 26

Yesterday we were bombed. Bombed! The noise, the fear, the confusion. It felt as if the whole city was turned into an inferno. They were supposed to hit the railway station at Campo di Marte. Rome was bombed dreadfully last week. Thousands injured and the Pope distributed money from one of the basilicas. He cares more about his precious Vatican not being bombed, Enrico says. We have been hearing for six months about the bombing of Milan and the dead and the damage but it was all like the cinema to us. Until now. You could hear it everywhere in the city. Anna Maria was screaming like a madwoman and Mamma could not comfort her. So the Allies are our friends. What good friends, killing us, she shouted. She was not even there. I was.

Annabelle walked her bicycle over the rough patches of the footpath. It was Saturday and she was going to visit Nonna's friend Alma who lived near Campo di Marte. Alma had no telephone and Nonna was worried about her. She is getting on, she said, she is finding it hard to get out. Nonna Lucrezia always referred to 'the old people' as if she herself were not one of them.

The state of the roads and footpaths deteriorated more every day and it was harder and harder to ride the *bici*, for the huge potholes.

There was no money, no time and no labour for mending roads. The Germans had other priorities. Towards the station of SM Novella, the surface improved and Annabelle re-mounted her bike to cross the piazza. At least with no cars it was easy to cross the great expanse in front of the station, though it was wise to be careful of Nazi trucks and fascist militia vehicles because these days they owned the road and never looked out for cyclists or pedestrians.

Thinking of that, she narrowly avoided running into the rear of a cart with a horse between the shafts. Laughing at herself for the near miss, Annabelle's good humour was restored. It was not as if she could be spending Saturday in the country or at the seaside. The sky was clear. It was steamy, not unbearably hot, though to the north, heavy clouds were gathering. Was that a roll of thunder? A storm would clear the air. She pedalled faster, as she had not brought a raincoat.

The low grumble of the B17s was audible long seconds before the bombs fell. The planes came out of the north and out of the clouds and filled the whole world with their rage. The air rippled and trembled and the ground vibrated. Annabelle's bicycle reared beneath her and threw her to the ground. The hot stones of the pavement scorched her hands and knees. In the seconds it took her to scramble to her feet, the scream of the bombs warned her the storm was upon them. Annabelle had never seen bombers before. She abandoned her bike and turned to run back towards the centre and then the bombs hit. There must have been thousands of bombs because they went on falling and falling and falling. Would they never stop? A curtain of noise and dust came down on the scene between Annabelle and the station. She could see nothing, feel nothing, hear nothing.

She was lifted off the pavement and thrown sideways against the walls of the cloisters of SM Novella. For long moments she lay immobile, blinded by the dust and unable to hear because ... why could she not hear? She was deaf! Don't panic, don't panic, she said loudly. She could feel now, and what she felt was terror; her heartbeat was louder than the crashing stone walls about her and she did not seem to be able to get enough air. She shook her head from side to side and beat her ears with her hands. But no, she was not deaf. The streets were filled with sound and she could suddenly hear it all – screaming of bombs and screaming of people and running feet and moaning. By now her lungs were working again. She could see too. The horse lay still, between the shafts of its overturned cart. Was it dead? The driver was nowhere to be seen.

The predator planes droned off to the north, leaving the dead in their wake. Annabelle pushed herself straight and sat against the wall. Her chest was heaving and she could hear a sobbing that must be hers. Carefully, she prodded her arms and legs. Nothing broken. There was a large egg on the side of her head where she had hit the wall, but when she got to her feet she was not dizzy and she could walk. By now, the police and ambulances added to the noise. It was still impossible to tell what had happened as the dust was too thick, but it looked as if the bombs had fallen to the rear of the station. People ran back and forth with little idea of what to do, and an elderly man sat weeping in the gutter before her, his face a mask of dust, etched with wet runnels of tears. She touched him on the shoulder but he stared right through her. He was not wounded.

I wonder where my bicycle is, she thought, then, I must get home. *Mamma, Mamma*, she thought, or did she call it? Stumbling, she caught her foot in the hem of her skirt, which was torn and hanging to the ground. She bent and ripped at the material, tucked the hanging bits into her belt and kept walking. Keep walking. Keep walking. All about her was hell – a swirling storm with people at the centre. The air was sulphurous. She tasted blood in her mouth.

Not thousands of bombs, said Enrico, the next day. But certainly dozens, perhaps hundreds. There were thirty-odd aeroplanes. They were American, he said. B17s sent to bomb Bologna, but the cloud cover was too heavy so they decided to unload their bombs on the shunting yards of the railway station in Florence, but their aim was poor and they only hit some of the target and lots of the population. More than two hundred people dead, hundreds more injured. Until then, apart from an air raid a couple of weeks ago, Florence had largely been spared the destruction of the rest of Italy. People said it was because the Allies respected Florence as the centre of art.

'Balls!' said Enrico. 'You watch. Once the Allies begin to move up, the bombs will fall like rain.'

It was three weeks since they landed at Salerno. The Americans will be here in no time, Anna Maria said often, unsure whether that was a good thing or bad. Annabelle was not confident. The grip of the *Nazifascisti* tightened every day. The streets were plastered with posters, proclamations, orders and deportations. The Germans, they're not all bad, you know, said the local greengrocer. Yes, they are, Annabelle thought. She had no inclination to see Germans as people.

After breakfast, she set off to retrieve her bicycle. The walk along via Panzani to the station was familiar and normal but her heart rate escalated with every step closer to the piazza. Her hands were sweaty. She came to a halt at the back of SM Novella and had to steady herself against the same wall she had been thrown against yesterday. Her breathing was ragged – she did not know what she had expected but the sight of the horse's body, covered in dust and flies, gave her an electric shock. She edged around the corpse, trying not to see the flies crawling in the horse's nostrils and open eyes, to where she had fallen from her bike. It was gone. Someone would be glad of it. There was no damage apart from loose stones, the horse and the overturned cart. The horse must have died of shock. The bomb damage was all to the rear and the side of the station.

She turned down the road to the west of the station and tumbled into another world. Mounds of rubble filled the street where people scrabbled and scavenged among the bricks and stone and plaster, for small treasures from the life they lived before yesterday. The air was already thick with the smell of death and escaping gas. In the middle of a street reduced to a slag-heap, a single wall of three stories stood alone, doors and windows open, on the second floor, an iron balcony with a chair, the cupola of the Duomo framed in the vacant windows. Houses were open to the street, their secrets exposed, entire walls missing, many with rooms still decorated as if their residents had just stepped outside. It was embarrassingly intimate, like an old woman in her underwear, without her teeth. There were no stairs: curtains fluttered limply at windows onto nowhere and sofas hung at oblique angles to the road. It reminded Annabelle of the open-fronted dolls' house she treasured as a child, now stored in the attic, but there were no figures in the rooms here – no-one sat to read beneath the ruched silk lampshade. No-one dreamed beneath the embroidered covers

81

of the beds. No-one ate from the bowls still sitting on tables. On the walls, portraits of Il Duce hung askew. From time to time, the portraits, or pictures of mountain scenes, or photographs of grand-children or calendars for the twenty-first year of the Fascist Calendar or crazed mirrors released their hold on the cracked plaster and fell, crashing into the debris with explosions of dust. A child's rag doll spiralled from the tilted edge of a bedroom to the bricks below and lay still.

To her left, a team from the Misericordia worked with shovels and picks while behind them, an elderly woman stood rigid, her face impassive and her eyes fixed on some distant point, as another, younger version of her sobbed and beat her fists against her temples. *Poverina*, said a man to Annabelle, her baby is under the rubble. Annabelle wanted to turn and flee but her legs would not move. Farther down the street, a whole palazzo lay on its side. The bodies of the dead and the wounded had been removed, but only those on the surface. Beneath the debris lay others, frantically sought by teams of family and friends and city workers. They worked silently, so as to hear any call from under the wreckage. But no call came. Finally she turned and wobbled away.

Annabelle's centre of gravity tilted sideways with the bombing. She developed a tic at the side of her mouth that twitched constantly. It was as if some part of her were damaged, though there were no external wounds. She would never feel safe again – there had been no air-raid warning, there were not enough shelters, not enough rescue-workers. There was not enough food and even less faith. She had stopped asking Enrico for news of Claretta but she gleaned bits and pieces of news from the newspapers. The family had been released from prison and sent north, she read. Enrico did not understand. Better not to raise it with him – it only made him angry. No matter what Enrico did, she would always love him. She would never leave him. She would be loyal to him forever. Why could he not see that Claretta had no choice?

The North 1943

September 23, 1943

I hear my beloved's voice. I will never forget the sound of his voice today. My prayers to Saint Rita are answered.

'Ben, my great Ben. *Amore mio.*' From Merano to Gargnano, the letters sped back and forth for a month. 'Everything I am is yours and belongs to you in every moment of your life. The only thing you have ever done wrong is to place your trust in the dwarves around you who let you down.' Her love for him, she wrote, despite all, 'retains the pure and spotless light of the dawn of life.' She begged him to send for her. His replies were muted and nerveless. '*Mia cara* Clara, if you only knew how bitter and full of ashes my mouth is.' He was too tired. Hitler however, was not inclined to let the romance lapse. He needed the Duce in better form and he ordered General Wolff to bring Clara to Lake Garda.

The surface of the lake glittered beneath a soft blanket of mist. It was almost October. The leaves were turning, there was a mist every morning. Behind the villa, the vines stretched up the hillside, golden, russet, yellow, ready for the *vendemmia*. From the terrace of the villa, Claretta watched Ben's car inching up the gravel drive. Shivering slightly, she crossed her arms and turned back indoors, wishing she had thrown a cardigan over her shoulders. She had spent hours deciding what to wear, then returned to her original choice of high-waisted slacks and an open-necked shirt with the collar turned up. She had put on lipstick then wiped it off. Now she glanced sideways in the mirror – too thin, too drawn, too old. No matter, it was the best she could do for the moment. She undid the top button of the shirt and adjusted her cleavage – at least she still had a little. Taking several deep breaths, she closed her eyes for a moment.

At the crunching of gravel and the slamming of car doors, she took another unsteady breath and stood very straight, a vein pulsing at the side of her throat. The heavy footsteps on the stone stairs could not be Ben, and yet there he was, in the French doors – too thin, too drawn, too old.

83

'Oh my darling, what have they done to you?' She rushed at him, and he allowed himself to be held and the front of his tunic to be soaked with her tears. She felt as if *she* were the taller.

With her hands on either side of his face, she gazed into his eyes, willing him to respond. His breath was sour. He patted her shoulder, nodding, nodding. She led him to a sofa before the fireplace and he allowed himself to be seated, as if he were blind. He was still nodding. He was here, wasn't he? That would have to be enough for now. Ben was more than sixty. He was shocked, frail. It would be all right. He still needed her. She poured him some tea and coaxed him into speech. He said nothing about ending it and he assured her he had no interest in other lovers, she was his great love, she had no cause for jealousy.

She had no cause for celebration either. This was a different man.

CHAPTER 7

Florence 1943

> *October 13*
>
> *We are officially at war with Germany. So Marshal Badoglio informed us today on the radio. From Brindisi where he and the King are hiding. What has this been then, if not war?*

Life had become a series of spies spying on spies spying on spies who in turn spied on others. In every bar and tobacconist, at every bus stop or bakery or fishmonger, gossip changed hands like black market goods. Everyone was under suspicion. The old men who drank their coffee each day at the edge of every piazza and in every bar, were certain they detected in this stranger or that visitor or even that neighbour, a spy for the Germans or a spy for the fascists or a spy for the partisans, depending on where their own sympathies lay. Only two doors away, that week, a body was found in the courtyard, executed it was said, by the rebels for having been a fascist spy. The boy was barely older than Enrico. His family were fascists. Was he a spy? Who could know? Enrico said he had heard nothing about it, but then he might not tell Annabelle even if he had.

Enrico said Claretta and her brother Marcello had been spying for the Allies. He is only saying that because he hates them, Annabelle thought. How would he know? And anyway, she was beginning to sound as if she were playing a game of 'Simon says'. Enrico says this and Enrico says that. Why won't you tell me? Why won't you trust me? Why won't you let me come with you and help you? She pestered him at every turn.

'Because it is not safe, it is too dangerous for you. Knowing puts you in danger. And anyway, *Ciccia*, you have the bad habit of writing everything down.' He kissed his forefinger and placed it on her forehead.

Sometimes she could hate him! The side of her mouth twitched. Why does everyone in the family simply accept that Enrico is in charge? Why do they all have to do what Enrico says? She knew the 'Simon says' game came from Cicero: Cicero says do this. Enrico is beginning to think he is Cicero. He is not Cicero – but if he is not careful, he will meet the same end.

The country was split into two: the Kingdom of the south under Victor Emmanuel III and Badoglio, with the Italian Social Republic, the Republic of Salò, under Mussolini in the north.

'Puppets at both ends of the Peninsula and the Allies fighting the Germans in between,' her father said.

Not that he said much these days, but he too warned her about her diaries.

'Even Anna Maria can no longer be trusted,' he reminded her.

They all knew Anna Maria had long ago fallen, as she often said, beneath the spell of Il Duce's deep and beautiful eyes, and could not understand the family's agnostic attitude to the regime. Or to life, for that matter.

'He is friends with the Pope,' she told Annabelle, replacing a pin in her thinning grey hair where the pink of the skull showed through. She retied the strings of her apron beneath her bosom firmly, to deflect argument. 'One of the best things Il Duce ever did was he put back the crucifixes in the schools and courtrooms when I was a girl.'

Like thousands of couples across the country, she and Sesto had given her wedding ring to Il Duce for the war effort in Ethiopia in the euphoria of 'The Day of the Wedding Ring'. Bishops and nuns gave their gold rings too, and even cardinals contributed their gold chains. Think of it, said Anna Maria, our Queen gave her ring and made a speech for us on the day.

Now Anna Maria and Sesto and their compatriots were afraid of the Germans and the Allies, and torn between Il Duce and the King. No-one had any confidence in the King, widely hated for deserting them. King Victor Emmanuel had never inspired much confidence. A lonely prosaic ditherer, he was too short, too bored, too French, to wield any authority. He could easily have ordered his army to stop Mussolini twenty years ago and he had been too weak to do so. Now the two men were bookends to a history of failure – parroting Enrico again, but this time Annabelle agreed with him.

Italy was divided by scratches on the map: the Gustav line, the Caesar line, the Albert line, the Heinrich line and lastly, the Gothic line. Enrico drew them on the map for her, but the country was divided by far more than ink marks on an atlas. Italy had almost ceased to exist. The city was littered with leaflets falling like summer snowflakes, urging all men and boys to join up, to enrol to fight for the RSI. They could join the Decima Mas, under Prince Valerio Borghese. Or there was the Muti Battalion of Blackshirts, or the Fascist Republican Militia. The important thing was to join, before it was too late.

Her father was spat upon in the street last week, for not supporting the new Fascist State. He had not supported the old one, but this was different. Men, workers who had tipped their caps to him, stalked past without greeting. Anna Maria gave in her notice and then, unsure how she would eat without the bit of food that came from Impruneta, baulked at the prospect and retracted it.

In households throughout the city, the quandary of whether to flock back to the known world of Il Duce, or run to the dubious protection of the King and the Allies, or throw in their lot with the partisans, divided fathers and brothers and cousins. In the streets, the sodden leaflets rotted underfoot into sludge, making the stones slippery and dangerous. Or more slippery and more dangerous. The war had been going on for nearly three years, but now the real war came calling, came right into their homes, and it wore the faces of foreign soldiers, both Allies and Germans. In every corner of the country people were forced to choose. *Nazifascisti* they said. Germans and Italians. Allies, Germans, Italians – they all killed you.

Further north, it was easier to choose between the Germans and the Allies, but the fascists made people choose between Italians or

Italians. Betrayal was in the drinking water. When Annabelle looked at the lines on the map, drawn in red ink, she saw only blood.

Anna Maria could have been any one of the thousands of elderly women of the city – gaunt, stringy, malnourished, enduring. Her mouth had been full and soft once. Sesto loved to run his tongue around the ridged outline of her lips. It always seemed to make her pregnant. That was long ago. Now her mouth was as thin as the rest of her, no more than a pencil-line of anxiety. She liked this family well enough. They were not bad people on the whole, but she struggled to understand their ways. They did not go to Mass, but the nobility could do as they wished in that regard; they were not like her kind. They did not belong to the Party and that worried her, even more since the unbelievable events of recent months. However, a job was a job, and without one they would starve. There was food here and these people were kind.

The comings and goings of recent weeks worried her more than ever but she had long since learned not to know things. The house teemed with silent activity. The *Signora* was not herself lately and it was hard to follow her orders, but Anna Maria simply nodded and then did as she wanted because it was ages since *Signora* Eleanora bothered to follow up her instructions. Spoilt they were, these women. Anyway, Anna Maria was an honest person and could be trusted to do what was right. *Signorina* Annabelle was also behaving strangely, and Jesus, Mary and Joseph, let us not even think about the *Signora* Elsa! A sly one, that. Up to no good. Had them all fooled, if you asked her. Put on airs and graces, floated about like a *deficiente*, but she was not as dumb as she made out. And the boy was trouble, Enrico. Always a wild one, him. His mother's fault. He would be up to no good in the mountains. She prayed for them all at night because if he got killed, *Signora* Eleanora would go mad. She loved him like her own son and she was not strong. She has never had to work. Not one of them has ever had to do a day's work in their lives.

They worried about her too, she knew. She heard the Count telling his brother to be cautious, even in the house, but there was no need. She and Sesto had their own daughters to worry about and they both agreed that Gino, one of the sons-in-law who was missing, was probably in the mountains too, God help us. This was not like any other war. It was tearing families apart. How could you know what to think? Her mouth got thinner and straighter with each day.

Her stomach was the one rounded thing about her and that was only because her uterus had dropped. It gave her trouble, yes it did, but there was nothing to be done about that. Old age. She rubbed methylated spirits on her knees every night but they still creaked and gave her pain. Her breasts, once full, now hung low, loose flaps of skin beneath her enveloping floral apron and the endless layers of undergarments she wore to keep warm. She never seemed to be warm enough. Her wire-rimmed glasses were no longer the right prescription but there were no more to be had now, so she squinted through gimlet eyes to perform even the simplest of tasks. Sewing had become a purgatory. She probably did not clean corners as well as she used to but no-one cared, though the Count could get very gruff if there were stains in the coffee cups so she was careful there. Reading had never been part of her job so it did not matter that she could no longer read. She had never been able to read more than a few words anyway. No-one like her could. What do we need to read for? It's all bad news anyhow. Her children had been to school and she was proud of that. See, that was Il Duce too. Four years of school, they had. One of them had nearly five.

Il Duce offered Anna Maria and Sesto a life they had never dreamed of. Her elderly parents embraced the Party with all their hearts and so did she and Sesto. They were wood-burners, *Carbonai*. Her parents were also wood-burners. They cut the timber from the forest, split it into large faggots, bundled it and hauled it down to their pits where they began the long process of carbonisation to turn the wood into fuel. Hard, hard work, it was. Made you old before your time. From early spring to late autumn they lived in a shack high in the valleys. While the men cut and hauled the timber and tended the fires that rendered it into fuel that filled their lungs with the smoke, the women hauled water and gave birth alone and tried to keep their families alive. Two dead babies and two live daughters, Anna Maria and Sesto had. Two little grassy mounds sprinkled with mountain flowers, on the high side of the valley where the sun would warm them each morning. Two little wooden crosses. Two little boys who seemed so perfect but did not breathe. Well, who could understand the ways of *Il Signore*. Our Lord. It was not for her to question these things. She just had to get on with looking after the ones she was given. Teach them their prayers and how to survive in this world. Some even tried to teach their children to read and write but few had time for such luxuries. No-one had ever told them they counted for anything.

'Tell me,' Annabelle said to her one day, perched on the edge of the kitchen table, 'tell me what it was like in the mountains.' She patted the old woman's veiny hand.

Anna Maria enjoyed answering the girl's questions about her life. She often came to the kitchen. She was lonely, *poverina*. So many people in this house, but they were all lonely. Anna Maria had never worked for the nobility before and their ways were certainly different. She clucked her tongue.

'You couldn't understand,' she said. 'We had nothing. No-one cared about us. Not the government, not the King, no-one. We had never been given anything in our lives. The socialists promised us everything but we never saw them. Maybe they helped the workers but not the *contadini*. Il Duce helped us. He gave us respect – and gifts: blankets in the winter and suchlike.'

Then there was the miracle of Sesto's teeth. Even if he did complain all the time that they hurt and made him look like an *asino*, and even if he did take them out to eat and leave them grinning at her from the sink or the kitchen table, he could not manage without them and he would not have had dentures at all if not for Il Duce. She herself, now, she did not need them. She still had a few good teeth left in her head and they would see her out. *Se Dio vuole*, God willing! She crossed herself. And a sewing machine, he gave us, imagine that! He told us we were Italians. He gave us a schoolroom.

'For years after that war killed my uncles and crippled my father, he looked after us. He loved us.'

It was the Blessed Virgin Mary that gave Sesto the accident that meant he was no good for this war, she thought. Her eyes misted. She said a rosary of thanks for that, once a week. 'We lived in a *baita* up in the valley. In a cowshed. It took days to walk down to the town and the townspeople looked down on us and our children anyway.'

She raised her hands, palms open, and dropped them again with a shrug, helpless in the face of a world overturned. 'We believed in him. It is our fault things did not go well for him. It was not his fault. *Se lo sapesse Il Duce.* If he knew about the bad things people did he would have been angry but they kept it all from him. We were not up to the faith he placed in us. He was the only thing we ever had to believe in and we failed him. What are we to believe in now? We let him down.'

The babies who died were boys and only the girls survived, so Anna Maria and Sesto had no sons to send to war for Il Duce. She was secretly glad of that but it shamed her even more. She should know these things, the *signorina*. She was a good girl, even if she was a bit spoilt. She cared. She hiked at the garters holding the heavy stockings sagging at her ankles.

'Though I don't know what more we could have done. And now this changing sides – it's wrong. I don't want any more war but it's wrong. It brings shame upon us. You don't know what it is like – you never believed in him. For us it is unbearable. We have nothing left to believe in if we don't support him now.'

Her tone was limp. It was hard to believe in this new Duce who seemed so far away – a ghost. She tied her apron tighter about her stomach and pounded the flour on the scrubbed wooden tabletop. They added all the seeds and husks they could gather to the bread these days. 'You all talk about hunger as if it is something new. We always knew hunger. We never had enough to eat. We had no medicine. We did not have water except what we hauled from the stream, an hour's walk away. Il Duce gave our village an aqueduct, you know. We had only the food we managed to grow. We only knew hunger until Il Duce began to look after us. It is that terrible woman who brought us all to this.'

She made the sign of the cross.

'What have you got all over your jacket?' Annabelle carried Enrico's tweed jacket from the hook inside the wardrobe under the main staircase. A large patch of the luminous greens and browns was matted into a single colour with a rusty paste. 'It looks as if you went hunting in it.'

'What were you doing in that cupboard? Give it to me.' He jerked it from her.

'Mind your own fucking business!' he shouted as she opened her mouth to answer.

She struggled to stop her chin trembling. She had been looking for a pair of old boots to give to a man who had come to the door asking for food. She tried to explain but Enrico was already gone, with a bang of the door. He had never shouted at her before. What had he been up to? The anti-fascists were active everywhere now. Communists, the butcher told her, all communists. But she knew Enrico was not a communist. She had seen a small paper called *La Libertà* in his room, belonging to something called the Action Party, but what action, she was unsure. He went out at night to meetings of this party and Annabelle was convinced his mother had gone with him on occasion, bizarre as that seemed. Reports of the clandestine newspapers and leaflets, and the cutting of telephone-exchange wires and derailing of trains and other acts of sabotage, were in the news every day – the acts of traitors and rebels who would be shot when caught. Bolsheviks, communists, saboteurs, socialists.

The eleven o'clock bulletin brought no good news but it was habit. Annabelle was almost asleep, curled into the high wing-backed armchair, a cushion under her arm.

'Why don't you go to bed, *Ciccia*,' Enrico said.

'Why don't you mind you own business,' she snarled. 'I'm not tired.'

Her father, busy tamping tobacco into his pipe, glanced up in mild surprise, shrugged and returned to the ceremony of the pipe – one of the few pleasures still left to him. As the deep gong of the clock boomed eleven, the news broadcast began.

> *A German officer of the 90th Panzergrenadier Division was assassinated in Florence last night by two socialist traitors. A hand grenade was thrown into a bar in via Faenza, where five officers were the last customers, enjoying a nightcap. One was killed and the others wounded. It is believed one of the assassins was wounded in the attack.*

Annabelle sat straight in her chair. Her pulse pounded in her ears.

The news bulletin must have continued but she heard nothing else. She looked at the wall, careful to avoid Enrico, who tensed but did not turn his head. Her father clucked his tongue and noticed nothing.

Annabelle said, very quietly, 'You are right, I am tired. I think I will go to bed.'

Her legs were rubbery. Of course it was blood on his jacket. As she left the room, the radio voice continued:

The German High Command has not yet announced the reprisals for the act of barbarism committed in via Faenza.

CHAPTER 8

Florence 1943

Into the mountains

'*Voi avete fatto un bel cazzo!*' Enrico's voice. 'You all did absolutely fucking nothing! You could have stopped him. Years ago, you could have stopped him. But you were too arrogant. You thought he was a buffoon and you allowed him to do whatever he wanted.'

Annabelle heard the shouting from the kitchen.

'You are joining the communists.' *Zio's* voice, loud, tremulous.

'Communists. That is what this is all about. You old men were so afraid of the communists you let Mussolini and his morons do whatever they wanted all these years and now you cannot stop them.' Enrico was hoarse. 'Look at what is happening here. What about the Jews?'

It was not a fortnight since a train pulled out of Santa Maria Novella with three hundred of the city's Jewish population, headed for Germany.

'They say more than a thousand Jews from Rome were on a train out of Ferrara on the twenty-third. They are killing them. And they are killing us.'

Annabelle pelted along the hall, barging into the library without knocking. Enrico stood at the doors to the garden in the far wall. Outside, shreds of fog were drifting spectres. Her father turned, raising a hand at the intrusion, and let it fall to his side.

'You might as well come in. You will only listen at the door anyway.' There was a white line about his lips.

Zio Francesco also turned to her, his eyes as red as the tip of his nose. 'Tell your cousin he's a fool.'

He's going. She knew it. He's going. Her heart was choking her. She moved towards Enrico who did not turn to her. From the moment they heard of the fall of Naples to the Allies, he had talked of nothing else but joining the liberation of Rome. After the reprisals for the death of the German in the bar, he really had no choice.

'She won't stop me, will you?' he said and then, with his hands on the door frame, he leant forward, his head on the icy glass, and said more quietly, 'And you needn't think telling Mamma will stop me because she would go herself if she could.'

For a moment, the four formed a mute tableau, each mind roiling. Annabelle's breathing was like the roar of the sea in her ears.

'If you get killed ...' she whispered.

Still Enrico did not turn. An aureole of condensation formed on the cold glass around his head. Like a Holy Picture, thought Annabelle, *i Santini*. That was another thing denied her in this liberal, unbelieving family. How she used to envy her little friends their pictures with deckled, gilt edges and beatific skies of gold and azure, background to a blond and glowing Jesus, or the Virgin Mary wrapped in shades of lapis lazuli and the saints in their flowing robes and flowers.

Finally, he turned, his mouth set in the mulish look they all knew well, his eyes glittering. He had never looked more beautiful to Annabelle. Everything about Enrico was vertical lines and sharp angles. Except for his eyes and his mouth. His grey eyes, set deeply behind round glasses, shone with a restless curiosity which, combined with his ridiculously full mouth, was not only irresistible to Annabelle but to most of the girls he knew. He had told Annabelle he had lost his virginity at fourteen and not – as was the custom – with a prostitute, and she had every reason to believe him.

Enrico sighed. 'Look,' he said more gently, 'I'm not going to join the communists. Nor the anarchists. Nor the monarchists. I am not going for any political motives. I have no choice. If I stay, I will be killed anyway. I'm going because if you put a chain around my neck, I will shake it off. As simple as that. I'm going to fight with *Giustizia e Libertà* and if I die, so be it.'

She knew it! Justice and Liberty. He had been going to those clandestine meetings of the Action Party in Dr Vanucci's house all this time, and Justice and Liberty was the brigade they had formed. She knew it all and she knew his mother would not stop him because her aunt Elsa had been going to those meetings too. With that, Elsa entered as if summoned. She was absolutely calm and she seemed ... taller.

Why, Annabelle wondered, did all family meetings and events and celebrations and commiserations, seem to take place in their apartment? *Zio* was the elder brother and head of the family. Or perhaps because theirs was the larger apartment, with the ground floor giving onto the *cortile*, the internal courtyard once used for the stable and workshops, as well as the first floor, or *piano nobile* with its tall windows and frescoed ceilings. Or perhaps because her own mother, Eleanora, had once been warm and motherly and welcoming and never found anything a bother and they all felt welcome. Once. *Zia* Elsa on the other hand, was always a little, well, absent. *Testa per aria*, they said. Head in the clouds. Dreamy. Always had her head in a book. Like me, really, thought Annabelle, though not to look at.

Elsa was tiny: slight, insubstantial, with masses of dark curly hair. So unlike the rest of her sturdy blond family. Annabelle had never known her to be ill, but with her air of fragility no-one wanted to bother her, no-one expected anything of her. She looked like the English paintings by Waterhouse in *Zio's* study, and he thought so too. *Zio* Francesco adored his wife. Uxorious, said Enrico. Annabelle had meant to look the word up. She had never seen her own parents touch, but Elsa and Francesco sought each other's eyes when they were both in a room, leaned against each other unconsciously, and he had the habit of absently stroking her hair as they talked. Francesco was never, for a moment, unaware of his wife's presence.

Elsa was afraid of the shiny polished timber-and-brass telephone recently installed on the wall in the foyer. She could see no use at all for it and made it clear that if she wished to speak to someone she would send a message or go herself by foot or by bicycle. She rarely took part in the arguments around the dinner table. She was excruciatingly shy with strangers. Yet here she was – taller, older, calmly taking control of this new situation with hardly a need for words. Elsa knew precisely what the situation was.

She placed a hand on Francesco's arm, one finger tapping gently. 'None of us has a choice any longer, my dear. I think you know that. Why would we be afraid to die when we are afraid all the time to live?'

He covered her hand with his.

Annabelle thought, *I have never known my aunt. Perhaps I have never known anybody.* She had been feeling as if she were in a play, or someone had stopped the clock. Elsa's entrance decisively restarted it.

Her father Achille too, now came to life, crossed to his desk, removed his reading glasses from a hard leather case like a small coffin and held it out to Enrico. 'Take this. Take all your glasses with you. You will be quite useless without them. When do you leave?'

'Tomorrow night,' he said, 'we will go out after curfew through the Boboli.'

'We?'

'Me and Roberto and his friend Giacomo.'

'Your cousin?' said Francesco.

'Roberto is a deserter now, Father.' They all noted the formal address. No more *babbo* then. They had crossed a line. There was no need to say more; it was only a week since three boys were publicly executed for refusing to enlist.

'Take all you can wear of your warm clothes and as many socks as you can carry,' said Francesco. 'Two pairs of boots. Boots will be important. This will not end quickly.'

November 20, 1943

I have no memory of this day. It took longer than a day to pass. Enrico leaves tonight. I am determined to join him.

The tension in the household was as thick as the fog outside. Anna Maria and Sesto had been sent on an overnight errand to Impruneta. They had only been with the family for five years, since Matilde had died. Were there any old and trusted family servants anymore? Annabelle did not know whom to trust. This war had prised open schisms between friends, between neighbours, between staff and employers and within families. Gaping chasms of principle, habit, fear and self-interest had opened beneath the feet of those who thought they knew each other. Annabelle was afraid these wounds might never heal.

Elsa spent the day resolutely making plans, arrangements, her face shuttered. Roberto and Giacomo were to enter by the service door at nightfall. Annabelle kept forgetting to breathe. It did not occur to her to wonder how Elsa felt. She did not care how anyone else felt. The loss was hers.

'I want to come with you,' she said to him that morning.

Enrico took her chin in his hand and tilted her face to his, giving her his full concentration in a way he had never done before.

'Annabelle,' he said.

When had he ever called her Annabelle?

'Annabelle,' he said, 'this is for us, for men. We are no longer boys. You cannot come, but you can help. Mamma will tell you what to do.'

He brushed a strand of her hair back, gently tucking it behind her ear, and held his fingers against her cheek for hours, or seconds. He made no jokes. He looked ridiculously large and ungainly in all his heavy winter clothing. He was sweating lightly in the indoor heating but it would be very cold out in the streets and freezing in the mountains. He was wearing two jumpers and two undershirts and in fact, two of everything he owned. She should have found it funny. She fingered the scalding imprint of his hand on her cheek.

Alea iacta est

Enrico let the French doors click behind him. He took two steps down onto the gravel path of the *cortile* and the cold nipped his nose. Tendrils of fog trailed from the dim trees like summer wisteria, or the soft curls about Annabelle's weepy face. He could always turn back. No. The world back there had ended. He made his way across the pebbled paths of the courtyard by Braille, trying to open the heavy iron gate to the back lane quietly, thinking a squeaking gate would soon be the least of their problems. Stepping through into the lane, he gave a low whistle and two ghosts emerged from the shadows. Enrico kissed Roberto on both cheeks and held him close for a moment. Giacomo enveloped him in a bear hug and the scent of pipe tobacco, and without a word the three men faded into the fog.

Enrico tried to put the house behind them out of his mind. He did not want to think about the pain his mother was feeling. And his father too. He knew it would be a long time before they had news of him and the family would be in mortal danger because of his decision. And Annabelle ... he would not think about Annabelle. The pain of others was an indulgence he could not afford at the moment.

Enrico pinched the bridge of his nose hard. As a child skiing in the high mountains at Abetone or in the Alps at Courmeyer, he learned to conquer fear. At first by not admitting to it. Then gradually, as his risk-taking became more heedless, by not caring. His adolescence was dwarfed by the looming shadows cast during the failing fascist dream and the war. In those years, the world around him was mad and he saw no reason to be sane himself. Unable to fight back against the fascist state, he fought against fear instead. Now he could do both. They would head towards Rome to join the partisans, fighting to slow the German response, to give the Allies time to take the city. Nello Traquandi had given him the name of a contact. How exactly he was to find this contact, he had no idea, but pushing on was the only choice now.

The streets were silent, empty, the penalty for being out after curfew dire. They slipped along walls and down *chiassi*, the tiny medieval alleyways honeycombing the city, assailed by the odoriferous familiarity of Florence winter drains. They were careful not to let the hobnails of their boots slide or strike sound off the uneven paving. They had few weapons to carry so their progress was swift.

Roberto had been in hiding for two months. He had his army-issue Beretta pistol and the Carcano rifle, which he knew by now was not much of a match for the Germans' weapons. In his *zaino*, Enrico had a Walther belonging to his uncle, carefully wrapped in rag and placed on top of his dog-eared copy of *Marcus Aurelius*, which he had carried since he was fourteen. Giacomo had nothing but three packets of tobacco and his hunting knife. But the bulky forty-seven-year-old had dispatched many a *cinghiale* with that knife and he was prepared to use it on human pigs as well. They would be properly armed by the partisan group when they met them tomorrow. More importantly, for now, they all had bread in their packs.

Enrico's jaw ached. He had ground his teeth at night since he had teeth and he was trying not to do it now. This journey had been ordained since the eighth of September really, he thought. The muggy weight of that hot night was still with him. Listening to the broadcast of Badoglio's speech in *Zio*'s study, his eyes had met his mother's. *Il dado e tratto*, she said. Caesar's words, and now the die was cast for Enrico and his companions too.

Giacomo, a journalist older than the others, had been in Spain where his lover Giselda, also a journalist, was shot. He had no-one else but his elderly parents. He had covered Mussolini's visit to Berlin in 1937 and Hitler's reciprocal visit to Florence in 1938. He always knew this night would come.

Roberto was a character who could have stepped straight out of the canvases of thirty generations of family portraits. Stocky, sturdy, olive-skinned, with a hawkish nose and an inquisitive gaze, he would rather have been a farmer than a fighter. All he ever wanted was to grow olives and grapes and till the soil of the country *fattoria* that was his inheritance. Enrico reckoned there were not enough faces to go round in their families, which was why Roberto was issued with the same one passed on from father to son for six hundred years.

Roberto was left high and dry by his King and his superiors on the ninth of September, and after doing his best to help his own men, he did what he had advised them to do – desert. For a whole day after almost the entire corps of army officers abandoned their posts and their men and their country, there was a vacuum: no-one in charge. In the eye of the storm, in the stillness, the sultry air tasted of fear. Then on the eleventh the sky fell and the Germans spewed down the peninsula like molten lava. A day later, Mussolini was rescued by the Germans – the King and Badoglio had forgotten to hand him over to the Allies. A few days after, he was back in power. Nominally. Everyone knew who was in charge and it was not Mussolini.

'Now we will see what war is really about,' Roberto said. His frown turned his heavy eyebrows into a single caterpillar.

Already, the murders, disappearances and torture – conducted out of sight in private villas throughout Florence and its surrounds – had begun in earnest. Fascism, always at its most brutal in Florence, was now unrestrained. In the early years, wealth, status and family connections protected the upper classes from the worst excesses, but that was over. All three of them were heartsick at the thought of the danger their families faced. A distant relative of Roberto and Enrico's, Mario, a good fascist, was executed in 1938 simply for refusing to betray young friends like Enrico who had been distributing subversive leaflets at night when Mario happened upon them. Another died fighting the fascists in Spain. By now, anyone who openly opposed fascism or gave any comfort to those who did, was either dead or in *confino*, exile, or in gaol. It was the turn of Enrico, Roberto and Giacomo, and they were ready.

Annabelle stood at the doors for long moments after Enrico was swallowed by the soupy fog. This is for men, he had said. What about us? What about women? Did we not matter? She would join the communists, fight with them, if he would not take her. She gulped back sobs, racked by anger, fear, loss. She wanted to rush up to his room and sit amongst his books: Yeats, Fibonacci, Galileo, Herodotus, Marcus Aurelius, Hadrian. The Stoics, his heroes. Or Dickens, or *Alice in Wonderland* and *Through the Looking Glass*, with the magical illustrations they had shared all their lives. She wanted to hear him recite Robert Burns' poetry for her in the funny accent he affected for the Scottish bard. She wanted to lie on his bed and look at his drawings, at his Ernest Hemingway books filling a whole shelf, at the maps lining his walls and the great topographical map of Australia that so enraptured him. She wanted to listen to his gramophone recordings of jazz and finger his collection of coins, and his crystal set, which she had helped to make and through which they listened in secret to Radio London. Inhale his special smell. As if he were already dead.

Too late. Behind her, the authority in the room had shifted.

'Annabelle ... Annabelle.' *Zia* Elsa took her by the shoulder and guided her to a chair. Firmly. 'Do sit down, my dear. We have much to discuss.'

The others obediently sat too, ranged about Elsa. Annabelle's mother sniffled quietly, her hair in disarray from constantly running her hands through it. Her eyes slid sideways to the comfort of the Par jigsaw puzzle, half done on a small walnut table by the bookshelves.

Eleanora's jigsaws made sense. Took her mind off things.

Elsa turned kindly to her: 'Eleanora, dear, what if we were to have some soup. It is going to be a long night.'

Pleased to have a task, Eleanora started, briskly now, to head to the kitchen.

'We have to organise ourselves tonight,' Elsa continued. 'The servants will be back tomorrow and we will need to be very careful indeed.' She turned to Annabelle. There were no children in the room now, only adults, all with a role in this coming travail.

'Annabelle, tomorrow you will start work for our friend Siviero. You will have many bits and pieces of art to carry back and forth. You will carry the messages. *This* is how we will keep Enrico and all our men safe. By doing everything we can to hasten the end of the Germans in our country.' She sat silently awaiting Annabelle's acceptance of this new role.

Annabelle was still plotting ways to join Enrico. Achille lit a cigar for himself and one for his brother, and made notes on a pad on his knee, her uncle reading over his shoulder. It was a list of ... what? Annabelle had no idea. Her mother came back pushing a trolley with a tureen and soup bowls.

Annabelle had been a lonely child who retreated into books and the world of story, adventure, romance – dreamy, ethereal. Ethereal was such a lovely word, but no-one of her height and build could lay claim to that adjective; that was more a word for Aunt Elsa. Evenings were spent sitting in her window watching twilight fall, reading Petrarch and Boccaccio and Leopardi and daydreaming of a life on the other side of the hedge, of danger and excitement. Her head was full of the classics and the lives of others. She had no idea what she wanted to be, but she would be *something*. The one thing she was resolved *not* to be was her mother, never to be her mother.

Everyone loved and respected Eleanora. Yes, but ... Annabelle loved her mother, but she would not live that life. Eleanora was given to fits of the vapours, with frequent recourse to her smelling salts, eliciting only concealed irritation from Annabelle and overt irritation from Achille. Her father, like most good husbands, treated his wife with fondness, respect, and a slightly dismissive indulgence. He knew it was better to give Eleanora her head in domestic matters, but in all other matters she deferred to her husband or the state. At least he did not beat her. *Chi commanda sono le donne,* the fiction that women ruled in the home, was the rule of the weak – a sop to a part of the population who really ruled nowhere. Apart from some local elections, they were not even allowed to vote – when anyone used to vote, that was. According to Enrico, the freedom of the dog was only the length of its leash. He meant it for life under fascism but it was doubly so for women. Annabelle would not content herself with that short leash. She did not want to be loved and respected by all. She wanted to be passionately loved by Enrico and she wanted to live the life he lived. She railed at the restrictions and constrictions of a life forever at the starting gate, thwarted in all her efforts to hear, listen, participate. Enrico had always egged her on in her wild imaginings. It amused him to fan the flames of subversion. Now, when it really counted, he too had fallen back on the old platitudes: men's work.

Tuscany 1943
'The wrong sector of the right side'

The city folded wordlessly about the three men as they slid around corners and slipped up alleys and flitted across the paving beneath the Vasari corridor to the Ponte Vecchio. They tucked back into the shadows from time to time as small knots of militia passed or drunken German soldiers loitered on their way to the barracks. At the northern end of the bridge they simply waited in the shadows until the two German sentries leaned against the far wall to chat and smoke a cigarette, then they were across, turning quickly up Costa San Giorgio to make their way through back lanes and gardens to the Boboli. Once they were in the Boboli Gardens they were protected by the trees until they emerged on the via Romana. Slipping through an arch in the buttress of the Porta Romana, they skirted the Piazzale and made it to the via Senese. By then there was no-one to be seen, but they kept prudently to the verge all the same.

'Pfffhew.' Roberto gave a long sigh after holding his breath for ages. 'Let's stop for a bit and have a rest. Where are we meeting this man?'

Enrico was much less certain than he had been earlier. 'No, we have to push on. We are to head for Siena and at dawn he will find us.' It sounded weak, even to him, but neither Giacomo nor Roberto argued.

It was already late but they trudged on for another two hours to Chiesanuova, utterly exhausted.

'*Senti amico*,' said Giacomo. 'All right for you, at your age, but I have to have a break.' He climbed the grassy bank to the left and slid his *zaino* to the ground. 'Wish I could light my pipe.'

Roberto followed, saying quietly to Enrico, 'He's right. We need to conserve our energy. Let's eat a bit of bread and sleep for two hours, then we can be at Montespertoli at dawn.' He passed around a flask of grappa and each man took a sip.

Enrico was relieved. He had never been so tired. It must be the anxiety. He was developing a taste for grappa. He was not sure who was supposed to be the leader here. The others had followed him because he had the contacts. Now what? They settled in, beneath the trees where they were not visible from the road, and lay down on the frozen ground. 'As cold as death,' Enrico said.

'No,' came Giacomo's muffled voice, 'if you were dead you wouldn't feel it. Get used to it because we will not be warm again for a long time.' He shook his head at the naivety of the young and closed his eyes.

'Lie on your side,' said Roberto, with the wisdom of the soldier, 'so you do not snore.'

They fell into unconsciousness.

Enrico rolled over to his back and lay quietly, woken by the flickering of the stars through the tree branches. He was heavy with foreboding. They were to join a brigade of *Giustizia e Libertà*, to defend Siena as the Allies moved north after taking Rome, but so far that seemed like a dream. The Allies were their only hope but they were still bogged down at Naples. Not that the Allies thought much of them. He made to sit up and could not. A boot came down firmly on his shoulder, the icy barrel of a gun at his temple, the metal so cold it seared his skin. The sound of bolts being drawn back woke the other two, who found themselves in the same position. So, it was not the flickering of the stars then. Stay calm. Stay calm, he said to himself.

'Sit up very slowly, my friend,' said the tall, bearded shape outlined above him in the early dawn. He gave Enrico a small shove with the barrel of the gun and took a step back. The others did the same. There appeared to be about six men in the group.

'*Di che rosa siete*? Who do you belong to?' The tall one was the leader. His voice was like sandpaper, his Tuscan diction as thick as *ribollita*.

How Enrico wished for a password or some single thing to identify them. 'We were to meet you at dawn,' he said instead, sounding like a character from his *Boys Own Annuals*. His patrician vowels did him no favours here and he knew it.

'We. And who might we be?'

Giacomo leaned forward slowly and said in much gruffer tones, 'No, kid. They're not ours.' To the men, he said, '*Siete Garibaldini*, you're with the communists, right? We are going to join the *Giellisti* in Siena.'

'Stand up, all of you. Let's get a look at you. You don't look like fighters to me.'

The six moved closer, all carrying a strong odour of sweat and gun oil.

'We are all fighters now, *Commandante*, and all on the same side.' Enrico had recovered. 'If we are against the *Nazifascisti* we are all on the same side.'

He was self-conscious about his expensive snow-jacket but there was nothing to be done about it. Besides, it was already filthy from the hours on the side of the muddy road and would soon look like theirs anyway. In the sombre grey of the pre-dawn, he could see the men were wearing an assortment of uniforms and working clothes and army greatcoats and all had a red kerchief tied at their throats. They were heavily armed: sub-machine guns, ammunition belts crossed on their chests and grenades dangling from wide belts. The only partisans Enrico had seen were the thin, painfully young boys armed with farm implements he'd once encountered just after the

Armistice, on the way to Impruneta. No wonder these were called after Garibaldi; they had all modelled themselves on that romantic figure. Enrico knew they were dangerous. The one with the beard wore a beret with the hammer and sickle insignia. Two of the others had the red star on their caps.

'So you want to fight the good fight, do you?' said the leader, with an edge of derision. 'You know it means killing them. Are you ready to kill? This is not a joke, you know. We are talking about killing people.' He turned to Roberto, who still had not spoken. 'You look like you could do it. What about you?' he said, turning to Enrico. 'Can you kill?' Then to Giacomo he said, 'And you, big man, you look as if you could do it with your bare hands and you would like to do it now. Maybe we should give you a go.'

'Boss.' A smaller man stepped forward. 'We can't trust them. We have no idea who they are. I say we kill them now. It could be a trap.'

Roberto spoke, slowly and evenly. 'I've been in the army. I can kill, yes. We are all here for our own reasons. I am on your side now, as long as this goes on. You are going to need all of us sooner or later because this is not going to end soon and it is not going to be easy.'

In the long silence, Enrico could hear his stomach rumbling. Could he kill? He would soon find out.

The *Commandante* turned back to them, boisterous now. 'Right. You're with us now. But watch your step.' He picked up Enrico's rifle and tossed it to him. 'Get your stuff, *Bello*. We've got a job to do and we can use the extra hands. We are going to raid the *Caserma* in Tavarnuzze and take all the bastards' weapons. And you lot could do with them.' He gave a deep laugh. 'Off we go, back the way you came. But we will be right behind you.'

Cristo, thought Enrico. We have joined the communists and we are going to raid the *Carabinieri* barracks. He thought of Robert Burns. *The best laid schemes of mice and men / go often awry.* Just how awry, he could not yet be sure.

Enrico was an only child in a country where having babies for the Regime was considered a duty. In his family, having babies had become a doubtful proposition. His mother spent most of her time reading or writing and his father spent most of his time fussing over his mother, whom he did not want to subject to the dangers of another pregnancy. They had little time for Enrico, much less for another child. His only company was his cousin Annabelle. She was his own, from the day of her birth, in a way no-one else had ever been. He was overwhelmed by the flood of love the tiny creature generated in him at the age of nearly four, and he never tired of watching her little hands with the miniature fingernails of a doll. As they grew older and the world about them grew greyer, she became his confidant in everything. Everything, that is, except his participation, with his mother – his astonishing mother – in the covert activities of the Action Party. Annabelle had to be protected from that. From everything that might harm her or make her sad.

At this moment though, he was in no position to protect anyone. He resolutely put Annabelle from his mind as they trudged in the floppy dawn towards the *Carabinieri* barracks in Tavarnuzze. He was far from convinced these bastards would not shoot them after they had served their purpose.

As if reading his mind, the leader, called Carlo, said to him, 'Don't worry, *Bello*, we are not going to shoot you now. You do yourselves well in this and you are with us. Understand?'

Carlo, he had told them earlier, was not his name but his battle name. No-one used their real names, but in fact, around here, most of them were apparently well-known to the local fascists because they were born here, so Enrico could not see that it served much purpose. Not that he was inclined to say so.

CHAPTER 9

Florence 1943

'*Avanti*. Come on in,' Annabelle said, beckoning. 'I am sick to death of the subjunctive.' She was glad of the interruption. It was ridiculous to drudge along with French homework while the world tilted on its axis.

Her cousin Lorenzo nudged the door to her father's study with his shoulder and smiled with his habitual diffidence. Where Annabelle sat, at the great mahogany desk in a far corner of the room, golden pools of lamplight spilled across the garnet shades of the Persian rug. The high walls of books with their leather bindings and gilt letter-ing gave shelter and the illusion of safety, inside at least. Annabelle pushed back in her chair and the boy ambled to her side, leaning to get a better look at the homework. He pointed to the notepad.

'You can't always assume the imperative will be the same as the subjunctive.'

Lorenzo had been invaluable these four weeks since Enrico had gone into the mountains. Four weeks. Four years, four centuries! They had not heard a word. Annabelle had entered a state of abey-ance. There had never been a time in her life when Enrico was not there. She drifted through each day, running the errands, carrying the documents, visiting the galleries and private art dealers who were now her cover for the work with Rodolfo Siviero, which, she told herself, promoted the cause and kept Enrico alive. If he was alive.

Lorenzo, recently turned sixteen, was her cousin on her mother's side. He too should have been at home studying. Instead, like Enrico before him, he was a slippery shadow on the stone walls of the city, flitting ahead of fascist and German patrols, delivering messages, collecting ammunition, secreting evidence and cutting wires to signals. How strange to discover that Lorenzo and so many others had been doing this work for ages and she had not known. Before the surrender they had all been attending meetings with communists and Christian Democrats and the Action Party. She knew this much but no more. Since the German invasion, they had gone underground, deeper than before. It was best for her to know as little as possible, they said. They all wanted to keep her safe. Safe. Safe. When would Enrico be safe?

Lorenzo tousled her hair as if he were the older, despite being two months younger.

'No news yet, before you ask,' he said. 'But if the news were bad we would have heard it. The word has it that they have finally reached the *Giellisti*. It just hasn't been confirmed yet.'

Finally reached the GL brigade! Where in the name of God had they been all this time then? She sighed from her head to her feet. The safe glow of the lamps was a lie. Lorenzo paced and shuffled, scratching the parting in his floppy, fair hair and rubbing his cheek. Did he have more news then? He looked silly and young, and his gentle tone, aristocratic lisp and shy demeanour belied the courage he had already shown in these weeks.

Lorenzo's father Michele had been arrested and was detained, they thought, in *Le Murate*, but no-one had been able to get that confirmed. 'Enzo! What is it?' Annabelle could take the tension no longer. It was not about Enrico or he would have blurted it at once. What then?

'I want to join them. Come with me. We could go tonight. We could be in the mountains tomorrow. I cannot sit still any longer. You know they killed Bruno last night.' His voice quavered.

No. She had not known. Bruno was his school friend, a year older. In a week, it would be Christmas. There would be no Christmas in that family. Annabelle drew in her breath. Her heart banged in her chest. Lorenzo was right, they could go tonight and no-one could stop them. They could gather warm clothes and provisions and they could take her father's guns. She was a crack shot, though Lorenzo was hopeless. They could easily slip away after curfew. She could be with Enrico. They could find him and ... and what?

'Bruno's body lay in the alley all night,' Lorenzo continued. 'People passed and crossed themselves but no-one dared to stop. That's how it is now.' He rubbed his forearm with monotonous intensity. 'I must go. Come. Please come.'

Annabelle exhaled slowly and the resolve leaked away on her breath. She crossed to Lorenzo and put her arms about him, her head on his chest against the racket of his heart.

'We cannot go into the mountains. You know it. No-one wants to go more than I, but they would send us back. Even if we could find them, which is unlikely. You said yourself, we still don't know where they are. I can help them more here, and you must finish your education.'

She did not say, you are too young. No-one was too young now. She said instead, 'There is going to be a world after this butchery.'

Is there? She straightened and went on, determined now. 'It would kill your parents. We still don't know for certain where your father is and your mother is in poor health. You know what it would do to her. And as for Nonna, it would finish her.'

Lorenzo sagged onto the edge of her father's desk, his own resolve punctured.

'Come on,' she encouraged. 'I've got a parcel you must deliver.'

He nodded glumly and pushed himself upright.

Annabelle was not convinced. 'Are we agreed?'

'Yes all right.' He was impatient now. Unspilled tears glittered against the cobalt of his eyes. He turned and left with the parcel, without another word.

Annabelle was shivery and chilled. With rationing, heating was scant but the cold was not in the room. She clutched her thick cardigan tighter about her and wrapped her arms across her body, biting her lips hard; she had learned not to cry. Instead, she packed up her homework, grabbed her heavy coat and went out to visit Nonna before curfew. She had not seen her for several days and was missing her. Nonna would make her feel better. She had never known the grandmother Annabelle for whom she was named, but she had, by way of compensation, been loved all her life by her great-grandmother, Nonna Lucrezia, her mother's grandmother. Born in 1850, Nonna belonged to a world before Italy was even conceived of as a country.

She had seen Garibaldi. She had seen unification. She had seen the Great War. She had seen the birth of flight and seen cars. She had seen everything. And now ... Annabelle wished she did not have to see this.

The house had the muffled quiet of deep winter. Christmas Eve. There was nothing of her father's usual courteous manner as he slammed back the door of Annabelle's bedroom, rattling the heavy frame of the Fattori picture on the wall beside it.

'Downstairs, please.'

Oh God. Don't let it be Enrico. No. It is not Enrico. He is angry. Furious. What is it? What have I done?

She lagged behind as her father strode ahead to his study where she found her mother, her aunt Elsa and Lorenzo's mother Elisabetta. No. Not Lorenzo. Please, not Lorenzo. Her thoughts flew to Bruno last week.

'What do you know of this?' Her father's voice grated.

'I have no idea what you are talking about,' she said. Her breathing faltered. 'Tell me.'

'Lorenzo has disappeared. Are you saying you do not know where he is?'

'Why should you think it?' She would not cry. 'Has he left no note?' But she knew.

'Nothing.' This from Elsa. Elisabetta had not spoken. 'He was at home last night but this morning he is gone, and all his clothes and his father's service revolver are gone too.'

It was already nine o'clock but it was still gloomy outside and in the long windows, the grey-greenish sky was a presage of snow. Elsa, who nowadays was always up early, was fully dressed and perfectly groomed. All the others were in various stages of morning disarray. Eleanora was in her dressing-gown. Elisabetta had a coat thrown over her house clothes. Her hair was still down, pulled hurriedly back with a comb. She must have run all the way from via Porta Rossa. She looked like a mad woman as she turned on Elsa.

'This is your fault. All of you. You all encouraged him. You think I am stupid but I know you are all in it. He is only a child. A child.'

Her voice got higher, her breath coming in gulps and hiccups.

Elsa put out a hand to her but she jerked away. 'No. What use is it to me if at the end of this accursed war, you are all dead?'

She sleepwalked sideways to the dark leather sofa, subsiding like an empty packet, her hands fluttering and flapping.

Like white butterflies, thought Annabelle. 'Papà,' she said, 'I swear I did not know. He talked to me last week, the day after they killed Bruno. He was in a state. He wanted to join Enrico. I thought I had talked him out of it.'

Elsa walked about the room lighting lamps. 'We will find out, Elisabetta. Try to be calm. As soon as we know something we will tell you.'

If we know something, Annabelle thought. Lorenzo was the only child of doting, indulgent parents. He was not equipped, mentally or physically, for the mountains or the snow or the fear or the danger. They still had little idea where Enrico really was and Lorenzo had even less. Tomorrow they should be celebrating the birth of a saviour who had clearly deserted the earth. No-one in the room thought of turning to him for help.

Lorenzo headed north. He had to be very careful around the railway station where there were lots of Germans and several fascist patrols, but once he got up to Fiesole, the night was calm; silent night. The piazza was ghostly in the starlight: doors shut tight, nothing moved except his own vagrant shadow. He headed for Monte Morello. From memory, he thought it was about twenty kilometres, and it was all forest from Fiesole on, so if he walked all night he should be there by first light. He was not exactly sure where 'there' was, but he felt certain Enrico would be there somewhere. Monte Morello had been mentioned at his meetings and knew a band of partisans was already there.

Lorenzo was glad of his new jacket, with its expensive sheepskin lining and crested buckle, made for him at the end of last winter and not yet worn. Despite the cold, he was sweating and his heart was choking him. His hands trembled as he tried ineptly to light one of the cigarettes he had stolen from the enamelled box in his father's study. He threw it down; he had never smoked anyway. It was hours since he'd left the road. Could he be in the wrong valley? The path he followed had narrowed to a boggy track. The cold gnawed his face. His hair, where it escaped from beneath his cap, was damp and icy – he should have cut it off before he left. The stars glittered, shards of ice in a moonless navy-blue night. He turned to gaze up at the sky and his foot caught in a root, sending him tumbling heavily down an incline where he finally bumped to a halt, stunned.

Lorenzo had never been alone on the mountain in the dark before. Tears brimmed but he swallowed them, ashamed of his childishness. He unlaced his boot and poked at his ankle, decided it was not broken, and pushed to his feet. He could still walk. He felt about for his water bottle and rucksack and his stick. The compass had disappeared from his pocket – not that he was very good with a compass anyway. He had fallen hard against what he had thought was a tree but he could just make out the handle of a plough, a stack of crates, and close by, the outline of a hut with a sliver of weak light at the edge of a door. Limping, he made his way across a slippery farmyard, leaned on the door and banged with his fist, a dull thud on the wet timber.

'*Chi c'è?*' From within, a woman's voice, tremulous, suspicious.

'Please. I need help. I am injured.'

The door opened a slit and he could barely make out a woman of about half his height. He could not understand her very well, but he understood the 'No. No. No.'

'I am a partisan,' he said. 'I need somewhere to sleep.' Well, he was going to be a partisan.

With another volley of dialect from which he managed to interpret that she was afraid for her children and of having her home burned down, she pushed the door shut and a wooden beam clunked into place on the other side.

Inside the farmhouse, the young woman leaned back against the door, breathing heavily. Her husband was already dead, in this war she did not understand. The mountains were crawling with escaped prisoners – soldiers from nations she had never heard of; deserters from the Italian Army, which had been the death of her husband; brigands

113

claiming to be partisans who were really criminals; real partisans who were just as frightening, with their ragged beards and huge guns and belts of bullets across their chests. All starving, they all stole your food and worse perhaps. She did not know whether she was more afraid of the partisans and the reprisals they always brought upon the peasants, or of a spy and the inevitable retribution of the partisans for betrayal.

That one, that giant, she thought, was too tall and too fair and only spoke Italian. He had hair like a girl. He was certainly not from this valley. *Tedesco*? German? Or fascist? Who knows? These days you could not trust anyone.

Outside, it was darker than before. Lorenzo's stomach grumbled and he swayed slightly. It was hours since he had eaten. He had a bit of bread wrapped in paper in his *zaino*. If he could find somewhere safe he could eat it and sleep a little before deciding what to do next. He should have brought more bread but at least he still had his water bottle. Perhaps he should have done more planning but there had been no time. Oh well, tomorrow it would all be clearer. He caught the odour of lucerne and manure and felt his way along a stone wall to the other end of the hut, until he came to an iron bolt holding the door of a stable closed. The bolt lifted easily and he slipped into the fetid warmth, sliding into the straw against the warm rump of a sleeping cow, and, forgetting his bread, he dropped into slumber.

The *Carabinieri* were too easy – they collapsed like the Queen of Hearts' cards. After a night of tramping back the way they had come, ahead of the *Garibaldini*, Enrico's enthusiasm had sprung a leak. After the high drama of setting off, all three felt like fools for having been press-ganged into the communists. The wrong sector of the right side! It was still dull on the horizon when the group of partisans, swollen by four more comrades who had joined them along the way, arrived outside the *Caserma*.

Only the town dogs were stirring. Carlo motioned to the group to form a half-circle and then, with no warning, lobbed two hand grenades against the heavy timber of the main doors. Through the smoke and confusion, windows flew open on the floor above, filled with sleepy panicked faces.

'Don't be heroes,' bellowed Carlo. 'What's the point of dying now, for nothing? We've got you surrounded. Your King and Badoglio have thrown you to the dogs, so why throw your lives away.'

He was right. When the King and Badoglio ran away in the early hours of a September night, Italians awoke from a bad dream into a nightmare. Italy as a country collapsed. The *Carabinieri* were left to fend for themselves, abandoned. The whole country had been abandoned, but none more so than the military. All soldiers – and those *Carabinieri* were soldiers too – awoke to a day with no orders, no food, few weapons and little ammunition, and no idea who the enemy was supposed to be. In barracks up and down the peninsula, men trailed about asking for orders, and when none were forthcoming, many hefted their packs and their weapons and what food they could scrounge, and began the long walk back to their homes. They did not know whether the country was still at war or not. Many were country boys who had never understood what they were doing there, now all they wanted was to get home.

Before long, they were called deserters and ordered back, on pain of death, into the army of the newly formed Italian Socialist Republic. Mussolini was back, they were told in a flood of leaflets and posters, and the enemy was still the Allies. By that time, the Germans had begun rounding them up and sending them in the Todt convoys to Germany as labour – the Germans did not want disillusioned and apathetic soldiers in the Italian Army. They had greater need of manpower in the factories in Germany.

To the dishevelled and disorientated mendicant soldiers on the road, it looked like the Germans were in charge and they were not friends. Many fled into the Fascist Army and militias. Others joined the newly formed Italian SS Legions. Others became refugees, their numbers swelled by equally stunned Allied prisoners-of-war, who had been released or had escaped from the camps when their guards walked away. Some of those same guards joined them. The country was beset by roaming bands of fugitives who threw in their lot with the partisans – in some cases for want of any other alternative.

At the windows of the *Caserma*, the expressions on the faces of the sleepy *Carabinieri* were of varying degrees of relief, like children some parent had forgotten to collect from school. One by one they withdrew, and through the grill of an open window, a white flag tied to a broom-handle appeared almost before Carlo's voice had faded. Then the big *portone* creaked opened and the *Maresciallo* edged through. It was clear he was the *Maresciallo* because he had thrown his jacket, with its maroon-edged epaulets and collar, over the top of his pyjamas. He was wearing his slippers and a look of stupefaction. Behind him trailed a dejected line of half-dressed *Carabinieri*, all in complete agreement that there was no need for them to be heroes.

As they came to a stop several metres from the band of partisans, Carlo raised his machine gun, levelling it at the chest of the closest one – a boy, not the *Maresciallo* – who lagged behind.

Roberto moved closer to him and said quietly, 'Make an example of them now and you might instil fear but some of them will join you if you take a different approach.'

'Well,' replied Carlo, 'it's not as if they are militia, I suppose, is it.' Unconvinced.

He lowered the gun slightly and indicated with his head for the scraggly bunch to turn back inside the *Caserma*, where the partisans shoved them into the empty cells and turned the keys. Carlo could quite willingly have executed the boy, Enrico realised, and he could not rid his mind of this new knowledge. It took little time for the group to collect all the food they could carry and the arms they had come for. It was still not light when they slipped away. Not a cat stirred on the streets – it was as if the grenades had not been thrown. Curtains twitched and citizens twitched behind them, but no-one else wanted to be a hero either.

That was a week ago. This was not so easy. Bunch of cretins, Enrico thought, as he eased his back against the icy rock. In the aftermath of the raid on the *Caserma*, the group moved fast, heading for the shelter of the mountains. Patrols of *Carabinieri* and fascists and even Germans, ranged the countryside in search of them. Finally, after two days and two nights without rest, they made camp high on Monte Morello, on a ridge above the village of Poggibonsi. They sheltered in an open-sided shepherd's hut where they dropped to the ground, ready to fall into exhausted sleep. Roberto enquired about watches, horrified at the reply that it was not necessary. When he responded that he thought it was, Carlo grunted, '*Senti bello*, I'm in charge here.'

'Well, not of us,' said Roberto in an undertone to Enrico, adding, '*cani sciolti*.' Mad dogs.

Roberto, Enrico and Giacomo agreed they would stand three-hour watches. It was gruelling to stay awake after being on the march for nearly three days in a row, but growling hunger and the pain of the rocky edges cutting into the flesh of his thighs kept Enrico alert. He had toothache, as well. Best not to think about that. The moon was not up yet, the stars veiled by wispy fog. Snow was close by. He stood and stretched, removed his gloves and unbuttoned his fly. The stream of urine against the frozen rock sent a cloud of vapour so high into the air he worried it could be seen from below. Hurriedly, he buttoned his trousers, dragged the jumpers and jacket back down, and shivered his body back to warmth. He was grateful for all the layers he had taken with him but he was still cold and he knew that it would only get colder. Winter was a long way from over.

Enrico was lonely. The word crept up on him and pounced. He had never been lonely before, or perhaps he had never been caught by it before, without a book to hide in. He did not believe in leaving himself prey to such emotions. Action was his antidote to weakness. Learning inaction came hard. Slinking along behind loneliness came yearning – for Annabelle, for his mother, even for his father and for their home. It must be because he could not smoke. Don't get maudlin now. He pinched the bridge of his nose, pushed his glasses up and rubbed the pressure spots where they rested. He took his mind with both hands and turned it away, silently reciting snatches of poetry and lines from *Marcus Aurelius*. He was good at committing words to memory, learning by heart. Could you learn with your heart? His thoughts wandered to Yeats but shied away at the memory of Annabelle quoting him Yeats. That was not where he wanted his thoughts to go. He must keep his mind on the present, this present, the one that needed to be resolved. His abdomen contracted painfully, coiling, uncoiling – he had never been as hungry in his life. He willed his thoughts to their current situation. Predicament, more like.

The *Garibaldini* might be a bunch of amateurs, but they were dangerous and he had to find a way of moving on for the three of them. He was the one who was supposed to have the contacts with the *Giellisti*. He was mortified he had got them lost. These communist idiots would get themselves killed before they could do any good, and all in the name of a dogma that most of them could not even read, much less understand. But where should he be heading? He needed to make contact with someone from the Action Party and get instructions. What a mess.

He took a sip from his water flask, stood and stretched again, rubbing his flank where it had cramped against the stone. He was considering another pee when he caught a sound or a shadow or a scent or an omen. He stood utterly still, straining all senses – nothing. Perhaps he was getting jumpy, but still … Holding his rifle very firmly so as not to bump it against the rock, and placing his boots meticulously, he slipped across the couple of metres to where Giacomo and Roberto lay against their backpacks on the ridge at a slight distance from the rest of the group. Enrico slipped the straps of his *zaino* over his shoulders. Very gently, he placed a hand on Roberto's arm and tapped twice. Roberto sat instantly, a hand already on his gun, and tapped Giacomo who did the same.

'Something is not right,' Enrico whispered.

And the night blew up in their faces.

In a fury of grenades and bullets and flashes and shouts and running feet and screams and oaths and groans, it was impossible to know who was attacking them and who was fighting whom. Roberto grabbed the back of Enrico's jacket and alongside Giacomo, they rolled over the edge of the ridge and down the embankment, scrabbling to retain their weapons and not break a limb amongst the loose stones and tree trunks. Glasses, glasses, thought Enrico. It was like falling in a dream – down the rabbit hole. After what could only have been a minute or two they came to rest at the bottom of the ravine where all was silence. Above them the battle continued. The sky flashed fire and the cold ground thrummed with the beat of mortars. Mortars! They lay still for a moment to orientate themselves and work out whether they had been followed. Roberto pointed upwards to a lip of the hillside concealing them from above. There were no pursuers.

The moon was up, the moonlight through the trees like pale milk. The battle sounds gradually died away. Still no-one came after them.

Enrico spat the ferrous taste of blood from his mouth and realised his teeth had gone through his tongue in the tumbling descent. He could feel the tongue swelling – that would hurt tomorrow. Unbelievably, it was his only injury. His chest was heaving. A strange desire to laugh came over him. Perhaps he was hysterical. Roberto and Giacomo too had taken inventory and decided that they were, more or less, whole. They also struggled to govern their breathing, which sounded too loud in the still night. All three, astonishingly, still had their weapons. Enrico had his *zaino* but he could not see whether the others had theirs. His glasses were missing but he had others in his bag.

Roberto put his lips to Enrico's ear – his breath scalding – and whispered, 'Give it ten minutes and then we will head east along the creek bed.'

The mention of water brought thirst clawing at Enrico's throat. He nodded and settled back on the tree roots and rocks to wait. Thank Christ we got away, he thought, from the communists as a much as from the *Nazifascisti*. He was not sure which pleased him more.

Cowbells. The tinny clanging just ahead sent them scuttering into the forest. Tepid sunlight sifted through to the rough path they had followed since dawn. To their left the low dry-stone wall gave way to a steep incline, and to the right the mossy bank sloped up into the forest in a tangle of twisted roots and ferns. They slithered into the fungal leaf mulch and lay still. It had rained in the night. They were saturated and chilled.

Lower down the muddy track, an elderly man rounded the curve, leading two cows by a single halter, their udders swinging heavily, their hooves squishing and sliding in the rocky slush. His head – no higher than the shoulder of his cow – was tipped back and he squinted from beneath the brim of a tattered cap that might have fitted him when he had hair, but now swivelled on his slippery skull. He slowed a moment, then came on, bringing the cows to a halt directly in front of where the three men lay shivering, clutching their gear. Each had their *zaino* – they had found Roberto's and Giacomo's at the bottom of the ravine as they'd edged their way along. Giacomo even had his knife. Enrico had his glasses too, which had been dangling from his jacket with one broken wing. Their world turned on those small, essential objects.

The old man dropped the tether, letting it trail as the cows wandered to the edge of the path, gently snuffling and dribbling, almost nose to nose with the three fugitives. The men stopped breathing. The heat of the cows' breath and the grassy scent of their slimy, mucus-covered nose-rings hung on the morning air. The old man untied a cloth he carried on a stick, spread it with care on a tuft of moss and sat with a heaving sigh, his back to them. A threadbare jacket hung off his scarecrow shoulders, much the same bony shape as his cows. He dug out a dark bread and a large wedge of dry cheese. Holding the bread beneath one arm, he hacked away at its end with a wicked knife. The smell of the cheese made their stomachs rumble.

Without turning his head, the man said loudly, in a raspy mix of dialect and Italian, 'Come on, *ragazzi*. If you're hungry you might as well come out and eat. I can't do you much harm with this.' He waved the knife and placed it on the ground beside him.

The sight of the bread and the cheese was stronger than them. Feeling foolish, the three men shuffled to their feet, brushing mud and twigs from their filthy clothes, and emerged onto the path. With cautious glances in each direction they lined up in front of the old man. With his knife, he gestured to them to sit, split three bits off the cheese, and proffered it on the point of the knife. 'Breakfast.'

As they gobbled it, he sawed three hunks of bread, offering them in the same way. It was all they could do not to wrest it from him and wolf down the whole thing. None of them spoke.

'*Guai*. A fine pickle you've got yourselves into from what I hear,' the old man said. 'You know they're out looking everywhere for you, those *porci fascisti*.'

Fascist pigs. So it was the militia who raided them.

'So you'd be on our side, would you?' Giacomo's tone was sceptical.

'I'm not on anyone's side, son. No-one is on our side. Us *contadini* – we just get in the way and get run over by everybody, us.' He grunted and chewed his cud harder. 'I don't like what you are doing. Any of you.' He was as desiccated as a late-winter apple.

'But you don't like what the fascists are doing,' replied Giacomo.

'Or the *Nazisti*,' the old man continued. 'It's all right. No need to piss yourselves, I'm not about to turn you in. Worse than the Nazis they are, our lot. The Duce, he was going to do everything for us. Promises!' He spat expertly from the side of his mouth. 'In the end they're all the same.' His stubbly jaw worked back and forth as he chomped his bread, which was like stone even for someone with teeth, and he had none. 'Your comrades are pretty much all dead, by the way.'

'Not our comrades,' said Giacomo. 'We're not communists.'

'Just as well, my friend, because seven of them are dead and two are taken. They'll have talked. I wouldn't give much for their chances.' He dug around in his piece of cloth and pulled out a shrivelled pear, which he divided carefully into three and gave to them. 'You're to come with me and someone will be in touch.'

With his chin he indicated a hessian bag, slung over one of the cows. Giacomo rose and extracted a bulbous green glass bottle stoppered with a cork tied with string. The old man nodded, and with a broad smile Giacomo pulled the cork with his teeth.

'Man. Now you're talking.' He threw back his head, swallowed with a deep gurgle and passed the bottle to Roberto, who did the same.

Enrico took his turn with more caution but it did not help. '*Caspita!*' He choked and spluttered, struggling for breath. His eyes watered. Not the finely wrought grappa of his father's *Fattore* at Impruneta. This was distilled in some *baracca* in the valleys, with God only knows what in the bottom of it. He averted his eyes from the crusted lip of the bottle. The clear liquid tasted vile and seared every centimetre of its pathway to his kidneys. It was revolting. He loved it.

'How do we know you're not a spy yourself?' he said, without much conviction. He ate the piece of pear, though it made him feel like a bastard – the old man was a gnome who barely came to his shoulder and was made of nothing but tobacco-coloured leather stretched over the loom of his bones. He would never have had enough food in his life.

'It's not as if you've got lots of alternatives, is it like?' the old man replied. '*Venvia! Un dire bischerate!* Come on, let's go. Don't say stupid stuff.'

The three snorted with laughter at the familiar bristly dialect.

Florence felt closer. Laughter felt foreign.

The gnome creaked to his feet, tied the grubby cloth at its corners and picked up the cows' tether. 'Come on, *Avanti. Avanti.* These cows can't milk themselves, you know. Too cold for them to be out long.' He ambled off in the direction he had come.

Feeling like three more of his cows, they fell in behind him.

CHAPTER 10

Florence 1944

La staffetta

Anxiety and fear filled each day right to the edges, yet the sense of purpose and satisfaction, and yes, of enjoyment, was a relief after years of impotence and futility. Annabelle would rather have been in the mountains with Enrico but at least she was a part of it now, an important part. Her work as a *staffetta* was essential to maintain support and information to the men who were fighting. At night she gathered with the rest of the family to listen to the broadcasts of Radio London. Her days were busy collecting and delivering leaflets, paper and ink to the clandestine printing presses, documents for escaped prisoners of war and Jews in hiding, and carrying messages.

She was disappointed she was not permitted to work outside the city, liaising with the men in the mountains, but many of the partisans were still underground and active in the city itself and her job was to aid them in their tasks as they interrupted communications and cut wires and derailed trains. She knew now what she was doing and why she was doing it. There was excitement. The danger was ever-present and real, the city a bubbling brew of mistrust, distrust and suspicion. The air reeked of it as of sulphur and it infected relations at all levels like malaria – *mal-aria*, poisoned air. Servants and mistresses distrusted each other; shopkeepers betrayed customers and vice versa; doctors could not be trusted with suspicious wounds; neighbours spied on neighbours, and malignant spores of the black market in all goods, spread and flourished.

Each day brought news of more people who had disappeared,

more bodies in the streets. Still no news of Lorenzo. The sweet stench of death became familiar in the city byways where once it was only found in the cemetery. Or, in earlier times, in via degli Avelli at the side of Santa Maria Novella where corpses were interred in the green and white marble niches, which often cracked, giving off the pungent odour of decaying flesh. Annabelle had read all about that in her history books and always avoided the little street on her childhood ramblings. There was no avoiding it now. Bodies were deliberately left where they were shot as a warning to others: to those who tried to escape after being arrested for defying orders to re-enlist or were caught distributing leaflets or manning the printing presses or trying to escape deportation in the Todt transports. So far, the bodies were men but the danger escalated daily and sooner or later both the fascists and the Nazis would begin making an example of the women who were aiding the men.

She went to sleep in fear and awoke in dread, yet every sense was heightened. Life was never so fully lived and colours never so clear and bright, and it all led to Enrico. After nearly two months, they had heard he was with a group on Monte Amiata, and every message she carried was really for him. In her pocket, she fingered a much-folded sketch which had arrived with a *staffetta*. On a piece of lined school notepaper was a head and shoulders portrait of a girl with sad eyes and wild hair, and beneath it in Enrico's hand was written: '*sursum corda*' – cheer up, lift up your heart. And she did.

The package of passports was almost too large to fit properly inside her pleated blouse. Lucky her breasts were so small or it would have been suspiciously visible. She hunched forward a bit and crossed the Ponte alle Grazie in step with a German patrol. By now she had perfected a calm confidence in her encounters with the Nazis, less so with the local *fascisti*, many of whom knew her. Today the sun was shining and the Arno, in its winter pea-soup colour, rushed by beneath her. Gino Bartali coasted to a halt on the other side of the bridge with a casual wave as if he had seen her by chance. She waved back, trusting that neither the Germans nor the fascists would dare to accost him. Gino was an Olympic cyclist, a national hero – no, an international hero, and the world was watching. Would that always be enough to keep him safe, she wondered. She sauntered across and stopped to speak to him, kissing him on both cheeks, as with any chance encounter. The flapping of her heavy cardigan, left unbuttoned so it would fall forward as she bent down, concealed her hands and no-one saw the package go from her blouse to his satchel as she bent to retrieve her dropped handbag.

Annabelle stood for a bit with the winter sun on her shoulders, grateful for the warmth soaking through her clothes and through her skin, reaching right into her body to her organs, allaying her fears a little. She watched Gino ride away, taking the passports to a group of Jews and an escaped English prisoner of war, hidden in a convent on the far northern outskirts of the city. The convents and monasteries were all hiding Jews ever since last November when Archbishop Dalla Costa ordered them to do so.

Her heartbeat was still slightly elevated and the sense of dread would persist for some time. She marvelled again at Gino's courage and endurance. He had won the *Giro d'Italia* twice, or was it three times, and then the Tour de France in 1938. Although there were no bicycle races for him now, he had not diminished in the slightest his training regimen and his commitment. Sinewy, intense, wearing a racing jersey, the brim of his cap turned up, he was a constant sight all over the region and throughout Florence as he pedalled on his 'training runs', delivering information and passports and maps. He ate up the kilometres of the mountains and travelled as far afield as Umbria and le Marche and even to Rome. He had hidden a Jewish family in his own home. He hid documents and notes and passports inside the frame of his bicycle and in secret pockets of his saddle bags, and once in a wagon attached to the bicycle, which he claimed was for weight to enhance his training. Many Jews in this city owed their lives to him, and Annabelle prayed he would be able to continue his work until the Allies arrived to spare the Jews the tragedy of deportation. If they can only hold on, she thought. Where oh where are the Allies? When oh when would she see Enrico?

Breakfast was ready – if it could be called breakfast. Annabelle drank some of her weak milky coffee and dunked a stale brioche in it, watching with revulsion as the oil from the brioche floated to the surface. She pushed both aside. She was badly out of sorts today. A copy of Dino Buzzati's newly published short stories, *The Seven Messengers*, was open beside her plate, but the stories only accentuated her bad humour. The cramps in her stomach meant her period was near. There had been no news of Enrico in the past week. No-one had heard anything of Lorenzo and he had not arrived at Monte Morello. Thank God. There had been a massacre there. She was contemplating the empty morning when Elsa entered, carrying a pile of papers. No-one seemed to knock anymore and everyone seemed to live here in their apartment, Annabelle sulked.

'Today's run is a big one,' her aunt said, without so much as a *buon giorno*. Elsa as the early-rising, bustling head of the family was still a phenomenon.

'Good *moooorning, Zia*,' replied Annabelle, but the sarcasm fell to the carpet with the crumbs of the brioche.

'*Va bene*. You want to work, you say, really work. You want to be a *staffetta*. You are always saying it. You are fed up with being on the edge.' Elsa's mouth was a straight line. 'Today you will work for us. It will be very dangerous. Do not tell your mother.'

Annabelle stilled. The day was improving after all. Her pulse scurried and she pushed aside the repulsive coffee, which had congealed at the edges of the cup and formed a milky skin. She tingled, her earlier torpor vanished.

'I have documents – passports, birth certificates and so on, for delivery. But. This is the problem: in this case there is more, something highly classified. They must be delivered in person and I cannot do it for reasons I cannot explain. You will have to do it.' Elsa pulled out a chair, abandoned it and paced. 'If you are caught with this you will be killed. Do you understand me? They will shoot you,' she continued after a moment, as if killed may not be clear enough.

Annabelle was thrilled by Elsa's perturbation and to be finally included in the dangers Enrico was running. To be sharing his perils.

'This involves Carlo Levi,' her aunt explained, 'and spies working with the Allies, which is why it carries such danger for you.'

126

Annabelle did not know who Carlo Levi was, but the name was Jewish. That was not good. As a child she had no idea names could carry such weight. There had always been a family by the name of Levi in Borgo Pinti but they had disappeared, leaving their lovely house deserted, brooding, forlorn. Things had been dire enough for five or six years now, ever since the passing of the Racial Laws and Jews being interned and persecuted. Now, in her work with Elsa's clandestine friends, she was accustomed most days to being involved in some form of help for the Jews secreted throughout the region. Her aunt's friend from Turin, Rita Levi-Montalcino, a brilliant doctor, was now one of many in hiding underground somewhere in Florence, protected by *Partito D'Azione* workers such as Elsa. The deportations increased daily and rumours from Germany, too horrific to be true, were no longer rumours and were certainly true.

The Germans began rounding up Jews as soon as they invaded, months ago. They said it was for labour camps, but now people were talking about death camps where the Jews were being systematically murdered. Gassed. The English had warned about this a year ago. Annabelle could not imagine such a thing could be true, and yet just this month the Italians had refused to hand over Jews from a concentration camp, so even the fascists knew it must be true. She did not want to believe it, could not believe it, and yet she knew in her heart it was true. The world had gone mad. By now, her pulse had gone mad too.

Carlo Levi was, Elsa explained, a dissident, imprisoned in *Le Murate* until the events of last July. He was hidden in a palazzo in Florence and was working with the Resistance. The penalty for hiding or assisting Jews or escaped prisoners of war was death. They all knew that. Annabelle had run that risk many times. The penalty was death. The mantra of the times. Posters on walls all over the city shouted it sternly, alongside tattered earlier ones declaring Germany is truly 'your friend'. Volleys of machine-gun fire were the background sound to their lives, along with the church bells. Her aunt was probably exaggerating – why would this errand be any different?

'Of course I will do it,' she assured her. 'And certainly, it is better if Mamma does not know.' She stood taller, though there was no need as she already made her aunt look like a *Lenci* doll. She attended soberly to her instructions and rushed upstairs to change clothes.

Annabelle clumped down the frigid stairwell awkwardly, owing to the slim package taped scratchily to the inside of her thigh beneath the wool stockings. Her bicycle leaned against the wall in the foyer. Struggling to open the small door in the gigantic studded *portone*, she jerked back as a platoon of fascist militia in their black uniforms marched past, almost running her down in the narrow street. Their *Capo squadra* strode ahead, arms swinging, filling the whole of the narrow street. The few shopkeepers and merchants and early shoppers did not so much as glance at them. A far cry from the past when bystanders smiled or waved or even clapped them. Annabelle resisted an urge to spit. She paused instead to regard the crystalline late January sky and breathe deeply of the thin air; the cold burnt the inside of her nose. Exhilaration had cured her stomach cramps.

She bumped her bicycle over the threshold and turned down Borgo Pinti toward Sant'Ambogio. She was to visit Rodolfo Siviero, to collect a package of documents relating to the provenance of two Renaissance bronzes. The package, and the one on her person, were to be delivered to a villa in Fiesole. That was all. Why so mysterious then? She had made many of these runs, and this was in daylight, with no need for subterfuge.

She rattled along, a happy part of the early chorus of bicycles clattering over the uneven paving of streets laid down a thousand years before. A good morning to be alive. Today she saw no bodies. She crossed the Ponte alle Grazie, heading towards Lungarno Serristori and the gracious home of the Jewish art critic and collector, Giorgio Castelfranco, who was the director of the Gallery of Palazzo Pitti until the Racial Laws. He had fled the city immediately after the German invasion. He was alive and working in Bari, Elsa said. His protégée, Rodolfo Siviero, conducted business at many levels from the honey-coloured Renaissance palazzo. The legitimate comings and goings at the house gave excellent cover for his work with the Resistance and Annabelle was used to collecting and delivering information there.

With the flat cardboard pack of documents attached openly to the rack of her bicycle, she re-crossed the Arno – wintry and sluggish – and headed towards Fiesole, passing the devastation of the bombing of two weeks ago. As she pedalled harder and higher, she could see snow on the surrounding hills. The sweet hills, topped by villages dusted with powdered sugar. Below her, the Duomo glittered with snow-diamonds and Florence snuggled into its basin, enfolded by the soft curves of those protective hills whose cleavage held so many secrets.

After standing on the pedals for the last of the steep incline to Villa Rosalia, Annabelle was out of breath and swallowing a creeping dread when she rapped the iron knocker of the *portone*. Inside the courtyard was filled with sunshine, the stone walls radiating warmth and reassurance. There was a well in the centre of the paved court-yard, with an ornate cast-iron rail and roller from which the wooden bucket hung. The wet rope and the bucket steamed gently in the sun. Two wooden carts stood to the side, their shafts empty, leaning on the flagstones.

A woman came to meet her. 'I am Adua.' That was all she said, but she smiled. She wore a brown cloth skirt of the sort the *contadini* wore, yet her accent was clipped and cultivated, with no trace of the harsh 'c' of the dialect. The skirt was the same brown as her hair, the brown of a Picasso Annabelle had once seen. Adua took the large package and led her through the door of the stables where two men waited. Any warmth and reassurance dissolved. The men were dour, businesslike, not inclined to pleasantries. Their faces wore the closed expression of the countryside; they would certainly use dialect. They nodded at her. Both had machine guns. Annabelle had never seen a Bren before. In fact, she had never seen a partisan before. One of the men held the iron ring to a trap-door, propping up the weighty wooden platform. His belt was heavy with grenades or bombs of some sort. The other indicated with his head that she should follow him, and clambered down the ladder under the floor. There was no sunshine anywhere now. Annabelle tucked her skirt higher, conscious of the package still taped to her thigh, and descended into the blackness.

The smell of hay and animal dung from above hung heavy in the gloom. Her stomach roiled again, but now with a terrible looseness in her bowels. Never admit to fear, Enrico always said. All very well for him. The man who preceded her down the ladder turned and took her arm gently, as if she had spoken aloud. Three spectral forms emerged from the straw where they had been lying like discarded sacks. All three were emaciated and unshaven. One was very tall, wearing a uniform Annabelle did not recognise; another wore the remnants of an Italian Army corporal's uniform, and the third was in a suit much too big for him. The tall one came forward with his hand extended. He said in quite good Italian, 'I am Major Mason of the First Transvaal Scottish Regiment.'

The other, the Italian, introduced himself as Corporal Mario Manzoni. He went to salute and then proffered his hand instead, in the English manner. His dark beard was long and thick and he had obviously decided to let it grow, by contrast to Major Mason who was obviously making some effort to shave when he could. Manzoni spoke Italian but his accent was not from anywhere around Florence – further north, Annabelle thought. He brushed at the straw and dust of his uniform in silent apology for its condition.

'We have both walked a very long way,' he said, nodding at Major Mason, 'and we have a long way to go. Thank you for coming, *Signorina*.'

The third man in the old jacket said, 'Max'. No more. He did not shake hands. His hair stood up in tufts and he ran his hands through it ceaselessly. The other two would have been in their twenties, she thought, but it was impossible to tell with Max. His cheeks were sunken and his eyes were black – the pupils, the deep circles around the sockets. He looked like someone peering out of hell.

Major Mason said, 'You have documents for us.'

Why oh why did I not remove the package before I got in here, Annabelle thought. And then in the same breath, no-one here cares about modesty. She pulled her skirt up and ripped at the tape holding the package to her leg. It came away awkwardly, with some of the wrapping tearing. The skin on her thigh burned. She felt a fool, but no-one was interested in that either.

As Major Mason unwrapped the parcels and went through the documents, Annabelle waited beside Max. He was very ill, that was clear. His breathing was uneven and his breath smelled of sadness. The large package she had delivered to Adua contained identity and travel documents in hollowed-out provenance folders, but the one the Major was examining now was typewritten sheets in some sort of code. Corporal Manzoni squatted and laid out the identity documents in a row before him, squinting in the dim light as he sorted the papers into piles. Major Mason spread the typed sheets on an up-ended crate and picked up a torch from a pile of belongings on the straw. It was a large tubular torch with a dull yellow beam, completely unlike the flat rectangular ones she had seen the Germans using. Max took no part in the activity but simply attended, an observant wraith.

One of the men with the guns said to her, 'Wait for us upstairs.'

She had been wrong about the accent. Nothing was normal here. She climbed the ladder into the light and air where Adua awaited her. Her stocky sensible form was reassuring after the dank underworld.

'Come with me and I will make you a coffee,' she said.

The normal courtesy surprised Annabelle. She had a rush of gratitude. She followed Adua through the end of the building to where the kitchen of the farmhouse abutted the stables. Annabelle sat at one end of a rough table while Adua prepared the coffee. Annabelle's bowels had settled a little but her whole body vibrated. Her mind was a ferment of questions but she did not know what to say to Adua. She had no idea what they could and could not talk about.

Adua relieved her of the worry. 'Max is a Jew. A scientist. His wife and two children have been deported. His parents are dead, his brother too. He escaped. There are many Jews fighting with us.' She sat, pushing one of the two small cups toward Annabelle, and continued. 'He shot two German guards with their own rifle. We have to get him to Switzerland. He has important information for the Allies.'

'And the others?' Annabelle asked.

'Both escapees.' Adua was happy to talk, apparently. 'Major Mason is South African. He escaped from a prisoner of war camp in Capua. He was caught in Tobruk, in Africa. Mario is a deserter being shipped to Germany with the Todt transports. There were documents for four of them today, but one ...' Adua faltered.

Annabelle did not want to hear. She realised she had seen Mario sort four groups of documents. Her bowels shifted again.

Adua fixed her very squarely and continued. 'Her name was Anna. She worked with us, helping people like these, Jews in particular. She was arrested and sent to *Le Murate*. Then to the Villa Triste. We managed to get her out but ... she had been repeatedly raped and tortured and ... she was in a very bad way and she died after we got her here.'

Her tone did not alter. 'She did not talk. You should know these things. These are the risks you run, we all run.'

Adua leaned towards her. 'It is not always a clean death. The Germans will shoot you but it is the *fascisti* who rape and torture. Our own countrymen!' She unbuttoned her blouse, let the fabric fall off her shoulder and shrugged it down, baring her heavy, left breast. A clotted mess of livid flesh with snaking white ridges of scar tissue spread across the burned area where the nipple should have been.

Annabelle's head snapped aside as though she had been dealt an open-handed blow. She thought she might vomit but swallowed hard until the contractions in her throat subsided. Your life is in danger. The penalty is death. Elsa said it, the posters all said it. Of course it was. She heard it all the time. Now it was real. There were worse things than being shot. She sat very still. Her breathing was very loud. Her mind tried to veer away but her eyes remained riveted to the wound. Oddly, she realised she no longer felt nauseous. Adua pulled her blouse back up and buttoned it but neither spoke or moved. Annabelle understood now how Adua could relate Anna's story without a change in tone. She knew she would not survive that. She was not Anna or Adua. She would talk. She was sure she would betray them. She was very afraid for Elsa. Why she had never considered what would happen to Elsa if she were caught?

Adua spoke again. 'Anna left two children and a mother, and a husband fighting with the *Garibaldini*. Her husband does not know she is dead yet. He may be dead himself. This is our life now, Annabelle.'

So Adua knew who she was. Anna's husband was fighting with the communists. Was Adua a communist too then? What does a communist look like? Annabelle knew so little about the dreaded communists, though she knew the majority of the partisan brigades were *Garibaldini* – communist. The men with the guns were not wearing scarves, red or otherwise. Were they communists? Elsa and Enrico were not communists, they were with Justice and Liberty. Annabelle had thought they were opposed to each other. She understood so little, so little. She felt hot tears close by. Adua would not have shed tears for a long time. Annabelle threw her head back and looked up to the ceiling and breathed deeply until the stone in her throat dissolved.

Adua put a hand on her arm. 'There has to be a better world after this. I am happy you share the fight. Sooner or later the Allies will come. The war will end. It is up to us to build a better future for Max's children, for Anna's children, your children.'

Did Adua have children? The two guards emerged from the stables. One nodded to Adua and they turned and disappeared through another door at the far end of the kitchen.

Adua stood. 'There is no message. They have what they need. You will be safe going down, with nothing to carry.'

'And Anna ...?' said Annabelle.

The conversation was over. 'Anna is buried here. *Stammi bene.* Be safe.' Adua embraced her, turning her leaden form by the shoulders towards the door.

Like a sleepwalker, Annabelle retrieved her bicycle from where it leaned against the well. The bucket and rope were dry now. The sun was low and the warmth had gone from the day. From the world. She led the bike across the bumpy stones through the gates to the pathway in the olive grove. From time to time she stumbled, the pedals grazing her ankles, but she did not notice the blood staining her socks.

Annabelle did not trust herself to mount the bike. She did not trust herself to walk. She did not trust herself. She thought of Max's eyes. She thought of Major Mason's upright bearing and punctilious manner. And his marvellous torch. She thought of Mario's decision to shake hands. She was in the long shadows of the villa walls by now and it would soon be out of sight. She did not look back. If she did, would she turn to salt? Would it all still be there – the farmhouse, the stables, the trapdoor, the men – or would it have disappeared, a mirage in the desert?

The now familiar stone in her throat was choking her. She felt light-headed. She felt old. She had been a fool: it was some sort of childish, romantic game she had been playing until now. How could she have been so selfish? Was that why Elsa had sent her? So she might finally understand? At the road, she mounted her bike and headed unsteadily down the hill towards the city, pedalling faster and faster, her hair flying, her mind roiling now instead of her bowels. She would never be young again. This fight is for our lives, she thought, for all of us and all of them. She needed to talk to Elsa. She needed to be with Elsa. She did not think of Enrico. She heard a door slam shut behind her.

It was dusk before Annabelle reached the outskirts of the city. Owing to the blackout there were no street lights, especially about the area of SM Novella. For several years the city had been preparing for bombing and now it had arrived. The outskirts of the city were bombed again last week, but with fewer casualties. Passing the Accademia, Annabelle thought of Michelangelo's *Prisoners*, walled into protective, kiln-like brick structures built around them, like the Trulli houses of Puglia. They once were prisoners of their marble but now they had become truly prisoners, forever bricked up alive. In the great niche where the David once stood was a forbidding cone of brick. David too was a prisoner. We are all prisoners, she thought.

The streets were drab, the winter evening drew in. Shreds of mist swirled about corners, the face of the Virgin Mary floating on high from ancient frescoed tabernacles. Annabelle shivered in her coat, too light for being out at night. She wanted to be home before the curfew and avoid, just for today, the stomach-churning anxiety of being caught out after dark. And she was hungry. Starving. How odd, she thought. What strange creatures we are, how could she possibly think of food after Villa Rosalia? She crossed Piazza Duomo and stood gazing up at the majesty of Giotto's Bell Tower. Surely there was still beauty and truth somewhere.

She turned the bike up Borgo Pinti and lifted it through the heavy doors into the main courtyard. For a moment she stood at the foot of the wide curving marble of the graceful stairway leading to the formal rooms. No-one in the family used it, all preferring the steeper, faster stairs previously only for the servants' use. The main staircase lead directly up to her uncle and aunt's apartment – Enrico's apartment, as she always thought of it. She considered going up immediately to Elsa, or should she wait and think about what to say? She turned right and took the back stairs.

As she opened the door to their own home her father pulled it inwards, his face sober. He sighed in relief, stepping back to let her enter. In the drawing room the lamps were lit, though the fire burning in the grate barely managed to take the edge off the cold. The heavy frames of the paintings lining the walls seemed to her so reliable, so solid. Had she ever actually looked at them before? Elsa was seated at the piano, her back to the keyboard, and it was plain they had not been discussing music.

Achille took Annabelle by the shoulders, kissed her on both cheeks and released her with a push towards her aunt. 'Your mother and I have to go out. I have asked Anna Maria to bring you both some food on a tray.'

So he knew, thought Annabelle. It was not his normal practice to greet her with a kiss. It was not anyone's normal practice in this family. Annabelle had rarely wondered about the emotions of her mother or her father and certainly not of Elsa. Now she was full of wondering.

Elsa had not spoken. Now she rose, took Annabelle's hand and led her to the small round table beside the fireplace, which was set with two places. Annabelle did not know where to start. She picked absently at the loose stitches of the threadbare brocade on the arm of the sofa nearby. The fabric was at least three hundred years old and was once red but had turned to a soft dusty pink, suddenly so familiar and so dear.

'They are communists,' Annabelle began. She did not look at Elsa. 'Adua and those men, I mean. I thought we did not join the communists.' She did not mention Anna. The stone rose again in her throat. She had an image of that stone – it was pale granite, hard, oval, smooth, and at times she thought it might suffocate her.

Coming to stand beside her, Elsa wrapped her arms about Annabelle, cradling her head on her breast, which was at just the right height for the seated girl. From nowhere, Annabelle was juddered by dry, rasping sobs tearing up from deep within her. Her aunt held her tighter, waiting until she quieted and relaxed against her. Annabelle realised she was clasping Elsa so tightly it was a wonder she did not break. She loosened her grip a little but did not sit back. She had no memory of ever being held like this. Surely her mother must have held her as a child? Perhaps not. Her nurse Matilde was the strongest image from her childhood, and though kindly, she did not offer affection. Her father was a stern and comforting presence but distant. The only person whose arms she knew was Enrico, who cuddled her and carried her everywhere, even after she learned to walk.

Elsa sat her back in the chair as Anna Maria entered slowly, wheeling a wooden tray with bread and cheese and soup. The old woman was more stooped than ever, her arthritic knuckles raw and inflamed. Each day she tied her apron tighter about her bony frame – a carapace against a dangerous world. Elsa nodded brusquely to Anna Maria who hovered.

'That will be all.' Her tone was cool. Then in a low voice, 'She has taken to hovering around doors.'

After waiting to be sure the servant was out of earshot, she crossed to the door and opened it to check outside, then returned and shook out a heavy white napkin each. She served some soup and a large chunk of bread to Annabelle, and then sat opposite, on the edge of her chair.

'You see now what is happening in this country,' she said. 'We must all work together. The communists are not the only opposition to fascism. For years now we in the Action Party have been working to combat fascism and we must work with the communists if we want to survive. If we want to win.'

She pulled off a small piece of the hard unsalted bread and chewed it. 'They are not monsters, Annabelle. That is the picture painted for us by the fascists, and by many of our own class too, who feared they would erode the feudal system we have lived off for centuries. We are fighting not just an invader but our own countrymen. This is a fight for our lives and our country and not all of us will survive it. But we must try.'

It was a lecture. This was how Enrico talked to her but now her diminutive aunt was the rebel. It did not even feel strange, where nothing was as it seemed anymore. Annabelle pushed some cheese toward her, wondering how many grams of food it took to keep such a tiny creature alive. Elsa's unruly chestnut hair was loose, an aureole about her face as she turned with the firelight behind her. A little myopic, Elsa always leaned into a conversation, allowing the listener to see deep into her eyes, which were brown – not the black-brown of her ancestors, rather a soft amber brown. It was no wonder *Zio* was besotted with his wife. So was Enrico. Now Annabelle too was beguiled by this woman who, she realised for the first time, was still very young.

'Partisan does not mean communist, Annabelle. We are of many stripes. In Justice and Liberty we belong to no "ism", except perhaps patriotism in its decent sense.' She stood and took Annabelle by the elbow. 'Get some sleep. You have a lot to think about. There is time.' She stood on tiptoe, kissed her again on the cheek and turned towards the door. 'And we will talk about Anna later.'

We. It was we, now. On her cheeks, the faint scent of Elsa's perfume lingered. It was called Joy. For the first time that day, Annabelle thought of Enrico out there somewhere. She prayed he was all right but he would take his chances as they all would. She had a lot to learn and was in a hurry now to catch up.

Florence 1944

Achtung! Zona infestata di Banditen, Banditi.

A nerve twitched in the calf of Annabelle's leg jammed against the seat in front of her. The sheer audacity of her mission almost made her laugh. It was three weeks since her visit to Villa Rosalia and nowadays she knew the risks. She knew everything she needed to know and no more. They were in regular contact with Enrico and his brigade and Annabelle was happy to have a role. Lorenzo was still missing though. He had not made it to Enrico. Elisabetta was deranged. Someone said he had joined the communist group up near Marzabotto but no-one could confirm it. He was not the only one missing.

As the bus ground uphill towards the village Annabelle gazed out the window at the frozen fields, snow melting in the ploughed runnels. February, the worst month of the year. Lent into the bargain. Why her unbelieving family gave up decent food for Lent she could never understand, though now every day felt like Lent anyhow. It would freeze again. She looked up at the grey-green sky, a certain harbinger of snow. And so she missed the road block.

The bus jerked to a halt. Fascists, not Germans. Even if she had seen them, she could do nothing. To the side of the road was a German sign nailed to a post: *Achtung! Zona infestata di Banditen, Banditi*. Attention. Zone infested by bandits. Infested by partisans, it meant. There were at least twelve militia – all heavily armed, all looking unfriendly in their grey uniforms and black shirts. Annabelle's heart was so loud they could hear it, surely. She breathed deeply and tried not to look suspicious. She was seated towards the back of the bus, which carried about fifteen passengers, mostly aged and slow to descend the rickety stairs. Using her foot, she awkwardly slid the wrapped parcel back under the seat as far as it would go, and then it was her turn to get off. At the side of the road a corporal questioned the elderly driver. The other passengers waited, their faces closed like the shops on Sunday. No-one spoke.

The commander approached her. '*Signorina Albizzi, buon giorno.*' His courtesy was formal but not encouraging. 'May I ask your business today?'

'*Commandante Neri, buon giorno,*' she rejoined. Was it a good thing she knew him or not? 'I am on my way to the Castello. My father is there and my bicycle has a broken chain, so I'm afraid it is the bus for me.' She rolled her eyes at the hopelessness of girls.

He nodded impassively and indicated for her to stand aside as his men mounted the steps of the bus. She wanted to run. She wanted to run. She wanted to run. But she stayed very still. Breathed very quietly. Spreading her hands at her sides, she managed to wipe her sweaty palms on her skirt. Incredibly, after what seemed hours, the men all climbed down from the bus without comment and without a great deal of interest. Commandante Neri indicated to the passengers they could climb aboard again. He saluted Annabelle. Not warmly, but, his face said the Nobles were the Nobles after all and it was necessary to keep on good terms with the aristocrats.

Annabelle's legs would not work; she almost fell but managed to get aboard. Would she sit in the same seat or not? Yes, better to do so. Was it a trap? With much grinding of gears, spitting and coughing on its methane fuel, the bus reluctantly chugged up the incline far too steep for the motor, inching forward a metre at a time while she stared straight ahead, waiting for shots. After twenty minutes her legs had cramped and she forced herself to relax, subsiding into the seat. She felt about with her foot but the package was not there. Not there! Her heartbeat bolted again. She did not look over her shoulder. There was nothing to be done until they reached the piazza in Impruneta. As the bus drew in Annabelle stood clumsily, and her bag slipped to the floor. With a sigh of exasperation she let the passengers pass and knelt to retrieve its contents, flailing madly under the seat until her hand touched a piece of the cloth. On her knees, she saw the worn and cracked boots of the driver at her side.

'*Signorina*,' he said in a low voice, 'if you have lost your parcel it will have slipped into the wheel compartment. Shall I get it out for you?'

She wanted to laugh with nerves, or perhaps scream. 'Most kind but I have it now, thank you.'

She leaned right under the seat, bumping her forehead on the frame, and with both hands, managed to pull the heavy parcel towards her, praying it would not unfurl before his eyes. Then, dusty and scarlet-faced, she stood with great dignity and turned to get off the bus.

The driver preceded her, waiting at the bottom of the steps. He touched his finger to his cap. 'Be more careful in the future, *Signorina*. Not everyone is trustworthy, you know.'

For long moments after the bus droned out of the piazza, she stood watching, stifling the desire to sob.

The yawn nearly fractured Enrico's jaw. Who would have thought that war could bring boredom? They were awaiting a drop of arms and supplies. He gave a heavy sigh and settled into the hollow in the cold ground. He was still learning the art of inaction. With not very good grace. Enrico was a fidgeter. He was no good at sitting without a book. Contemplation did not suit him. He preferred to read about the contemplation of others. He drummed his fingers silently on his thigh, scanning the sky and the surrounding countryside. Nothing. Just the glitter of the stars and the passing shadows of low cloud. Occasionally a far-off dog barked, the call echoing across the empty space of the valley. Three days now with no activity. Still, it was good to be fighting on the right side, finally. Roberto too was thrilled to be fighting alongside soldiers again, men who knew what they were doing. Major Mason was South African, and the rest of them were all either escaped Allied prisoners of war or ex-Italian Army. The major had walked all the way through the mountains from up near Parma when the guards of the prison opened the doors and abandoned their posts on the day of the Armistice. The *8th Raggruppamento Patrioti Monte Amiata* was a fine group of fighting partisans and Enrico was proud to serve with them. They were well-equipped too, and even had enough to eat – most of the time.

Enrico checked his watch and unpacked the field-radio to make his report. The group had excellent contact with the Allies, and Enrico's fluent English and excellent radio skills were in demand. He could send in morse too. He knew – they all knew – the Allied attitude to the partisans was ambivalent at best. At worst it was patronising and antagonistic. The British and the Americans did not want the communists to gain any credit or power at this point – they were already looking ahead to after the war. Being a Justice and Liberty group, however, and having many Allied members, the suspicion did not fall upon them to the same degree. Arrogant bastards they were, really, especially the British, and devious too, but Enrico was used to them and for now they needed each other. He would be relieved of his watch in half an hour and could not wait to get some food and some sleep. They got enough of both at present. It was funny how when they were busy they never got enough sleep but they did not seem to need it and yet on days of inactivity such as this, when there was no reason to be tired, all he could think of was sleep. He scratched his beard, running both hands up and down the sides of his face. Not lice again! He would shave off the beard. He had razors at the moment so he might as well be comfortable. Time enough to grow it back when they ran out of razors.

He brooded over the meeting with Annabelle. It was the second time he had seen her. Their *staffetta*. It was good that she was working with them, though he knew it would be a worry to his mother and to *Zia* and *Zio* too. It certainly worried him. He had seen his mother, his astonishing mother, once, as well. She brought important maps and the news that his teacher, Giovanni Neri, had been executed by the fascists. Everything worried him, but there was nothing he could do about any of it. His mother was always calm and strong. So tiny, so determined.

If only Annabelle were not so anxious all the time. Too much thinking; every little thing had to be examined and re-examined. Too cautious. Annabelle was a worrier. It got on his nerves. He was happy to see her but she was so tired and strained and tense that she made him feel that way too, and they had not really talked, but what was there to say? He hated the knot in his stomach as she left on the dangerous journey back to the city. He would feel better if he did not see her, then he would not have to worry. Perhaps. He needed to keep his mind on the tasks out here. He turned with relief at the low call from Matteo, coming to take over.

The waft of garlic and tomato drew Enrico along the last few metres of the track, his stomach racing for home at the thought of food. He unbuckled his ammunition belt and stacked all his gear on the ground, careful to keep his gun upright and at hand. The experience with the communists had taught him early that life was full of surprises. Here they were all well-trained to be alert at all times.

Roberto and Giacomo were still awake, waiting for him. He patted Giacomo on the belly and said, 'Getting fat there, old man.' He sat with another sigh. Giacomo seemed perfectly attuned to feast and famine – when food was unavailable he appeared to be able to go without ever thinking about it. When it was there, he gorged on it.

'Piss off, skin-and-bones.' Without rising, Giacomo ladled out a heavy plate of stew and passed it to Enrico.

Meat! It was ages since he had eaten meat. He did not ask where it came from. Giacomo leaned back and lit his pipe. They had plenty of tobacco at the moment. Days of plenty. It would not last.

'Heard an English joke today for you, *amico*,' he said to Enrico. 'Been keeping it all day.' His store of jokes was endless.

'Go on then.'

'A Roman walks into a bar, holds up two fingers and says, I'll have five beers, thanks.' At Enrico's snort of mirth he added, 'Knew it would appeal to your classical pretensions.'

Enrico finished his food and lay back with a sigh, this time of contentment. Roberto had not spoken apart from a grunt and a pat on his shoulder as he got back.

'What's the matter?' he asked, giving his cousin a shove.

He held his breath a little, because Roberto had not had news of his wife and two small children for weeks now. 'Bad news or no news?'

'Not bad news at least,' Roberto replied, 'but it gets harder and harder not knowing if they are all right. None of us knows much, but still, it's hard not to think about them.'

His wavy chestnut hair had grown long. Enrico was used to his cousin with the short tidy army-issue haircut – the long soft waves made him look young and vulnerable. The other two nodded. There was so much not knowing. Many families of the prisoners of war here in the battalion did not know the fate of their husband or brother or father or son. They had begun trying to ensure that information got back but it was difficult. Giacomo had news of his parents recently but he never, ever, discussed them and certainly never talked about Giselda. He told jokes.

'I think we all need more sex! Well, not you, my boy,' he said to Enrico. 'I think you seem to get our share too. I reckon that's why those *staffettes* are keen to give the messages to you. Ah well, you're young.' He passed the grappa.

Enrico took a deep swig of the liquid fire, smiled and shrugged. 'I think it is time we all got some sleep.'

CHAPTER 11

Florence 1944

The Verona trials

January 12

Loving Mussolini got Count Ciano nothing but a firing squad. The Verona Trials have finished and they have already been executed. Well, four of them. One got a life sentence. Loving Mussolini will go badly for many more of them. Poor Claretta!

The old romantic notions of Claretta had dried up like a scab on a wound. Annabelle pitied the girl who could not have known what she was getting into when she was so young. An image flitted into her head from long ago: of a purring, gleaming car with a beautiful girl in the back seat. It must have all seemed so romantic then. But Clara stayed with that megalomaniac who brought all this upon us and she would pay a high price now, like Ciano and the others. Annabelle had never, not for a moment, considered the object of Claretta's passions.

Il Duce was the wallpaper of her life. He was the figure in LUCE newsreels. He was the gesticulating dictator on high, raving from a balcony. He was an actor. He was the face in the framed portrait in every office and school and home. He was not a person. Not a man. His image repulsed her. In Annabelle's cloistered world, Claretta had represented daring and passion. In love with love, Annabelle was – then. Embarrassing now, those childish notions. The life before real life when she stepped across the invisible line. It was hardly her fault though. If she had ever had a normal life, it must have been as such a small child that she had no recollection of it. Enrico was a boy and it seemed he could do as he pleased but she was allowed no outlet for her bursting desire for action and romance.

It was all different now. Elsa offered her a much better model for action and romance. Let the Allies get here soon! Whatever end awaited Mussolini and his supporters, let it be soon! Before too many more of ours die. Before Enrico dies.

'It is only a matter of time,' said Elsa. 'They were all in love with him,' she added. All obsessed with Mussolini: Bottai, Ciano, Claretta, even Hitler, and certainly most Italians. 'In love with an empty vessel who could never have given what he promised. He did not have it in him.' Mussolini was, said Elsa, a cult.

'Look at that face,' she added, flicking the corner of *La Nazione* with Il Duce's jaw thrusting across its front page. 'Nothing but empty bombast. If you want to see an image of power, real power in its lasting form, look at a portrait of Doge Loredan or even of Cosimo il Vecchio. Not this braggart.'

Annabelle knew the Bellini portrait of the great Venetian Doge only from art books. He meant nothing to her, but she knew Cosimo, that stern old merchant, the oldest of the Medici. It was Albizzio Albizzi's money that got him out of jail, but without Cosimo's steely wiles most of her family and her class would never have made it through the fifteenth century to the castles and the seats of power. Another of Enrico's heroes. Yes, she knew him and she could see the difference.

'The so-called trial is over. We think they will be executed at once.' Elsa had told her this a couple of days earlier.

The hearings trailed on from December but the show trials had concluded over the past two days with indecent haste. Wasting no time, the executions were carried out by firing squad on the eleventh in the leaden gloom of a January dawn. All the members of the Grand Council of Fascism who had voted against Mussolini were tried and sentenced to death, but only five were actually there; the rest, including Grandi and Bottai, were tried *in absentia*.

'Mussolini himself is *in absentia*,' said Elsa. 'This is a German occupation. Make no mistake.'

Edda Ciano's frantic efforts to save her husband's life were the subject of much discussion, the newspapers full of snippets, but it was through the Action Party meetings the real information filtered in, via Allied contacts. It was commonly known that both Edda and Galeazzo Ciano lived their own lives and their own loves, but at the end, Edda rallied to her husband's side, utterly disbelieving that her father could do Hitler's bidding and have his own son-in-law executed, the father of his grandchildren. After initially resisting Hitler's order, Mussolini was, it seemed, no longer really interested – in the death of his son-in-law or anything else. The great love expressed by Count Ciano for his father-in-law was no longer requited.

Edda dashed to Rome to hide Galeazzo's diaries, with a plan to have the whole family escape to Germany. Elements within the upper echelons of the Nazi hierarchy were keen to trade the diaries, in particular Himmler, who hoped to use them to discredit Ribbentrop. The Allies too. Everyone had a vital interest in the diaries and by now, everyone was talking to everyone else. The family's flight to Germany was futile, however. They had barely arrived with the three children before Hitler, having learned of the plan, refused them sanctuary. Hitler was combustible, enraged by the King's illegal arrest of Mussolini. Even if, as Ciano and the others claimed, they too were caught unawares by the King's ploy, someone had to pay the price. And as Hitler was unable to have the King executed, much as he wanted to, then someone must pay. He insisted Ciano be sent back to answer for his betrayal. They were forced back to Italy, where Ciano was immediately arrested and imprisoned in Verona. In febrile conditions, the ripples spread.

'There are more spies than loyal citizens now,' said Elsa, 'even at Gargnano or Rocca delle Caminate.'

Finally, Edda made a last, futile dash to Switzerland with the Count's diaries, in a doomed attempt to barter them for his life.

'More to save herself and the children than Galeazzo, if you ask me,' snarled Elsa. 'I am glad he is dead, but it changes nothing.' Her voice had a vicious edge to it.

Annabelle regarded her with astonishment – Elsa rarely gave

opinions and never indulged in sniping. Annabelle's awe for her grew deeper each day, and as she understood more and more of Elsa's life and the bravery of her recent years, she was ashamed of her own childish ways. For the first time, she noticed the fine cross-hatch of lines around Elsa's beautiful eyes and deeply drawn around her mouth. Lately, her face in repose sagged into a portrait of sorrow.

Elsa waved a hand, as if dark thoughts could be warded off like a bee or a fly. 'I'm sorry, *Tesoro*. Take no notice of me. You know it was Ciano who had the Rosselli's murdered?'

There was more and more she did not know. The Rosselli brothers, founders of the Justice and Liberty movement, had been murdered by the Regime in France. It must have been six or seven years ago. Was Elsa was involved even then? With a hot burst of mortification, she realised that Elsa had given her only child to this battle and Annabelle had been too immersed in losing Enrico to understand that sacrifice. It was not easy, this being engaged in the adult world.

'We need those diaries,' Elsa continued. 'They will be crucial when this is over. No-one kept more detailed accounts than Ciano. In a way, it is just as well the Regime or the Nazis did not agree to buy them back for his worthless life because then they may well have been destroyed. The Allies will continue to search for them.' She shook her head slightly. 'Well, enough of that. I need your radio skills. You and Enrico spent enough time building crystal sets to make you useful to me.'

Diaries, thought Annabelle. Yes, a record will be important. She would insist on being allowed to attend the meetings of the Action Party. It was time to throw out the newspaper cutting of Clara. Delusion was the word that came to her mind. And love. Was all love finite? She knew so little about love and what one might do for love. She forced her mind to the present.

'I doubt a crystal set would be much use. What have you got in mind?'

In a street of ghosts where cars never boded well, the sleek black car stood out like ... well, like dog's balls, Enrico would have said. Its occupants were making no effort to be discreet. Annabelle brought her bicycle to a halt, one foot on the gutter. With a great show of digging about in her pockets for a handkerchief, she blew her nose. It seemed to be always running anyway, so it was no pretence. The car cruised by, an antenna revolving from side to side, sniffing for a signal. On the far side of Piazza dell'Indipendenza it made an agonisingly slow arc and her heart dropped into her stomach. She thought she might be ill. But it continued on through the piazza, turning down via Nazionale. She stood for an age, wiping her nose until it almost rubbed off.

They must have been off the air – the morning transmission would have finished only moments ago. Had the car picked up the signal and marked the house? She waited for three minutes, her whole body straining for the sound of tyres or running feet, or unusual movements. Her knuckles on the handlebars of the bicycle were white. The piazza was empty save for several elderly women and a horse-drawn cart piled high with mattresses. Annabelle turned slowly, very slowly, to survey the piazza one last time, then pushed off and pedalled across the open space, which felt kilometres wide. Nothing moved except swirls of mist. At the side of the building she turned down the narrow lane and propped her bicycle against a wall. The stroll to the front doors was torture. Still nothing moved. As she let the big doors close behind her, panic set in. She took the stairs two at a time and had to stop on the landing, breathing deeply so as not to panic the others. It was time to move.

For three weeks, they had been transmitting from the apartment Enrico Bocci had rented for the purpose. *Commissione Radio, Radio CORA*. The first transmission for the Information Service of the Action Party was received by the Allies in Bari from the publishing house of Bemporad in via degli Albizi, with the words 'The Arno is running in Florence'. Almost immediately, they transferred to the current spot and every single day, two transmissions went out, giving details of German movements and receiving information for weapons and supply drops for the Resistance, both in the city and outside.

'What?' Bocci still had his headphones on and one look at her face told him and the others that things were grave. He removed his headphones and stood, nodding to Carlo who had understood at once and was already dismantling the radio.

'They were outside. Outside.' Don't babble, she told herself. 'Just now. In a car with an antenna. They must have missed you by seconds.'

There were four of them in the room today and by now their routine was clear. Annabelle felt as if she was the only one shaking. The others began quietly packing up.

'I waited,' she said. 'There was no-one else. I was not followed.' She was calm now.

Carlo nodded and put a hand on her arm. 'We have the next place ready. You will do the afternoon transmission. Let the others know and Luigi will tell you where to find us.'

He gave her a gentle push towards the door and she left them to empty out the room. Thank God she had learned about radio from Enrico.

Florence 1944

Feb '44

The Allies have broken through the Gustav Line. If they can only take Rome! Please let them get here quickly. We are afraid for so many reasons but in particular for the Jews. The bombing is much more regular now, to our north and south.

The hard winter was made harder by fear, hunger and grinding uncertainty. Everyone hoped for a quick sweep up the peninsula by the Allies but it seemed less and less likely. 'Let it be over soon' was beginning to sound plaintive. The Germans were implacable. Their teeth sank deep into the despised, defeated Italians.

Annabelle was feeling unwell, but so was everyone. The malaise went deeper than the winter weather. Despite constant efforts from all, there was not a word on Lorenzo. No body had turned up and no-one reported seeing him. His mother had taken to her bed and refused all visitors. Annabelle's own mother rose later and later, drifting about, wafting orders here and there, muttering lists of household tasks as if the concrete and mundane might save them. Her mother had the knack of irritating her no matter what she did – always had. Her father suffered more and more from his bronchial attacks. He had long since run out of his vast stores of Dunhill tobacco but had found some sort of replacement, which did not have the fragrance of old. Her uncle was almost invisible. They were never accustomed to sharing emotions and Annabelle did not know how to reach out to them now, except by trying not to be impatient. The only energy in the household came from Elsa and Annabelle. Anna Maria, her apron and her mouth tighter and tighter, made meals from ever less food. They needed to conserve wood, coal was rationed, the house was dark and icy. All over the country the elderly froze to death.

Annabelle snivelled with a heavy cold a week old now – she was sick of it. The pain in her sinuses made it difficult to concentrate on anything for long. Luckily there was little time to dwell on it. She made at least four weekly broadcasts for Radio CORA – there were about twenty workers to take turns. Then there were the clandestine night-time meetings with members of the Resistance in the city, and daytime bicycle or bus trips into the villages in the mountains as a *staffetta*. She slept little and tried to think even less. She was surprised her pulse rate was permanently high – she'd have thought she'd get used to it, but each furtive exit on a dark night set her heart racing.

Twice she saw Enrico when he came in from the mountains for meetings, and once when she met him to the south of the city with information for his group to raid a COOP, to steal a consignment of cheese and supplies about to be requisitioned by the Germans. He was an older version of himself: bearded, his fingers yellowed from nicotine. He was drawn and fatigued and so was she. There was little to say. No news of Lorenzo. They had to assume he was dead, he said. We are all on close terms with death now, he'd added brusquely, to forestall further questions. She had none anyway. Enrico was gruff, closed, old. Annabelle was brisk and probably old too, she thought. They had all aged fast, but each day she knew he was alive was good. The rest of her time consisted of avoiding her mother's anguished unasked questions and running errands to Siviero's house with information, or packages, with meetings to organise assistance for Jews and escaped prisoners, or finding medical help for wounded partisans. Thank God for Gerhard Wolf, the German Consul, who was aiding them to get as many Jews out of the city as possible. He intervened on behalf of many arrested by the fascist militia, and they heard through a spy in the consulate that he had blocked Goering's manoeuvres to transport several of the most valuable of the paintings in the Uffizi to Germany. Annabelle shuddered at the risks he took.

In the city a semblance of normal life continued. The theatres, the opera and cinemas were all open. Art exhibitions were regular. For some people, it seemed it was still possible to inhabit a pretend-world of once-upon-a-time. On the road down from Piazzale Michelangelo, Annabelle saw an elegant couple – the woman in a cloche hat and glossy fur coat, the man in cashmere overcoat and fedora – being photographed against the backdrop of the Duomo in its medieval nest. Tourists! A spurt of hot rage gave her indigestion. She seemed to be angry a lot of the time lately.

Four months earlier, Mussolini's 'Philosopher of Fascism', Giovanni Gentile, shifted The Royal Academy of Italy from Rome to Florence. Everyone knew Gentile had ghost-written Il Duce's *A Doctrine of Fascism* even though it was meant to have been the leader's own manifesto. Having remained loyal to Mussolini throughout the Grand Council session, Gentile threw his weight behind the establishment of the Republic of Salò.

'Our finest intellectual,' Enrico scoffed. 'But,' he added, 'at least Gentile is no anti-Semite and we must hope for a reasoned voice from him.'

To be fair, he said, it was certainly true that under Gentile the academy appeared to favour both fascist and anti-fascist endeavours, but Enrico found it difficult to care about art or philosophy at present. He had lost his faith.

Annabelle did not have a faith to lose. She was more in search of one, in search of who she was supposed to be. It would have been good to be pretty – like Elsa, for example. People found her mother pretty and so she was, she remembered. An image came to her like stills from an old film, which then unspooled. She was small. It was a birthday party. It must have been her fourth, because she did not remember anything before that. She was sitting on the piano stool and Enrico, who would have been nearly six, brushed her hair and tied a ribbon in a big bow on top. It was blue, the ribbon, pale blue satin.

His tongue stuck out the corner of his mouth in concentration and his fingers were fumbly. His breath smelled of caramels. She would not sit still for her mother to brush her hair but she would allow Enrico to do it for ages. Her dress was blue too, something stiff, like organdie, and it itched where the smocking gathered across her chest. Lorenzo was there, clinging to his mother's skirt. There were several other children – out of focus. It was before fascism drew a jagged line through their family, so there would have been other cousins but she had little recollection of them. Finished with the bow, Enrico put his arms about her and lugged her off the stool, even though she was nearly as big as he, and she examined her small self with satisfaction in the long mirror at the end of the room. She was pretty.

Still, she thought now, it would be nice not to feel so large and awkward. Being taller than everyone else was not much fun. It was useful though; she was strong, that counted for something, especially now. Should she learn to smoke? They all seemed to do it. She could not imagine it. Women did not smoke, well, not women she met, respectable women. Women smoked in films and it looked romantic and sophisticated. Did she want to look sophisticated? She was embarrassed even to have these thoughts, so shallow at such a time. It must be the cold and the gnawing fear that the Allies were not going to be their saviours for a long time yet. What if they did not succeed, the Americans and the English and the others? Her heart thudded against her ribcage at the thought. No-one even considered such a thing, not out loud. What if this battle could not be won? What if they were all going to die, just when she had begun to live?

German occupation was ambiguous occupation. A proxy occupation. In the city, the Germans ran operations from their headquarters in Piazza San Marco, which Florentines avoided unless they had business there. There was no doubt the Germans were in charge but they were not the greatest fear. They stayed largely at a distance from the affairs of the city, leaving things in the hands of the local fascists – and that was the problem. Scum floats to the surface, Enrico said and it was plain to see.

Mario Carità was loathed and feared. With about a hundred other misfits and miscreants, he directed the torture and murder of rebels or spies or dissidents or, in fact, anyone who was, or who was denounced as being, or who might possibly be, or was related to someone who was opposed to the new Socialist Republic. Most did not come out of the *Villa Triste*. Not alive. In a sickening irony, his name was Charity. There was no shortage of good citizens ready to settle a score by denouncing someone to Major Charity. The war lifted a rock and from under it, unimaginable creatures emerged, creatures who could not survive in the sunlight, who could thrive only in the dank shady corners of a civil war. Carità and his minions and informers were not alone. The Muti Blackshirts were largely criminals from the jails, the members of the Decima Mas were professionals, but no less brutal. The Germans were short of men, munitions, rations and patience. It suited them to allow the worst of the ordure of the occupation to fall upon the fascists.

For the partisans, their supporters and all the members of the Resistance and their families, the city throbbed with menace. The monsters in the shadows were real. Mothers were terrified to emerge from the house for fear of the sight of their son's body hanging from a lamp-post. Or a butcher's hook. Elderly parents and siblings and wives and lovers gathered daily outside the *Villa Triste* in via Bologna, or the jails, awaiting news or a glimpse of someone they loved as he was transferred to another prison, or in the hope of getting food or supplies or some word of comfort to the prisoner. Or of one last look. Let him know, that gaze meant, let him see us, let him know we are with him. He is not alone in his death. Then old ladies would faint and their older and infirm husbands would be left struggling to lift them and carry them on their tears, home to a house full of loss and death. Younger boys would be restrained by their parents, to prevent them from venting their rage then and there and dying in a hail of fire, alongside their older brothers. Wives would turn away and trudge home, knowing the child in their womb had no father. Sometimes a bullet-riddled body would be dumped at the door of his home with a militia guard so the relatives could not approach for hours, could only stand at the door or the window.

Stand watch.

This was the real Florence, the Florence of sobbing and wailing and tearing of hair, not the painted and decorated Florence put on show by the authorities to distract the populace, like the dance of a painted harlot before an audience of terminally ill patients in a madhouse. The communists suffered the most. They were the largest and most experienced group of fighters and bore the greatest numbers of captures and deaths. But the members of the Action Party were every bit as engaged in the fight. They were fewer, younger, lacked the experience and the ideological drive of the communists, but they did not lack the courage or commitment or determination to drive the *Nazifascisti* from their city and their country and their lives. They were young. They were tired of being children where childhood was only a fable.

When Annabelle was very small, for a short while her life seemed endless, in a leisurely, pleasurable way – a whole week of Sundays. In later years, every day was Sunday – life more like a stagnant pond blighted by the reflection of heavy clouds on its surface. She felt like the prisoner of Zenda. There was no freedom in the city or the country. Mussolini's secret police force, OVRA, was omnipresent, with its spies and the reintroduced death penalty. It did not help that the death penalty was hardly ever invoked; its very reinstatement cast a dull pall across their lives. There was no freedom in the house. Every word was considered, measured out in doses that would not poison the air. The children were put to bed early so the adults could listen to Radio London each night. The first notes of Beethoven's 5th Symphony opened the transmission, followed by the clipped, BBC tones of Colonel Harold Stevens, known as *Colonnello Buonasera*. The greeting, 'London speaking, *Parla Londra*', was a low murmur behind the closed doors of the study. The telephones had been tapped for years. Her parents barely spoke to each other. Except for the social courtesies, which was something, she supposed, in retrospect. And that was not the result of the war outside the walls. Her mother who, like most women, had never known freedom and did not bewail its lack, smiled at everyone as a reflex, almost a nervous tic, but she never laughed. Laughing, giggling, silliness, lightness – Annabelle had only ever known these with Enrico.

She used to have terrifying dreams. Monsters with glinting steel talons, eyes ablaze, roamed the landscape of her nights and lurked beneath her bed. Gargoyles, trolls, minotaurs, Cerberus, Cyclops. Creatures whose breath could singe your hair lay in wait in dark corners of the room where the rivulets of moonlight could not flow. She would not ask for a night light. Shadows flitted across the face of the moon outside her window and hordes of raptorial wretches with misshapen heads surrounded her bed and gabbled in divers tongues. Divers tongues. She had no idea what that meant, but it made her shiver and examine her own pink tongue in the mirror, for signs of divers. Too much reading, her mother said. Too many books. She often awoke sobbing, but she curled into a tighter ball under the bedclothes and never got out of bed. She never wet her bed.

Enrico did both. He had the same dreams but was not afraid to draw his sword to do battle with the shadows. Or with anyone who crossed him. He was *mancino*, left-handed, and that was not allowed. The only thing worse in those superstitious times would be to have red hair! Not that superstition was tolerated in their household. Oh no! Enrico set his jaw against being forced to learn to write with his right hand, his tantrums command performances reverberating throughout the house. In the end, his parents called a truce. What would become of him they did not know, they said in resignation, and retreated.

'Highly strung' was the term used in the family for the cousins. Of course Enrico would have gone into the mountains. Of course they would both have joined the Resistance. Of course she would have learned rebellion from Enrico. They had no ideology like the communist groups, the *GAPisti*. They wanted a future of freedom, though they had no experience of freedom. Even just the freedom to fight and die was better than nothing, better than the shackled life before. They were exhilarated by 'the dizziness of freedom'. That was Kierkegaard, Enrico told her. Enrico loved Kierkegaard. When he first encountered the philosopher's remark: 'Once you label me, you negate me', he decided to love Kierkegaard. Annabelle could not argue Kierkegaard with him, but, she wondered, wasn't he religious? Oh that doesn't matter. With an airy wave of the hand, Enrico conveniently chose what suited him and let the rest go. And not just with

Kierkegaard. You take everything too literally, he told her.

While Enrico wielded his sword with Justice and Liberty against the monsters in the mountains, Annabelle hefted hers with the members of the Action Party in the city. In her case, it was more pen than sword, the work of getting *La Libertà* printed and distributed a constant preoccupation. Supplies of ink and paper were dire. They were 'The Resistance' – they were communists, Action Party, liberals, anarchists, democrats, rebels and Jews. They waged civil war or revolution or resistance, according to their politics or personal beliefs, and often their lack of understanding of either. In the dark and the cold and the fear they engaged in sabotage, kept the radio running, printed newspapers, stole weapons, and set up committees to help escaped prisoners of war and Jews and deserting soldiers. Many, like Enrico before them, attacked fascist offices, fomented strikes, bombed bars and places where German soldiers gathered. Some were not as measured as others; some were rabid dogs, plainly dangerous. Many would have been delinquents, with or without a cause. When a fascist colonel was shot, five hostages were summarily executed. In the twenty-second year of the Fascist Calendar, no-one was playing games anymore. Civil War. What a stupid expression, thought Annabelle.

'*Ciao Bella.*'

Annabelle tried not to show her disappointment at the greeting and the woolly bear-hug from Giacomo. Enrico was not there.

'He's on a mission, pet,' said the bulky old fighter before she could ask.

She brought information, copies of *La Nazione*, maps of troop movements, medicines: aspirin powders, castor oil for constipation and magnesium for diarrhoea. She brought matches, tobacco, a razor, another pair of glasses for Enrico. She gave Giacomo the news of Pietro, wounded a week ago and recovering well. She passed on what she knew about the bombing the week before, of the monastery at Monte Cassino on the Gustav Line. Lines on a map could kill you. The Allies had been bogged down there for too long and the Americans decided to raze it to destroy the Germans' defensive position. Annabelle knew nothing of the abbey before the bombing – there were abbeys on every hilltop. Since then she had heard little else. Nearly three hundred dead and irreplaceable art treasures destroyed. The papers and the airwaves were full of it. The barbarians at the gate, ranted *La Nazione*.

Giacomo already knew the story. 'Word is, they were not even in the monastery, the Germans. It was all for nothing.' Relations between the partisans and the Allies were not the most cordial. The Allies made a grave error, Giacomo warned, and they would pay dearly for it now. 'They killed every living thing around it and the Germans will dig in now and use it as a fortress.' He lit his pipe with the new tobacco.

What of the priceless art, thought Annabelle, but it troubled her that she thought of art when so many lives were lost.

'But,' Giacomo continued, 'are art and history more important than lives?'

The debate was as acrid as the air above the ruins. There was a time when Annabelle took for granted the centuries of art treasures she'd grown up with. The Greek and Roman statuary, the exquisitely fine gold work of bejewelled chalices and crowns and vestments. The ugly Renaissance babies – could Jesus really have looked like that? The beatific Madonnas, the bleeding and tortured saints, the acres of gold leaf in haloes and sunbeams. The chubby Venuses and the improbably conical breasts of Michelangelo's women. But since she began work as a *staffetta* she had begun to see it differently. What are we without art? What links us to our past? Surely, artists and their works are our highest expression of civilisation. Yet, the same person who produced some of their most precious art, Leonardo da Vinci, also designed the cannons and the bridges that enabled it to be destroyed. Was art worth a human life? Well, she supposed it depended on whose life. But if there was nothing left afterwards, what were they all fighting for?

'What I think, pet,' Giacomo concluded, 'is that between death and talking about death, there is a huge chasm, and it is always easier to talk about the death of others.'

He re-lit his pipe and chomped hard on the stem. His front teeth were chipped and cracked from the constant chomping, his fingers tobacco-yellow. 'Art,' he went on. 'What would I know about *Art*?' He capitalised it. 'These questions are all for later. If there is a later.

156

All I know is, they made a bad tactical mistake. They killed a lot of people for nothing and handed the Germans a fortress for free. It will be a long time before we get rid of them from there.'

He gave Annabelle another hug and plodded off into the icy rain, leaving only a rich waft of tobacco. She turned and headed off in the other direction, in the same rain and the same cold and the same confusion.

CHAPTER 12

March 15

Ettore disappeared three days ago. Dear Ettore. Alone in the snow of the Passo del Forno. He would have wanted it that way. It is where his life was lived. They have not found his body. When the snows melt he will be found. They found a body in the valley near Monte Morello last week, a boy, and we got our hopes up, but it was not Lorenzo.

It was still cold for March but the mimosa was flowering in a tumble of golden blossom. It was three months since the Allies had landed in Anzio and a month since the bombing of Monte Cassino. After the bombing of the monastery, the Germans went on the attack by radio, accusing the Allies of wanton destruction of Italy's art treasures. Suddenly everyone had an opinion. President Roosevelt and Churchill found themselves in need of a convincing stance. Even the Archbishop of Canterbury joined the argument, on the side of the preservation of art. Letters to the newspapers stridently declared sides. Allied lives or monuments? The Americans announced the formation of a special group of officers sent to protect the monuments and art treasures of Europe. The protection of historical sites and art became a matter of utmost importance and was to be governed by strict rules. Rules of War.

Annabelle was scathing. Like a board game! A childish idea, thought up by men, always men, who think war is a game. Detailed aerial 'Shinnie maps' showed bombers where they could and could not drop loads, with Florence and Rome high on the list. The marshalling yards of SM Novella railway station, however, were too important to leave intact. At the beginning of the month, when the planes came over, they made no mistakes. More than seventy B-26 bombers destroyed everything within the target area, leaving the priceless treasure of Santa Maria Novella church untouched. See, people said, they can do it. They did it again a week later. Treasures survived. Human bodies were less durable.

It made Florentines feel, however, that rescue was near. It emboldened more and more citizens to fight back. News that their most famous mountaineer, the patrician Ettore Castiglioni, had disappeared into the void, crossing back over the Alps after escorting escaped prisoners into Switzerland, strengthened the resolve of many to join the fight. Ettore had written that he was 'shattered by the shame of being Italian, by the shame of my own powerlessness to rebel and redeem'. Captured on the Swiss border, Ettore escaped and made a run for the mountain pass in the midst of a furious blizzard. He had no warm clothes and no boots and no hope and he knew only death awaited him. The old stone in Annabelle's throat rose up hard and hot. Tall, beautiful, brave Ettore. Somewhere beneath the snow, his slender hands would be clasped in repose. He would not have been afraid.

Via Rasella, Rome, 1944

Finally, a spring day in Rome. It was not hot yet, but the claws of winter had relinquished their grip. The sun was out, the sky was cerulean, the air was crisp and starlings wheeled above the rooftops. Carla Capponi stepped lightly, despite the weight of the pistol in her pocket and a certain cautious dread. She was hot and sweating with the big raincoat over her arm, but that owed more to tension than to the soft sunshine. She worried the raincoat looked suspicious. Carla too knew about Ettore Castiglioni. Everyone did. He was not a communist, but every day the numbers grew of people who were no longer prepared to bend beneath the yoke of the *Nazifascisti*. They were, after all, on the same side and she admired courage.

Today was to be their most important attack yet. She steadied her breathing with difficulty. Living on the move with the men in hiding, sleeping where they could and finding food when they could, with not enough clothes to keep them warm, had exacted a heavy toll, particularly on the women who had to battle menstrual problems and indignity on top of all the other hardships. Carla was thin, ill, tired, and her cough worsened each day. Her chest pain was agonising and she found it difficult to take deep breaths. Not good for running.

Loitering. Window shopping. Dallying. She could see Paolo waiting further down the hill. How much longer, she wondered, could she do this? Where were the Germans? She wandered idly past the offices of *Il Messaggero* in via Nazionale and dawdled up the hill into Piazza Barberini. The raincoat over her arm was looking more and more suspicious as the sun glared warmer and warmer. Down the hill, two policemen turned and began their third pass up that side of the street. Things were not going according to plan. How much longer could she hang about before the policemen decided to investigate? Her watch creaked slowly past the two, then half-past two, then three o'clock. Jesus Christ, she thought, here they come. She put her hand in her pocket again, resting lightly on the reassuring smoothness of the gun.

The policemen stopped before her. 'Are you waiting for someone, *Signorina*?' said one, the other looking around and behind her as if she might be hiding someone.

Carla was beautiful, even after the privation of the past months. She took no particular credit for it, but she knew very well that huge eyes in a heart-shaped face did no harm at all when it came to deflecting male attention from things they must not notice. It was just another weapon in her armoury.

'Yes,' she replied with a friendly smile and a helpless look, 'waiting for my boyfriend. I was bringing him his coat, but he seems to have stood me up.' Another smile: wry, rueful, but don't overdo it, she chided herself, 'and it looks as if it isn't going to rain after all.' A sigh and a glance at her watch.

Where oh where were the Germans? Her heart racketed in her chest. Beneath the raincoat, her arm was drenched with sweat. She half expected to see it dripping onto the footpath.

'He's a fool to keep you waiting.' With a jocular wave, the policemen moved off.

Still no-one came. What could have gone wrong? The plan was perfect. The organisation was smooth. So much hung on this attack. It would show the Nazis what the GAP fighters were made of. Call it off, she thought. This is wrong. Call it off now. She had almost decided when she heard the tramping of boots, hundreds of boots. The sound of a regiment on the march in those narrow, stone streets was like tanks on the move. The ground rumbled. When the marchers rounded the corner at the bottom of via Rasella she could see there must have been more than, well, she thought, doing a quick count, a hundred and fifty, at least. That was all of them then. Carla stopped sweating. Her calf stopped twitching. She turned in a slow arc, checking everyone was in place.

Then, out of nowhere, as the column approached Paolo at the bottom of via Rasella, a group of young children ran towards her, shouting, laughing and kicking a ball, which flew into the garden of Palazzo Barberini. Jesus Christ, she thought, they will be right in the middle of the battle. They could not have been more than eight and nine years old. Carla almost vomited. No time now. She turned, her arms waving, her face contorted, and roared, 'How dare you play ball in that garden. Balls are forbidden. Piss off! Get out of here at once! At once! At once! Fuck off!'

One look at the face of the mad woman was enough to convince them. As they scampered off up via Quattro Fontane, she whirled to see Paolo engulfed by the tide of marching policemen.

When the bomb went off Carla thought her eardrums had exploded. How could anything be that loud? It was by far the biggest explosive device they had made. The footpath buckled and rocked beneath her. Buildings swayed and bowed. The shock waves knocked her to the ground and a bus was blown almost on top of her. Then Paolo was there beside her. The boom, boom, boom of the mortars sounded like a medieval battlefield and Carla fired her gun over and over, but blindly – impossible to see in the dust and stone chips and falling tiles that filled the narrow street. Bullets came from every direction, ricocheting off the walls. Down the slope, via

Rasella was a frenzy of running, yelling soldiers, dazed residents at high windows and police firing weapons and shouting orders. Bodies lay strewn amongst the wreckage of paving stones, window-frames, doorjambs. Limbs seemed to be everywhere. So many limbs. Dust swirled like winter fog. Was that the wheel of the rubbish cart hanging from a lamp-post? Carla saw it all, as if a reel of film had jammed for an instant. Paolo juggled his gun in one hand, shrugging into the raincoat over the top of his sweeper's uniform. He grabbed her hand and they ran and ran and ran. In the distance, the sounds of sirens and bells and screeching wheels fanned the excitement. They were jubilant.

Carla was twenty-five and she was in love with Paolo. Paolo was not his real name. His real name was Rosario. Paolo was his battle-name and hers was Elena. Carla was in love with Rosario Bentivegna and they were alive. They had never, ever, been more alive. They ran and they hugged and they exalted and life coursed through them. Finally they were making a real difference. 'We did it!' they shouted. 'We must have killed dozens of them. Now they will know we mean it! We showed the bastards!'

Far from via Rasella, as the light faded in their cellar, Carla and Rosario and the others awaited news of the response to their daring escapade. They had all escaped. Information filtered through in excruciatingly slow dribbles. At first, they were delighted to hear that twenty-eight German policemen had died, then chastened to learn that a man and a young boy had also died. Thank God she had scared those children off in time. All the news came from their own sources. They were puzzled by the official silence, and wary. On the evening news broadcast, there was nothing. No-one slept that night. *Il Messaggero* of the next morning carried nothing. No radio reports, no announcements. Had they been betrayed, was it a trap? Should they move from the cellar? Their elation congealed as their anxiety grew. They began to worry in earnest. Soon there were reports of prisoners being rounded up, hands above their heads, before the gilded gates of Palazzo Barberini. Then, at midday, they listened in sickened disbelief to the radio announcement by the German command under SS *Obersturmbannfuhrer* Kappler.

In reprisal for the unprovoked terrorist attack yesterday, March twenty-third, in via Rasella, by elements of Badoglio-Communists, which left thirty German policemen dead, the Führer himself has decreed that for every death, ten Italians would be executed.

Three hundred Italians. The announcement ended with the stony words:

The order has already been carried out.

In Florence, Annabelle sat before the wireless, a gargoyle, her mouth a rictus of shock. The door opened slowly and Elsa entered. She had no need to ask if Annabelle had heard it.

'No-one knows yet who they are. Were. Or where they were killed.' Elsa put a hand on Annabelle's shoulder, patting absently. With the other hand, she jiggled the ornate comb holding her hair until it gave way and her hair tumbled about her eyes. 'This changes things.'

'Yes,' said Annabelle. 'This changes things.'

PART THREE

CHAPTER 13

The Apennines 1944

The men were not happy. Enrico knew that, but *cazzo*! What was he supposed to do? It was not as if he planned it that way, was it? He did not mean Annabelle to join them. He did not mean her to pick up the rifle and shoot that fascist bastard either, did he? He did not mean to make love to her, but there it is and now they had a woman in their group. And they all had to admit that she fights as hard as they do and shoots as well and complains less.

They'd had to go down into the city that night. It was the only way they could get hold of the new guns they had been promised. Him, and Pietro and Maurizio. Annabelle was to meet them with the directions and the code. The usual place. The Lungarno was tranquil, the sky clear. The moon was high and round and the stars were out: not ideal. But they were careful and stealthy and slipped down from Piazzale Michelangelo beside Siviero's house without seeing a soul. Then suddenly, as they began to cross to the bridge, there were *fascisti* everywhere, bullets flying like confetti, and they were running and the side of Pietro's head was missing and the icy steel of his rifle skittering across the stones was like fingernails on a blackboard. Then Annabelle was there.

In the noise and chaos, Enrico had no time to think of Annabelle until the rifle was in her hands and the fascist turned away to fire again. She seemed so calm, as if she could not hear the shots and the shouting or smell the cordite or the fear. She raised the rifle, sighted carefully, and shot him in the back. He fell forward, his forehead bouncing off the edge of the pavement. He looked dead. Enrico slipped and as he tried to recover his balance, the fascist had propped up on an elbow with the rifle pointed directly at him. He did not see Annabelle. She was metres from where he lay on the footpath. She did not run. She took several steps very coolly to where he lay, placed her foot in the middle of his back, carefully put the barrel of the rifle to his temple and pulled the trigger. It seemed to take forever but it was over in a matter of seconds. Then she ran.

They all did. Enrico and Annabelle and Maurizio. Maurizio had been shot in the leg and he couldn't keep up. Go! Go! Go! He shouted. Get me out later. And they ran, and ran and ran, slipping and sliding on the icy stones, and they did not stop until they reached the thick *uliveto* behind the Belvedere where the moonlight barely penetrated. There was no sound of pursuit. Crazily, they wanted to laugh. Their breathing was raucous and then Annabelle was sobbing. The tremor of her arms made the rifle dangerous. Enrico took it from her, put the safety catch on and lay it carefully under an olive tree. He drew his arms around her and held her close until the convulsions ceased. Then he held her, still, and then they were on the grass and their breathing was more raucous than ever and there was no way back. It was always going to be this way. He had always known it.

Annabelle knew it too. When she picked up the gun she had never felt calmer, more certain, in her life. She was not even conscious of feeling fear. Time stopped and so did sound. She shot the fascist officer as he turned away. He fell forward then she fired two more shots at the others. It was hard to tell how many there were. It was an old militia rifle so she had no difficulties at all. She could not see Maurizio, but Enrico slipped, and as he struggled to his feet the fascist, who was not dead, dragged himself upright with his rifle pointing right at Enrico's face. It was only a few steps but if she missed from there it would be too late. She took the few steps and felt the recoil as the barrel of the rifle struck the back of his head and it exploded. She could hear only her own breathing.

She had always been good with guns and would soon learn to use a Bren with deadly accuracy. Hunting amongst her people was as popular as it was in England. The private walls of many *palazzi*, such as theirs, were hung with hunting scenes by owners who rode to hounds. Annabelle had never participated in a hunt to hounds. Her father did not approve. 'The unspeakable in full pursuit of the uneatable,' he said, paraphrasing someone. She had learned to hunt wild boar or *cinghiale*, from as soon as she could hold a gun. Once she picked up the rifle as it skittered across the cobbles, the thing was done.

Later, sinking to the damp floor of the olive grove in the freezing velvet dark, she knew there was no way back from that either, and she knew she had been waiting all her life. The understory of the olive grove was fragrant and welcoming. She did not feel the twigs and branches scoring her knees. She felt the branding of the pattern of moonlight through the olive branches on her bare breasts; were they too small? He did not think so. Above her the stars were icicles, and on her throat Enrico's breath was warm. He kissed her eyelids. She was already wet to her knees. There was no blood, no pain. Wasn't there supposed to be blood? There was enough blood being spilled in the world around them, perhaps her pointless virginity was the way to expiate it. In the night sounds of the forest, she had a glimmering of what love might really be. She had thought she was already in love, but *this* was love. Real love. An ocean of rightness. Homecoming.

They made it back to the camp as the sun returned from the other side of the world. The sentries along the way whistled them through and Roberto was waiting at the edge of the clearing where the tentacles of day had not yet unfurled.

'We thought you had been taken.' His gaze flicked from Enrico to Annabelle and between them to the rear, though he already knew it was only the two of them. 'Tell me everything once you have had something hot to drink.'

He held a rough blanket, which he wrapped about Annabelle and led the way back through the *bosco*.

'Pietro is dead, Maurizio is wounded.' Enrico pushed Annabelle gently ahead, all three in single file. 'He was captured. We will know soon enough where they have taken him.' They all knew he would not have been killed there and then. In these times, that was often the better fate. Now the dappled light was soft on the track and on their faces, and Annabelle's shivering had ceased when they reached the hut where the others were waiting.

'Boss. *Ben tornato*. Welcome back.' This from Falco. At the sight of Annabelle, his heavy eyebrows met across the bridge of his nose in a simian frown. The others came forward one by one, greeting Enrico quietly with a word or a touch. They nodded at Annabelle but no-one spoke to her. She felt the scorch of the glances and the raised eyebrows and the silent interrogation. They all knew who she was and had all, at one time or another, carried a message from her or to her, but was their whispered question, 'What the fuck is she doing here now?'

Roberto pressed a cup of the chicory essence coffee into their hands and they sat on logs ranged about the entrance to the hut. The sun was higher now and the chestnut leaves dripped diamonds as the night's frost melted.

'You were betrayed,' said Roberto. It was a statement, not a question. They knew they had walked into a trap and the next task would be to discover who had betrayed them.

Enrico nodded. He sipped the bitter, scalding liquid and a wave of exhaustion almost drowned him. He turned to Annabelle, realising that she must be much worse. Her eyes were dull with fatigue and shock and she had not drunk her coffee. Her skirt was torn and caked with mud and the blood and brains of the fascist; her hair hung in loose tangles. Thank Christ she was wearing sturdy lace-up shoes because they did not have a pair of boots to fit her. Later he would find her a pair of trousers. The shirt and knitted cardigan, beneath a canvas jacket would all do well enough up here. He tucked her hair behind her ears and said, 'Go to sleep now. We will talk later.'

He nodded at Falco who took her by the elbow, not ungently, and she allowed herself to be led without resistance into the hut. Annabelle sank to her scratched knees and was asleep on a pile of sacks almost before her head touched the rough jute.

'She can't go back.' Enrico said to Roberto and Falco. 'She killed that bastard, Fabbri. She executed him. She will have to stay with us. They all saw her. The door is closed to her past now, as it is to ours.'

March 1944

I am not sure of the date today. It is still very cold. This is the first time I have been able to write since that night.

Should it have been harder to kill a man? I felt nothing. Then we walked all night. We made love. We made love. I want to write that over and over again.

Two days ago, Francesco was killed and they have given me his boots. My shoes were already split at the seams. I had only what I was wearing that night. Thank God I don't need glasses. Or medicine, like Primo, who is not going to last long up here without his Anginine. This is no place for someone with a weak heart, but then we are all strong in our hearts in a certain way and so is he and life is really only for the day you have it now.

The men do not want me here and many of the peasants hate us. I understand but we cannot change anything. For the men I am a weak link. They worry I will not be able to keep up and they are angry that Enrico and I are lovers while their wives and lovers are far away where they cannot protect them. They worry I will be a distraction. For the contadini, we are the very Devil himself. We need to take food from them that they can barely spare and though we try to pay them, we have little with which to barter. As well, they know we bring danger: if they are caught helping us they will be shot, and every time we attack the Germans or the fascisti they suffer reparations. There are also many brigands, or bandits, as the Germans call us. There are bands of malcontents who call themselves partisans but are nothing but criminals, and treat the contadini badly and give us all a bad name. But we must go on fighting and I can no more go back now than the men can. We heard last week that the fascists and a German commandant raided our home and took Zio and Papà to the Questura. Not to the Villa Triste, thank God. They let them go after two nights and they were unharmed, but it will happen again.

Yet I am happy. How strange life is. We all know that we could die at any moment and I want to live. But not at any price. For the first time, we feel we have some control over our own lives. We have never had that. We have

grown up without knowing how that might feel and we
like it. We will not be turning back. I am always afraid
and always tired, always hungry, always exhilarated. I
would change nothing. Now I have paper and pencils,
so precious and so hard to find, I feel I have my voice
back too. Not being able to write for these weeks has been
hard. I should call Enrico by his battle name, Corvo, but
I keep forgetting. We all have a new name: Mine is Silena
because I arrived by the light of the moon. This is supposed
to help conceal our identity but if we are captured and I
am tortured I doubt they would not know at once my real
name. I worry about it constantly because we all know
that we should die rather than be taken and betray each
other, but what if there is not time or what if my nerve
fails me for a moment or what if I do not have my gun?

Lake Garda 1944
The prisoner of the lake

> *He takes my hand and supports me. We look at each other,*
> *trembling violently.*

Clara sat back, her head resting on the back of the sofa, the diary
open on her lap. It was nearly six months since she wrote those words
after their first meeting on the lake. Ben was distant and exhausted
then and he was worse now. 'My soul', he called her, but their future,
he said, depended on the war. Which war? She wondered. The war
against the Anglo-Americans or the war within the country? The war
was everywhere.

I am nothing but a prisoner on this accursed lake, Ben complained
constantly, but, thought Clara, looking about her at the bizarre collection of artefacts and oppressive furnishings of *Il Vittoriale*, I am a
prisoner too, alone in a museum. The house – you could not call it a
home, and really, the word house did it no justice either – was a living
monument to its dead creator, Gabriele D'Annunzio. It gave her the

creeps. There was a guard on the door but it did not help. At night, it reminded her of when her father had once taken her as a small child to see the Vatican museums after everyone else had left. Clara felt she was wandering through a stage set as an actor in … a comedy or a drama? She was beginning to think it was more a tragedy. She was still jumpy and anxious after the terrible scene with that peasant, Rachele, yesterday. Dreadful woman! The shouting and the screaming! Clara was not above a good scene herself but really, that woman was too much. The whole situation was most unsatisfactory. She riffled the pages of her diary, admiring the careful tiny script, but the pages were not reassuring.

On their second meeting, before the family moved in, Ben had sent the car to bring her to Villa Feltrinelli and they spent a whole night together. It was a true reunion. She thumbed back through her diary to the day after that visit.

> *We enter the room in silence. I feel I am fainting. He is bitter, grief-stricken, nauseated. The torment of seeing twenty years of work destroyed. We get cold and we go to bed and talk the whole night through. He tells me that he has thought about me every minute, that I am the last and the true love of his life.*

The poor darling. It was not his fault it had taken so long to get her and her family out of prison and up here with him. Clara thought things would be better from then on, but really, nothing had improved. When a journalist wanted to interview him, he said, 'Why? Seven years ago I was an interesting person. Now I am a corpse.' It frightened her to hear him talk like that.

Once the whole family arrived and was living with Ben in Villa Feltrinelli, his life became insupportable. He could not avoid them. How could there be so many Mussolinis? Hundreds of them. Vittorio and his family were living at Maderno and there were relatives everywhere, imported weeds planted in every village. It was like the colonies Ben always dreamed of but it was a nightmare. He complained that Rachele was making his life hell and he could not get away from her. Chaos, it is, he thundered. Chaos, I say! It was not that he did not love his children, but they pestered him day and night and the grandchildren had the run of the house. Rachele whined endlessly about expenses and the running of the household, spied on his every move and either fussed over him like an invalid or refused to speak to him. She insisted on doing her own ironing, if you please, as if they were on the breadline!

There *was* the problem of money. Ben had never been interested in money but now, with these hordes to support, it was becoming a real problem. He earned a little from his books and articles but it was not enough. The only ones who were any use to him were Elena and Vittorio. Not that Vittorio was much use. Things had improved slightly since Ben shifted his office into the village, in the Villa Orsoline, but it was still necessary for him to meet Clara at *Il Vittoriale*, for them to have any real private time together. He could hardly come often to her at Villa Fiordaliso. He was always busy and always distracted. Their daily letters were their lifeline; he was more loving in his letters than when they were together.

Outside, the air was soft but it was still cold. Clara drew her cashmere cardigan closer about her shoulders. The globular pearls of the buttons were exactly the shade of the wool and one was loose, she noted, hanging by a thread. She must be careful of it. She tried to ignore her toothache. What if the tooth had to come out? Oh God! Only old people lost their teeth. The evening shadows were closing in. April was not her favourite month. Spring was here and in the parkland and gardens of *Il Vittoriale*, crocuses poked their heads up tentatively to see if it was safe to come out yet, but most of the plants and animals were as hesitant about this spring as the humans were.

Indoors the atmosphere was still wintry. Clara picked some fluff from her navy woollen slacks, thinking, I should have worn the navy cardigan, this cream is too pale with these slacks. And then, regretfully, I won't be changing into linen for some time yet. She rang for some tea, then changed her mind – why not have some hot milk instead? Ben had given up milk on the orders of the German doctor Hitler had put in charge of him. It did seem to be helping and Dr Zachariae was very kind. Ben had put on a little weight. But Ben was not here, and she *did* like milk every now and then.

She hated having to meet in the house of that revolting man, D'Annunzio. He had been dead for more than five years now, but

Clara attributed much of Ben's misfortunes to him. He had always been horribly jealous of Ben. Why Ben was so bewitched by him, she never could understand. She could not see all the fuss about his books and poetry either – he was some kind of war hero from the Great War, but that was so long ago. Ben had been very brave in that war too. Everyone said so. She had only known D'Annunzio slightly but she found him repulsive – how he could have thought himself a great lover, she could not imagine. He was incredibly old, his teeth were rotten and he had bad breath. Yet women flocked to him, even then. He was so tiny he looked like a mummified child. Having sex with him would be like being raped by a praying mantis. He made her flesh crawl.

From a heavily embossed silver frame on a side table, Eleanora Duse smiled out at her. *La Duse.* One of the most famous actresses of her time. She died years before Clara was born but her aura lived on in Italy and in this house. Why would she have bothered with that repugnant man? He could not hold a candle to Ben. Claretta was in no doubt it was his drug-crazed lifestyle, the flagrant abuse of cocaine and every other drug he could get his hands on that influenced Ben's dependence on all the pills and potions and medicines and injections. What with years of the ridiculous diets and all the drugs the Italian doctors prescribed – which she was convinced had made his illnesses worse, not better – it was no wonder he was unable to run the government properly. Dr Zachariae's injections of hormones and vitamins definitely seemed an improvement.

She shifted around on the sofa, regarding the floor-to-ceiling bookshelves lining every wall, the marble busts and gilt picture frames. Every flat surface was draped in heavy, scarlet brocade cloths with gold tassels. Embossed cigarette cases, lighters, silver cigar-cutters, paperweights of glass and silver, silver and more silver, an ornate hand mirror also of silver. You could barely move in this room, or for that matter, any other room in the house. *Victoriana*, Ben said. Though what the dead English queen had to do with it, Clara could not see. Clutter, is what it was, clutter. The candelabra was from Murano, its light was soft and golden, but the atmosphere in the room was too close to breathe properly. Still, she thought, at least it is all authentic and, as her mother had remarked, in good taste, unlike the ghastly

fake antiques surrounding Ben and his family in the vast and pre-
tentious spaces of the Villa Feltrinelli. Rachele thought that was all
marvellous. She would!

'Get out of my way! I want to see that whore.'

Clara paused with her vicuna coat over her arm, ready to go to
the car as Rachele stormed into the library, followed lamely by the
sentry whose hopeless expression said he had no chance of imped-
ing her progress. Rachele was taller, broader, much more torrid and
florid than Clara. She ground to a halt, like a locomotive applying the
brakes just in time, with the steam still hissing.

'So, you are going out, are you? Out to fuck my husband, no
doubt. Well, my girl, I have had enough of you.' She knocked the
coat from Clara's arm. 'Nice clothes. Paid for by my husband, no
doubt. I see you do not stint yourself.'

Clara had still not spoken. She rearranged her expression, refused
to take a step backward, stood as tall as possible. Thank God her
mother was out. She could feel the heat of Rachele's breath on her
forehead. Finally, she turned away and sat calmly, a pulse ticking in
her throat. It was important to maintain one's dignity.

'How dare you break into this house.' Her tone was frosty. 'I could
call the police, I hope you are aware.' And tell them you tried to have
me murdered, too, she thought, but did not say aloud.

'Go on, you bitch,' screamed Rachele. 'Go on then, call them.
And I will tell all of them what a lying whore you are, you and your
whole family.' She rushed on before Clara could utter a word. 'You
with your nose in the air. Your brother – a doctor! What sort of doctor? A spy and embezzler. To think it was your own mother who first
took you to my husband, to fuck him. Your mother, with her ladylike
pretensions, pimping her daughter.'

Now it was Clara's turn to lose her composure. On the floors
above were the German and Japanese diplomats, who would be hearing all of this. Heat burned across her chest and up her neck. Her
breathing was ragged.

'How dare you mention my mother or my family! You! Of all
people to talk about family.'

Her voice had that screechy edge she hated but it could not be helped. She rushed at Rachele, hands raised, and would have hit her with anything that came to hand, but finally the sentry, who had been paralysed by the entrancing scene unfolding before him, stepped between the two women. Clara burst into tears and collapsed onto the sofa. Rachele deflated as if he had punctured her though he had not touched her, and she too began to sob. The sentry put an arm about her shoulder and led her, wailing plaintively, from the room. His hands were shaking.

Clara rang her bell and unsteadily called for tea. Ben, she thought, I must warn Ben. She rushed to the telephone, bouncing up and down on her toes as she waited for the operator to put her through. Please, please, she thought, do not let the lines be down today. The German listeners will love this! It was six kilometres from *Il Vittoriale* to Villa Feltrinelli. She had time. After an age, Ben's voice at the other end was dull and listless.

Although Clara was feeling perfectly calm again by then, she thought it just as well to make him understand what she had been through, so she sobbed just a little. It would do no harm. It certainly brought Ben to his senses. Right, my love, he said, brisk now. I tried to talk her out of it. I thought I had. Right, I will go to the office immediately and I will sleep there overnight. That *troia*, he said. She has gone too far. He rang off. He was fed up with Rachele and her tantrums and, thought Clara, he does not want to be beaten by his wife with a rolling pin, again. She opened her purse and took out her enamelled compact, reassured by her reflection. Some women could look lovely when they cried but Clara was not one of them. Her eyes were a little red but not too swollen. Her tea arrived and she sat back to drink it, thinking, well really, that could have been much worse.

The heat from the green majolica stove was insufferable. To everyone, that is, except Ben. Clara unbuttoned her jacket and opened a window. No, close it, close it, said Ben, who was cold no matter what the temperature. He complained that his SS sentries would not let him go swimming in the lake, but the water was freezing and she knew he would not go into it for anything.

Ben sat at the side of the desk, stirring his tea – round and round, the spoon tingling, ringling, as if he had forgotten he hardly ever took sugar. He had developed a habit of stirring his tea and staring into space, even when she was talking to him. Clara glanced about at the shabby room. The sitting room of the Villa Orsoline was as awful as the study. The whole house was shabby and run down. Ben slept there last week after the scene with Rachele, who rushed home and drank bleach to kill herself. It was not the first time she had done that and not the first time he'd slept there. He quite enjoyed being alone, with a worn sofa and a table and his books and the wireless. It suited him perfectly, he said. Although he dressed every day in his full militia uniform with its red epaulets, Rachele no longer kept it pressed and laundered and Ben did not even care that it was too big for him now. At the gaping sleeve of his jacket, Clara could see the scar from where he cut his wrists when he was a prisoner on the Gran Sasso. He had the barber come once in a while, but did not care if he was unshaven either. Thank goodness he still had his nails manicured every fortnight, at least that was something, and he no longer slept half the morning away.

Ben worked in the study and received his guests in this room. Nowadays though, he seemed so happy to have visitors he no longer kept them standing but invited everyone to be seated on the scruffy old leather sofa that sagged in the middle, while he talked to them about the situation in France, or his study of Nietzsche, or his opinion of Kant or Schopenhauer. Or Aristophanes. Clara knew all about Nietzsche because he never ceased to tell her, but really, the others she had never heard of, and she had a feeling many of his visitors had not either. He did not bother to hide his spectacles any more but wore them all the time, no matter who saw him. The heads of all the government departments came here to meet with him but there seemed no order to the visits. I am no more than a provincial governor now, he said.

The government was strewn haphazardly across the whole region, with various departments in different towns and villages, with often not even enough fuel for travel between them. Ben's office was in Gargnano. Everyone called his Regime the Republic of Salò but there was nothing at Salò except the Department of Foreign Affairs and the

Ministry of Popular Culture from where the propaganda broadcasts issued. So people said, Salò says this and Salò says that, but Ben was not at Salò. It was all very confusing and uncertain, typical of the unreality of the whole thing. It was enough to give her a headache.

'Why,' she asked him, 'does your government not operate properly from your own office?'

'My government!' he shouted. He rushed to the window, flinging it wide with a theatrical flourish. 'It is not my government. Even the Pope has more power than me. Look outside. What do you see? You see Germans. Every tree has a German behind it. I have SS guards, my telephones are monitored by the Nazis, my driver is German. My doctor is German. My life is run by the Germans and my country is run by the Germans.'

He was puce in the face, the only time he had been anything but deathly pale for weeks. 'Fascism is dead. The Italian Socialist Republic we are now. Fascism no longer mentioned. A failed experiment. We run this little toy government from a corner in the playpen. Not from Rome, not from Milan. But from a village on some godforsaken lake in a gloomy and ramshackle Villa like a *capanna*.'

Clara never knew what would set him off. At times like this she thought he might have a stroke and he seemed to be in danger of losing control, more and more often. Then the air went out of him. The Allies will take Rome within weeks anyway, he told her, his tone querulous, as if she should know that. Clara closed her eyes, tried to think calming thoughts. They had so little time together, she must be careful not to spoil it. She shivered. She was living on her nerves. Perhaps she should take another pill.

'*Amore,*' she said, 'I thought we were going to go for a drive?' She slumped in her chair and picked at a thread on her skirt.

He looked at her over the top of his spectacles, and sighed. 'Can't you see how much correspondence I have to attend to? It will not be possible to go for a drive today and what is more, we have not received our allocation of fuel so my car cannot be used.'

'But it would do you good. You need to get out.'

'Don't be a wife. I already have one of those.'

So they were not going anywhere today. On the desk to his right was the tiny revolver he kept there out of habit, though no-one was likely to attack him here, and if they did, that odd little gun would not do much. To his left was a basket full of letters, but really, none of them was important. Only people wanting things and Ben did not have much to give them any more, as he said himself.

Before him was a letter in his daughter's handwriting. Not recent, because Edda had cut off all communication with him after her husband's death. It caused Ben much pain and he often could not sleep for thinking about his son-in-law. They made him do it and he was very angry with Hitler and Pavolini and the others. Poor Ben. He could never stop going over and over the gruesome details of the botched execution. He could not get it out of his mind. He was also worried about Edda's threats to make public a great deal of her husband's information about government relations with the Germans. As if his situation were not bad enough without that.

His situation. The situation with Ben's family was dreadful, Clara agreed, but what about *her* family? They were all driving her mad too. No-one had a normal life anymore. Nowhere to go and nothing to do, nothing to fill their time. And money was short. What about my life, she sniffed. Ben filled his time writing his memoirs and articles for the paper, but even those were censored by his guards.

Marcello's schemes got wilder and wilder. Only the other day, her brother intimated to her that he was in touch with Winston Churchill. The British Prime Minister used to be a great admirer of Ben. Who knows, she thought, it could be true but she couldn't trust Marc. You never knew what was truth and what was, well, not quite truth with Marc. If only they were talking about ending the war. Then she and Ben could be free.

Then there was Elena the Paragon. At home, Ben relied on that fool of a son Vittorio and in the office, on Elena. She seemed to be a permanent part of the family now. Ben thought she was wonderful and she had become his favourite child. She had made herself indispensable to him, which was very irritating. It was bad enough when the mother, *La Cucciati*, was always on the scene. Now she had to put up with the daughter. If she really is his daughter, she thought, not for the first time. Clara was jealous, but she did not truly think Ben was sleeping with Elena or indeed anyone. He was not sleeping with *her* and he was not interested in even talking about sex. Sex seemed a distant echo from another life. Ah for the days when, after having sex with three women, one after the other without so much as removing his boots, he would come to her, a raging mountain stag. She knew how to make him roar, yes, she did. I adore you, he would say. You are my only love, he would swear. No-one else can do that, he would exult. At the moment of ejaculation he would throw back his head and roar like the king of the mountain and then fall spent upon her like a dead body. Sometimes the bites and bruises took a week to heal, her secret badge of honour. The unshakeable pact between them. These days she had no bruises of any sort – he no longer beat her either.

Ben's office was close to Villa Feltrinelli and he went in early, went home for lunch each day even though Rachele would not speak to him, came back to the office after lunch and stayed until 9 pm. But most of the time he wanted to be left alone. The Germans were all criminals and the Italians nothing but ungrateful slaves, according to Ben. It was Elena who sat with him, gazing at him adoringly, agreeing with everything he said, running his errands. Clara sighed and bit the inside of her bottom lip. Bite my tongue, more like, she thought. She would not give ground to Elena, but it was unwise to upset Ben over it. Really, she could not afford to. It was the one thing she had in common with Rachele. They both knew their fate depended upon Ben. She smiled at him and settled onto the sofa with her pen and her diary while he went back to his correspondence. She began writing her entry for yesterday.

> *We all keep diaries now. Ben says it is important for a record of these times. Ciano's diaries are hidden (only Edda knows where) and Ben writes in his every day. I know he is right, and heaven knows I record everything. Ben's ulcer is playing up. He is very angry today because Giovanni Gentile was murdered several days ago in Florence, by the communists. He is so furious he can barely speak. This shedding of blood must absolutely stop, this anarchy, he says. He is angry with the rebels, as he calls the communists. The Germans call them bandits. Ben is angry with the Germans and the fascists too because he says they provoke the so-called partisans and the whole*

thing is getting out of control. My poor country, he says. When I ask him what will become of us he gets angry with me. Surely I suffer more than Christ himself, he says. There are more important things in this world than your next fur coat! Really, sometimes I think he will have convulsions.

She put down her pen and glanced over at Ben, who had finished his tea and, with intense concentration, was minutely gathering the crumbs from his biscuit into a tiny pile on the tablecloth. She did wish he would not do that. It was becoming a nervous habit, very irritating. She made a note to call her dressmaker after lunch.

CHAPTER 14

Tuscany 1944

Primavera: 'di doman non c'è certezza'

April '44

> So we make love or have sex, whichever you call it, at
> any opportunity and in any place and sometimes it is
> wonderful and often not. At least we are alive to do it. If
> tomorrow never comes.

Spring! It felt like a hoax, a mockery. All about them was a hectic
efflorescence of blossom and bees and dragonflies and birds and
beauty – an excess of nature in an ocean of loss and desolation.
Shortages tightened belts already cinched down to their last hole.
Until the past winter, although rationing cut deeply, there had been
enough vegetables. No crops could be sown in the devastated south,
and now, as the bombing drew closer, the fields below Florence could
no longer be tilled. In the roads and byways, even close in to the city,
people foraged for whatever weeds and herbs might show their head:
wild fennel, *rucola*, dandelions, thistle. It all helped.

It put Annabelle in mind of the times of Saint Francis and the
famines when the local populace was out of its mind on hallucination-
inducing poppy seeds because they were starving, adding whatever
came to hand to their bread. Saint Francis had probably been mad
with it – much of his behaviour would indicate that. It would happen
here too. The thought reminded her of old Anna Maria kneading the
bread, in her saggy stockings and her layers of underwear. Did she ever
take it off, the underwear? Annabelle had only once seen a large pair

of flesh-coloured bloomers hanging on a line in the back courtyard. You all wash your clothes to death, Anna Maria had admonished her. A wave of longing surged through her. For what, she wondered. We are never happy, are we.

In calm, bucolic scenes between battles, the scent of nectar-filled flowers and the drone of pollinating bees commingled with the sweet decay of rotting corpses swinging in the gentle breeze and the hum of blowflies. Every encounter with the fascists or the Germans left someone dead or wounded – if the brigade was fortunate the deaths were not theirs, but they often were. After each appalling episode, Annabelle and Enrico made love. Sex was urgent in the aftermath of death. Urgent and often awkward and uncomfortable. It felt as if they had been lovers all their lives, and in a way they had. Enrico was the adept, and she the willing acolyte. They made love wherever and whenever and however they could: against the rough trunk of a chestnut tree, leaving her back raw; stretched over a sun-warm rock full of peace; in a pebbly stream-bed with water like iced champagne; behind the altar of a tiny church in pleasurable heresy; against the back of a barn with splintery timber; once, in the sweet hay smell inside a barn while the cow slept through it beside them. They did things she never dreamed of and things she could not have imagined. Things that made her think of those books high in the shadows of her father's library. She wanted to live forever so they could go on doing those things forever. To carry the caramel scent of him on her skin forever – the Prince and the Princess lived Happily Ever After.

Or if not, to die right there, with Enrico's head between her thighs, where the dark honey gold of his hair was exactly the colour of the dark honey gold of hers. Did you know, he told her, that Caesar had every hair tweezered from his entire body? Or that John Ruskin had a horror of pubic hair? Ruskin was disgusted by women's bodies. Enrico was entranced by women's bodies, adored women's bodies. He adored hers. Venerated it. Enrico's gaze made her beautiful. He recited her a poem by a man called Cummings: '*I like my body when it is with your / body. It is so quite a new thing.*' So did she.

And he made her laugh. When Roberto, who prided himself on his memory, forgot a code, Enrico said '*Cazzo*! He has a photographic memory; it has just never been developed.' In the midst of fear and blood and death and excrement, he made her laugh. Every day when they opened their eyes, they wondered, who will death come for today? The world outside war ceased to exist and they strained to glean even the smallest nugget of domestic information. They had stopped asking about Lorenzo and neither had heard news of their parents for weeks. A lot could happen in a week. Would the Allies never get to Rome?

The night was dark: dark enough, not too dark. Perfect for the drop – their first supply-drop since they got up here. Now the Allies knew they were not a communist formation, they got more of the drops. The message from Radio London had arrived in the afternoon, and at 10 pm they were tucked into the forest around the high clearing, straining for the low grumble of a Liberator.

Annabelle had a twitch at the corner of her right eye and she saw Enrico had bitten the quick of his thumbnail until it bled again. They were strung out like piano wire; only Giacomo, cold pipe between his teeth, showed no sign of tension. He never did. Every moment was crucial. The signal beacons were burning so they could not wait too long. The fires would not go unnoticed. It was only spring during the daytime and they all shivered in the chill night air, which carried an oily whiff of kerosene. Annabelle's stomach contracted as she heard the growing rumble of the plane – please do not let too much of the stuff miss the target. It was not easy to find a clearing large enough for the drop, without ravines and gullies close by. Hurry! Hurry! A searchlight swept over them and the first thunks sounded, as crates and packages hit the grass and the ground trembled with the low pass of the plane. Then it was gone, leaving only the quiver on the night air and the swish of red and white silk parachutes settling onto the grass with a polite sigh.

Annabelle's pulse hammered and beside her, Enrico rubbed the bridge of his nose, leaning into a crouch, ready to spring forward. Roberto gave the signal and they leaped into activity. Annabelle's task was to extinguish the beacons as quickly as possible. It seemed almost everything had landed within the clearing. It would be a long night – they must make it far away from the clearing before morning. The weight of the canisters told them there were much-needed weapons inside, and the silk of the little parachutes would be handy too. Even the ties and cables would be cannibalised for some purpose. She tried to ignore the burn on her forearm from one of the beacons.

It was not yet light. The barn had a shepherd's stall with a cot. Enrico unbuttoned her shirt, one, slow button at a time. He licked circles around her nipples, took her by the shoulders, lowered her backwards to the lumpy, stained horsehair mattress. He drew off the muddy boots as if they were glass slippers; the sweaty socks, like silk stockings. Giggling, she raised her legs and he pulled off the army shorts as if they too were of the finest silk. Oh look, he said, a girl! And put his tongue to her, to confirm the find. Together they fell away through the mattress into a world of enchantment on the other side of the wardrobe where the pounding of mortars could not reach them.

Glittering sunlight and warm fingers of sunshine through the slats of the barn coaxed Annabelle awake. Outside, she heard activity and whoops of delight as the canisters from last night were unpacked and distributed. She squatted against the back of the barn to pee, splashed her hands and face and had a drink at the well on the way to the farmyard – what luxury to have water without having to carry it. She had hacked her hair off again, straight across at the nape of her neck, because it was impossible to get enough water for hair-washing. Elisa, the *staffetta* who had taken her place, had given her a wide headband to keep it off her face.

In the brick-paved space in front of the stables, the men worked rapidly to empty the containers. Medical supplies. The burn on her arm seemed a lot better. There were explosives and charges and boots, oh boots! Brens, Bredas and Brownings. A couple of Stens. They were thrilled about the powerful and reliable Brens in particular. And ammunition – lots of ammunition. The guns were no use without that. There were some rifles too and grenades and mortars and, thankfully, some British army uniforms. It felt like Christmas. Then it felt like Christmas and New Year and birthdays all at once, as they opened a canister to find it contained ready-made cigarettes, tobacco, matches, lighters and tinned cake. Annabelle had taken to smoking as if she had always done it. They trembled and hopped from foot to foot like children as Enrico shared it out with a sip of grappa for each, and the air of the courtyard was as thick as the inside of a cinema once the cigarettes were lit.

'Why do you wear those things? A woman should not be seen in men's clothes. It offends *Il Signore*.'

The dialect was as thick as porridge and Annabelle could understand few of the words but the sentiments were clearer than the water of the mountain stream. The woman beat her wash on the rocks, rubbed the potash into them, beating them again on a board. She had spread most of the white sheets over the surrounding bushes to dry and the smell of urine and lye hovered, acrid, on the air. She could not be older than Annabelle's mother but her hands were much older, reddened and chapped. She bent with difficulty. Under the kerchief tied about her head, the hair was sparse; she was missing three teeth. In her rough brown clothes she was a small dull bird. She wore no socks with her clogs and her heels had crevices like the erosion of the Val d'Orcia. Her face was shut and barred, her back stiff with animosity.

The other women ignored Annabelle but she could hear them thinking *puttana!* Whore! It was not only that these peasants feared the partisans, but they were shocked and scandalised to see the few women in the brigades wearing shorts and trousers. These mountain people were not like the workers on the farm at Impruneta. They belonged to an older time, a time Annabelle had never inhabited. A country she did not know. She washed her face and gave up the idea of taking off her clothes to bathe; that would certainly scandalise. There were more and more women with fighting brigades and yet, she thought with a spurt of rage, it was not only the peasants who did not want them. In her own brigade, the stench of disapproval from most of the men was as strong as their sweat. Fucking morons, she thought, how do they think they can manage without us? She must stop swearing. She was beginning to sound like Enrico. She nodded brusquely to the women and climbed back up the bank to the camp.

Their brigade had been there for nearly two weeks and the peasants were terrified of reprisals. They had little food to share and Enrico had instructed everyone not to touch the meagre supplies of these people in the scattered huts. Giacomo explained it to them in their dialect so the peasants knew their food was safe. But, they said, what use is our food if the militia shoot us and burn down our homes because you are here? Or worse, what if the Germans come? They had never seen a German but had heard they were giants. They had good reason to be afraid of the giants.

Boves. Everyone remembered the first reprisal last year in the immediate aftermath of the Armistice. Annabelle remembered General Eisenhower's radio broadcast on 29 July: 'We are coming to you as liberators. Your part is to cease immediately any assistance to the German military forces in your country. If you do this we will rid you of the Germans and deliver you from the horrors of war.' And deliver us from evil, amen, she thought. Hold the line, we are coming, the Allies said, and in Boves up near Turin, a thousand Italian soldiers tried to hold out until they got there. But they did not get there. The Germans burned the whole village with everyone in it, including the priest. Even those who had no idea where Boves was knew the name. Now, every village was Boves. Villagers down the valley collected leaflets snowing from German planes. The leaflets were in Italian. It only needed one person who could read. Word spread the infection.

> *Whosoever knows the place where a band of rebels is hiding and does not inform the German army, will be shot. Whoever gives food or shelter to rebels will be shot. Every house where rebels are found will be destroyed. All food and animals will be taken away and the inhabitants will be shot.*

Clear enough. But other planes – English, American – also flew low overhead, their leaflets, also in Italian, wafting into trees and bushes and streams. Resist, they said. Hold off. We are coming. Join the rebels. Do all you can to sabotage the Germans' progress. Many villagers and even some *contadini* risked the reprisals. Their sons and fathers and brothers had been sent off to fight in Mussolini's war that no-one understood and they had their pride, after all. Who were these Germans to tell them what to do? Many did not believe the Duce was still alive, anyhow. Up in the valleys they had no radios. Who has seen him? Who knows what the Germans had done with him? They asked their questions in low voices. In the high valleys, for most of them politics did not exist – fascists, Germans, communists, rebels, bandits, partisans – all the same to us, they said. Hungry escaped prisoners of war roamed the region: exotic fauna in uniforms no-one had ever seen before. And, they said, some were even black, imagine that! Now there were the Americans and English and their bombs to be afraid of too. Some shared their last bit of bread with the partisans and knew the risks, and many decided, for their own reasons – some more creditable than others – to join those rebels.

Back at camp, Annabelle stiffened at the sight of Elisa, seated on a log in deep discussion with Enrico, their heads inclined towards each other, shoulders touching in easy intimacy. Annabelle compressed her lips. Elisa might be brave and reliable and even likeable, but she smiled too much at Enrico and leaned in too close to confide her messages. Too familiar. Enrico stood, his expression preoccupied. He nodded, gave Elisa's shoulder a squeeze and turned back into the hut, a sheaf of papers in his hand. At the door was a pile of ammunition Elisa had carried up to them. It must have weighed a ton. How on earth did she hide it?

The girl smiled warmly and gave Annabelle a hug. 'I brought you some soap. And some old bits of sheet I thought you might need ...'

Annabelle smiled her thanks and gave her a pat on the arm. She would be glad of some clean cloth. Menstruation was not the simple matter here it was down in the city. Nothing practical was simple here, and yet in many ways, life had never been clearer or simpler. The mountain women, she had learned, wore nothing: no underwear and no pads. She was shocked, but then, what else were they to do but what they had done for centuries? She had not known how anyone else dealt with that uniquely female conundrum. It was not a subject anyone had ever raised with her, except for her mother's one and only fumbling, disjointed attempt to explain sex on her thirteenth birthday. With the presentation of a menstrual apron and a dozen monogrammed, sewn pads. Enrico had taught her more in the past months than she had ever known about her body. Here in the mountains life was fundamental, elemental, precarious and precious.

She had come to love these Alps. They were so different from the gentle, voluptuous hills linking Florence and Impruneta, forming the boundaries and contours of her other life. Here the stony zigzagging footpaths and mule tracks had steep banks filled with wild strawberries or thorny blackberries that tore her legs. Beneath the dappled shade of the chestnuts, footsteps crackled on fallen nutshells. Faded Madonnas peered from makeshift wayside grottoes, offering interception with the Son for the daily needs and fears and hopes of wayfarers. From the gaps and spaces between the trees, on the edge of precipices, an oceanic sky rolled endlessly over valleys and villages and church towers and huts. In unexpected clearings, cut logs offered a rough seat. Netted bird traps served as hides for other prey. Springs gushed from musky grottoes, the water icy and pure. It had become her landscape. She had become another person.

Elisa kissed her on both cheeks and turned to the path in the forest, on her dangerous return to town. Roberto and two of the men would accompany her some of the way, but for much of the long journey she would be alone. Annabelle knew how that felt.

She stooped into the hut to get the latest news from Enrico. A small fire burning in the hearth made the room a furnace. He stood, leaning his forehead on the dirty glass of a tiny window in the back wall, just as he had stood at the French doors the day he left to go into the mountains.

'What's wrong?' she asked. *Please do not let it be the family.*

He sighed and rubbed the bridge of his nose beneath his glasses. 'They killed Giovanni Gentile.'

'Who did?' She was confused. 'The Germans?'

'No. That cretin, Fanciullacci.'

'But I thought Gentile was helping to negotiate the release of our prisoners.'

Enrico nodded. 'From what I can gather, Gentile had just come from the prison after discussing a prisoner exchange. This will be a nightmare. Fanciullacci is a loose cannon, *cane sciolto*. Someone should stop him before he gets us all killed.'

Amongst the groups, the talk was all of the urgent need to set up some sort of central command for the fighting brigades and the formations in the cities. It was only weeks since some 'partisans' in town, with no warning to anyone else, assassinated one of the fascist militia officers, and five civilians were executed immediately in reprisal. A few weeks ago in the village of Stia, to the north-east of where their own brigade operated, someone fired on German troops from a window. We do not even know if it was deliberate or not, said Enrico. The Germans killed every one of the hundred and thirty-seven residents of the village. The stories were the same in every area. No wonder the townspeople and the peasants were afraid of the partisans. No wonder the reprisals got more and more vicious. Now this. Many of them were a little afraid of the communist fighters – ideologues who did not care about consequences. Many other so-called partisans were nothing more than misfits, out to settle personal scores.

'When did you sleep with Elisa?' No! Why did she say that? It came from nowhere.

Enrico turned distractedly from the papers in his hand, lines of fatigue and impatience scribbled all over his face where the dirt had settled into the sweat.

'*Che cazzo*! Are you mad? Elisa! Elisa will probably be fucking dead tomorrow and so will you and so will I.'

He ran a hand through his hair and threw the papers across the rough table where they slithered to the floor on the other side. 'What is wrong with you? I've got more on my mind than Elisa.'

He was right, of course he was. She burned with the ridiculousness of the whole thing.

'And what's more,' he went on, 'we know who betrayed us on the bridge that night. We've got work to do.'

He collected the splayed pages from the floor and fed them one by one into the fire, taking great care they burned fully.

He had not answered her question.

They all knew things had to change. All very well, they said, but we cannot go on like this. High time for some form of proper command

and control, they said. Everyone said it. They all nodded sagely at one another but no-one wanted to be the ones taking the orders.

'How much do *you* want to take orders, my friend?' asked Giacomo of Enrico.

Enrico shrugged. He busied himself rolling a cigarette with the tobacco Elisa had brought them. 'Depends on who is giving them.'

Yes, agreed Giacomo, puffing on his pipe, which had been empty for days before Elisa's arrival. It depends. He knew the suspicion between the groups. Hadn't he seen it all before, he said, in Spain? The Justice and Liberty brigades did not want to take their orders from the communists. The communists did not want to take orders from the discredited, cowardly Badoglio government in the south – most had forgotten there even was a putative Italian Government down there in Bari. The few brigades composed of real soldiers despised the ramshackle nature of the others. Some had been fighting fascism for years; others had only just begun. Mussolini had betrayed all of them – their country, their armed forces and the citizens ... and not just since Salò. He had sent them to wars in Africa, in Russia, in Greece, with no weapons, no tanks, no planes, no food, no uniforms and no hope. Roberto's loyalty was to his country, he said, not the Regime. He was a soldier, he had a duty to do; he would take orders, but he was better at giving them.

'What about you, sharpshooter?' asked Giacomo, turning to Falco, who narrowed his lidded eyes still further and shook his head. Falco did not waste words. He ate little, said little, worked hard. He was there to kill Germans and fascists and that was all he wanted to do. In this brigade, they all took their orders from Enrico and Roberto and that was enough for him.

'Just don't be thinking the Allies will be rushing to thank us. We're doing this for us, not for them. We need to get everything we can from them but we don't have to love them. Or them us.' Giacomo's final words on the subject issued from a cloud of perfumed smoke.

Meanwhile, fascist murder squads roamed freely, leaving bodies rotting from trees or deposited at front doors. Nazi round-ups, Todt transports, confiscations and atrocities weighed more and more on the civilian population, as men and women flocked to the anti-fascist groups of all stripes. What choice have we got, they said. We have to do the best we can. They knew they were a threat to the Regime but it was a brittle, volatile situation with no-one properly in charge, except for those in the GAP groups. Many of the rebels were like Roberto, ex-soldiers, and thank God, said Enrico, we have enough of them; their formations were very good at attacking the fascists and Germans. Not all the ex-soldiers wanted to fight, though. Some wanted to hide until the whole thing was over. Some would do anything for food and shelter. They all knew the Allied support was reluctant, half-hearted. Churchill was dismissive of them. They all heard the broadcasts; they all smarted at his disdainful tone. They all needed each other. When Ferruccio Parri and the Action Party formed the National Committee of Liberation, comprising the various anti-fascist resisters, he contacted the Allies with a view to forming a proper partisan army, but got a cool response.

The communists did not wait, but formed the Garibaldi Brigades, and the GAP groups to foment terror amongst the Germans and Fascists in the cities.

Yet, despite little help from the Allies and vicious reprisals, the number of fighters grew every day. Boys who had never picked up a weapon. Mothers who knew their children would have no hope otherwise. Husbands whose wives and children were dead in the bombing or in the reprisals. Girls like Annabelle who preferred action to submission. Wave after wave of unlikely heroes stepped forward to offer their life, for what it was worth.

In the past nine months, according to Enrico, the *Nazifascisti* had killed nearly sixteen thousand resisters, but still they came. An amnesty for all 'rebels' was proposed for the twenty-fifth of May, which shows, Enrico said, that we are hurting them. And now, they had killed Gentile, one of the few in power who could have made a difference.

The Arno was in full spate: a foaming, tumbling ribbon of chocolate swollen by melting snow in the mountains. Higher up, in the dissolving ice of the Dolomites, the body of Ettore Castiglione emerged from the snow. How many more bodies lay beneath the snow? Still no word of Lorenzo. Racing under the bridges, the Arno carried branches, trees, planks and debris of all sorts, which lodged against the bridge-stanchions and swirled about in the eddies of the shallows. The body of a dog, too slow for the rushing water, bobbed along at the edge. Annabelle was a stranger here now and yet it was all so familiar, like the city of a childhood dream.

She had not been down into Florence since she joined the brigade but she was insistent on coming now. They needed a woman. Elisa had brought the information about the betrayal of their group on the bridge in March. Pietro had died instantly and Maurizio, shot in the legs, did not survive the Villa Triste. Paolo Ambrosiano was a member of the Justice and Liberty group and yet he had betrayed them to the fascists. How? Why? How do we know? Annabelle asked. Who knows why, said Enrico. It does not matter why. What if we are wrong? she said. We are not wrong, he replied.

The late afternoon shadows fell long across Piazza Santa Croce as the three of them sauntered, separately, along the footpaths behind the stone seats. Annabelle wore a coat of taupe lightweight wool. A jaunty hat sat low over her left eye. Her hair was tucked tightly behind her ears, and her gloves, clutch-purse and shoes were of matching taupe. She was not given to taking so much trouble with her appearance and had never owned such adult clothing. It was not easy to get hold of the ensemble, but without it she could not have ventured into the city that, once her home, was now enemy territory.

Across from her she could see Enrico, also wearing a hat – a fedora – and looking really rather gorgeous. She was completely calm. A few metres behind Enrico, a scruffy elderly man shuffled slowly, a cane held awkwardly against his left leg. Giacomo did not have his pipe. One by one, they turned down via Magliabecchi and into Corso dei Tintori, by now in deep shadow. Ahead of them, a short solid man in early middle-age made his way home in time for dinner. Beneath the hat he was apple-faced and rosy. Rationing has not done him any harm, Annabelle thought. By the time he reached the Lungarno, all three were directly behind him. Annabelle lengthened her already long stride and caught up with him as he turned across the bridge.

'Excuse me.'

He turned to her and slowed, waiting for her to catch up. He did not smile.

'Excuse me,' she said again, proffering a piece of paper, 'can you

194

help me with this address?' The last light cast her face in shadow.

The man leaned forward to read the scribbled address. He was much shorter than Annabelle, but bulky and surprisingly heavy as he sagged against her. The long knife had met no resistance at all and Annabelle staggered slightly as, linking her arm though his, she propped him against the parapet. All four figures remained, evening friends, leaning on the stone of the bridge until a cyclist passed them. Then Paolo Ambrosiano went over the edge without even a splash. In the glinting light, the body bobbed along like the body of the dog. No difference really, she thought. It worried her that killing was not harder. But then, many things could worry her. You had to choose what to worry about. It did not bring back Pietro and Maurizio but an example had to be made. Example of what, really, she wondered.

She hoped her parents were not in the city. It was no longer safe. She would give anything to see *Zia* Elsa. They crossed the bridge and faded away up through the shadows and the trees towards Piazzale Michelangelo. Her heel was rubbed raw, the shoes too tight. She only hoped she had not got blood on the coat. She would have to get the outfit back to Falco's sister. She would be happy to be back in her trousers and boots. This city and these clothes did not suit her.

CHAPTER 15

Rome/Florence 1944

Roma città aperta

> *May 26*
>
> *The amnesty for partisans ended yesterday. According to the fascists, thousands handed themselves in, but we do not know of a single one who was fool enough to fall for that. Monte Cassino fell to the Allies last week and their way is clear to Rome. This might be over by the end of summer.*

Rome has fallen. Rome is liberated. Rome is free. All over the country the air crackled, a raging forest fire of static from every field radio and telephone, as well as Radio CORA and all the other clandestine radios and Radio London.

> *Parla Londra. London calling. The Allied Army has taken Rome. We will now begin the transmission of some special messages: The rain is over. My beard is blond. Felice is not happy. The cow gives no milk. The shoes are too tight. The parrot is red. End of transmission of special messages.*

The propaganda from Salò could not compete. There was not any way to present the fall of Rome in a positive light and Mussolini's sympathy for his 'poor people' was widely regarded as risible.

'The Huns are leaving,' came a message from a journalist in Rome. 'There is widespread jubilation.'

Jubilation. The word elicited dread in Annabelle. It was

reminiscent of the time of Mussolini's fall. Hold on, we are coming, said the Allies. Hurry, hurry, we are ready, responded the populace. Let it be true. Let it be true. Or, just as before, they wondered aloud, would the ground open beneath them and this time would they plummet to a deeper circle of the Inferno than any of them could have imagined? For Annabelle it was harder and harder to hold onto optimism without sounding like Dr Pangloss. Everything they knew came to them filtered, second-hand. Was it real or true or not? The world of the partisans was not the real world. It was a world of too little sleep, too much fear, too little information and too much uncertainty. Even though Enrico never admitted aloud to fear, there was never a time when they were not afraid. Even Florence, since that last fleeting visit, was beginning to seem an illusion, no more real than Atlantis or Memphis. Was there a real world, she wondered. She had never known one.

'Rome, "open city". What a joke!' said Enrico.

The Germans might have left it unbombed, but they massacred everyone in their path. Naked, executed bodies lay where they fell as bullets thwacked home. Departing fascist battalions fired into groups of civilians: take that, their bullets said. As the Allies closed in on Rome, the partisans surged back into the city like water filling low-lying land. A trail of limping, dejected Germans extended from south of the city to the north and beyond. The German 10th Army in retreat was a pitiful, vengeful creature, a writhing dragon of anger, confusion and hunger, devouring everything in its path on its torturous way north. It was very bad for everyone but worse still for the Jews. Please let the Allies arrive to save us, prayed the populace. Prayers wafted to the heavens on the dying rays of the sun and the Pope came out onto his balcony to bless the hopes and dreams of his flock. But the first column of the Allies had no time to stop in Rome, racing on through the Eternal City with barely a glance, in exhausted pursuit of the Germans. The leaflets falling all that day bore the Ten Commandments: 'Do as we say. Rome is yours. Go back to work. Our job is to destroy the enemy.'

Who could go back to work as if nothing had happened when their saviours were at hand? In the early evening, crowds milled beneath Mussolini's balcony in Palazzo Venezia, the piazza now choked with strange foreign vehicles. The 5th Army, the knowledgeable muttered, nodding heads and wearing reliable expressions. But most wondered, fifth of what? In the cool early morning of the next day, the via dei Fori imperiali was a colourful swirl of citizens – priests and prelates, cardinals and prostitutes, thieves and grandmothers – all ready to welcome 'The Allies', whatever that meant. Many had no idea who the Allies were. Weren't Britons and Americans supposed to look like the Germans? Tall and blond? Many of these rambunctious soldiers were not tall and blond at all, and some were, frankly, very dark indeed. Darker by far than a Sicilian. What could that mean? No matter, they said, the lights are back on and the Allies are here, so they showered the men in the strange uniforms with flowers and kisses and wine as they rumbled over the cobblestones in their vehicles called jeeps.

That night President Roosevelt of the Unites States addressed them all: 'One up, two to go. The first of the three cities of Europe has fallen.'

'He's getting ahead of himself,' Giacomo muttered through his pipe smoke. It's not going to be as easy as all that. And,' he added, 'the Allies are no saints and the great General Clark is not *Il Signore*. Remember that.'

Grumpy old bastard, said some of the men, but jubilation did not seem to travel well over the long, inhospitable distances between Rome and the mountain valleys behind Florence.

SPQR: Senatus Populusque Romanus

Rome was a zoo. Someone had opened the gates and walked away, leaving the animals without food and water. For days before the Germans left there were sightings of long columns of cows and oxen and beasts of all sorts being herded north, along with vehicles of every description, carts and wagons being pulled, as were cars without fuel. Then came the bedraggled columns of trudging, weaving, staggering German soldiers, all exhausted, many drunk; some in stripped-down cars with no tyres, some on bicycles, some attempting to sell whatever came to hand for a few lire. Prisons and hospitals spewed their hungry cargo of patients, political prisoners and common criminals onto the streets. Jews who had been in hiding emerged, blinking, into the uncertain daylight of a city given over to bacchanalia. All were emaciated and depleted. All had been without power, food and water. Many were starving. They all wanted to believe, though – oh, how they wanted to believe. And surely now, friends, neighbours and strangers said to each other in bars and on street corners, surely now, this new government bodes well?

A government. Fancy that! The Bonomi government. Suddenly spores of hope swirled in the air. Right will triumph, good will prevail. Only now did Annabelle begin to realise how little time there had been in her short life to learn of government. She had not yet turned nineteen. Would she turn nineteen? In her life there had been no government, there had been only 'The Regime'. The so-called government of Badoglio and the King, hiding away far to the south and calling itself the official Italian government, was nothing but a joke played by cowards upon the gullible. Mussolini's Italian Socialist Republic was not regarded, even by the fascists themselves, as a real government. Now for the first time in her life she was being asked to understand the composition of a proper government such as other countries, normal countries, had. She should have paid more attention to her studies of English history. If she survived, she avowed in secret, she would learn to understand these things, so that she could judge for herself. In the meantime, she would have to rely on Enrico, who seemed to have always been paying attention. Why had her parents never talked to her of these matters?

In the wake of the Germans' retreat, as their place was taken by the partisans, Rome began to breathe out again. The anti-fascists occupied the railway, radio, administrative buildings and all municipal structures. The National Government of the South declared all partisans to be soldiers, fighting officially. Enrico showed Annabelle a *communiqué* making clear, though, that Stalin and Churchill did not want the new government installed. To Churchill, Togliatti was a communist who would cause problems after the war. Stalin's objections were more opaque. Roosevelt, however, made it clearer that the Rome CLN, the National Committee of Liberation in government, was the only way forward, communists or not. Finally, thought the members of *Brigata Leone* and partisans everywhere, finally, our worth is recognised. Florence still felt a very long way from Rome but if jubilation did not travel well, hope was a hardier creature and could not be ignored. They began to hope.

Annabelle turned for explanations to Giacomo, who was old enough to know things.

'So, pet, here's the situation,' said the wily old fighter. 'Bonomi has taken the place of Badoglio. Badoglio is out and the King has abdicated in favour of his idiot son, so you can forget about all of them. Bonomi is a good man but it won't be easy. But,' he continued, *'Mantovano fu.'*

Try as he might to maintain his disillusion, Giacomo could not hide the tiny green shoots of hope struggling through even his parched hide. Annabelle had been paying enough attention to her studies to know he was referring to Virgil. Could Ivanoe Bonomi from Mantua be their guide, lead them out of this? Ivanhoe, she said. A hero. Surely a man called Ivanhoe could save them? Giacomo laughed and went back to sharpening his great knife with the stone he kept wrapped carefully in his buttoned pocket. As he often said, a man could run out of bullets but a good knife was always ready.

Florence 1944

June 4

We had word that two days ago the British sent in parachutists to help with Radio CORA. Thank God they finally realise how important the radio is. Things have changed since we became official. Carlo, Enrico, Maria Luigia and the others could not go on alone for too much longer. I wish I were there to help them.

All quiet. Outside the tightly sealed windows, Piazza D'Azeglio baked in the heat that only a city like Florence, nestled into its basin, could generate. Inside, the air was fuggy with humidity and tension. Hunched over the desk, sweat dripping from his chin, Luigi Morandi spoke in a low clear voice into the microphone, reading from a long, handwritten list on the desk beside his pistol. The others worked quietly at their tasks and kept watch at the door to the apartment and out the window for telltale vehicles with an aerial, but in the piazza nothing moved. The transmission was almost finished when the door crashed to the wooden floor.

Luigi spun about, his pistol already in his hand, and the first of the Germans through the doorway took the bullet in the centre of his chest. He was followed by dozens more, all too big for the small space. The room filled with cordite and bullets and shouting and the stamping of boots, and Luigi folded to the floor, crimson leaching across his chest, his pistol silent. A German soldier kicked it from his inert hand. The other five fought with the courage that had seen them through every day of their clandestine broadcasts but their pistols were no match for the Germans. They were overwhelmed within minutes.

Enrico Bocci, Carlo Campolmi, Maria Luigia Guaita, Giuseppe Cusumano and Franco Girardini: the list of those carried off to prison. Shortly after, Gilda La Rocca was arrested. At the same time, in another part of the city, Captain Italo Piccagli of the Italian Air Force handed himself to the fascists in exchange for the others. His valour was useless. After five days of torture, he was taken into the woods and executed with the four Allied paratroopers and an unknown Czech partisan. With them was Anna Maria Enriques Agnoletti, who had been held and tortured in the Villa Triste and then *Le Murate*, but who had not betrayed her brother, a member of the CLN. Unable to capture him, they contented themselves with executing her. By now, they did not care as long as the numbers increased.

> *That vile man Pavolini has taken over the Excelsior Hotel as the headquarters for his new bunch of killers. The Black Brigades. They look like the SS. Florence is no place to be. We do not know whether Pavolini was involved in these murders. So many murders to remember. Gilda and Maria managed to escape. Escape from the Germans, but not from their nightmares. They killed the British parachutists too. All dead. All gone. If I had been there, I would be gone too …*

Achtung! Zona infestata di Banditen. The posters went up all over the valleys and mountains and villages. It seemed there was nowhere not infested by bandits, no-one not guilty by association, but the worse the repression became, the more people flocked to the partisans. The *Carabinieri* of Montepulciano deserted to the partisans, taking all their weapons with them. Their own *Brigata Leone* got three weapons drops in May so they were all well equipped to take on the Germans. A month ago, The *Brigata Stella Rossa* fought a pitched battle with Germans and fascists on Monte Sole and won. According to Giacomo, *Lupo* and his 'Red Star' band killed nearly two hundred and fifty Germans – he and his group were becoming famous. Notorious, more like, in the eyes of the Nazis.

Now we are talking, Giacomo said, but they will make us pay. He was right. Montepulciano made the down-payment on what was to be a high price. Hostages were taken, houses razed, hopes dashed and one partisan was hanged from a lamp-post in the piazza. No-one was allowed to cut down his cadaver.

As the Germans become desperate, they became spiteful. Kesselring issued his edict that no-one was safe. 'I will protect any Commander who exceeds our usual restraint in the choice and severity of methods he adopts against the partisans,' he wrote.

'Usual fucking restraint! That means open slather,' said Enrico. Do anything you like, to anyone you like, at any time, was what Kesselring really meant, and the Nazis and the fascists took him at his word.

Under a scalding afternoon sun, a truck screeched to a halt in via Fortini. As onlookers tried not to be onlookers, six youths were shoved out of the truck, bound together in threes with thick cord, like bundles of wood. So young, whispered the old people on the footpath. Four German soldiers prodded and shoved them along into the piazza where they were lined up and the soldiers levelled their guns. They wore no boots. Boots were too valuable to be wasted on the dead. Just as the boys closed their eyes and steeled themselves, as the watchers hunched their shoulders against the shots, as the soldiers steadied their aim, the commander changed his mind. He set them off, shuffling in their ropes, until they reached the gates of the cemetery. But no, said a man passing by, the cemetery is closed, it is no longer in use. In only their socks, the six were marched on yet again: mute, resigned. They looked neither at each other nor at the sad faces of the people in the street. Only one boy turned to a small knot of locals and said, 'Please. Please tell my mother where I died.'

But no-one knew who he was and his dialect was hard to understand.

'*Poverini*, they are not from here,' old ladies whispered and crossed themselves.

Finally arriving at the other cemetery, the six were lined up against the wall and a volley of fire to their faces and heads ensured that no mothers would get any news for a long time.

'They were from Siena,' Roberto said later. 'General Alexander ordered the partisans in the Siena area to execute all captured Germans. This was the reprisal.'

Panic trembled on the thick air as if Pan truly lurked in the woodlands. Terror drove herds of people in this direction and then that. Children woke in fear and parents stroked them gently, whispering disconsolate words of consolation. Fascists began to panic. Real support for the Salò regime barely existed; only the most fanatical fascists were still committed, or those who knew their lives were over if they fell into the hands of the Allies or the partisans. The others defected in their thousands to the Allied soldiers and the partisan groups. Those who were left, though, they were the ones to be afraid of.

'The Black Brigades and the fascist militias are far more vicious,' said Michele, the crippled tobacconist who fought in Africa. His aunt had been tortured and raped by Pavolini's militia. 'She knew nothing, mind. Her son *was* a partisan but he was already dead. *Bestie*. Animals. Always have been. The things they did in Africa, the things they have been doing in Trieste for years. You would not believe it.'

The fascists used rape and torture of a kind that made the Germans cringe, but the Germans too were in a panic of despair and defeat. Terrified of the ghostly raids of the partisans, they reacted with madness to any attack. When partisans captured the fascist headquarters in a small town outside the city, the Nazis retaliated with a dawn raid, seizing nearly thirty fighters and farmers, and hung all of them on butcher's hooks. Where could you get so many hooks?

The partisans are murderers too, said people. Partisan massacres of fascists and Nazis, and torture – at times even of civilians – was another great terror of the populace. The peasants especially, but all civilians were trapped between the Allies, the Germans, the Italians and the partisans. The local blacksmith had his hands smashed on his own anvil by a partisan for refusing to mend a weapon, and two old men were shot as spies. 'People are starving,' wept the daughter of one. 'They will do anything for food.'

'Didn't Cicero say that in war, the rules dry up?' said Roberto.

'Not partisan, communist,' said Giacomo of the murders. 'Much of it is lies, but me, I wouldn't want to get on the wrong side of those bastards. Revolutionaries make me afraid. All for a cause.'

Genitals burned off with branding irons, feet branded with horse-shoes, eyes gouged, tongues cut out. No. Annabelle did not want to believe any of it and so much was true. She had only questions. Are we heroes? Are we murderers? When do we become what we are fighting against? So many questions.

'Look at this!' Roberto waved a newspaper in one hand as they sorted through the satchel Elisa had brought. *Il Pioniere*. 'Communist publication, but who cares as long as the information is getting out. The first really professional-looking one.'

There was no doubt the communists were the best organised. Roberto flicked through the six pages and then back to page two, his expression fading from light to dark. He passed the paper to Enrico, folded over at page two, stabbing with his forefinger. 'Oh *Cristo*!'

Beneath an article about the strikes in Turin and Genoa, and one about some women who had had their heads shaven for fraternising with the Germans, was one commemorating the dead of the *Fosse Ardeatine* – the Ardentine Caves. Enrico read aloud. After the fall of Rome, the Allies excavated the caves where the hostages of the reprisal for the bomb in via Rasella were buried. The Germans executed three hundred and thirty-five men in Rome that day. Seventy-five of them were Jews, but it was not for that reason. They rounded up civilians and locals but when they could not meet the numbers for Hitler's edict of ten for one, they took them from jails and off the street. The Germans shot them all in the neck one by one. It was exhausting work. Many soldiers wept. It took all day. They threw the bodies into the caves and tossed hand grenades to seal the entrances. They took ten for each of the thirty Germans who died in via Rasella, but they miscounted and killed five extra Romans.

'One Roman more or less, what's the difference to them? Bastards!' Enrico sat back and ran his hands through his hair, which looked as if it was wearing off from the constant friction.

'What are five extra lives to them?' It was the dreadful confirmation they had hoped not to have. People blamed Carla and Rosario and the others for the massacre, but they did not know and could not have given themselves up in time, even if they had. The Germans would still have gone ahead with the reprisals.

As Elisa and the girl who had accompanied her made to leave, Giacomo shifted the axe and sat on the chopping block beside where Annabelle stood, glaring after Elisa, her bottom lip jutting.

'Be sensible, pet. You will get hurt.' He did not mean the axe. 'Men …' His gaze too followed Elisa as she dissolved into the dappled depths of the forest. He patted Annabelle clumsily on the shoulder and lumbered away.

Giacomo was right, right, right. She gave herself a good talking to. Keep your mind on the job. There are no saints here. There never were. It is the work that is important. Reprisals do not work. Soon every zone will be infested with bandits. We will never give in.

CHAPTER 16

Tuscany 1944

Things fall apart / the centre cannot hold

In a time of plenty, she would have run to fat. But this was not a time of plenty. It was the time of the seven lean cows and so the woman was broad, lean, raw-boned. She looked to be about Eleanora's age but much tougher. Her nails were black and ragged, her hands calloused, scarred. The two brigades met on the banks of a wide sluggish river where regions and principles overlapped.

Together they had left a German convoy in ruins and the task of hiding the corpses and wrecked vehicles and shifting all the weapons and ammunition was finally over. It was rare for the *Giellisti* and the *Garibaldini* to work together but it had gone well. This woman from the Emilia-Romagna was a GAP fighter and there were three other women with her in their brigade of eighteen. It was the first time Annabelle had been in close touch with a communist brigade and the first time she had met other fighting women. She called herself 'Caterina'. She was as curious about Annabelle as Annabelle was about her, but determined not to be interested. Her clothing was an eccentric assembly of field labourers' garb except for her boots, which were British. Boots were too important for principle to get in the way. She was not inclined to chat but Annabelle's patrician accent raised an eyebrow and her curiosity overcame her guarded antipathy.

'What on earth brought you here?' she asked.

Annabelle told her story, short as it was. Caterina was unimpressed.

'This is the workers' struggle. What would you know about the workers or the *contadini*?' Her own Italian was pure and cultivated.

Caterina was no peasant-worker either.

'I know nothing. About anyone,' Annabelle replied. 'Nothing at all. I know nothing of my own world either.'

Caterina lifted one shoulder. 'Well, you're here and you did damn well today.'

For the short time they had left before melting back into the mountains in opposite directions, they sat on a log and smoked and talked as women. Below them, the estuarine eddies rattled over clean stones. Caterina had a son and a husband fighting. Annabelle asked her about Carla Capponi. She had been hearing worrying rumours.

'They blame Carla and her group for the Ardeatine massacre,' Caterina said. 'The Germans would have done it no matter what. It was only a matter of time. No-one could have foreseen it. Everyone is looking for a scapegoat and we, the dreaded communists, we get the blame for everything. And she's a woman, of course!'

Yes, women. They had both followed men into the mountains but, they agreed, they stayed now for their own reasons.

'It's the way of the world,' said Caterina, 'but it's changed now. After this, things will be different. We won't just follow the men ever again.'

Annabelle wanted to believe that. She could not believe in communism or Catholicism or fascism. It was only in these past months that she realised how singular her upbringing had been. She had nothing, nothing at all in common with anyone here except Enrico. The men all crossed themselves before going on a mission, carried rosary beads. To the mountain peasants she was a whore for living with the men, and in their hearts the men, except for Roberto and Giacomo, thought so too. She had no religion, no politics, no philosophy to shield her. She wished she knew more about these matters. All she could do was parrot Enrico. Fascism had been simply the background scenery of her life, impossible to see with any detachment. Fascism and communism seemed to her to have a lot in common, except for the very attractive freedom for women offered by the communists. She liked the way Caterina talked about things. It reminded her of that fleeting encounter with Adua. How she longed to talk to Elsa about these things. Elsa would be able to explain it all to her.

'Well,' said Caterina as they began to move out, 'you had better ask yourself what you are doing here and what you will do if you are caught. Be prepared. We pay a higher price than the men.' She nodded, not unkindly, and shouldered her heavy pack.

Annabelle put out her hand but Caterina had already turned away. She had a lot to think about but she was more and more certain of what she was doing there. She had brought no practical or domestic skills with her, but she had discovered she was good at most things and learned quickly. The one skill she did possess had turned out to be the most important here. She could fire, clean and dismantle a gun faster than any of the men. She was no longer as terrified of making mistakes that would cost lives. The only fear now was of failing her companions, of giving in under torture and betraying her group. They all were afraid of that.

> *Allies: what does that mean? The British and the Americans, but they are so many nations. Monte Cassino fell to the Poles apparently. Then there were those like Major Mason from South Africa. These are places I only know through books, and then vaguely. Shouldn't we be afraid of the Russians? Weren't we supposed to think of the French as our friends, but look what they have done in Siena? Goumiers. Ghouls, more like.*

Two days they were gone. Two long, anxious days, but finally Enrico and Giacomo materialised from the forest in the early light as Annabelle washed her face from a tin cup of water. Water was short again and already the sun was high, shaking its fist at them with the threat of another July day in the furnace.

Enrico listed slightly to the left, still in pain from the infected toe-nail Falco had removed with a pair of pliers a week ago. As Annabelle started towards Enrico he nodded at her and raised a hand meaning, no, wait. He was clenched, lined, sweaty, and they had obviously walked all night. What now? She tamped down dread as he beckoned Roberto aside. Giacomo poured coffees, put one in Enrico's hand, and all three sat in a triangle, heads nodding together, hands chopping the air. Whatever it was, it was not good news. Enrico pushed his glasses onto his forehead and rubbed his nose and eyes ceaselessly. He looked older every week; they all did, and probably she did too – she had not seen herself for so long that she would not know. The strain on Enrico scored deep furrows down his face, crevices that did not relax even in sleep. His hair was thinning into a widow's peak. Giacomo puffed furiously on his pipe, which did not bode well – he usually rationed his precious tobacco. Finally they all stood, stretching and running hands through their hair, attempting to throw off the pall of the news.

Annabelle took Enrico by the arm. 'Tell me. What has happened?' Not knowing, was to imagine much worse.

'Not now.' He shook her off. 'I will talk to you all about it later.' Then, in response to her face, 'No. Not the family. I saw Elsa. She is well. It's war news.'

He pushed past her and dropped into a deep well of exhaustion on the wooden cot at the back of the barn. The smell of hay and manure was clean, comforting. Annabelle stood for some time, gazing down on him, watching his chest rise and fall, muscle twitches flickering and flashing across his face. He had seen Elsa. How she wished she could see Elsa. She knelt by the cot and put her head on his chest, against his heart.

Eleven hours, Enrico slept. He could afford it today. They were lying low, awaiting another drop tonight. Beneath the press of the heat and the drone of flies, he slept as if he might never awaken. Annabelle fought the dread of a child whose mother was ill. She had work to do, as they prepared for the supplies they hoped would float from the heavens like manna that night. Giacomo was already up, working silently, preparing their flares for the launch. He had not spoken to anyone.

Finally, Enrico awoke with the cool of evening. They sat on a wooden stool built before the hut, with a view through the treetops as the sun flamed from sight into the valley. Things have changed, he said. Things have become much more dangerous. This has a long way to go, he said, but they are losing and when you are losing, you become desperate. They are all using desperate means, our Allies too. He said much more, and between the lines Annabelle knew he was talking about her. I will not go back. I cannot go back. She was defiant. No, he said. You are right. You cannot go back. None of us can.

So we need to be much stronger and much more careful. Very bad things are happening.

'*Goumier*,' said Enrico. 'They're not French. Mercenaries, nothing but fucking Bedouins from the twelfth century. The Dogs of War.' His mouth worked as if he might spit.

Giacomo put a heavy paw on Annabelle's shoulder and heaved down beside her. Giacomo was a bear of a man, but his bear-skin hung loose on his rangy frame, his hands and feet too big for his body. He was not designed to be thin; it did not suit him. As his flesh evaporated, so had his hearty good humour. He was right, she thought. The Allies are not saints: there are no saviours, no Messiah.

'Berbers from the Atlas Mountains. Arabs. Infidels, if you like. They wear great capes and headdresses. And earrings. The locals are terrified of them. They carry huge scimitars.' Giacomo patted his own great knife.

Berbers, Bedouins. It was all the same to Annabelle. Reports of the brutality of the French Moroccan forces were not new, but now they told of a horror previously unthinkable. In Frosinone, Enrico said, a partisan from Siena had told him the wild tribesmen went on a rampage of rape and murder and pillage that made the Crusades look like a polite outing. They were true mercenaries, recruited on the promise of the spoils of war – rape and pillage.

The civilised French. 'Surely the French cannot know?' said Annabelle.

'They know, all right,' said Giacomo. He blew a cloud of fragrant smoke.

'You have to know how to act quickly so that you are never taken.' Giacomo said. 'It isn't just them, but they are the worst.' He took his notebook out of his top pocket, flipped a couple of pages, and read aloud. 'We must expect more of these sorts of outrages if we use Africans. The British and Americans would not behave like that and we cannot suppress it everywhere.' He closed the book. 'That is what the upright British officer said. We cannot upset the French, is what he meant. Rape, murder, pillage. Warfare as it has always been over the centuries. But,' Giacomo continued relentlessly in his journalist's voice, 'the Americans did awful things in the south and we Italians did this in Africa.'

Annabelle did not want to hear this.

'Graziano and all of them, they poisoned the Ethiopians with mustard gas, raped their women, stole their goods. Haile Selassie took it to the League of Nations, but no-one would listen to him. Not us, not the famous Allies. Our reputation in Africa stinks like dead fish.'

So there was no right side. Giacomo read her face.

'Some men do these things. Not all men … some men. Some Allies. Some Germans. Some fascists. Some communists. Some of us. Perhaps only some of the Moroccans, I can't tell.'

Suicide. Never be taken alive. It was one thing to say it but another to really understand. Be sure you could put your own gun to your head and pull the trigger. Worse, as Enrico pointed out, if she could not do it he would have to. No. She could do it. If Caterina could do it, she could do it.

'*Contessa! Contessa! La Polizia!*'

Eleanora put down the basket of beans but did not turn to Anna Maria as she came panting into the kitchen garden. She stared straight ahead at the rosy brick of the kitchen garden wall. Anna Maria took her by the elbow and turned her as the three policemen came through the back door without invitation.

'I told them to wait in the *salotto* but they would not listen to me.'

'*Buon giorno, Capitano Neri,*' Eleanora said as they approached. She appeared surprised at the sound of her own voice, weak but calm.

The captain shuffled uncomfortably but the others glared at her with the mute dislike they reserved for the nobility but usually managed to conceal. There was no longer any need to pretend.

'*Contessa,*' said the captain, without greeting. 'We need to speak to your husband at once.'

'The Count is not here,' she replied, unsteadily now. 'He is at the Castello.'

'It is true,' Anna Maria said, but it was as if she had not spoken.

'Your daughter has committed a murder. A man called Ambrosiano. We need to speak to your husband at once. Do you know where your daughter is?'

Eleanora looked at him as if he had spoken in another language and then, before anyone could move, she pitched face-forward onto the captain, her face striking the burnished metal of his buttons as she slid down the length of his body.

A summer day
July 20, 1944

The heat was an iron fist. Annabelle was drowsy. A single fly was driving her mad. She eased back on her haunches, rubbing the small of her back. She would give anything for a cigarette. They all would. The sweat stung her eyes, ran between her breasts, burned between her buttocks, where it was already red-raw with heat rash. It dribbled from her hair into the soggy green kerchief knotted at her throat – the *Giellisti* still wore their green *fazzoletti*, though the *Garibaldini* decided last month to renounce their red ones for the time being: too visible. They all wore oddments of the British army uniforms scrounged from supply drops. Annabelle had stripped to her singlet and tied the woollen shirt around her waist. She mopped at the hair of her armpits with the dangling sleeve of the shirt. Everything itched. They were all persecuted by lice. No wonder: heat, dirty clothes and dirty raggedy blankets often taken from cattle stalls or shepherd's huts in the mountains. Despite the heat it was cold at night this high up and they needed the blankets. The men had grown beards because it was so often impossible to shave, making the lice worse. Enrico told her John Donne had written a poem about body lice, called 'The Flea'! He kept his beard as short as he could with a small pair of nail scissors he found in a hut. She had cut her fingernails with them. What a relief. It seemed a lifetime ago that she used to chew her fingernails. A torn and broken fingernail could cause a very painful infection and they all used their knives to pare their nails. Scissors were not as important to her as the raggedy toothbrush, but a luxury.

Thank God for the wonderful khaki British Army desert shorts. Her woollen socks were rolled down over the top of her boots in the style they all affected. But nothing lessened the heat. The stink of her made her sick. It was more than a week since they had been able to wash. The only spring was two kilometres down the mountain – too dangerous to make more than one trip a night and they could only carry drinking water. Please do not let her menstruation start, although that was getting less and less all the time, thank God. Poor nutrition, fear, anxiety and privation had some small benefit.

The ammunition belt, heavy with bullets and two long grenades, cut into her midriff, her back aching from the weight of it. She had still not recovered from a fall down a ravine and her back was no better. If she took great care with her posture, it was bearable. The metal of the Bren was too hot to touch, even though it was in the shade. She had covered the barrel with a jacket so that no sunlight might strike off it and give away their position. From time to time, in the dappled light, they caught a glint from the sights of the sniper across the valley and they knew he was not alone. At least three of them, Enrico said.

Where were the Allies? They had made it to Perugia by the twentieth of June and here it was, a month later, and they were still bogged down, to the south. Allied planes droned constantly overhead. At times when the wind was right they could hear the noise of battle. 'The Front' was a chimera – ever moving, ever changing but hardly ever, it felt, moving closer. It was not a line, not even an imaginary line, but a jagged series of pushes into this valley or up that hill or across some river. The Allies were so close now but still, Annabelle thought, still we are alone.

She tried not to dwell on the battle raging about Impruneta. No news of her parents for weeks now. Her father had not recovered well from his arrest and God only knew how her mother was. They were questioned after she went into the mountains and released after a day or two, but when she was recognised in the city during Ambrosiano's execution it was different. After Achille's arrest on his way back into town from the farm, they held him for a week in the Villa Triste. *Carità!* Her mother did not know which way to turn. Elsa waited every day outside the prison until finally, the doors opened and a different, older man, with his fingernails extracted, shambled into the heat haze of the late afternoon. Achille was not a naturally brave man but the times bred bravery and, he said, he was proud of his new courage. There was nothing more anyone could do to him.

No. She would not think of them now.

And where on earth were the Germans? This convoy? It should have been here hours ago. No *staffetta* had turned up to tell them of changed arrangements but perhaps no-one could get through. Had they been betrayed? Or had the route changed? Or had there simply been a flat tyre or some such normal delay? Normal answers were the last things one thought of these days. The sun climbed toward the zenith. The zinging of the cicadas reached crescendo. There were eight of them perched up here over their guns in the green light of the chestnut forest. It should have been cooler this high up. The fly was back.

To her left she could just see the large, unkempt head of Gino, whose talent was that he could kill a man with a single blow to the face before he had time even to shout. He had the largest hands she had ever seen, gnarled and scarred from his life as a cart-builder. On his left was the taciturn Massimo who could shoot the eye out of a bird at hundreds of metres. Once, in another time, Massimo had been a concert pianist, but here that was not needed. Unseen, but very much present, were four more members of the *Brigata Leone*. They were tucked in amongst the trees, suffering the same boredom and discomfort and tension as she was. Two were mountain men, like Gino, farmers who knew the area. Two were city-dwellers like Annabelle and Enrico and Massimo. They had all adapted to killing as part of their job, but often their job was simply to wait. They waited with a patience none of them had possessed in their other life. Each had learned to sit silently for long periods with only their own thoughts for company.

Apart from the occasional low sigh as someone shifted their weight, Annabelle might have been alone. To her right, Enrico surveyed the far side of the valley and the dusty road steeply below them in slow sweeps of his binoculars, careful to keep the sun off the lenses. The silence was absolute. She had to give it to the Germans. They were just as quiet.

She heard a sharp intake of breath from her right where she knew Alfonso was hidden. '*Che cazzo*?' 'What the fuck …?'

Far below them on the white dusty track, Annabelle saw the slight figure of a woman emerge from the forest, from the direction of Loro Ciuffena. Her figure rose and fell, a mirage on the waves of hot air.

Plodding doggedly into the heat haze, she carried a child heavily in a sling across her chest, a cloth full of something tied over the other shoulder. It was too far away to make out her features. Annabelle stopped breathing.

Close to her ear, Enrico whispered, 'What the hell is she doing?'

The Germans had forced all the locals to evacuate three days ago. The villages were abandoned and the Germans had been told by Field Marshall Kesselring that they now had *carte blanche* to do whatever it took to instil terror into the local population, as they were all collaborating with the partisans. The Germans were exhausted and angry – trigger-happy, the Americans called it. If they could capture a partisan they were merciless, but if they could not, they would attack their families and friends or unrelated and innocent villagers. It was getting harder and harder to tell the difference and the Germans no longer tried.

'No. No. No.' Whose voice was that? Was it her own? Enrico's hand was over her mouth, forcing her teeth into her upper lip, his other a vice on the nape of her neck. Annabelle did not hear the shot. Why didn't she hear it?

For a moment – a long, long moment – the woman stilled, upright, the blood of the infant a crimson flowering across her chest. Then she crumpled to her knees in slow motion. For seconds she remained kneeling, immobile, then she sagged like a rag doll into the dust, folding protectively over the baby. A puff of white dust settled on the brown of her garment. Small birds startled into the air by the shot snuggled back into the trees. In the field beside the road, scarlet poppies shook their heads. The valley shimmered, the heat haze imparting movement where now there was none. On the far side of the valley a dog's bark echoed across the space and rolled away. The cicadas had ceased. The silence was too loud.

It seemed to Annabelle she only heard the crack of the shot then. Time wavered, slithered, shimmied as if she were under water. The big old stone in her throat was choking her. She thought she might suffocate. She closed her eyes. She opened them. The dusty brown bundle was still there. Flies already swarmed about the spreading, brownish-red stain beneath it. Annabelle and the others were frozen in their positions. She thought of the bodies captured in an instant in

215

the volcanic ash of Pompeii. Then Enrico released her, with a slight shove to break the spell, and signalled to Falco, who inched to his side.

Enrico's low voice was frayed. 'They're not coming, the convoy. Pack them up,' he said, nodding at the men. 'We're going higher. We will spend the night at the *baita*.'

'*Si, Tenente*.' Falco's faced was closed. He came from here. He knew whose wife and baby were dead.

Don't look down. Don't look down, don't look down. Annabelle began to dismantle her machine gun without a sound.

> *Elisa brought news of Nonna Lucrezia's death today. She died a week ago. She was ninety-four. How strange to think of a death from natural causes. Yet down there, normal life, incredibly, goes on for some. Babies are born, people die of natural causes, parties are held and people argue about small and unimportant things. I am happy Nonna is gone. I shall miss her terribly but this world displeased her mightily now and she was worried sick for us. When I was small I could not bear the thought of her death, heartsick, but I am used to death now and hers is timely. What she has given all of us can never be taken away. It is the only form of immortality for any of us – that we live on inside the soul of those who loved us. I think of Spinoza up here: there is no God and our soul dies with us, but memory is passed along. We must pass on these times. But who will believe it?*

The sunlight glimmered through leaves, a lacy pattern on her bare stomach, reminding Annabelle of childhood summers, of their secret world beneath the grapevine. Her world with Enrico. Now *this* was her world with Enrico. The imprint of his hand burned on her breast. She cupped her breast in her own hand. She put two fingers inside herself, touched them to the tip of her tongue and to her nose. If only this moment could be their life. No before, no after. She stretched and yawned, luxuriating in the lethargy and lassitude of the late-afternoon sun. For a while, a little while, Enrico would be less withdrawn, less grim, less coiled, but not for long. The boom of the guns from the south resonated in the ground, the bellowing of a subterranean monster making the oily air tremble. Grudgingly she scrambled to her feet and dressed, to follow Enrico back to camp.

Resting. They were resting. It made them sound like an acting troupe between plays. Annabelle could not go down for Nonna's funeral. Would there be one? Of course there would. People still held funerals but it was hard to get the emotion right. Up here, they had buried so many people, left behind others who could not be buried, collected the pieces of those who stepped on mines, and the purple, bloated, maggot-ridden corpses of those who had lain for days under the broiling sun. They tried to keep account, to record the deaths and to mark them in some way that was human, but Annabelle wondered if any of them was truly human any more. A creeping numbness had entered them from the feet up, through the blood-soaked soil.

Enrico had become used to command. He was one of the youngest but so many of the old ones were dead. Succession was automatic. No-one questioned his authority. You grew up quickly here. He was bearing up well, Annabelle thought, but she worried about him. They made love ferociously whenever they could, more to prove they were still alive than for any erotic impulse. He was withdrawn and pensive and chewed his nails to bloody stumps. The men stepped around him carefully, listening intently so as not to have to ask anything a second time. Roberto had left the brigade to organise the fight in the city but Giacomo was still with them. The only old one still alive, he joked.

It was only a matter of days before they would get word to move down into Florence and take up their positions for the battle for the city and they knew they must be ready. No-one wanted to think about what they would find there. After Bruno Fanciullacci's recent raid on the women's prison of Santa Verdiana, reprisals had blazed with a final ferocity. Fanciullacci was brave but always reckless. Captured, he committed suicide, but the Germans were not assuaged. No-one in the city was safe.

Do not think about it, Enrico said. So much to not think about. Enrico had instructed them all to rest, sleep, eat and drink plenty of water.

'Do as I say, not as I do,' quipped Giacomo, but he too was preparing for what was to come. He had run out of jokes and tobacco two weeks ago. A sty in his left eye made his face asymmetrical and his gaze had a look of leave-taking.

After the euphoria of Rome, confidence had oozed away into the dreaded realisation that this could go on forever and the fear that, unthinkably, they might not win. The whole of June and July was like the game of Monopoly that Annabelle's father brought back from his final trip to London when she was thirteen, as one after the other, with agonising slowness, the towns fell behind Allied lines. The Americans built bridges called Baileys over ravines and rivers with a speed that astonished the partisans, but that was the only thing that happened fast. Everything else was mired in a sticky morass of heat and time. Kesselring had declared Florence, too, an 'open city'. The Germans had been evacuating the city for weeks but many remained, and Major Carità's Italian SS and the Fascist Republican Militia were more and more active. Tension vibrated in the air between the Germans and the locals.

Annabelle opened her little tin cigarette-box of treasures and took out a needle and some black thread. She had found two bone buttons in the dirt. They were not the same size but it did not matter. Now she could sew them onto her shirt, which had been gaping and flapping for weeks. Her fingers worked industriously while her mind swelled with thoughts of Enrico, his scent, the silky feel of the hairs on his forearms, the sharp taste of his sweat. The needle pricked her thumb. She dragged her mind back from the edge. With the rusty nail-scissors she snipped her hair to keep it off her neck. Enrico had lost his good scissors. The men lay about the clearing, some propped on rocks, cleaning weapons, mending uniforms, others dozing in the heat. Most were plagued by boils and infected cuts and were as thin as the weapons they carried. Their numbers were swelled by eight more escaped prisoners – five Poles and three New Zealanders, none of whom understood a word of Italian but knew how to fight. Many scribbled in notebooks or on bits of paper they carefully folded into a pocket, in case ... Some of the men crossed themselves and some still prayed – how was it possible to still believe, Annabelle marvelled.

For now they must rest and gather their forces. This afternoon, when they had made love, Enrico had brought her the precious gift of an egg. An egg! It might have been a Fabergé egg, it was so precious. He gently pricked the end with her sewing-needle and held it to her lips as she sucked the albumen and yolk. As a child she was disgusted by the raw egg Nonna tried to make her drink, but now it was nectar. The consistency of semen. Life.

The radio was their lifeline. It was hard for the *staffette* to get through with news of the city, but when they did it was all bad. The fascists had stopped pretending life was normal. The exhibitions and concerts had dried up. Gas was rationed, electricity was short and so were tempers. Drinking water would run out soon. The Arno was a sludge almost solid enough to walk on. Cigarettes were impossible to obtain and people smoked herbs and leaves wrapped in bits of paper. How Annabelle wished she had not begun to smoke. How she wished many things.

News of massacres were so common they had lost the power to shock. San Polo in Arezzo – everyone killed. Eugenio Calò, one of the Jewish fighters, captured and tortured and murdered. Fifteen partisans tortured and executed in the Cascine. Then suddenly, by radio, they learned that the fascists had fled north. Carità and Pavolini had disappeared, and so had another fascist official, with most of the city's funds. The CTLN, the Tuscan committee of liberation, issued a decree declaring itself the official government of the city. Then the Germans issued their own edict: all residents of the streets along the Arno were ordered to leave their homes. To take no furniture, no goods. To find shelter with friends or family and if not, to report to Campo di Marte.

Elisa arrived with instructions for preparations for the arrival of the Allies. She too was drawn and tense, no intimacy in her demeanour as she leaned in to Enrico. She brought a graphic description of the state of the city. Power cut off. All bridges mined. The Germans were in retreat and would blow up the bridges as they left. Decrees, edicts, exhortations, ultimatums – the air was thick with imperatives. Do this. Do not do that. The streets were strewn with American leaflets urging citizens to unite against the retreating Germans. The Germans ordered them to ignore the leaflets and evacuate the city. The CTLN urged them to join the Resistance: old men, women and children – what do they think we can do, they groaned. They put their heads down and ignored all but survival, as they struggled to carry anything still connected to their old life. The bridges across the Arno became clogged – heaving rivers of trudging humanity. Women limped along in unsuitable shoes, clutching at the straps of petticoats and brassieres. Wedge heels endangered ankles. Floral dresses lent an air of false gaiety. On the Ponte Vecchio, a florist offered bouquets while black marketeers slid from house to house. A bicycle cart with three wheels and a large rectangular tray full of goods, trundled past the hospital, which had all its columns bandaged like damaged limbs. Exhausted children in sandals and singlets snivelled and clutched at the skirts of mothers who did not have a hand free for them. Babies bumped along on thin shoulders in improvised slings. Old men pulled handcarts laden with goods that would be no use to them.

The Uffizi and the Pitti Palace were to be spared and they flocked to the Pitti as a bastion of safe haven before the bridges went up. The scene of families of every social caste, encamped, splitting firewood and rummaging amongst their meagre possessions in cardboard suit-cases within the august salons of the greatest of the Medici palaces, beneath the imposing gaze of gilded potentates and majestic artworks was, said Elisa, bizarre and oddly touching – medieval.

The order would come soon now, very soon, to move right into the city. Enrico bit his nails, gnawed the quicks and stayed close to the field radio. The Allies were barely a few kilometres away. Hurry, please hurry, Annabelle prayed. The Jews were being wiped out just as they had been in Rome. Those left were in hiding throughout the city but how long could they hold out? Not long now, she chanted in her mind, not long now. They will be here soon.

CHAPTER 17

Ferragosto 1944

August 3

The bridges have gone. One by one, we heard them blow. It is not light yet but almost dawn and everything has gone quiet. The last explosions were some time ago. We could feel them in the ground. The sun is struggling through a ghastly coppery light of thick dust. I can see out a broken window and I hardly recognise anything. The Ponte Vecchio is still there! I did not believe them but it is still there, just where Kesselring stood yesterday. Borgo San Jacopo has disappeared. Nothing but rubble. There is a thick silence. We hear a shot from time to time and then the Raffica of a Sten. Every now and then a beam gives way and the wreckage moans and settles with spirals of dust.

For weeks the Germans had been leaving the City of Art. Deserting the city. Abandoning the city. Without a backward glance, as if leaving Gomorrah. Without most of the art they would like to have taken with them too, thanks to the foresight of those who had long since filled the country houses with treasures, like the tombs of dead Etruscans. Florence was ravished, looted, despoiled. But still alive. If she lay quietly and waited, the marauders would be gone. Beneath the spent calm, the violated city roiled with rage and impatience and plotted vengeance.

The New Zealanders and South Africans were very close. At San Casciano. They would be able to see Florence. On the morning of the twenty-eighth of July new street signs appeared, phosphorescent for night vision in different colours. Blue, red, yellow and white arrows. Pointing the way to the bridges for the Germans in retreat: a white one to the Ponte di Ferro to San Niccolò and a yellow one to the Ponte alla Vittoria. The only bridges without arrows were the Ponte Vecchio and the Ponte alle Grazie. What could that mean? Then two days later, leaflets with General Alexander's signature wafted down upon the Florentines, urging them to 'impede the enemy from blowing the mines, protect the telephone exchange, clear the streets and protect the essential services'. If we could do that, people muttered, we wouldn't need the British. Protect the railways! It was the Allies who were bombing the train stations, not the Germans. It is vital, continued the proclamation, that the Allied troops can cross Florence without loss of time. And the people? No-one cares. We are expendable. We are starving and they are telling us to hide our food from the enemy. What food? All over the city, people were ordered to evacuate and the streets were crammed with the homeless and terrified, all trying to salvage something precious to them. Making the odd selections people choose when it could be their last.

The CTLN responded to the leaflets with plans, plots, programs. Ideas spawned with the mosquito larvae. There was a plan to save the bridges by throwing Molotov cocktails to stop the trucks. Another plan to mount a machine gun on a truck to attack ordinance troops. But the Commandant of Justice and Liberty vetoed it for fear of the reprisals it would visit upon the civilians. In the end, the plans wilted in the August fug. Only the mosquitoes flourished.

A forbidding sign said: *Achtung*! As Florence is now an "Open city" a permit is required to enter.' We *have* a permit, said Enrico. The Germans cleared the city, street by street with their usual methodical ways, and the Florentines were like rabbits running before them. The tram tracks of the Ponte alla Carria were barely visible for pedestrians carting bedrolls and suitcases and pushing wheelbarrows piled with objects. Children cried and wailed and women sniffled and sobbed and no-one knew whether they would ever see their home again or if they would live. Servants and mistresses carried each other's things. Sometimes. Others displayed the worst possible human traits, even asking for money for the rent of a cart on wheels.

Finally, a great silence fell over the city. The footpaths of all the bridges were mined, with double tubes of explosive joined by wires running from support to support, the length of each bridge.

Not every German was yet in retreat and summary executions were happening everywhere. By the Germans, by the fascists, by the partisans. Two Germans were found attached to a truck with chains. Two more were shot by their officers for looting. But real looting was authorised: three wagonloads of goods were shipped to Bavaria from museums and private homes. Spoils of war. The streets were littered with empty explosive crates. Across the city, citizens were shot by German paratroopers for trying to get back into their homes or shops, or for not understanding the orders. One elderly woman was deaf. 'She can't hear you!' screamed her daughter. They shot her too. Behind it all, the sound of the heavy artillery of the Allies closing in from the south.

In the suppurating heat, the insects and parasites were the only winners. As a child, Annabelle had averted her eyes from the messy decay of death: mouldering corpses of pigeons dissolving into wet streets or the furry cadaver of a fox, its entrails strewn about by a wild boar. The sickly-sweet stench of the niches of cemeteries, with their flickering candles and wilting flowers and gruesome photos were theatres of horror. Now the stench of guts and excrement rotting into the parched soil in a black swarm of blowflies and maggots was as familiar as the stench of a country latrine. Every element of the periodic table was present in the stinking, glutinous air.

They said Hitler loved the Ponte Vecchio and would not have it blown up, but Kesselring was there and that did not bode well. What was one bridge more or less, after all the lives and bridges already lost? Field Marshal Kesselring was furious that his gesture of sparing the bridges of Rome had only allowed an advantage to the enemies and he was not about the repeat the mistake. The boom and pound and thud of mortars resonated through the ground, constant, seismic tremors.

Annabelle did not tremor. A steely calm descended upon her. Her whole life had led her to this moment. On the bridge, the Germans worked in sweat and dust, their caps pushed to the back of their heads, rolled-up sleeves soaked with sweat turning to mud, some working bare-chested with runnels of muddy sweat coursing down into their belts, as they wired the tall conical mines. In the sultry afternoon light the Field Marshall strode back and forth, a raptor ready to pounce, flinging terse orders about as his men, faces scored by deep lines of resignation and exhaustion, worked like automatons. Nothing if not efficient, thought Annabelle. She adjusted her rifle, rested it squarely on the windowsill, the muzzle barely poking between the shutters, and lined up the general clearly in the crosshairs. His face, right between his eyes. No. She moved the barrel down to the swastika at the centre of his Iron Cross. No, that might deflect the bullet. She moved to his left. On his chest, above his heart. Yes. Smiling Albert, they called him. He was not smiling. She could do it. She was that good now, a practised sniper. Her finger gently caressed the smooth trigger and her breathing slowed. She squinted along the sight, her shoulder leaning into the heavy butt of the gun.

Then she sighed deeply, took a long, raggedy breath and stepped away from the window. How easy it would have been. He was right there in front of her and he could be dead now. There would never be another moment when she would have a chance like that. But one general was not worth the lives it would cost. It was all mathematics now. One general equals ... how many women and children? Ten civilians for every German. Even that equation had long been exceeded.

Beside her, Enrico relaxed his shoulders. Let them go, he said. Let them leave. They are not our concern here. We will fight them further north. The problem in Florence was no longer the Germans. The problem was the fascists, the loyalists who had nowhere to go now that Pavolini and his men had fled north, taking the whole stolen armoury of the *Caserma* with them. Those militia remaining knew there would be no role for them in the new national government. They had nothing to lose, and would remain in their lairs throughout the city, killing every passer-by until they ran out of ammunition and were killed themselves. People scrutinised every window and every doorway before venturing across open space, but still, a single shot and a falling body were common sights.

The first explosion went off in via Guiccardini. Then one after the other they blew, with long silences between. Every two hours.

The banks of the Arno afterwards were a giant quarry, nothing but gravel left of what had been medieval streets and homes. Tiny *vicoli* and *chiassi* and workshops, little shops and little lives, all gone. Much of this, thought Annabelle, we can never get back. Borgo San Jacopo and Por Santa Maria. Gone. Where once the buttresses of the bridges were reflected in the Arno, they were now under it. The rubble at either end of the Ponte Vecchio groaned and shifted, expanding and contracting with the heat of the day and the cooling of the night. Bricks clattered and dropped into gaps between shifting beams. Puffs of dust arose in small geysers. Thank God the gas was off, As far as they knew, no-one had been trapped beneath the rubble. The only things buried there were hope and memories. So many homes gone. So many lives shattered. But at least those left were still alive. They could rebuild, they could begin anew. Annabelle was unsure what that meant because it was hard to recall a life before, but whatever it was, it could not be worse. Somehow they must make it better. A new government. A new world. She would work harder to understand politics.

She shook herself from head to foot like the working dogs on the farm. It would be a long time before most people could think of new lives, the losses so catastrophic that many people would never recover. The Germans were being driven from Florence, but what that would mean for afterwards was beyond her imagination. Please let it be better than this.

For weeks, their brigade had been in the mountains close by, cutting telephone lines, attacking lone convoys, blowing up bridges and roads, stockpiling weapons. With each step closer to the city the danger grew. Everywhere they stepped the land was mined. In order to minimise the reprisals, they had been warned to concentrate on sabotage and attacks on the fascists rather than the Germans. The *comandante* of the 1st Division, Justice and Liberty for Florence, had ordered them all in. Each night they filtered back into the city in small knots of twos and threes, in readiness for the Allies. The communists were doing the same. One by one, they slipped into the unsleeping city under cover of shifting clouds. The *pffumf pffumf* and *crack-crack-crack* of battle were constant, the air raids and summer storms leaving everything damaged and broken. The air was sulphurous and stank of cordite.

The heat built daily to the climax of summer. Not even two weeks to *Ferragosto*, 'Holiday of Augustus'. There would be no Emperor's holiday this fifteenth of August and certainly no *festa* to celebrate crops and harvest. The sun singed the skin of the living and inflated the dead until they burst. Civilians tried to stay off the streets, afraid to go out, even to forage for food or water. The South Africans were still bogged down at Impruneta. The fighting there had been terrible. So close to Florence, so very near, yet it might as well be another country. Please let them be safe, thought Annabelle of the family. No. Nowhere is safe.

The front limped towards Florence. Time unspooled and looped and dragged its heels. Reprisal was everywhere. Many Germans were drunkards, desperate and out of control. Not all were monsters. Many were country boys who did not understand how they had ended up like this. Many were principled army officers who had served their country loyally. Now they were nothing more than The Enemy. The massacres in the countryside built to a crescendo, and as the Germans pulled back from Florence, every street and piazza was the site of vicious executions of partisans and prisoners of all sorts.

> *They are determined to destroy us. Why did they declare Florence an open city when they really want us all dead? Do they care about the monuments? What about the people? Every day when you open your eyes you wonder, who will die today? Who will death come for today?*

'How the Duce will hate it when Florence falls,' said Annabelle.

Enrico shrugged. 'Mussolini does not care. About anything. He was always hollow. He never believed in anything. Hitler copied him in everything, but for Mussolini it was all on the surface. Hitler is the one with the deep beliefs – the apprentice become master.

The benediction of evening was not far off. Soon there would be a little relief from the heat, but the dust hung, clammy and heavy, over the humans, the animals, the statues. The sound of industrious

Florentines at work competed with the noise of war. Inside Palazzo Pitti the air was redolent of leather-working, coal fires, babies' nappies, frying oil, boiling chickpeas and garlic. It congealed with steam and spitting oil or lard. Women wiped sweat from their eyes with the back of their hand and stooped, stirring pots on makeshift pans of coals or spirit burners. Washing draped the marble statues and iron railings and chairs. An old woman with swollen ankles lay on an iron bedstead with no mattress. All about, children played as children do, with whatever came to hand – bits of paper, small stones, broken bricks, dry twigs, the occasional toy salvaged during the evacuation. Not all children. Some clung to their mothers, thumb in mouth, eyes blank. Wondering what the noise had been all about and why their father was not there and what all the blood had meant. Some had not spoken for days. Might never speak again.

Women in summer frocks wore necklaces, brooches, earrings, bangles – keepsakes saved just in time. Who knew when they might come in handy for sale or barter? Others treasured rosary beads or a candlestick. Some had chosen a book or a framed photo, selected in haste. One old woman with translucent skin, wearing glasses with only one wing, sat silently before three framed photographs, arranged on the pedestal of a statue as they might once have been on her mantle. Despite all, there was laughter and chatter and jokes and gossip. Shrugs were common: might as well make the best of it, at least we are alive, could be worse, it will soon be over. Many braved the bombs, cooking outside over open fires made of bricks, in the Boboli Gardens. God knows, they said, there were enough bricks. Thus they consoled and supported and sighed and hoped. Men in shirtsleeves and braces gathered in small knots to exchange information, roll a cigarette, commiserate, share wine. Many of these new residents of Palazzo Pitti were visiting the famous palace for the first time. Its grandeur was lost on them. People who had owned precious tapestries and bronze statues shared tin dishes with those who had never entered a museum in their lives. The marble figures that had populated the great courtyard for centuries betrayed no surprise.

The city was full of waiting. Florence's time had come. Four days ago, the Allies had smothered the city with leaflets: 'Citizens of Florence, these are your instructions. The future of the city is in your

227

hands.' Now it was. Or what was left of it. They will come tomorrow. Will they come tomorrow? Will they come in time? To the south-east, the noise of battle rose into the evening sky from the ground-fighting, mingling with the roar of wave after wave of bombers receding into the hills. As darkness wrapped the city, the preparations were complete. The clocks were still. The eve of battle; nothing more to do now until the fighting began.

The eve of battle. Such words – they thought in portentous sentences now. They knew they were part of something very grand. Three weeks ago, the Tuscan Committee for Liberation had called on all the formations to unite under the one banner to defeat the Nazis. They were all, for the time being at least, ready to fight together as the 'Arno' Division. Most of the brigades were *Garibaldini*, but their own brigades, the *Giellisti*, were also there in force. The city was a time bomb primed to explode at the first signal from the Allies.

From their vantage point on the roof of a medieval defensive tower, Enrico and Annabelle could see across the river to where the sky flashed and echoed with the drumbeat and dreadful splendour of mortar shells. In the blackout, the indigo sky was a tent of stars. Moonlight winked off shards of shattered glass in the rubble. They sat against the stone parapet, still warm from the day's heat. The warmth was kind to her aching back. With every explosion, her pulse raced and she gave a start. Closer. Closer. She wanted very badly to cry but this was not yet the time. Gradually, the stored heat of the day seeped into her, filled her with the sun's energy and slowly set her body alight. Enrico pulled her against him into the curve of his shoulder. With two fingers beneath her chin, he softly turned her face to the velvet night.

'*Had I the Heavens' embroidered cloths* ... *Amore mio*, do not be afraid,' he said. 'Think of this. If we die tomorrow I will have loved you all my life. Whatever happens or however long, when I die, I will have loved you all my life. Never doubt it.'

Tomorrow was to be his twenty-first birthday. They made love on the warm stone as if they might never be warm again. It was 11 pm when the war began.

228

PART FOUR

CHAPTER 18

Ben is tormented by the thought that black soldiers are polluting the streets of our 'Eternal City'. He says they steal from our churches and rape our women. Thank God we are not there. I have said a special rosary for our friends in Rome. Ben has not forgiven the Germans for the deportation of Rome's Jews, and now Florence. He says Himmler and some Moorish Mufti in Berlin want them all exterminated. Naturally, we all despise Jews but Ben would never have done that. He says the Pope will collaborate with the Allies now. Not that the Pope ever raised his voice about what the Germans were doing to the Jews everywhere else. Ben says Il Papa would have done anything for him once, because he gave the Church back its state after it lost everything in the Risorgimento. Divine Providence, apparently, brought Ben to him! Papa Pacelli would never oppose Ben. Once. But they heard little of him now. Despite her father's and Marc's loyalty to him too. Why does Ben bother with him? Ben does not even believe in God! He repeats over and over that he, Ben, is the most hated man in Italy. He says he does not care but it eats at him, I know. How can people be so ungrateful!

'Florence will be taken by the Allies within days.' Ben's tone was dreary. 'They are already at the Arno and the Germans have abandoned the city. They have been leaving for weeks now.'

His tea sat untouched on the table at his side, a tea-leaf floating on the surface like a dead insect. He had not recovered from the fall of Rome. He had not been the same since. He had ordered three days of national mourning. Rome was, he often said, his Imperial Dream. It broke his heart.

'I do my best,' he mourned, 'but the whole thing is a farce.'

Now Florence, the city he loved perhaps most of all. He slumped in his favourite mangy old armchair, picked up his cup and stirred his cooled tea, sighing over and over and over. Round and round and round, the spoon tinkled against the cup in the silence. *Non me ne frega* ... the old fascist 'I don't give a damn' slogan. Ben does not actually say it, but more and more he means it, about everything, Clara thought.

'Don't leave papers lying around,' he said with a nod at her diary, his lips pursed like an old woman.

She would hardly leave papers lying around! As much because of those surrounding him, as for anyone else. Things were quite grim enough without him treating her as a fool. Wasn't it him, always saying we need to keep a record of these times? For a while now, he had been fretting about her diaries and letters and papers, but he too scribbled constantly, it was history. Clara took a long, slow breath and composed her expression – the times were too dangerous for her to lose her temper as she once might have. The colourful shouting matches of old, ending in riotous sex, were a long way in the past.

'Don't worry, *amore*. You know how careful I am. I have made arrangements to safeguard all our papers.'

Her exasperation just showed, like the hem of a petticoat beneath a skirt, but Ben had lost interest. She would certainly safeguard her diaries, but also the hundreds, no thousands, of letters between them, extending back to her adolescence. It was true the letters and diaries of the past year or two were the most important, but they were all important to Clara. He knew that! *La mia cara, Clara* ... All his letters began that way. He never used the childish 'Claretta' her family and the press used. Even here on this cursed lake, he wrote to her every single day and she answered every letter. They had no choice. Life was a constant game of hide and seek, of ruses, passwords, assignations, trysts and secrets. If not for the tower of *Il Vittoriale*, it would be almost impossible for them to have time alone together. It made life difficult, but also injected excitement into an otherwise dull existence.

This was the time of testimony. They all knew it. It was a time of fervid scribbling, typing, relating, recording. It seemed every drawer in the country must have a secret bottom with papers hidden beneath. Clara had meticulously filed and annotated all their letters and tied them in orderly, dated bundles. She'd even had copies made of them – that caused her a lot of problems. For a while there, even Ben was almost persuaded by her enemies that she was about to use them against him. Poor darling, so easily swayed by the dreadful people around him. Sometimes, she had to admit, his letters were cold and distant but others were passionate and loving. Poor Ben, he knew he could not do without her, but sometimes that made him resentful. He said things he did not mean. One moment she was the great love of his life, and the next, women meant nothing to him.

Now that woman, Romilda Ruspi was here on the lake. What did she want with Ben? He claimed he was not involved with her but he cared about her. Cared about her!

'No. You fucked her. Admit you had sex with her.'

'Oh all right. But it means nothing.' He groaned. 'It is like blowing my nose.'

'Don't make me laugh, Ben!' There was no danger of that.

'Stop whining,' he said, 'you sound like a wife.'

Clara was haunted by that woman. Back in Rome, Ben actually had her living in a cottage in the grounds of Villa Torlonia for years. In his home! Clara could never relax even when he was at home, had to make him telephone her constantly all evening to be sure he was not sneaking off to a tryst with Romilda. When she did catch him out, she remembered his letter: *I'm bad. Hit me. Hurt me. Punish me, but don't suffer. I love you. I think about you all day, even when I am working.*

Romilda meant nothing to him. Clara knew that, of course she did. He even claimed to have once had sex with another woman in front of Romilda. Probably nonsense. Not all the stories about Ben were true. Did not that awful man, Boratto, when he was Ben's driver, tell everyone lies, saying that Ben was sleeping with both Clara and Mimi? Romilda Rospi was just one more feminine thorn in her side. She was always there in the background, and now, Clara shook her head, here she was again. It really was too much.

Florence has fallen. Each city is a nail in his heart – Arezzo, Pisa, one after the other until all the beautiful bridges of Florence are gone and the Allies are in the city.

The Germans have taken over all of our factories, they are sending all our food to Germany as well as all our workers and they have even, according to Ben, stolen all the country's gold. What more does Hitler want? Can he not see that it is hopeless? Ben even thinks – I am never to breathe a word of it – that General Wolff and others would surrender now if they could find a way of doing it without Hitler knowing and if they could get the right terms.

Ben worries about the rebels. The partisans as they call themselves. Ever since they killed Giovani Gentile, things have got out of hand. Communists, nothing but filthy communists they are. Ben is upset by Pavolini's tortures and massacres and the Germans have become completely murderous. They are killing everyone. Women, children, even babies. These people are his people. It will be counterproductive, he argues. Major Carità has apparently moved to Padova. The stories from there are too horrible to contemplate. The man is a monster.

It was actually the rebels, the partisans, who took Florence first, before the Allies arrived, but Ben did not wish to discuss that. So we have come to this, he muttered, the Gustav Line is breached. Clara had only the haziest idea of the mountainous countryside between Florence and Bologna – geography had never been her strong point. She remembered Florence, a wet day of glory – could that have been only three years ago?

There were only fanatics left now. Ben had never been a good judge of character – too trusting. Just as Pavolini convinced Ben to kill Ciano, so he talked Ben into approving the setting up of the Black Brigades. He enjoyed any excuse for violence. The Black Brigades were to kill the rebels, he argued, but they were killing everyone, right, left and centre. It was having the opposite effect. This was what they got for making Pavolini the Head of the Party.

'We shall be implacable,' he said. Strutting turkey! Called himself a philosopher! Ben thought he was a genius just because he had a university degree. Ben had an exaggerated respect for scholars, in her opinion. Pavolini strode about with his thumbs hooked in his belt as if *he* were the Duce. Now Ben regretted allowing him to set up his vicious army. Counterproductive, he called it. Even Pavolini had abandoned Florence and was setting up his headquarters right here, in Maderno. The swine.

It was not only the RSI troops causing problems – the Germans were just as bad. Ben tried not to let her hear it, but people were saying the Germans had even bayoneted babies! He did not want to believe these things. After the last massacre ordered by Kesselring, he wrote to Ambassador Rahn, saying, 'The act was contrary to every Italian sentiment and an offence to national justice.' No-one was listening to Ben anymore.

> *We all have blood on our hands now, he says, and he is fretting about it. No wonder we need to take great care with our diaries and letters. We all want to be acquitted now. We are all writing letters and notes and diaries and hiding them for later, for after, for a time when we can claim to have not been guilty. 'I am not innocent. Your little war criminal.'*

Ben was reading *The Life of Jesus Christ*. He understood, he said, the depths of anguish, of betrayal and solitude. Someone had given it to him when he was in prison. It was not good for him. Clara preferred it when he read aloud to her from great love stories or biographies of men like Mazzini. She particularly liked it when he read her stories of great men and their beloved women. Clara herself once read him a beautiful passage from the romantic novel she was reading but he thought it shallow. Ben was more heroic. He talked often about making a last, heroic stand, of taking his loyal troops into the Valtellina and dying with a final, grand gesture. They will never take me alive, he said. But, she wondered, what about me? Heroics were all very well but ... She clucked her tongue and made a mental note to have her nails done when Ben's manicurist came tomorrow.

A week ago, the *Legione Ettore Muti* shot fifteen partisans in Milan. It had a terrible impact on Ben. Ettore might be dead but the SS Legion named for him continued the glorification of death and violence that Ettore had learned from D'Annunzio. Ben used to adore Ettore – well, he would – a great pilot was Ettore. Clara had once heard a rumour that Ettore was yet another son of Ben's. That was ridiculous. Certainly, the death of the rebels in Milan was undesirable. Ill judged. Or rather, it was the way the corpses were piled up in Piazzale Loreto. Thrown down together, like dead animals tipped off the back of a truck. Deliberately mutilated. Left for days in a rotting, tangled heap on the ground, with a sign on a stick and a guard to stop the families taking back their bodies.

Yes, it was all very unfortunate, untimely. People were very angry. Yet all of this violence was no more than Ben's own troops had done in Africa. He had not been happy about that either. He had shown Clara images of long lines of Africans dangling from scaffolds, and she had heard him damning Graziano and Pavolini for rapes and poison gas. They bombed Red Cross hospitals. They committed atrocities too unspeakable to consider, but that was Africa.

Ben was not so sure D'Annunzio's 'theatre of violence' worked any more. It had lost its appeal. It worked for twenty years but did not seem so 'purifying' any more.

'It is because we are losing,' said Ben. 'The more you realise you have lost, the higher you raise the stakes, but this is not a game of *Scopa* and we cannot win this way. We will pay very dearly for the blood of Piazzale Loreto.'

Florence, August 1944

'Be careful, pineapples can kill,' said Enrico, handing out the American hand grenades as they crouched in the lee of the General Post Office. Pineapple grenades only had one pin. They bumped on either hip as Annabelle ran, bent low, across the open space of Piazza Strozzi, praying the pin would not pull out. From the top window of the hotel diagonally opposite, the muzzle of a Beretta 38 glinted down at the chaos of the piazza but it did not move, did not fire, the only still thing in a scene of utter confusion. The sniper might be dead. Or he might not be. From the Oltrarno, the battle thundered. The Allies were already on the southern banks and the fighting there was ferocious, but they could not cross the river.

Ducking and weaving, she listened for the shouted instructions of the commanders of the four groups fighting here. They were to take the old centre from the last of the retreating Nazis and Black Shirts, who were dug into vantage points on the tops of the buildings. Every weapon she had ever seen, and some she had never laid eyes on, were present, firing and misfiring. The city held a couple of thousand partisans now. Used to small fast skirmishes, this pitched battle was a terrifying novelty. They had never had the chance to engage the enemy so brazenly in full battle before and the sensation of liberty was intoxicating. She had never fought alongside so many women either. Every organ in her body was on high alert, all heaving, fizzing, racing, pulsing. From behind Palazzo Strozzi a division of militia tried to hold them down with machine-gun cover, but they could not fire around corners and this was a maze of corners.

They had a clear idea of the situation because earlier, Enrico Fischer had managed to get into Palazzo Vecchio under the eyes of the Germans and make it across the Vasari Corridor to the South Africans on the other side. He wanted to lead them back across to the northern side, but the corridor was too weak to take the weight of the troops and munitions. Instead, he threaded a telephone wire all the way through, a link to the Allied Command.

For the first time Annabelle and all of them were fully engaged in the war, the real war, the battle for Florence. In the smoke and dust and flying stone-chips and bullets, her eyes watered and she struggled to see. She prayed Enrico's glasses would not be smashed. He had tied them fast with string. The shouted orders and screams of pain and the clang of bullets on the iron rings in the façade of the building mingled with the thunder as mines went up. Sometimes mines exploded, hit by gunfire or falling masonry, but mostly as someone stepped on one of the hundreds of tiny S-Mines the Germans had placed under the metal covers of the gas and sewerage points and between the paving stones of the streets and piazzas. Their parting gift.

Launching herself for the protection of the wall, Annabelle skidded and fell heavily in viscous blood pumping from a severed arm. The man lay beside her, his face close to hers, watching her with detached interest as his life ebbed away. Silently. In shock, she thought. In shock. For long moments, they lay together, stricken, then his eyes closed. She felt her own arm roughly grasped and Giovanni tugged her to the back of the building. A man crawled past, firing from the ground.

'Carlo, wait,' Giovanni shouted to him. 'Follow Carlo,' he yelled to Annabelle, 'get the machine-gun post.' He gave her a shove.

She scrambled to her hands and knees and crawled after Carlo to where they were able to lob the grenades through a grill to the street behind. Their aim was good.

Giacomo ran past, bent double, calling, 'Good work, pet. You'll make a soldier yet.'

In the swirls and spirals of dust and smoke, his beard was putty-coloured, stiff, like the beards in old Dutch paintings. His eyebrows were etched in plaster-dust. She felt better for hearing his voice. He winked at her. Then he rose into the air, slowly, so very slowly. How could such a large man rise into the air so gracefully? Time collapsed inwards, she did not hear the explosion, all sound ceased. Giacomo rose and rose and then ever more slowly, his shirt ballooning like wings, he fluttered to earth.

'*Scusate.* Excuse me.'

Six heads snapped to the left. From the shattered doorway, standing perfectly still with his hands in the air, the German soldier regarded them calmly. No-one moved. Falco burned his finger on the flame of the kerosene burner and dropped his pan with a *Cazzo!* Still the German did not move. He had lost his cap or helmet, but was otherwise wearing the full grubby uniform of a Wehrmacht private. When Enrico rose to his feet he was the same height as the boy, who looked to be about twenty, but the German was much broader and much blonder, with the square Aryan jaw that Italians thought every German was born with.

'What the fuck do you want?' said Enrico. Behind him the others got to their feet, spreading around and behind the newcomer. Were there others?

'Don't go near, he might be mined,' said Michele.

The German shook his head and raised his hands higher. In good Italian, he said, 'I am alone. I am not mined, not wired, not armed. I am alone,' he repeated. 'I do not want to die, I only want food. I hand myself to you as a prisoner of war.'

'We don't take prisoners of war.' Without moving or turning his head, Enrico said to Annabelle, 'Check the entrance and see how he got past Falco.' To the German, he said, 'If you have killed our sentry you are dog-meat.'

The boy shook his head as Annabelle edged around him through the door. 'No. I saw him but I was already here. I have been here for two days. If I wanted to kill you, I could have done so by now. Not,' he added ruefully, 'that I have anything with which to kill you. I have no weapons.' Circles of grime under his eyes gave him the look of a tawny owl.

Annabelle returned with Falco at her heels and they all stood like passengers waiting for a bus, shaking their heads. The German did not take his eyes off the powdered pea soup, by now burning in the tin pan over the flame. He flinched very slightly at the muzzle of Falco's gun in his back, the fingers of one hand twitching slightly. His begrimed fingernails were bitten, not just to the quick, but the flesh around them was chewed too. Like Enrico's.

Enrico nodded towards the back wall. 'Sit there, back against the wall. You can put your hands down.'

Falco prodded him and he crossed the room slowly, his hands still high, until he slid to the floor. Enrico nodded to Annabelle who spooned some of the pea porridge into a tin and passed it to him. Without taking his gaze from the group around him, he scooped the food into his mouth with his fingers, emptying the tin in a few seconds. It was nearly three days, he told them, since he had eaten anything but some mouldy corn he had found in the *cantina* of this building. He had been in hiding since the mining of the bridges. Falco raised his hands in a great shrug that said, what the hell are we going to do with him. Germans by the dozen where trying to hand themselves in, but usually to the Allied forces.

'We don't take prisoners,' Enrico repeated.

'I *am* your prisoner.' The German grabbed the second helping handed to him. 'I have nowhere to go. I want to hand myself in to the British.'

'Thanks to you, my friend, the British are still on the other side of the river,' Enrico said.

The German nodded like a fairground puppet. He knew, yes, he said, he knew, but what could he do. In the army, you followed orders. Not that he cared about the bridges. All this talk about the bridges, as if some statues could count in the face of the things they were ordered to do. There was a limit. He became garrulous. He had joined the army straight from school to fight the enemies of his country. Not to kill old ladies and children, not to murder innocent people. His own grandmother had been Italian. It wasn't murder if you shot a soldier, or ... his eyes flicked around, or a ... combatant. But it was murder if you shot an old man who could barely walk ... and him a Catholic, from a good Catholic family, and murder a mortal sin. No, he could not go on. They had lost the war, everybody knew that. He wanted to go home to his village outside Hamburg, to his mother and his father and his sisters, if they were still alive. And he did not want to go to hell if he died on the way.

Annabelle had never thought about Germans being Catholics. She had only known Lutherans. It was the first time she had been this close to a live German since before the war. She passed a plate to Michele, but he pushed it away.

'Give it to our "prisoner".' His face was the colour of suet and he could barely move for the distended stomach that made him look pregnant. It was more than a week now that his bowels had been blocked and he was in agony. Enrico had tried to help him with suppositories made from candle-wax but it did no good. 'You could die of so many things besides being shot,' he'd muttered.

Enrico pushed his glasses up onto his forehead, rubbing the bridge of his nose. He expelled a long breath. '*Christo*! All right then. I cannot guarantee you anything though.' At least, he added, the fool was not in an SS uniform.

He nodded to Falco. 'Finish the food and escort him to the Divisional *Commandante*.' He could not tell what would happen to the boy after, but more than that, he said, he could not do. Prisoner of war! The Geneva Convention was long forgotten here.

'He has cheek, the kid, you have to give him that!'

> *'Il Comitato toscano di Liberazione da oggi ha assunto comando della città.'*

> From today, the Tuscan Committee of Liberation, in collaboration with the National Government of Italy, has assumed command of the city. Every citizen is urged to rise up and defeat the invaders. We welcome the Allied Forces.

It was seven o'clock on the hot dry morning of the eleventh as the proclamation issued from number 8 via della Condotta, the head-quarters of the CTLN. It was now official.

The man, Carlo, had apparently dragged Annabelle to the safety of a doorway at the back of Palazzo Strozzi as the battle rolled away from the river, down via Tornabuoni. In its wake were the dead, the dying, the maimed. She had no memory of that. She had only the image of Giacomo. They were to bury him today. When she closed her eyes, the image of Giacomo rolled across her eyelids as if on a cinema screen.

When she reached his body, that great bear of a man had deflated into a flattened version of his old self, a bearskin rug. He was leaning forward as he ran, so as his boot tripped the mine it exploded in his stomach. For those first moments there was no damage to be seen. His briar pipe lay close by. She picked it up and put it in her pocket. It still carried his body-warmth. The great hunting knife was just visible in its sheath beneath his jacket but she left it there. No-one else could wield that knife.

Five of their fighters died that day but Enrico and Roberto and Falco were alive, and she was alive. And Giacomo was not. It was no easier to bury the dead in the city than it had been in the mountains. They wrapped him carefully in a heavy tapestry curtain torn from a shattered window and carried him to a piece of parkland to the north

– not too far north, as the Germans had only retreated to Fiesole, from where they rained down mortars and bombs.

Giacamo weighed a lot, for someone so emaciated. The men wanted to say prayers. Annabelle and Enrico let the incantations wash over them and stayed silent. These men had lost so much; it was not the time to deprive them of the one thing that gave them some sort of comfort. But there was no comfort for Annabelle. The brief euphoria of the pitched battle had evaporated in the August heat, leaving her spent and depressed. All around them the city was free. All day, the bells of the Bargello and of Palazzo Vecchio boomed across the city announcing victory, but it did not feel like it. Enrico had already told her he would go on, go north, that the group would fight on all the way up the peninsula until the Germans and the fascists were all defeated. She was not to come.

They were not yet free. From less than eight kilometres away, the German guns roared. The feeling that they could return at any moment haunted all Florentines. Word came of an unspeakable massacre in a village called Sant'Anna di Stazzema. Walter Reder – the name tolled about the valleys like a funeral bell – was a vicious drunkard slashing a trail of destruction through the countryside just to their north. Civilians herded into churches and burned alive. Hundreds and hundreds of innocent people who had fled the city and surrounding towns for the safety of the mountains. Obeying the German edicts to evacuate. The soft encircling hills crouching to the north. From their flanks came the heat and growl of battle. Their hills had turned on them. To the south was devastation. Florence was wounded, as she had never been since the days of their ancestors.

Enrico and the brigade were fighting up there and Annabelle was here, an exile in the rubble. Tomorrow she would try to find her parents, her aunt and uncle. She had no news of them. Tomorrow, if the palazzo in Borgo Pinti was still standing, she would go home. Whatever home meant.

She was dressed as a woman. Well, a girl really, which was amusing, because she was certainly no girl any more. She wore a tan-coloured, pleated linen skirt and a white blouse with pearl buttons, and brown sandals with grosgrain ribbons threaded through them. It felt like a disguise. She was dressed in the clothes of a girl called Oriana, who had brought them to her this morning. And a new toothbrush – what joy. Oriana was a *staffetta*. She was only fourteen but her clothes fitted Annabelle perfectly – she had lost a great deal of weight. Oriana acted as a *vedetta*, a lookout, for their groups and distracted the *fascisti* and the Germans when they were moving arms or medicines or people. Better still than clothes, Oriana had brought her some notebooks. Annabelle never stopped scribbling. They were all keeping diaries. Writing was the only way they had of making any sense at all of their lives. They wrote perhaps to be forgiven later, to be exonerated. To use in their own defence. To accuse others. To speak the unspeakable. To say, 'we were alive'.

In a mound of rubble, a circle of sobbing, keening men and women. A child's body. The care that had been spent on that little body. The minute, handcrafted smocking of the tiny mauve sundress. The smooth perfect skin, gently bronzed by that summer's sun. One impossibly small sandal. The baby girl lay at a right angle to her mother, whose outstretched hand had failed to save the child. The mother's chest was open but the child's body seemed untouched. Yet there was no life in her. Annabelle's throat ached, the great stone rose up and choked her. Thank God she did not have a child. She would never have children. Herodotus wrote that in peace sons bury their fathers and in war fathers bury their sons. In this war, there would be no-one left to do the burying.

She had not been able to get to the house. The city was crawling with snipers and Borgo Pinti was completely blocked off. Her home was intact, though. She knew that much. Soon, soon, she would get there. News had come of the family. They were at Impruneta, but no-one had been able to contact them. The men had decided she must remain in Florence. Why, she argued. The communists are happy to have women fighting alongside them.

'You are needed here,' Enrico had insisted. 'Elsa will be here, you all have a job to do here. Look around you. You cannot leave all these people in this mess. And then there is the art you care so much about.'

Elsa. How she needed to see Elsa. They'd had a terse message from her – she was not in the city, she would be there soon. No more than that. At least she was alive. Then came the news that Achille had died in the bombing at Impruneta. Her father was dead. Her mother and *Zio* were alive.

Achille. With his upright posture and serious mien. His scent of cologne and aromatic pipe-tobacco, his carefully trimmed, drooping moustache. She had never seen her father dishevelled. Even when he emerged from prison, even stooped and without fingernails, he retained an elegance. She felt orphaned but she was not: she had a mother, brothers. She had forgotten she even had brothers in recent times. Australia was another planet. There were Australians fighting here and the New Zealanders were just across the river, but that strange continent at the bottom of the world was like a dream. Now her father was dead. Achille had always been kindly. Distant, but kind. A loving and conscientious father. She had never really known him. Did you ever know your parents? Her parents were not unhappy, but theirs was not a passionate union. Not like Elsa and *Zio*. Were her parents in love once? Where does love go? Surely, her love for Enrico could never change? Surely?

Enrico blamed their parents for Mussolini and she knew Achille blamed himself. But those were the times. That was his social caste. Her father was brave in the end. In many ways, he had always been brave, Annabelle had simply not noticed. He resigned from the university rather than join the Party. He sent the boys away to Australia. When he removed Annabelle from school, he said if their Jewish friends could not attend school, neither would she.

'The Count was a good man.' Anna Maria said.

It was clear she had no time for Elsa or *Zio* and thought Eleanora spoiled and indulged, but she had a lot of time for Achille, and a certain fondness for Annabelle and Enrico and especially Lorenzo. Not that she ever said as much. Anna Maria had worked for a Jewish family but had had to leave after the racial laws forbade the employment of Italian servants. Who could have known they were Jews, she told Annabelle. They were like this family. Non-believers, she meant.

Even they seemed surprised to find themselves called Jews. Hard to believe, she said, that in October they were still people just like her and Sesto and by November, they were 'Persons of the Jewish race'. Suddenly, Jews could not even go on holidays, or stay in a hotel, or go to school, or go to work, or own a radio or the house they had always lived in or the shop they had always owned. Hard to understand, she said, but still, Il Duce must know what he was doing … No?

The professor, her employer, had lost his job at the university long before, but then, even all those big books he had written on mathematics were thrown out of the university. Even out of the library. A real pity, she went on, not, mind you, that she had ever read the books, but important, they were, and she had liked to work for someone so famous. At least he had not killed himself like many of them, like that big publisher from Modena and him not the only one. They might have been godless but they paid her well and treated her well. Just like this family, she said again.

Yes, the Count was a fine man. Annabelle felt herself all over, looking for the right emotion but it would not come. Tears would be appropriate but she had none.

Annabelle had changed from Oriana's clothes back into her trousers and shirt, proudly donned the green kerchief and shouldered her gun for the march through the crowded streets of the liberated city. Together the multifarious brigades of the 'Arno' Division – communist, anarchist, monarchist, and *Giustizia e Libertà* – all marched beneath the banner of Pegasus, united for that brief moment. Screaming, weeping, cheering crowds lined every street as the Allied army rolled into the city. At times men almost fell under the tracks of a tank or the wheels of the motorcade as they tried to climb or were joyously pulled aboard the vehicles. Girls plied shy English corporals with flowers and wine and kisses. The soldiers responded coyly in some cases and with alacrity in others. Boys who had never been outside a working-class suburb of Liverpool, whose crooked teeth were a marvel to the Italian girls who wanted to kiss them, who had never drunk anything but a warm beer in their lives, swigged from raffia-covered bottles and swaggered about as victors. It was a new role entirely and they enjoyed it for the moment. Their officers eyed them severely and they knew it would not last.

This is our city. The voices speak of even more terrible massacres in the hills as the Germans retreat. In piazza Ognissanto partisans tied a Fascist to a wooden chair and executed him. There will be more. The Arno is low, putrid and sluggish, filled with stone and mud and masonry and bodies: human, animal and sculptural. The statues from the Ponte Santa Trinità are all at the bottom; the people and animals have floated to the surface but the muses of spring and summer and autumn and winter lie deep beneath the sludge. Our seasons are suspended here.

We walk through a city of dust and heat and flies and rubble. I walk upon shards of Limoges plates and twisted forks and spoons that were once Georgian silver. Shreds of Persian carpets drift from gargoyles to lie among leather-bound volumes saturated in blood. Children's toys. I pass girls with shaven heads and bloodied faces. Collaborators. What have we become? Nothing outside me is real. Only what I manage to squirrel away inside can survive. Bodies everywhere. 'The body that is sown is perishable.' Was that Saint Paul?

The few vehicles are mostly military trucks and vans and we are under a different, more benevolent form of occupation. The bridges are all gone except for the Ponte Vecchio, and it is almost impossible to cross that because they blew up all the buildings on either side of it. The air is rank with the stench of rotting corpses and it must be 40 degrees today. The Germans executed all the prisoners and mined the streets as they left, so there are bodies everywhere. Ferragosto. The dead and the living alike are covered in dust.

The first Allies to arrive were the South Africans, followed hot on their heels by the New Zealanders. Or the other way around – they were racing to be the first in, as if it were a school carnival. The New Zealanders are largely blacks; that caused a stir. The British arrived soon after. People rushed to greet them but the city was still full of German and fascist snipers. We were still fighting. We fought from street to street and corner to corner. We lost many of our brigade that day and many citizens were caught in between. To die just when they were liberated. I don't feel liberated. Dozens of people pick their way across the ruins of the Ponte alle Grazie like ants on the dorsal ridge of a dead dinosaur in the water. A girl totters across, wearing wedge-heeled strappy shoes as if she were going to a picnic. The city has been cut in half for days. The Allies have suspended publication of La Nazione, *so we have no news. From Fiesole we hear the cannon. In Piazza Signoria, a truck with a canvas canopy dispenses purified water to a snaking line of householders, all with their flask or jugs or bottles to be filled. The men in the truck are Palestinians. We have no running water or food or communication and only bicycles and horse-drawn vehicles, but we have gold. On the Ponte Vecchio, three British soldiers have climbed over the rubble to gaze into a window full of gold jewellery. Souvenir stands are already set up in the piazzas, offering the soldiers mementoes of their time in Florence. I feel I am going mad.*

The Allied Military Command might be a benevolent dictatorship, but to people used to another sort of dictatorship, it was a great relief. These *inglesi*, they said to each other at the water truck or in the bread queue, actually seemed to care about the city and its people. The English loved orders even more than the Germans, they marvelled. Orders, so many orders. Even issued a new currency, they had. Fancy that! One lira was a blue note, five lire was green, ten lire was brownish: all of them square. The one-hundred lire note was rectangular with a green centre, not that many saw those.

Proclamations in both languages papered city walls, again, but this time signed by generals or captains with English names.

Florence, 7 September 1944. Allied Military Government: Restrictions on the sale of alcoholic Liquors. Order #9. The sale within the Municipality of Florence, of wine or any other alcoholic liquor, in bottles to a member of the Allied Armed Forces is hereby forbidden except where the buyer is an authorised mess or club. Any person convicted by an Allied Military Court of contravening the order, will be punishable by fine or imprisonment or both.

People shook their heads and wondered what could possibly be wrong with selling wine, but then, these *inglesi* really could not hold their liquor, especially the grappa. Not that they became like the Germans, but still, it was embarrassing. And 'authorised mess'? What was a mess? Wasn't that a *pasticcio*? Disorder? Strange people! Then there were 'Hygiene Instructions for Barber Shops', and instructions for the Postal Service. Further, and more sinister:

Every Citizen of German, Austrian or Japanese nationality, must present themselves to the Central Police Headquarters no later than the 2nd of September to be newly registered.

Japanese? Here, in our city?

'Japanese? Never seen one in my life,' muttered the butcher, looking about as he wrapped the tiny ration of meat.

'Never seen so many signs in me life,' replied his customer, handing over his coupon.

Borgo Pinti was reopened, the rubble cleared by columns of dusty, emaciated men carrying sacks of debris on their shoulders. Snaking lines of stumbling workers like slaves, unbuilding the Pyramids. The soldiers helped where they could, but they were occupied with restoring essential services to the city and building their extraordinary Bailey bridges across the river, so the troops could move north. A partisan had managed to save the aqueduct, upriver, from the Germans, so the flow was restored to the fountains in the piazzas and people could draw water, gather together.

Crossing beneath the arch into via dell'Oriuolo, Annabelle slowed, gazing down the length of Borgo Pinti, half expecting to be stopped by guards. At the far end she could see into the parched grounds of the English Cemetery, with its earlier dead. Apart from the loose rubble, Borgo Pinti looked the same … but nothing was the same. At least their palazzo had not been commandeered by the Germans, though there had been a gun emplacement in the Gherardesca gardens.

Each step dragged. Finally, standing before the great *cancello* to the street, she half wanted to turn back. Peering through the grill to the central courtyard, she could see apricots hanging like Chinese lanterns from the espaliered trees on the far side of the garden. To the left of the gates was the tiny door through which her ancestors once sold wine directly to citizens in the street. She hooked her finger in the hole in the centre of the wooden hatch and pulled. It was stuck fast. With her knife, she worked around the edges of the hatch until it gave and yanked it outwards with a gravelly rasping. In the gritty recess towards the back, she felt the lacy iron key to the door inset into the studded *portone*.

The key turned at once in the lock and she found herself standing in the internal courtyard, the carriageway. She crossed the courtyard and picked six of the velvety fruit, warm from the heat of the wall. Most of them lay rotting on the ground, fruit flies buzzing over the gelatinous mess. In the centre of the courtyard, the ornate iron structure over the *pozzo* hung at a rakish angle, the bucket lying by the shattered side of the well. Part of the northern wing seemed to have been hit by something too – not a bomb, probably flying debris. The other three wings appeared untouched. The key to the side stairway was still in the niche of the brickwork under the great formal stairs. For the first time in her life, she used a key to enter her home.

Annabelle climbed the stairs in a silence thick with utter absence. The back door to their apartment on the *piano nobile* was unlocked, as always. The long corridor was in darkness, the internal shutters closed. A shiver rippled across her body. She was not afraid of ghosts – she *was* the ghost. Everything was exactly as it had been. How could everything be the same when everything had changed? She opened the door to her father's study and tried the light switch, but there was no electricity so she felt her way to the windows and opened the shutters. A gauze of dust softened the scene, took the edges off, gave it a dreamy quality. Made it bearable.

High in the shadowy reaches of the library shelves, the gilt lettering of the forbidden tomes gleamed. On the desk lay a copy of her father's favourite childhood book, *Cuore*. Heart. He had given her a copy and one to Enrico, but neither of them liked it very much. Dated, said Enrico. Her father had been disappointed. There was no bookmark in the volume. What, she wondered, had he been reading? What childhood comfort had he sought? She replaced it carefully in its own clean rectangle on the dusty desktop.

She drifted along the corridor to her bedroom. From the doorway, she surveyed the narrow walnut bed of the young girl who once lived there. There were dolls and teddy bears, cardboard boxes of treasures such as the stones and shells from her collecting phase, a small glass horse, an hourglass and a magnifying-glass, a kaleidoscope and other toys of childhood – little from recent years, apart from her books. She had barely inhabited the room. Reading at night was almost always done in the sitting room or study and almost always in the company of Enrico. Time in her own room was passed in the deep window seat as evening fell, with a book in her lap, imagining another life.

She backed out the door and wandered down the hall to the echoey bathroom. She would have a bath. What luxury. She had not had a bath since she went into the mountains. There was water again now, though it was obscene to waste it on a bath. She filled the high, cast-iron bathtub and tossed in an extravagant glop of Balenciaga bath-oil from her mother's table. Dropping her clothes onto the black and white tiles, she climbed in, without remembering to find a bath towel. Didn't Odysseus bathe off the blood of his enemies in a gleaming marble bathtub? Or was that Nestor? With the shortage of water, the rusty colour and no heating, it was hardly luxury but it felt like the distilled essence of joy. She ate one of the apricots and lay back, the iron cold on her spine. She was *bathing*, in the old, sensual, languorous, almost forgotten sense of the word. There was no soap. She scrubbed at her feet with a loofah sponge until they were red, then she scrubbed her whole body with it, more gently.

Dust from the loofah floated on the water with her own accumulated grime. With a shaggy wooden nailbrush, she scrubbed and rubbed until her fingernails and toenails were surgically clean. She wanted to scrub forever. Could her soul be scrubbed? She marvelled she was not afraid, alone in the immensity of the deserted palazzo. There was nothing to be afraid of anymore.

Finally, she felt clean – truly clean, for the first time in five months. Could it only be five months? She stepped out of the bath, and dripping naked, retraced her steps to her room, leaving a smudgy trail of wet footprints in the dust. Opening her wardrobe, she surveyed the clothes, the stuff of childhood. She returned to the bathroom to collect the apricots then followed the hall to her mother's room. The empty house breathed in and out. This far from the streets, all sound was muffled. She halted at the door, surveying the beautiful room. It was only the second time she had been in this room alone. She liked the deliciously shivery feel of intrusion. Through the almost closed shutters the high summer sun scoured golden tracks across the boards and fairy dust motes danced.

She opened her mother's tallest wardrobe and fingered ball gowns of shot satin and bias-cut silk. Velvet, purple as the night; pond-green water-marked satin; black jet-beaded organza; filmy cream lace. She slid one from its embroidered hanger and shrugged it over her head. Deep emerald-green satin, cut on the bias, poured down her body like dark water, falling cold and silky against the skin of her thighs. She turned to the mirror and ran her hands over her body, over the cool material. On her mother it would have swept the floor but it barely came to Annabelle's ankles. To the left of the wardrobe, a mahogany chest of drawers held lacy underwear in cream, ecru, white – brassieres with satin straps and cups stitched in a circular pattern. She considered trying one on, but she had never worn one and could not see the sense of them. Moreover, the cups would be much too big. Another wardrobe held racks of shoes in jewel colours of suede, or silk-covered, dyed to match a particular frock. She chose a pair of strappy high heels in the exact shade of her dress. No, she looked silly – too tall by far and teetering forward. High heels were not for her. Anyway, her mother's feet were too small. She would buy some flat shoes in black velvet, like those she had once seen on Elsa.

From the dressing table with its mirrors that turned her into triplets, she chose a red, red lipstick, in a gilt case with a mirror the size of a mouth inside the lid. She drew her mouth, expecting to feel like a clown and instead she saw a strange woman who might be beautiful. It shocked her.

Being dressed as a man for so long had changed her, given her a feeling of power. To put on men's clothes and go to war – so different from the servant role her mother and other women accepted so readily. Except Elsa. She was reluctant to abandon her trousers and boots, reluctant to hand back the power they conferred. Surely, women would never go back to the old ways now. Surely? She thought of Heloise with a shudder; she wore men's clothing to get into the university, to get the education forbidden to women, but in the end she entered a convent. Perhaps not the best example. Annabelle had gone from a dowdy adolescent in wartime drear to a fighting soldier – from egg to butterfly, without ever passing through the chrysalis stage, the 'coming out' as their English relatives called it. She had never been *out*.

Holding the hem of the ball gown in one hand, thinking of Cinderella, she floated barefoot back down the hall to her father's study. Her *dead* father. Could that be true? She tested the word in her mind but it had lost its currency. Her father was dead. Of a heart attack, of all things. During the shelling. Saddened hearts, it seemed, often turned and attacked their owners these days. The scent of his tobacco lingered on the air with the leather smell of his books. Gone. How could he simply not be there? How many people were asking themselves that now? A deep shudder rolled over her and she only just fended off panic. She grasped a dusty, nearly full bottle of grappa from the drinks tray and swirled out of the study, slamming the door behind her. It echoed like gunshot.

In the doorway to her mother's room she paused, took a deep swig from the bottle and surveyed the gaping wardrobe. If she climbed inside, would she find herself in Narnia? Perhaps purple velvet would suit her? She stepped out of the satin and left it, a puddle of emerald on the floor. The purple was an off-the-shoulder gown – perhaps one needed a bigger bosom to do it justice. Strange word, bosom. She turned sideways, hands on hips, shrugged and let it drop, took another swig and selected the cream lace. No, too virginal. She giggled. She let it slither to the floor and took another glug from the bottle. She was beginning to see what the men saw in this stuff. It certainly took the edge off things. When had her mother worn all these dresses? She had little memory of seeing her in ball gowns.

Vague scenes flashed by, not memories, more traces of perfume and face powder as her mother bent to kiss her goodnight – her parents on their way out for the evening. Must have been a long time ago. Perhaps Eleanora was beautiful then. Annabelle had no memory of that either. She was beautiful in the photographs in the study, and in the large oil portrait hanging in the corridor with all the other ancestors. Between slugs of grappa, she counted up on her fingers – her mother must be … forty-seven. Was that right? It was getting harder to count the fingers. Was forty-seven old? Everyone seemed old. Giacomo was forty-seven and he was dead. Papà was forty-eight and he was dead. Most people were dead. Was Enrico dead by now? She'd had no news since the brigade moved up towards Bologna. Through the tall windows, the last yolky light of the setting sun shimmered on the sea of ball gowns at her feet.

Naked, she kicked away from the tangle of garments. In the mirrors, she noticed the red lipstick was smeared. 'Well, that's no good,' she said, and sat at the dressing table before the box of cosmetics. She placed the grappa very carefully on the dressing table. *Oops*, just caught it as it tottered. Pushed it further back. To the side, was the petit point box holding her mother's jewellery – the paste stuff. The real things had been stored away long ago. The pretend jewels were nicer anyway – more extravagant, more colourful. Another sip. She tried to clasp a heavy necklace but fumbled the catch and let it fall. 'She left the web she left the loom …' *Hmmm, used to know that by heart.* She bit into another of the apricots and the juice spilled down her chin and over her breasts. Another sip of grappa went very well with the fruit. She ate another, sucking on it and dribbling the juice deliberately. It ran down into her navel. *So greedy!* Gluttony. What circle of the Inferno did the gluttons go to? Wasn't gluttony one of the seven deadly sins? Were there seven? She should remember these things. She wished she could remember, so she could commit them all, all seven, now, before she too died. *How could that bottle be nearly empty?* She selected another lipstick from the box. 'Vermilion, I would call that,' she said aloud. Vermilion. What a beautiful word. She carefully applied the lipstick but it was more difficult than before. It did not look right. 'Oh, who cares,' she said, more loudly than before. And drew a gigantic mouth over her own, a mouth so ... voracious – another wonderful word. Voracious. That was what she was. She enlarged her mouth still further and then, slowly, slowly, squeezed the last apricot over her breasts, over her stomach, letting the sweet, sticky juice dribble through her pubic hair until it scorched its way between the lips of her vulva. Dropping the seed to the rug, she squashed the last of the fleshy fruit until it spurted between her fingers. With both hands, she massaged the almondy perfumed pulp over her breasts and stomach in dreamy swirls, then slower, slower, traced the pathway of the juice lower, lower. Arching her back, she slid to the floor, convulsed by wracking sobs and gasps and a crashing, rolling, deafening deluge.

For long minutes, she lay spent, then tugged the tapestry cushion from the chair and pulled it beneath her head. She dragged the velvet gown across her sticky body, curled into a soft, purple ball and closed her eyes. Tomorrow, tomorrow she would give up smoking.

'Beware of Snipers.' The worst poster of all, on every street corner. The hidden killers found their mark amongst the British soldiers, but the citizens too. A small boy in a cloth cap, carrying a cello nearly as big as himself, stumbled and tripped over the rubble, and fell. The cello on top of him. Why! Why! Why would they shoot him? Annabelle wanted to scream. She was sick at heart. The sight of an elderly couple, peering anxiously around a corner before crossing the street to the fountain, was sickening. These people were supposedly free of the Germans but every day, *i cecchini*, the Republican snipers, picked them off in sheer vengeance. In the vicious retribution of defeat.

Annabelle was busy, very busy. It was true she was needed here. They were all needed here. Elsa and *Zio* had returned to the city, taken up residence above her, filled the house again. But it could not be filled, not really. Eleanora remained at Impruneta for the time being. The villa there was intact and the *contadini* were working the farm as best they could, in the light of the mines and the mortar damage and the dead animals. It was for the best, Elsa said, as Eleanora was in no condition to return to the city.

Achille was buried in the family cemetery in the village and Eleanora did not want to leave him. She wanted to know why Annabelle did not come. Annabelle did not have an answer for her. Her mother was in the care of Anna Maria and Sesto, Elsa assured her, adding, 'Not that they are much use, but at least she is not alone. She will be all right for now.' They all had other things on their mind, in a city full of widows.

Before the brigade left without her, Annabelle and Enrico had been sent on reconnaissance of many of the buildings that had been occupied by the Germans. They were to prepare reports on the state and condition of the public buildings for the Allied minesweepers and bomb-disposal teams as they prepared for occupation by the victors. The Hotel Baglioni was to become a club for the NZ soldiers. She liked those laconic southerners who said *sex* when they meant *six*.

From the rooftop of the Hotel Excelsior, the damage was sickening. The bombed bridges lay in the silt, a series of islands of debris already connected by planks and crates and bits of iron, as people picked their way from island to island. Many of the nearly five thousand people who had sheltered in the Palazzo Pitti had come from the northern bank and they were desperate to get back. The task of feeding and caring for the limitless numbers of homeless was overwhelming, but with a degree of order that put the Germans to shame, the British had set up systems for everything. The Boboli gardens were now filled with open mass graves and bodies awaiting burial. Palazzo Pitti became a refugee centre for the Red Cross, with desks set up for alms to the indigent. Throughout the ruins, young boys wearing ammunition belts swaggered about in testosterone-fuelled excitement. Many were too young to have fought, except at the very last moment in the city. Now they were at a loose end – no school, no job, no home – no role. They were the next problem to solve.

The city was wounded, but the wounds were not mortal. Although Fiesole was still the site of a German artillery base, they did not bomb the city. The towers of the Bargello and the Badia still reached for the sky, the belltower of Palazzo Vecchio still pointed an admonishing finger upwards and the tremendous cupola of the Duomo still lorded it over the rest of the city, a crouching Sphinx.

In a room of the Excelsior Hotel, on top of the great desk used by Pavolini, Annabelle and Enrico made love. Taking back their town, he called it. And to think, he added, it was originally a church dedicated to the Virgin Mary.

Voltagabbana – turncoat. A new word was born the day after the liberation. Or perhaps an old word resurrected. In a chocolate shop in via Cavour, two girls who had sold boxes of chocolates to the Germans cowered all night as reprisals raged. Outside their window, a crowd watched as men dragged a woman by the hair. *Puttana, troia*, slut, they shouted. They spat upon her for having gone dancing with a German officer. Much of the spittle came from the mouths of good citizens who had been ardent fascists the day before. Many coats had been turned inside out overnight. Many wore red scarves now, who last week had worn black shirts. Hardly a day passed without the sound of running, shouting, kicking, punching groups of 'partisans' who dragged men to a piazza and shot them, leaving the bodies in a tangled heap. Impossible to tell whether the dead had been fascists or whether their executioners had been partisans. Vengeance, retribution, reprisal, *vendetta* – many words for it, but not justice. To Annabelle, justice seemed far off, but the CTLN was working hard to establish order. You had to believe. If you could not believe, it was all for nothing.

Some citizens were stronger than others. Some shouldered the task and got on with it; many were cheerful in the face of privation, many were not. Some had lost too much, and did not know how to find their way back. Everyone had their limit. Gerhard Wolf suffered a nervous breakdown; the German Consul had given everything, his loss was too great to sustain and the toll on his health too high. Since the German invasion, his position had become intolerable, but still he went on. He helped to save the Ponte Vecchio, and when the Americans they called the Monuments Men arrived to work on the retrieval of the art treasures, he helped them too. Many Florentine Jews owed their lives to him and to Cardinal della Costa. The art was important but the people were more important. The strain of the betrayal of his Fatherland, the pain of knowing what that country had become, the daily anxiety and fear for himself and for those about him, eventually overwhelmed him.

Annabelle was saddened by the Consul's illness. He would recover though, and he was not alone. For many, the accumulated pain drove them over that thin line. So many lines. From childhood, she had a fascination with the edges of things. Borders, intersecting lines where two things meet and one thing becomes another. The sharp line where houses finish and the countryside begins. *Dove va finire la strada*. The point on the horizon where the road disappears over the edge of the world. How is it possible that life or death depends upon an imaginary line: the Gothic Line.

Florence itself was a border, a line between the free and the unfree. The war was over for those south of it, and yet only a few kilometres to the north the war went on. Every day people died, and Bologna got no closer. On one side of an imaginary line, people were saved. On the other side, they were still condemned to die. If you were Jewish in Rome, you were saved that day when the Allies arrived, but if your relatives lived in Florence or Bologna or Ferrara they were in grave peril.

Now in Florence the Jews who were left gathered in via delle Oche to give thanks for being spared by the arrival of the South Africans and the improbable, smiling, noisy New Zealanders who were very, very dusky. Black! Oh well, they said philosophically. Oh well! But still, their families, above that line called The Front, were being deported, to die in German camps. They could not be philosophical about that. No wonder people's minds were at risk.

It was ridiculous to worry about back pain in the face of the suffering all about her, but Annabelle's back was much worse. She was finding it difficult to adapt to the new phase of the war. They all were, in their different ways. She was not the girl who picked up a gun so long before. It was for Enrico she had done it, but now there were more important considerations. Enrico, if he were still alive, was fighting somewhere up near Bologna. Roberto, at heart a regular army officer, joined the army again to fight alongside the Allies. Many of the prisoners of war did too, but some stayed on to fight in the brigades. Lorenzo had disappeared as if he had never been. Elsa was taking more and more risks. Elisa and Oriana continued to work as *staffette*.

On the street each day, Annabelle regarded her city like a neighbour she once knew but no longer recognised. She left as a child and returned as a killer. To a city full of killers.

CHAPTER 19

Lake Garda 1944

Every dawn has its heart injured

In the frigid water, her nipples strained against the clammy cotton swimsuit. As she pulled herself up the slimy iron ladder, Clara savoured the surreptitious glances of the two bodyguards treading water around the swimming platform. She stood on the last rung and arched her spine, her breasts pointing to the sky, threw back her head and let the sun warm her face as the water streamed from her hair. *Che noia!* The boredom of it all! Worse than Easter Mass. She did not really enjoy swimming in the lake. The lakes were miserable. Even now, almost August, the water was gloomy, deep, inky. Who knew what was down there. It was still too cold, the water, and with no salt, you had to work too hard at staying afloat. She much preferred the warm blue salty waters of the Adriatic and the flat sands of Rimini or Riccione or some such seaside playground.

She stretched out on her back on the hot, splintery timber of the platform, letting the sun soak into her pores. Loosening the straps of her top, she shrugged them down over her shoulders so she would not get white marks, taking care not to let her breasts actually show. She fingered the clasps on her heavy gold earrings; she probably should not have worn them in the water. Ben would be angry if they came off. High above her in the pale chiffon sky, a flock of birds wheeled and shot off in an arrow to the south. Ducks perhaps. She was not good at birds. The lake was always full of duck poo so they must be ducks.

The bodyguards circled the platform, doing laps now. They'll be cold, she thought idly. It always seemed cold here in the north. Really, she was not a northern person. Northerners were all so cool, so closed, so restrained. Ben hated it too, though he was a northerner of sorts, but he was different. She wished he would get back. He was not much fun these days but it was worse with him away. There was nothing to do. Trapped in the bosom of her family – Ben's family too for that matter. Ben joked that the Mussolinis and the Petaccis were like the Montagues and Capulets. At least *her* family did not hate her, want her dead. Her mother was fractious, her father was bored, underfoot all the time. Mimi pined for the bright lights and Marcello, well, Marc was constantly engaged in some activity or other, bound to land him in trouble again. This was how it must have been, in exile, *al confino*.

With a deep sigh, she rose and arced gracefully into the lake, heading for shore in long strokes. Ben should be back from Germany tomorrow, his birthday.

Ben is back but he is even more worried than before his visit. Hitler is mad. Ben says the Führer has lost his mind.

Clara placed her diary open beside her on the sofa and leaned back, surveying the tiny script crawling across the page. Like a hairy caterpillar, Marc said, of her writing. He should talk! She almost put the end of the onyx pen in her mouth but remembered just in time. A childish habit she was trying to break. What to make of Ben's visit to the Wolf's Lair? What did it mean for them?

Hitler had, it seemed, survived an attempted assassination.

'Now he too has betrayers. We no longer have a monopoly on treachery,' said Ben.

He sounded a little pleased. It seemed to have turned Hitler's mind. At first Ben agreed with him that it was an augury, a miracle, that he had survived and therefore that his cause was just and he would prevail. Ben even thought it augured well for him too, as he would have been there himself but for a delay in train travel. He always found these trips to Germany a trial but he felt he had to go to counteract the defeatism he saw everywhere about him. She could not tell with Ben anymore. One day he was all confidence and determination, the next he was planning his last stand. Now, after only a few days back, he was again plunged into misery and depression.

'Hitler cannot win. He swears there will be no retreat, no surrender, but,' said Ben, 'he cannot see clearly anymore. The bomb attempt has turned his mind.'

He had found the Führer old, infirm and hysterical, the whole of his left side shaking uncontrollably. He was never seen in public or heard on the radio anymore. The problem, said Ben, was that Hitler had assumed absolute control and no-one in his circle had any authority at all. He had become a megalomaniac.

'No-one man can run everything, without rest, without sleep. But then, perhaps the Germans can win, they say they have a new deadly secret weapon.' His tone said he was not convinced.

'Tell me,' she said. 'What was the meeting like?'

'The meeting – well, it certainly was not impressive. Hitler looked terrible, yellow and sick. He was sitting on a fruit box and I had only a wobbly stool. Imagine! It has come to this. I was so upset, I drank a cognac!' He shuddered. 'Vittorio, the idiot, stuffed his face with cakes and biscuits but at least he did not make a fool of himself.'

Clara restrained a snort. Ben's eldest son was a moron with the manners of a pig. Everyone loathed him. Why Ben put up with him she could not fathom, but Ben was, after all, a family man. He loved his children. All his children. Even after all this time, he still wept at the photo of Bruno on his desk. Bruno's death nearly killed him. Then recently, when he thought Romano had gone missing in the lake, he became a raving madman. Then there was little Anna Maria, *poverina*, who was not normal and he loved her tenderly.

The greatest pain and suffering of all was that Edda had never spoken to him again since he had her husband executed. The Countess Ciano resembled her father in temper and passions – they had shouted and argued and Edda had screamed and wept, the usual way. Edda thought Clara had been in on it too but nothing could have been more wrong. If they only knew how she tried to talk Ben out of it; no-one is ever grateful! It was all Pavolini's doing. Clara *had* tried at first to dissuade Ben, but really, Ciano was a traitor and he did deserve to die, to be made an example of. They both knew that Ciano's death was essential to keep Hitler on their side. Hitler! Ten years ago, he came to Italy like a provincial politician who did not even know what clothes to wear. He had never even been out of Germany before – and now he was telling Ben what to do as if he owned the world.

Ben had tried and tried to make up with Edda, but she was implacable. Edda had always been his favourite. His heart was broken. He wished later he had not agreed to Ciano's execution, but what could he do?

'From that morning I began to die,' he told her.

It was true. He had not been the same since January. He was a little afraid too – well, not afraid, Ben was never afraid, but worried, let us say worried. Worried in case Edda really did hand over the Count's diaries to the Allies. She had tried to barter them, but thankfully that did not work. Diaries were becoming the new currency. God knows the old one was not worth much. Clara eyed her own diary beside her. When Ben had asked Edda what he could do to make it up to her, she said he should kill himself. Edda was a very hard-hearted woman. To not even speak of that *troia* Rachele, who was no support at all and always took the side of Edda. Wasn't it always rumoured Edda was not even her real daughter!

Poor Ben, he was assailed on every side. He was so thin and he had begun to slouch. He once loved to sit tall, astride a stallion, but now he rode his bicycle like an old person. The doctor prescribed red meat but Ben refused to eat more of anything than the official ration. He would not, he swore, eat more food than any other hungry Italian.

Then there was Elena ... Clara heaved a deep sigh. Elena was no fool and Ben relied on her more and more. 'The eyes of Mussolini', as she had heard Elena referred to. The eyes of Mussolini indeed! It was true Elena was spying for him, everyone knew it. He admitted it. When Clara had offered to do that years ago, he had been amused. She must deal with Elena, she could not afford to lose influence in Ben's life. Their life.

In Rome Clara was invisible – *l'eminenza grigia*, Marc called her. People came to her to intercede with Ben on their behalf and Ben listened to her. She had her finger on the pulse and she had a certain respect. Now, though, especially since the dreadful things all the papers published about her while Ben was a prisoner – when they thought he was not coming back and she was defenceless – now, she was only too visible and their lives here were always under scrutiny. The Germans kept him under close surveillance and fewer were interested in an alliance with her – she had to work ceaselessly to maintain her networks and keep abreast of what was going on. She was caught between Ben's family gang on one side and Pavolini's fascists on the other; they all hated her and they all wanted her dead. Twice now they had tried to have her murdered.

Her family were relentless in machinating on their own account and were at her constantly to get Ben to do this or that for them. The wider circle of in-laws and relatives, all encamped in a series of villas around her, drove her mad with requests. Her mother had a new complaint to carry to him every day. Her father appeared to still have a conduit to the Vatican, but would not discuss it. Even Marc had some sort of secret going on with Ben. Churchill, he replied in a dark voice, with a finger to the side of his nose and a silly conspiratorial wink when she asked him what it was all about. Churchill indeed! It was true Mr Churchill had once been a great admirer of Ben – a Roman genius, he called him, but she could not imagine Marc having anything to do with the formidable British Prime Minister. Sometimes Marc got ideas above himself. That had always been his problem – a bit of a dreamer. Always schemes and plots and mysteries, with Marc. The English were nothing but 'umbrella-carriers', according to Ben, but he thought very highly of Mr Churchill. He had no respect for the American President – a cripple, he said. How can a leader claim respect when he has to be carried to the lavatory! The English were our enemies, but Mr Churchill, now there was a man!

Clara rose and rang for tea. Ben would not be long but she could always have a fresh pot made when he arrived. Should she change, she wondered. She wandered to the mirror, unpinned her hair, turned this way and that and then decided no, it was better up. She unbuttoned the top of her broderie anglaise blouse and turned the collar up to deepen the effect of her cleavage. Not that there was much likelihood of him wanting to make love, but still, it was as well to go through the motions. She did have a yellowing bite mark on her shoulder but really, it had not been much of an event. Ben could still be seduced by all those stupid women who threw themselves at him. Trying to reassure himself, or just habit. Sex and politics – the two things had become inextricable for her and Ben. Clara wondered if she truly missed sex. Perhaps she was never really very interested in sex, for its own sake, that was. Certainly when she was married to Riccardo it had not been anything to go on about. Violence, yes – he had once pushed her off a train at the station – but not much pleasure. In many ways, it was easier without the tumult and without the injuries too, for that matter. It was sad, though, that Ben no longer wanted her in the old, wild, violent way. She, and only she, could give him that, and he knew it and it held him to her, even when he tried to leave her. At sixty-one he was not the same man and did not have the same drive and energy. It was not, he assured her, that he did not love her or that he did not find her desirable. He did still love to have her dress him. He did still, occasionally, call her 'my dear little Walewska'. It was just that passion no longer burned as fiercely in him.

'I sometimes think my flesh is in hibernation,' he told her.

'But my youth still burns brightly for you,' she replied. 'How often have you told me that orgasm is good for you, sharpens your thoughts?'

He suggested she should masturbate if she wanted more sex, but she was not good at that – perhaps he was right and she had a low libido. If Ben was right when he told her years ago that 'genius lies in the genitals', then there was not much genius around anymore. She was rushed by a wave of nostalgia and melancholy, a yearning for the old days when they were happy and the world was theirs. Her eyes filled with tears and she rushed to her handbag for a handkerchief before her mascara ran. Ben must not see her like this. She cried too easily these days and it got on his nerves. Even if they rarely made love, he did still love her. He did still need her. She could not afford to have him tire of her – for his sake and for hers. Neither had another life now. It was her job to ensure it went well and she would!

At the crunch of Ben's car on the gravel, she quickly checked the mirror again to be sure mascara had not run onto her white blouse. She straightened her linen shorts, brushing at the creases, and adjusted the navy belt firmly. She took two steps then turned back, closed the diary and put it away in the drawer. With a wide smile of welcome, Clara strode out onto the terrace.

Florence 1944

The hunting season

'Wait for me. I will be with you after the war.' Enrico's last words to her. He had leaned down and placed his lips gently on hers, no more than a touch. With his eyelashes he brushed the tip of her nose, the butterfly kiss they used as children. He removed his glasses and held her eyes with his own for long moments.

'We *can* win this war!'

Annabelle was not so convinced. At least the heat had broken and with it, disease and illness diminished. They had water, gas and electricity. The rubble slowly receded and people were gradually re-housed. Inch by inch the city was restored. Bodies in the street were less common.

Qui, Radio Firenze – This is Radio Firenze – with those welcome words the first broadcast went over the airwaves on the twentieth of September. 'This is the voice of liberated Florence.' It was hard not to be moved and people gathered about radios, weeping at the sound. 'To all our listeners, *Buon giorno*. Today, Wednesday the twentieth of September, here is today's program.' A semblance of normalcy.

Annabelle divided her time between work with Siviero and work in the hospital, which was staffed by Allied soldiers and anyone who could spare the time. Local doctors too old to work, worked all day and all night, glad to be alive to help. It overflowed with the ill, the wounded, the dying and the dead, from the city and from the fighting. There were more every day as fighters were carried down from the mountains, often on the backs of mules, or stretchers improvised from weapons and branches. Here was something Annabelle could believe in. She no longer chafed to be on the front line. Tired of killing, she was grateful to be saving lives, improving lives.

In many ways, it was just as well Enrico was out of reach. For long stretches she was able to resolutely turn her mind away from what was happening to him. She had her hands full in the shattered city. Her mother had returned, old, vague, without volition. Her only role – good wife and housekeeper – torn away from her. She pinned her hair up each day in a crooked knot on top of her head, but that was as far as her grooming went. Not only did she no longer bear any resemblance to the portraits; she did not even look like the woman wringing her hands the day of Enrico's departure.

'And you,' she said accusingly to Annabelle, 'you did not even say goodbye.'

Annabelle shrugged and patted her mother's shoulder. She could not explain. She did not have the energy. There did not seem to be enough pity to go around these days. It was usual to find her mother seated at the long dining table, pages of newspaper spread out over one end, all the silver arranged about her, rhythmically polishing each object, rubbing and buffing the lustrous spoons and teapots as if hoping a genie would emerge and put it all right. They must have had the cleanest silver in Italy.

Anna Maria and Sesto had returned too. *Zio* Francesco gave them the task of keeping the whole palazzo in some sort of order. A young girl with eyes like a stunned faun, whose whole family had died in the bombing, came in each day to help them. Slovenly, Anna Maria called her.

In the rooms of the ground floor, Annabelle helped to set up a centre for refugees. There were thirty of them: seven families crowded into the space of the courtyard, workshops and carriage-house. One was Jewish. Another, a girl of sixteen and her four much younger brothers, had walked down from a mountain valley after the rest of the family was killed in a bombing. They had no shoes, only wooden *zoccoli*, with callouses on their feet as thick as the soles of the shoes they had never worn. Others came from the bombed area near the station. They were a disparate lot and they were not getting on with each other. None of them was very appealing. It worried Annabelle that she could think such things. Eleanora seemed confused by their presence. She shook her head, tut-tutting, 'Your father will not like all that confusion.' They were not like her *contadini*, she muttered. What were they doing there? They were not familiar to her at all. Nothing was the same. Annabelle was unsure whether Eleanora understood that Achille was dead. She did not enquire.

Indeed nothing was the same. Anna Maria was no longer ready for a chat in the kitchen. Sesto hardly appeared. Annabelle barely noticed what went on in the house anyway and did not care. Meals somehow appeared, made of whatever could be bought with their coupons and whatever could be produced on the farm, as the mines were slowly cleared. Last week one of the children of the *contadini* stood on a mine and lost a leg. How could you care about meals or whether the house was clean? Anna Maria turned to her for whatever orders were needed, as they all knew Eleanora was in another world and, Anna Maria sniffed, 'The *Signora* Elsa is above such practical matters.' 'Her Ladyship', as Annabelle knew the old woman called Elsa behind her back, was not interested in the running of the household.

Elsa was a wraith, materialising and receding at all hours and in all weather, her mass of hair tied into a scarf. She was more and more deeply engaged with the fighting. Annabelle saw much less of her – her own work in the city exhausted her and she dropped into bed, often fully clothed, falling, as Dante said, *come un corpo morto cadde*. She was sick at the thought of the dangers Elsa ran, certain she was taking on ever more perilous assignments behind enemy lines. Elsa had seen Enrico though. That was something. For the time being, he was alive and he was well. He had a jeep given to them by the Allies – not that a jeep was of any use in the vertiginous valleys of the Emilia-Romagna, but it was very useful in moving men and weapons up from the area around Florence.

Autumn and the hunting season was open, so at least they were not too short of food. *Funghi, tartufi, castagne and fichi.* Porcini, truffles, chestnuts and figs, wild boar and rabbits and birds. It sounded like a feast, but there was not enough to go around. Even the prolific chestnuts were rationed. The people of the mountains had their own patches of forest, which they guarded jealously. The hunt for *cinghiale*, the wild boar, was never so hotly contested. For the county folk it was all familiar, but for many of the displaced, town-bred people who had not hunted or foraged for *funghi*, it was fraught with danger, and many accidental deaths occurred by ingesting poisonous mushrooms or by careless shots.

The wild boar and birds had less to fear than the humans. The fighting season, the Allies called it, as if it were a game. The massacre season. The Germans and the fascists in retreat were in disarray: exhausted, spiteful, vengeful, pitiless. The partisans, whom Kesselring once regarded as undisciplined guerrilla rabble, were now a real threat, and his edict to spare no-one was officially enacted. The hunting season opened on partisans and civilians alike.

Enrico was with the *Brigata Stella Rossa* on Monte Sole. The Red Star Brigade was autonomous, one of the unaligned brigades like their own. A crack fighting unit, it had a large contingent of experienced British soldiers, escapees from a nearby concentration camp. The British officially recognised it and supported it with supply-drops. Its leader was *Lupo*, Mario Musolesi, anti-fascist, conscripted into the army. After the eighth of September he deserted and formed his own brigade to fight for Bologna. They all knew *Lupo*. He did not look like a wolf, reported Elsa. With his thick curls and full lips, he was more like a cinema actor, but his cunning and judgement were equal to any wolf. Annabelle did not know whether to be relieved or worried at the daring and exploits of this already legendary figure, who had survived several assassination attempts. From him, Elsa reported, Enrico had learned to deal with spies summarily. Fascist spies and infiltrators were now a serious problem, and the partisans too had issued their own edict. No mercy for spies, no holds barred. *Lupo* had a lot of friends, but he also had a lot of enemies. Annabelle and Enrico and their brigade were used to being much more anonymous. The war had entered a new phase.

The contrast between the work in the city and what was happening to the north was an unbearably sharp line. Everyone had expected the momentum to continue, the liberation to drive on inexorably, but it bogged down long before the Allies reached Bologna. Annabelle's nineteenth birthday came and went. As heavy banks of October fog rolled in, the Germans sensed fatigue in the Allied progress and dug in. Walter Reder's name carried evermore dread. Elsa reported a rocky mountain pathway lined with the hanging bodies of eleven partisans. Not, she reassured, from the *Stella Rossa*. There was no reassurance.

Annabelle tried to get through each day at the hospital, where the battle to save lives inched forward. At home *Zio* Francesco was almost invisible, Anna Maria ever more mulish, her mother polished silver with increasing zeal, Elsa was absent most of the time and the refugees squabbled amongst themselves. At the museum, Giorgio Castelfranco had returned, and a large team coordinated by him and Rodolfo Siviero worked on an inventory of the missing works of art. There was comfort in the compiling of lists and inventories and notes on the artworks. She *did* think it important. Under the oversight of the Director of the Uffizi, Giovanni Poggi, and the Monuments officer, Keller, the painstaking project was fascinating, somewhere progress could be counted. It was easy to become caught up in it. The art of Florence stood for something larger and grander than the daily scrabble to stay alive. Something older, enduring, permanent, something for the past and the future, Annabelle told herself.

Much of the art once stored at Monte Cassino and many other towns and cities had already been stolen and transferred to Germany. A separate team was working on that. Annabelle travelled to the castle of Montegufoni with the team sent to inspect and catalogue the works stored there. The Monuments team had been there for ages. The beautiful home of the Sitwells was a higgledy-piggledy mess of priceless art. Masaccio, Botticelli, Ghirlandaio, Giotto, Fra Angelico, Donatello, Michelangelo – every name she had ever read in any book of Florentine art was there. Paintings, altar-pieces and statues that had made little impression on Annabelle in their previous homes now held her mesmerised.

She stood before the great Botticelli painting of *Primavera*, the Venus she had always regarded as chubby, pasty and insipid. This would be the lover whose charms besotted Botticelli. His patron, Cosimo, had him locked in his rooms so that he would finish the commissioned works but Botticelli, or 'Little Barrel', climbed out a window to go to her anyway. Was that the nun he later ran away with? Or was that story about his teacher, Filippo Lippi? Renaissance art was too dense for her. Enrico would know. His face hovered for a moment and swirled away. The painting, she did know, only survived Botticelli's frenzy of repentance when he tossed all his 'profane' works onto the Bonfires of the Vanities of Friar Savonarola, because it was in the secret collection of a bishop or a cardinal. That the hatchet-faced friar later died on one of those bonfires in exactly the same spot, seemed like poetic justice to her. People do eventually tire of despots, she thought.

The work with the Monuments team was not enough to distract from the news to the north. In Bologna homes stood abandoned, stark evidence of dispossessed Jews, their goods confiscated, the rooms empty, the people vanished. By now, it was clear they would be annihilated. They were not alone. Torture of captured partisans or those who harboured them reached new levels of horror. The mass murder of civilians began. The worst of the stories were coming from the villages on the slopes of Monte Sole. Annabelle no longer slept. Her vow to give up cigarettes lasted only as long as she had none. She renounced grappa, but wine took its place, not that there was nearly enough wine or cigarettes. She paced and smoked and fretted, impotent and desperate.

When the news came it was worse than any of them could have imagined, worse than the nightmares, worse than anything Dante ever described. Marzabotto. A name they had never heard. In a village called Creda, another unknown spot on the map, the SS surrounded a group of partisan at dawn, in a *stalla*. The ninety-odd occupants of the village – the children, the women, the elderly – were stripped of their few possessions and herded into the barn with the *ribelli*. The SS soldiers strafed them with machine guns, threw hand grenades into the barn, lit incendiary bombs and threw those in, set fire to the homes and left the whole lot to burn. They continued through the forest and up the mountain tracks, slaughtering as they went. Over three days, the Waffen-SS massacred the residents of villages all over the mountain, leaving fires pouring columns of smoke into the sky by day, the night-sky lit with orange flares as if comets had dropped to earth. The SS soldiers slogged on with images of jerking limbs aflame, the stench of incinerated flesh heavy on the air and on their uniforms and on their minds. A young captain shot himself. Most simply drank more of the alcohol issued in copious quantities. They butchered almost two thousand people in only a few days. It went on and on – as the murder squads moved north, they mined the villages and pathways so relatives searching for the bodies of their families would die too.

'We have reached a new level of evil,' said Annabelle.

'No,' replied Gino, a veteran of Africa. 'I wish it were so but it is not. We too, we have done these things. Even the Allies gunned down prisoners in groups in the south last year.' He was inexorable. 'We all have this on our consciences.'

There were no good stories, no shelter.

Enrico has been killed.

Killed. What does that mean? Killed in battle or killed in an accident or captured and killed? Annabelle chanted the word over and over until it lost its meaning. *Ucciso ucciso ucciso.* The more you repeated a word the more the meaning leached out of it. The more it lost its power over you. The more it might not be true. Enrico. Dead. *Morto, deceduto, scomparso.* He had been alive and now he was dead. She was alive and now she was not. Not inside, where it counted. Eventually Annabelle ran out of words. She had lost her language. Her words failed her, deserted her, abandoned her. Betrayed her. She had no use for them. Enrico had failed her, deserted her, abandoned her. Betrayed her. How dare he go where she could not follow? She could not understand how things could be exactly the same all around her, as if the water had simply closed over him. 'Here lies One Whose name was writ in Water.' She had seen it on Keats' gravestone on a visit to the Protestant Cemetery in Rome many years ago. We are all just written on the water.

After all the death she had witnessed, this was different, like being given a mechanical toy with no instructions for its use – she did not know how to do this. *Elaborare un luto,* the expression old ladies used – work through mourning. No, she did not know how to do that. She sat, staring ahead of her in a trance from which no-one could rouse her. Her mother was galvanised to do the only thing she knew – she made soup. Anna Maria edged around her as if she were mined. Elsa might have helped but she was not there. Where was Elsa? Gino visited twice a day and sat with her. She muttered to herself – she always knew this would happen. She had been warned, hadn't she? Before he left, Roberto warned her: Enrico is like fire. You will be burned. He will take you to places you could never go but the price will be high. Giacomo had said the same things. But she'd had no choice. He was her twin, her other self … He could not be dead. Not while she was alive.

Then, as a milky dawn found her sitting in her windowsill, came a banging on the street door, a message. Enrico was alive. He had been shot, the bullet lodged in his leg. Michele had carried him over his shoulder all the way down a mountain track to a *baita* where he lay alone for a week as he slowly recovered. Michele did not make it back. Two more of their men *were* dead, one hanged by the Germans and one died of pneumonia.

The *staffetta* carried a note for Annabelle:

> *Non sono morto e ti amo sempre / I am not dead and I still love you.*

October '44

> *The facts. First the facts. What was it Pirandello said of the facts? They were brown paper bags that could not stand up alone or something like that. Well, let us fill the bags with all the information. Later, surely there will be a later for some of us, the facts will be important.*

San Quirico. Another name no-one had ever heard of.

San Quirico, where Elsa died.

Etched now and forever, in acid, on Annabelle's mind, on Enrico's mind, on Francesco's mind, just as the minds of so many others were seared and scarred for the rest of their lives. Now they too had truly joined the ranks of the condemned. When the news came, Annabelle stayed calm. Very calm. There was much to do. A *staffetta* was sent to find Enrico but they did not know whether he had received the news. There was the organising of retrieval of the body. The body. That was what Elsa had become.

Was it today the news came? Or was it months ago? Had she been here in this slough for days or weeks or months? Time has a different quality when grieving is present. It swirls and curls and curves, and swoops back on itself and flows and halts and circles its prey. An hour can take all day. It gets late early and is always night.

Now, beside the scrubbed wooden table of the scullery where Elsa lay, Annabelle was no longer calm. She closed her eyes and swayed. The sound of waves roared in her ears. She forced her eyes open. She would like to have put out her eyes like Oedipus at the sight of the dead Jocasta. The image burned into her retina, the etching of a silver photographic plate. Indelible, permanent. Unbearable.

For the first time in her life, Annabelle howled. She clutched her arms across her stomach, sank to her knees on the cold flagged floor and, with her forehead on the stone, she moaned, the pitch getting higher and higher until she howled: an animal sound she had heard only once, in the mountains, as a mother struggled to cut down the body of her son and then fell upon him. A sound she did not believe was coming from her.

Then Enrico was there. He pulled her to her feet and shook her, his fingers biting into her upper arms. His face was boarded up. She did not know him. He pulled her roughly to his chest and held her until her convulsions petered to a halt. Then he went to his mother. He did not see what Annabelle had seen. The sheet covering Elsa to just below her chin hid some of the damage. But not enough. Her wild and beautiful hair was a tangle of blood and dirt and glutinous brain matter. The cuts and bruises had not altered the fine planes of her face because they were sustained after death, the doctor told them – even the livid imprint of the cord on her neck. The clean bullet-hole below her jaw, in the soft curve beneath her ear, ensured that.

Enrico ran a hand through the tangled curls then kissed the closed eyes of his tiny, beautiful, beloved mother. In his own throat, a vein stood out like a cord, pulsing as if it would burst. He said, 'You are in charge here. I am going to Father.'

He meant, get control of yourself. She did. *Zio* had been given an injection by the doctor and put to bed. Her mother, strangely, had avoided histrionics. It was Anna Maria who had gone to pieces. Sesto had taken her away. Annabelle kept her mother out of the scullery for now, until Elsa's body could be washed and dressed and made more presentable. She would do that herself. She wanted to do that, to make it true. Enrico was right, she must get control of herself. This was not going to stop. More women than ever had been caught and executed in recent weeks and more would face the same fate.

The name of Irma Bandiera was a black pit in their minds. Tortured, blinded, massacred and dropped before her parents' windows, she had resisted, held out, betrayed no-one. None of them felt confident they could do the same.

Elsa had been captured in a farmhouse outside the walls of San Quirico. She had been to a series of meetings with British intelligence officers and four of the partisans liaising with them. She had been gone a week. The army officers had just left and Elsa and the men settled to sleep, when blinding Klieg-lights blazed onto the tiny windows. Fascist militia. They had a megaphone. A megaphone! Well planned then, yelled one of the partisans.

'You are surrounded,' they blared. 'You have no chance. Come out with your hands up. Leave your weapons inside.'

Before the end of the first sentence, the men were on their feet and firing. The fascists fired back but with care. They threw no grenades. They did not use a machine gun.

In the flying chips of stucco and the dust and the noise, one of the men turned to Elsa, shouting, 'This stinks. They want someone. You were followed.' Then he fell.

Through the splintering glass of a narrow window, a tear-gas canister hit the floor and rolled, spewing fumes. Another of the men was hit in the throat.

Coughing and sobbing and squinting against the fumes, Elsa crawled to her bag and dragged out her revolver. She placed the muzzle calmly to her throat and pulled the trigger. Elsa had never fired a gun until then. The first and the last time. She knew what to do. She knew she would only get one chance.

'It was her they wanted,' the only survivor told Annabelle and Enrico. 'She realised it. Someone betrayed her. They were so careful. They really wanted her alive.'

The man, Pietro, escaped through the cellar. When there was silence from the house, the militia men entered with caution. They dragged Elsa's body outside and set fire to the house. They threw her onto a truck and took her back into the town, where they flung the body to the stones of the small piazza in front of the church. They kicked and spat on the cadaver and hanged her from a lamp-post. Villagers peered from darkened windows and wondered, trembling, whose son it was this time, swaying and turning in the moonlight. No-one slept. The militia stood guard all night and all the next day, as the villagers edged around the scene, eyes averted. It was not a new sight. They shook their heads, a woman! What was the world coming to? They muttered prayers for her soul. By evening, the guards were gone. Two men dragged a small table onto the uneven paving of the piazza beside the post, clambered onto it and awkwardly cut down the body.

'She'll have a family somewhere, *poverina*,' one said.

The women crossed themselves again and fingered their rosaries, which seemed to have lost the power to soothe, to ward off evil.

They laid Elsa's poor broken body to rest in the family crypt. Rest, thought Annabelle, what a stupid, stupid word. It was not really a funeral – no priest for them. No tolling bell. Francesco was drugged and shambling. Eleanora did not seem to grasp much. Enrico stood, as stony as the crypt. No-one had words, incantations, to utter over *i resti*, the remains. What does remain after life is gone? Annabelle wondered. There must be something, some trace of us? Elsa would live on in her. That was the best she could offer. But what would she do without her? As the others moved away, she remained, immobile before the crypt. It was too hard to turn and walk away and leave Elsa there alone.

Do not fear, she is not there, Enrico told her, turning her towards the entrance to the cemetery. His eyes were dry. She did not weep. Her own unshed tears made it difficult to breathe. What sin had Elsa committed to die like that? Sin. Where had that thought come from? 'Forgive us our sins,' she heard Anna Maria praying. Annabelle did not believe in sin. Despite being reared with no religious practice whatsoever, both Enrico and Annabelle had been baptised. Cleansed of Original Sin. The hypocrisy! It would take more than some mumbled incantations and drops of stale holy water to remove the stain of the history they all carried. Now the war had ground to a halt. We *can* win this war. We *will* win this war. No matter how long it takes. Enrico was right. Annabelle surged with renewed determination. Or else it was all for nothing, she wrote.

> The facts. We must gather the facts and leave them for others.

CHAPTER 20

The Apennines 1945

The snows came

'Do you think he will go mad?' Johnny chewed on his bit of leathery chestnut bread and though he did not nod towards Enrico, Eagle knew who he meant.

It was so long since Enrico had spoken except to issue orders, that the men were nervous wrecks. Since his mother's death even his body had altered; everything about him was harder, sharper, condensed to sinew. His jaw was permanently clenched and he no longer lost his temper in the old colourful way. He hardly even swore. Where once he used to *bestemmiare* or blaspheme constantly, he now truly ignored God, to the point of not even insulting Him. The men were worried. But then fewer of them crossed themselves these days too. When they were not fighting or foraging, Enrico sat apart, smoking, reading his tattered little book, or gazing off into a space filled with things they could not see. When you did look into his eyes you did not like what you saw there, they muttered.

They had no cook now because when that cretin Alfonso raped the crazy girl from the hut up on the ridge, Enrico beat him to a pulp and handed him over to the family – all crazy, that family. He knew they would kill Alfonso and he did not care.

Last week when they brought in that peddler with the oily smile, to see what to do with him because the villagers said he had been spying, Enrico asked him three questions, then shot him between the eyes before anyone could move.

'Bury him so he can't be found … and slaughter the mule. We

will live on it for a week,' he said over his shoulder as he walked away.

'Oh!' said Michele. 'It's a wonder he didn't tell us to eat that bastard as well!'

Turned out the peddler had a revolver, a map of their position and a wad of lire hidden in the saddlebags of his beast, so he was a spy – but still …

The woman arrived between two sentries, both looking bemused. She was as tall as one and taller than the other. And much straighter, with a long stride. They emerged from the *bosco* into the clearing and moved in step towards the hut, the men unsure as to who was escorting who. Enrico was expecting them because news had been sent ahead. The late autumn light cast them in sepia and it was very cold. Enrico let the axe down onto the woodpile, waiting quietly, and in response to his raised eyebrows, Johnny lifted both hands before him, meaning 'nothing to do with me, Boss.'

The last of the dappled sunlight caught her hair, fine as a baby's and completely white. No, not white. Silver. It was cut off straight and tucked behind her ears. She wore men's clothing and mountain boots, well-worn, and carried a heavy rucksack. She had patrician written all over her.

'*Signora?*' he said. She seemed familiar.

'I've come to join you.' She stood very still, the heavy canvas of the *zaino* dragging on her shoulders.

Shit, he thought, she must be eighty. He was not encouraging. 'Do you know the *signora?*' he asked, turning to Johnny, who nodded.

'She is the mother of the professor.'

Oh *Cristo!* Enrico exhaled. Ferrucio's mother. More than eighty then. He extended his hand. 'Contessa, I am very, very sorry about your son.'

'As are we all,' she replied evenly. 'As am I, to know of your mother. I shall take my son's place.' Before Enrico could speak, she pushed on, 'Do not be foolish. At this stage, you need all the hands you can get. I am in perfect health. I am a good nurse and an excellent cook, and a very good shot.'

It would suit her better, she assured him, to die here, actively, than it would to die down there, of doing nothing. 'I've burned my bridges down there. I have nothing left to lose.'

After Ferruccio had been caught by Mario Carità's thugs, his mother had moved heaven and earth to find out where they had taken him. She did not plead for his life because she knew it would be useless and she knew he would not want it. She orchestrated an escape from the *Villa Triste* but it failed. She waited outside every day, hoping to see him. She refused all pity or support. Then they killed him. They brought him out alone, early one morning. He could not stand but a man on either side held him under the arms. As the rope was placed over his head, he kissed his fingers to his mother but was otherwise completely immobile. He had not talked, but they all knew that. She did not close her eyes. She sat on the stones of the piazza all day and all night, her gaze never moving from her son's body as it swung and turned, until they let her cut him down the next day. Not once did she speak. Not once did she shed a tear.

Behind Enrico, the others who had come out of the hut stood silently at his back, holding their breath. The woman's composure was absolute. She did not even shift her weight from foot to foot. The sun had slipped away and the evening sounded of the forest settling for the night. Enrico caught the scent of his mother's perfume. Joy. Very gently, he eased the straps of the rucksack off her shoulders. He would work it out later.

'We could certainly do with a cook, Contessa.'

The winter-coloured wind carried the scent of snow. The forest was already undressed and defenceless, as vulnerable in its nakedness as a sleeping child. There was a brutal beauty to the stark landscape. Huddled over the meagre flame, Enrico's face shifted and flickered in the firelight as human faces had done since fire was first discovered. The flames were dancing pinpoints in his pupils – an illusion of animation in an otherwise drawn and shuttered face. He drew heavily on his cigarette, which tasted like straw, but smoking had taken the place of eating.

The long, long dreadful winter dragged its feet across the land. They lived mostly on chestnuts collected before the snows. It was almost impossible for *staffette* to get to them. They stole food where they could from the country people, knowing they were hated for it, survival their strongest instinct. A good night was when they found a barn with an animal inside to generate some heat. A bad night was when they slept where they fell in the open after walking in the dark. The leafless trees afforded no cover and any movement against the white of the snow was visible from great distances. German and fascist snipers got better and better at picking off tiny figures against the snowy background. The full moon was the enemy. They tried to move at night and hide in the daytime. Move fast and often. If they had to, they could run even when they had not eaten for three days, even if they were slogging thigh-deep in snow.

With little or no food, lying in ditches for days at a time, soaked to the soul, coughing and spitting and trying to be quiet, death was with them every day. In the frozen ground, it became impossible for exhausted men to bury the dead. For many, the only shroud was an overcoat stiff with ice, but even that had to be taken from the corpse for someone who was still alive and needed it. Gino died of exposure. He had never been strong. He came from Florence too. He was an architect, not a fighter, and he'd had a weak chest even as a child. Paolo, on the other hand, died because he sank in the snow and slipped down a ravine. The landscape had turned on them. Enrico and Falco risked their lives to clamber down and retrieve Paolo's body. The men held them firm on long ropes and fretted, but they understood. By now they all knew they would probably die. It was important to mark each death, salute each body.

This war had become about bodies – about how the dead were treated; it was all that separated them from the animals. They had tramped through tiny villages where every living soul had been incinerated. Worse were the bodies hung on butchers' hooks, even women. Perhaps especially the women. All constraints had evaporated, free reign given to the basest of human instincts. It was a ferocity employed to instil terror and degradation – a deterrent. No-one died like Job, 'old and full of days' any more. The only possible response was *not* to be deterred, to live as long as possible, to meticulously acknowledge and bury the fallen. Even Neanderthals, Enrico once read, buried their dead with flowers, with ceremony, with incantations. A form of prayer over the dead seemed to have always been universal. They could do no less. There should be a tenth circle of the inferno especially for this time. *Dio infame!* Enrico carefully squeezed the end of his cigarette between his thumb and forefinger and put the butt in his pocket. Time to attend to Falco. He groaned to his feet. What will be left, after all the killing finishes? How will we learn to live? Will we want to?

Falco had taken a fascist bullet in his calf. They dug out the bullet but now his leg was septic, the wound full of maggots even in the freezing weather. He moaned despite himself.

'He will need a gag,' said Enrico. Sound carried over the snow and the naked forest. Falco bit hard on the dirty rag and his animal gurgling was the sound, not of words in any language but a cry from the distant past. Enrico knelt on the leafy mould and pulled the stinking wrapping away, taking bits of pus-coloured flesh with it. He did not turn his head away from the stench or the suppurating mess.

'All we can do is cut away the rotten bits and hope for the best.'

'No, cut it off, cut it off,' groaned Falco.

Johnny's hand, holding the flask of grappa, tremored.

'He will die if we cut it off and he'll probably die if we don't,' said Enrico, who had nothing with which to amputate a leg, even if he wanted to.

He nodded to Johnny, who placed the lip of the flask at the cracked lips of the patient. Then passed the flask to Enrico and held Falco's arms tightly. Enrico poured a little grappa over his knife and placed the flask carefully aside where it would not spill. He scraped the putrid flesh down to the bone, poured some of the precious grappa over the wound and bound it with a strip he had cut from an undershirt. Falco fainted. Enrico released a long breath, nodded at Johnny, climbed heavily to his feet and trudged away. His face was marble.

Taking care to keep the sparks away from his beard, Enrico re-lit the stub of his cigarette. With his knife, he sharpened his bit of pencil, now not much longer than the cigarette. He balanced his notebook on his knee. He did not keep a diary – he left that to Annabelle and others – but he needed to write now. It would reach Annabelle. Not that he had words of comfort.

The snows came and we died like flies. Go home, General

Alexander announced. Go home and we will take up the fight again in the spring. The fighting season will begin in the spring. What does he think this is? The fucking fighting season! A game, is it? Like the tennis season in the summer! We have no homes to go to! We are hunted now, like wild boar. Dio infame! That bastard, Alexander. We are up here with no ammunition and no food and no air support. Go home they say. Home! We are not on a day outing from the lunatic asylum! We cannot go home. Where should we go for the winter? How am I to feed the men?

The long Allied pause after Florence gave the Germans time to regroup and gather their strength. It was a mistake. The partisans knew it. So many clear, crisp autumn days of sunshine. Why oh why, they wondered, do they not seize the advantage of this great fighting weather? The Allies did not agree and did not care for their opinion. Communists and cowboys, was the common view of the partisans. The regular fighting forces needed to be rested. Winter arrived in a hurry. The Germans could not go home. They dug in. The autumn pause had given them time to gain the advantage. They were incredulous that the Allies had gifted them such a truce. They wielded it against the partisans and the Jews. In September, one of Kesselring's communiqués slyly linked all partisans with the Bolsheviks, making those 'low criminals of Moscow' fair game for extermination by any means. As for the Jews, there was no-one to help them. The transports became frantic. Every day dawned to the sounds of rifle-butts on closed doors, tramping boots on icy streets, shouted orders in German and the misty shapes of SS squads herding stumbling confused families into trucks and trains at first light. The Reich was determined to transport every Jew left in Italy above the Gothic Line. By now, there was no-one who did not know what the names Auschwitz/Birkenau, or Bergen/Belsen, truly meant. Concentration camps, labour camps, prisoner of war camps. Hundreds and hundreds of them, and they all only meant one thing – extermination camps. In touch with the outside world only by radio now, Enrico and the men listened, impotent.

One icy morning, in a deserted barn, hanging crossed on a hook among the farm tools, Enrico found a pair of old skis. They were as long as he was tall, narrow, turned-up slips of wood with only ties to attach boots. The poles hung from the rafters. His brigade, or what was left of it, would not survive without help. They needed a plan. He set off on the skis to make contact with others in the *Stella Rossa* – a solitary figure, leaning into the wind, nearly doubled over, a tiny question mark on the blinding snow.

He left Johnny in charge, thinking, Christ only knows if he is up to it, but until Falco recovered – if Falco recovered – there was no choice. It was nearly Christmas. From a tiny hamlet on the steep slope of a valley, came pin-pricks of wavering candlelight and the voices of farmers singing *'tu scendi dalle stelle'*. The reedy voice of children trembled on the thin air. Christmas carols would give scant comfort this year. He remembered the story of the British and German troops emerging from the trenches to sing *Silent Night* in 1914. It had changed nothing.

Florence 1945

Winter's claws gouged deep in Florence too. Many of the ill and elderly who had survived the war could not survive the winter. News from the north was as bitter as the January weather. Ferruccio Parri was captured in Milan, handed to the Germans, then suddenly released. It was whispered he was in discussion with Allen Dulles, the Mission Chief for the Office of Strategic Services – the OSS, and the Wehrmacht. Dulles was the most important of the many spies. Had Parri been exchanged for German prisoners? What deal had been done? What did it all mean? Flurries of secret negotiations blew about on the winds. Rumours had not been so fervid since the days of '43. Things were hectic, telescoped, kaleidoscopic. Expectancy thickened the air but answers were few. Was the end of the war near? It surely must be, but how would it happen?

Everyone wanted peace now – except, it seemed, Hitler. Everyone wanted peace, but on their own terms. Everyone wanted peace, but everyone wanted to be exonerated, their sins expiated. Everyone wanted something. Clandestine visitors slipped in and out of Italy and Switzerland on stealthy night-time flights – Germans, Italians, British, Americans; generals, politicians, negotiators, go-betweens. Even Churchill, whispered one of Annabelle's patients. No Russian names, no-one wanted the Russians. Documents, diaries, and reports were traded, bartered, debated, weighed and valued, as the Italians and Germans sought to buy safety, indemnity, and the Allies sought to manoeuvre for control of the peace. Venezia-Giulia must at all costs, not go to the Russians, or to Tito.

Annabelle read Enrico's letter, crouched before a weak fire, wrapped in layers of woollen garments. The cable-knit cardigan belonging to her mother was tight on her; it gave her the air of an aged crone. Not that she cared. Nor did her mother; Eleanora no longer cared about anything. Fifteen thousand dead soldiers, Annabelle had heard at the hospital, as many of pneumonia as of wounds. This winter killed indiscriminately – guilt or innocence irrelevant. What of the Germans then? Their losses were terrible too, much worse.

She understood why the Allies had to stop, but that did not help the partisans. Alexander's speech was insensitive at best. Lay down your arms, he said, conserve your ammunition, await further instructions. The Action Party's response was outrage – outrage at the plight of the fighters and outrage that they were expected to fight on again later without official recognition of their status. The response of the fascist press was delighted *schadenfreude* at the plight of the rebels callously deserted by the perfidious Allies. It was not what General Alexander meant, not at all, said Captain Smithson from British High Command. No, no, not at all. General Alexander had the highest regard for the partisans and was only thinking of their welfare. It was true General Alexander regarded the partisans more warmly than most, but many of them would not be there to take up the fight anew – they would be dead.

Annabelle knew though, from the work at the hospital, that they were not alone. Never was she as well informed as now, through the patients and staff. So many of the wounded came straight from the battlefields. Supply lines were ruptured, resources desperately scarce.

Some of the British troops had not even had winter uniforms until a few weeks ago. She would not want to be wearing her beloved Khaki shorts in the mountains now. Civilians huddled in shelled houses open to the weather, without food or heating, as battles raged over the top of them. Many were living in caves. Most of the RSI soldiers were short of food, clothing and ammunition. They only remained because of the threats of reprisal against their families. Up in the marshes of Comacchio, the Germans died unmourned and their bodies lay in the icy slush, eaten by roaming animals.

Spring was on its way and hope was in the air. The Fighting Season began again. On the third of March 1945, the elite 10th Mountain Division of the US Army broke through the Apennines under General Hayes. The stalemate was over.

After sheltering for eight weeks in a monastery to the south of Bologna, Enrico and his group were behind the Allied lines for the first time since Florence. The relief, if temporary, was numbing. As they pushed on with the 10th into the Po Valley, the roads were clogged with surrendering Germans, so many that the soldiers of the 10th could barely deal with them. Most just wanted to go home. On the body of a dead German captain, lying under the soft yellow blossom of the mimosa, Enrico found a letter: 'To my dear children. I write this letter, certain that it is all over. We have lost the war. My shame and sorrow are deep but the joy at seeing you again will also be great.'

In a town with hardly a wall left standing, a woman beat her washing in the stone tub in the centre of the piazza. The Americans gave us food, she told Enrico, after eight months of starvation and bombing, they gave us food. We are happy.

In Florence, young males roamed the streets like stray animals: boys between the ages of ten and fifteen, wearing an eccentric assortment of uniforms and stolen clothes. Their spindly legs were too thin for the British Army shorts and their bony wrists too fine for the stolen guns they carried. They practised swagger, with little talent. They wanted to be partisans, they wanted excitement. They wanted to do something, anything. They came from everywhere – refugees, even if they came from Florence. They had had no schooling, no food, no discipline and in many cases their parents were dead. They stole food and got into fights, and their anger, confusion and loneliness hovered in a cloud about their heads.

The *reduci*, the war-wounded, were also angry, confused and lonely, a crooked army of ghosts lurching about the cold streets with grimacing expressions that frightened the children as they made their way to the reopened schools each day. They were a problem, the boys and the men, the detritus and by-products of war, all war. They were one more problem to be somehow addressed with the few resources available to the committees and organisations striving to stem the crisis in the city. Yet the progress made in those weeks was extraordinary. Florence was unique in having its own government.

With so much despair around her, Annabelle turned inwards to the work of each day, finding herself strangely at peace. It was spring. A late spring, to be sure, but the trees had buds and the fields were full of green shoots. To wake up each morning, alive, seemed a gift that imposed a responsibility, a duty. For many, their God, their faith, still offered comfort. For others, it had curled around the edges and dried up, leaving them floundering or embittered. Annabelle had no answers but she felt the need of none. Each day brought its own demands and she responded. For now, that was enough.

Bologna has fallen to the Allies. April 21, 1945.

More than a year since Annabelle had gone into the mountains, seven months since Enrico left to fight in the Apennines, he had moved right up to the Dolomites. Her last news of him was near Milan. After all those months, Bologna was finally in Allied hands. Giacomo had been right about Monte Cassino. It was a terrible omen. Giacomo had been right about many things. It was a matter of days now, only days. Everyone knew it but still people died. Not only in the fighting, but in the liberated cities. As the frontline receded, the vendettas surged. It was worse now, people vying for position in the race to be the purest, to be on the right side, to be among the victors rather than the vanquished. In Florence, no-one had been a fascist, yet bodies appeared overnight as if by magic. Everyone had scores to settle. It was hard to condemn. Forgetting, if it were ever to come, was a long way off. Forgiving – there was no sign of that.

For those on the front, the other side of the enemy lines, it was an inferno. Every path, hillside and roadway was mined. Retreating convoys of marauding Germans poured along the roads. Allied planes bombed with napalm, forests burned and civilians died. Those months were the most spiteful of the war. Shattered homes, towns, villages and lives. Italians, Americans, British, South Africans, Brazilians, Poles, Gurkhas and Germans, all united in death.

Enrico slogged north from Milan with the 10th. Then, suddenly, shockingly, it was over. When they finally arrived at Riva at the top of Lake Garda, it was all over. It felt, he wrote, like running full tilt into a brick wall. They stood and listened to General Hayes addressing his troops. Surrounded by fields of white crosses, he said: 'The Lord held us by the hand.'

And bells pealed from every *campanile*.

'And then,' Enrico wrote, 'they went home, leaving their dead behind in our fields, but our dead are always with us. And no-one held us by the hand.'

Lake Garda 1945
Cadde il sipario. The curtain falls.

> *Ben is distraught over what Hitler has done to the Jews. They certainly are the scum of the earth, the Jews, but Ben would never have had them all murdered. They may have killed Christ but Ben cares little about that. What about La Sarfatti? She was one of his greatest lovers, according to him! He loved her biography. She was Jewish. Ben helped her leave the country.*

Ben's attitude to the Jews was difficult to predict. He always said the Racial Laws had nothing to do with Hitler, yet it was straight after that man's visit that Ben brought them in. So many Jews fought in the old war, so many were his friends. Not that Clara had ever known a Jew, for heaven's sake. The old Pope was horrified, her father told her, by the Racial Laws, but this new one was able to see the problem more clearly, though he agreed with Ben that killing them was wrong. No-one could have foreseen that.

'We have never had a Jewish problem,' Ben told her. 'I have been a racist since 1921, but I cannot condone this massacre.'

It had certainly turned people against them – against Ben and therefore her, against the Regime. Ezra Pound too had turned against them, and to think how Ben loved Pound's poetry and how much he helped the man. Then that evil unfrocked priest Preziosi accused Ben of siding with the Jews and Freemasons! The world was topsy-turvy. Ben threatened to resign over the treatment of the Jews but the Germans ignored him and did not even pass on the message to Hitler. No wonder Ben was depressed. He had been writing an article on suicide.

Clara shifted her weight on the sofa, to ease the soreness of the purpling bruise on her left buttock, smiling a secret smile at the thought of the teeth marks turning green, black, violet now after four days. It had been like the old days for a little while. Ben was wild and panting, and took her from behind with a violence she had not felt for more than a year. A storm, a tempest, an earthquake. Yes, yes, she thought, there is hope. But no. As quickly as the storm arrived, it passed, leaving him spent, morose, more dejected than before. We cannot go back, old times are over, she realised, but still, the livid bite glowed in the night, a shiver of pleasure in those dark times.

The Pope had abandoned them. To think he attended her wedding. He was Cardinal Pacelli then but everyone knew he would soon be Pope. She had still had to go to Budapest to get an annulment from Riccardo. So much for the Pope. So much for Riccardo. She was much more married to Ben. From the moment Ben said to her mother, '*Signora*, will you permit me to love Clara?' he was more married to her and to her family than to Rachele. He only married Rachele under protest before the second child was born – his first daughter, Edda, was born out of wedlock. How Clara would have loved the status of the *Signorina* Braun, official companion of the

Führer. Clara remembered the *Signora*'s visits to Italy in the days when they were all at peace. So elegantly casual, so confident, a little unadventurous in her style, but then that was the Germans, wasn't it? If the Germans could accept an official mistress, why could the Italians not? It seemed unfair. Though there *was* Rachele. Clara shook her head. The woman was deranged. She claimed Marc wanted to kidnap Ben and that Clara was poisoning him!

Ben was desperate. He talked endlessly about suicide. He was a failure; it had all been for nothing. He was despondent at the failure of his people, of his great vision. Even Stalin had succeeded where he had failed. In Tuesday's letter he lamented:

> *Today I am feeling a bit down, not to say, black. Communism has succeeded in creating a militant population, but fascism, no. Does it depend on the race and the doctrine, or does it depend upon men? For twenty years, I fought to give the Italian people the greatest of all glory, Military glory. Stalin managed it. I did not. If you only knew how bitter in my mouth is the disappointment. Despite all, I send you all my kisses. Your Ben.*

There were strikes all across the north, and the situation worsened every day. Ben refused to sign the orders for the violent repression of the General Strike. The Germans were furious. Allied planes were constantly overhead and the noise wore away at the nerves.

'And yet they never bomb us,' Clara said.

Franz, her driver, said the British did not want to bomb Il Duce because they wanted to take him alive. The bombs did fall close by, but Ben refused to go down into the bomb shelter with the rest of the family because he said most Italians did not have access to a bomb shelter and he would not hide from risks the rest of the population must bear. Huh, thought Clara, it is really because he cannot bear to be in a confined space with Rachele, who made his depression worse.

'She tries to make me look ridiculous,' he complained.

They could bomb all of us so easily, Clara thought, perhaps Franz is right.

'Anyway, I will be dead soon. The game is over for me. I am finished'. Ben slumped in the armchair, his buttoned jacket ruched up under his chin. The pouches beneath his eyes sagged. His chin sagged. Clara's spirits sagged. Yesterday we were going to make a last stand, today, we will all be dead. Day by day, hour by hour, things changed.

Ben's mood was not lightened by the fact that some weeks ago, Edda had handed all the Count's diaries to that man Dulles, the American spy. So now the Allies had everything. It had all been for nothing and the Count was dead. It haunted Ben. Clara had only recently found her own letter to Ben, saying, 'Ben, save that man. Fate perhaps will be kinder to us.' The Count had actually written her a note thanking her for her intervention but Edda still blamed her. Gratitude! Ben continued to send Don Giusto to Switzerland, begging Edda to come back, to forgive him, but she refused. Edda was a Red Cross nurse in Russia and in Sicily. She learned to be tough. She had tried to get her family to Spain to save them while the Count was alive but the Germans tricked her. Now Ben arranged to get them all to Spain and her own family too. He suggested to the Allies and to General Franco that he would prepared to go into exile in Spain. When he was not talking about suicide, that was.

At least exile in Spain seemed possible, unlike some of the schemes bandied about. Tullio Tamborini wanted to build a giant submarine and take them all to Japan. The man was mad. Pavolini raved about last stands in the Valtellina, or in Milan. He too was mad. Clara loathed the man, but he at least was standing firm with Ben, instead of running away like most. Vittorio urged Ben to negotiate with the Allies and perhaps for once, she thought, that moron was right.

Ben would not do that. He scribbled endlessly about Great Britain being responsible for their situation. If there ever was a time when he might have negotiated with Mr Churchill, it was now too late. It was very vexing – they could not stay here and do nothing. That was only too clear, but there were not many suitable places – that was also clear.

Clara pursed her lips. Oh no, she thought, now I am doing it. Bad enough Ben. She had read in a magazine that smoking cigarettes and pursing your lips gave you lines around your mouth. She leaned in to the oval mirror but the glass was too old and foxed to see her lips clearly. Still, she must not do that again. She traced her forefinger around and around the cool, silver edge of a tall cloisonné urn. Antique. Chinese. Blue, yellow, red, gold, valuable. As high as her waist. Ben was explaining, explaining, explaining. She could see where this was leading. He did not want her to go with him to Milan.

Milan. Last time he went, he spoke to a huge crowd at the Lyric Theatre and they loved him – for a brief moment. Then he came back and plunged into lethargy and dejection.

'I have ruined Italy. Life is nothing but dust. I am a Guelf,' he said, 'Hitler is a Ghibelline.' Clara was hazy about Guelfs and Ghibellines: wasn't one on the side of the Pope and one on the side of the Emperor? What did Popes and Emperors have to do with this? It was very hard to be patient. Dr Zachariae was worried Ben was heading for a real breakdown. Ben wanted to transfer his government to Milan but Milan was about to be overrun by the Allies at any moment and Ben did not really have a government any more.

Not that Clara wanted to go to Milan. There was nothing left of the city. What the bombs had not destroyed, the people had – the freezing, starving people of Milan. They had stripped every branch off every tree and cut down the trunks, they had chopped up all the public furniture and park benches, all the architraves and doors from damaged buildings, anything made of wood – for firewood for warmth and cooking. No, she did not want to go to Milan but Ben could not go alone, he was not in any state to be left alone. It was up to her to save them. Now both families were safe, it was only the few of them and she must keep her head. The money from the sale of her jewellery would see them through.

'You cannot stop me,' she said finally. 'I can go to Milan anytime I wish. I can book into any hotel I wish. I will go myself.'

Marc did not want either of them to go to Milan. He thought the only safe way was to make a run for Switzerland. It was certainly time to run somewhere.

Clara could feel heat, rising like steam up the narrow neck of one of her father's glass laboratory beakers. From her stomach to her chest to her throat, until her cheeks flamed and her hand trembled. Still, Ben droned on. He only stopped when the urn shattered on the tiles. Who could have imagined the enamel would be so brittle?

He stopped. She stopped. The ormolu clock ticked on in the void. Neither moved. He did not turn to her. It was a long time since she had smashed something and she was uncertain what else might have fractured. She had promised herself not to do this, to stay calm, to take care. She waited. Apprehension settled heavily on both of them. Ben's hand was unsteady. He was upset. *He* was upset!

With a show of weary patience, he finally turned to her, raised both hands to the ceiling. 'Do what you like. I cannot stop you.'

He righted the urn and tipped it back into place with a hollow clank, leaving the floor sparkling as if strewn with precious stones. He pursed his lips, rounding the urn slightly, to the left and then the right, until it was in precisely the same spot as before. Neither knew what to say. Outside, the tyres of Ben's car hissed to a halt on the asphalt. Clara started towards him but he turned away, raised one hand and trudged to the door.

Franz was waiting outside for her too, but he could wait. She sank to one of the rigid, uncomfortable sofas. She fingered her rosary in the pocket of her slacks. The late afternoon sun threw swords of light across the room, striking sparks off the accusing urn. She thought of an English story Ben once told her, in Florence. It was about a golden bowl which, once cracked, could never be repaired. Ben loved English writers. He read her bits of the story, translating as he went. It was very beautiful but it made her sad. Clara did not like sad stories, and now look what she had done.

She stood and smoothed the creases from her slacks, straightened her jacket and glanced again into the crazed mirror, tidying her hair back behind her ears. Very erect, she walked to the doors to meet Franz, saying aloud, I will worry about that tomorrow. Tomorrow, she would decide what to do. Ben would not fight with her. She could see that now. He had no fight left. It was up to her and she would not let him down. He needed her more than ever and she would be with him. She had always been with him and she always would. Now the family was safe, she could concentrate on saving Ben and herself. Poor darling.

Spain was out! Marc had done his best but the general had refused them. Ben was shocked. The ingratitude!

'It will be the end of that wretched dictatorship,' he shouted.

Her parents and her sister Myriam would be safe with the

Spaniards. She did not trust the Italians. She had given Myriam a document to open once they reached Spain, making Mimi executor of all her papers.

'I follow my destiny, his destiny,' she told her.

Now that General Franco had refused them, there was only Switzerland left. She did not even think of the Valtellina. That was the past, for her at least. Anyway, wasn't it under the control of the partisans? There would be no last stand now.

She straightened, smiled and inclined her head as Franz opened the door for her. At least she had her precious Alfa back. Although the sun had fallen below the treetops, the gleaming bodywork of the Berliner gleamed like a glass of old wine. How she loved that car. Ben's most precious gift to her. She would love it to the end. Wherever they were going, the Alfa would go with her. She sank back into the glove-soft leather, inhaling the smell as if it were the scent of her own child, and closed her eyes.

An occasion worthy of the Caesars

The Allies had taken Bologna. It was all over. What an awful city, Clara hated it. Always a stronghold of the Bolsheviks, dark, gloomy, and the food was too rich. Well, perhaps not now. It was nearly a week since Ben moved his office to Milan. He had begged her to accompany her family to Spain but he knew she would not go. Yesterday Colonel Dollmann came to see her, urging her to flee, or at least remain on the lake where she would be safe. He had tried to talk Ben into doing the same, the week before. The colonel was deeply involved in talks with the Americans to surrender, Marc told her. That very day, a radio broadcast had instructed the Germans in Milan to pack and be ready to leave. Colonel Dollmann again urged Clara to flee.

And leave Ben? 'Never!' she retorted. 'I loved him in the good times and I love him even more now that things are bad.'

What had Ben said, she asked. He said, the Colonel admitted, exactly what you have said. That you had been beside him in the good times and you would be with him in disaster.

She knew it! She ordered Franz and her car and made the dash from the lake to Milan. There was no time left.

'We are to leave. Now.' She leaned in towards Ben, willing him with her eyes.

She would never give up. She did not want to die, and really, neither did Ben. He wanted peace. He wanted to be able to help his people after this cursed war was over. He deserved to live, to see himself vindicated. She breathed deeply, taking air into the deepest parts of her body and expelled it, in a long, long breath she prayed would breathe life into Ben. She had been breathing for him, all of these past weeks, made so much more difficult by being able to see him so little.

The letters arrived in daily swirls. Each began with 'My dearest little one' and ended with 'Your Ben who wants to hold you.' In between, they were filled with longing, desperation and misery or ranting, repine and rage. It took her all day to formulate the words to reassure him, to strengthen him, to prop him up. It was her job, she had no other, and everything depended upon it. Too much of their planning was by letter, when it was her presence Ben needed. She ran her hand over his head, lightly fluttering her fingers over the bony ridges of his cranium, massaging his neck at the base of his skull.

'Amore, we must go to Switzerland, you know nowhere else is safe now.'

Beneath her fingers, the muscles in his neck tensed. He hated Switzerland. 'Switzerland is nothing but a hotbed of spies and intrigue. I cannot leave my country. You do not understand the delicacy of these matters.'

What Clara understood – the only one who understood anything at all – was that there were no possibilities left. Thank God for Marc. He could be difficult and erratic but he was now the only person she could depend on, the only one not paralysed by indecision and fear. He could have fled to Spain but he did not, he stayed with her and with Ben.

Marc was saying run, Clara. Run now. No-one said Claretta

any more. Run Clara, while there is still time. Not much time, but enough, if they left now. Berlin, he said, was a defeated city, the Führer a shambling madman whose life was over. The city was completely encircled by the Russians, with the Allies standing off to allow the Soviets to take it when they chose, in the next day or so. Churchill had come to an agreement with the partisans. Wolff and the Germans had come to an agreement with Dulles. Everyone had come to an agreement with everyone, except Hitler and Ben. Not that Ben had not tried. He sent offers to Churchill, he sent offers to that man Dulles, but they scoffed at him. He sent offers to the CLNAI but the partisans would not guarantee the safety of his men. His men! The fascists had been surrendering to anyone who would take them, like the rats and cowards they were. The American President had dropped dead. Ben was delighted. Struck down by his God, he said. Ben had never believed the crippled President would enter the war against them. What a mess.

'We must pack up your office now.' With an arm about his shoulders, Clara nudged him forward in the chair.

He nodded, allowing himself to be led to the desk, where the cases for his documents sat open, waiting. 'Rachele … the children?' He felt guilty because he had not been to see them before he left.

With a gentle pat, Clara pushed his leather briefcase towards him. 'They are all safe, Ben. You know they will be safe.'

Rachele, she thought. Rachele could look after herself. Had not Ben told her to turn to Mr Churchill if she desperately needed help?

'We are going to Switzerland, *amore*. All of us.'

Beyond the windows, the SS Headquarters in the Hotel Regina wore a wreath of black smoke from the burning of documents. Every road out of Milan writhed with cars crammed with the families of fascists in flight. The Chief of Police had signed a surrender document. In every city north of the Po, the Germans had thrown down their arms and were in frantic retreat. Close by, shots reverberated, running feet slapped at the stones, machine-gun fire rattled, shouts echoed.

The partisans had begun their uprising. Ben had been with Cardinal Schuster for three exhausting hours last night, in another vain attempt to arrange an armistice between the partisans and the fascists. All he came away with was a book about St Benedict. Even Gerhard Wolf had tried to help, but all to no avail. The CLNAI issued a proclamation, which effectively called for Ben's death.

> *All those guilty of suppressing Constitutional guarantees, destroying popular Liberties, creating the fascist Regime, compromising and betraying the country and leading it to catastrophe, are to be punished with the penalty of death.*

'At this point of my existence,' Ben said, 'death begins to look like a rest.'

Clara sent him to bed and called Dr Zachariae. Not that Ben slept anymore. The doctor pleaded with him to claim asylum in a sanatorium in Switzerland, but he no longer listened even to his doctor. Instead, he sat scribbling some drivel about what to do with the Baltic States! Reminiscing about his past triumphs. His speech at the Munich Conference. An occasion worthy of the Caesars, he called it, but that was five years ago. Clara and the doctor shook their heads at each other. Nothing to be done. Vittorio had been to see his father to beg him to flee, or offering to hide him in the apartment of a friend. Ben shouted at him and swore he would never leave the others to their fate.

Now, outside Ben's office door, the bustle of departure and the rustle of papers took the place of words. The air of the corridors quivered with hectic activity.

Finally, Ben stood a little taller and with a show of resolution, began to empty a drawer of his desk, not that there was much in it. Ben and his ministers had only been there days, a macabre semblance of government, which had now imploded, collapsing in on itself along with the bombed buildings of the city. Panic hovered at the edges.

'What about you? What about all your papers? Letters?' His voice was petulant, too high. 'I tell you to destroy things and yet you keep every tiny scrap. I am surprised you don't keep my fingernail clippings.'

'All done, all attended to. Everything is in a safe place.' Clara did not roll her eyes, she did not sigh. She did grind her teeth.

Days ago, on the eighteenth, when Ben had left Gargnano with an SS convoy for Milan, she had deposited her diaries, letters and every scrap of paper she had carefully conserved for ten years, with Rina Cervis. The Countess too, begged her to reconsider.

'I do not know what will become of me. I have chosen my fate,' she replied.

Rina promised her the papers would be safe and she knew she would be able to retrieve them all as soon as peace was restored. As soon as they could return. She said a quick prayer to Saint Rita, that it would not be too long.

Ben had returned to himself. The colour flooded back to his face; he straightened and strode about the office. Abandoning the drawers, he carefully packed the briefcase with the documents he had preserved for just this moment. Before leaving Villa Feltrinelli, he had burned every paper he was not taking with him. Most of his important papers, including his diary, he had entrusted to Carlo Biggini and some, mysteriously, to the Japanese Ambassador. He stood, a hand resting on the leather case.

'I doubt Mr Churchill is as tranquil and serene as I am at this time. I undervalued the intelligence of the masses. I have done all I could for my people.'

Clara gently slid the briefcase out from under his hand. She snapped the locks and handed it to his secretary. Luigi Gatti could be trusted.

'If necessary, I will die with him,' he told her.

Those papers and the heavy case with the gold were all they would need. She could leave Ben now and get on with her own packing. 'It will be very cold, my dear. We will need heavy clothes. It will all be over soon.'

She should have known it! No sooner had she turned her back than Ben fell under the sway of that dreadful man again. Pavolini would get him killed in the end. He had talked Ben back into making a run for the Valtellina that night. In Milan, the partisans had taken over the newspapers and most of the buildings, and issued a decree taking over the government. The Allies would be there within a day and now this! Chaos, it was, chaos.

People were behaving like … whatever those animals that jumped off cliffs were called. Preziosi and his wife jumped off a building. Good riddance to them. Clara pushed the cap up and scratched her head. She itched in the Republican Guard uniform and the cap was too tight. All her plans thrown into the air! She sat forward in the car as it sped away from Milan, tensed, urging the vehicle faster and faster though the black night over terrible roads in lashing rain.

Marc had rushed to her earlier in the evening to report that Ben had told his ministers the CLN was attempting to kill him and he must leave at once. Farinacci and his lover had already been caught and shot. Ben showed one of the ministers a revolver, saying he was ready to die but not at the hands of the CLN, and ordered his car for Como. They begged him to ask asylum of Cardinal Schuster but he laughed. He had an SS escort and Gatti, Bombacci and the others followed in cars. Pavolini was apparently to join them tomorrow. Vittorio too had left in pursuit of his father. A lot of use that cretin would be! Ben was apparently wearing a machine gun across his chest. A machine gun! What would he do with a machine gun, poor darling. He had not fired a gun since the last war! She had to catch him.

It was nearly dawn and still they had not reached his convoy. En route, they heard people had flocked to die with their Duce and been sent home. *Madonna mia*! It was like some ridiculous American film – as soon as they arrived at one place, they were informed Ben's party had fled to another, then they arrived there and he had moved on. Finally, as daylight dribbled over the horizon they caught up with him in Menaggio.

There, as if it were not already enough, Clara found Elena in Ben's party. It really was too much! She could not help it, her voice climbed. Don't be shrill, Ben said, but without conviction. She was so upset she slipped and fell and he did not even help her up. The German sentry turned his head and looked away. We must rest, Ben said and lay down on a camp bed. Go, he said wearily. Go. Save yourself. Too late for that, she thought. Then Elena brought news the Allies were in Como, then a convoy of German trucks arrived and they set off again, this time with Ben in the lead, driving himself in the armoured Alfa and Clara and Marc and the family at the rear in Marc's Alfa. Then an outrider brought news the roads were full of partisans. Another stop, and this time Ben was dressed like a scarecrow and pushed into one of the trucks. Pavolini had caught up with them. Then, and then, and then … a roadblock.

The rumble of the convoy rose on the thin air, high into the valley. Tyres grumbled over the road surface raddled by the long winter and melting snows. The canvas canopies of trucks creaked and groaned, motorcycle outriders roared and revved on the slippery surface, cars ploughed on with protesting gears. From high on the side of the steep cutting, three men with binoculars followed the German procession. Truck after troop-truck rounded the curve far below, all heading for home. A fog of dejection hung over the endless articulated crocodile of vehicles.

When the loop of the mountain road filled with trucks and armoured cars and the lead one was almost at the turn, one of the men raised his arm and spoke quietly into his radio. The rest of the brigade emerged from the steep mossy banks with the barricades ready and the *mitra* in place. It was only moments until the lead truck swayed around the bend, to be confronted by a roadblock of crossed tree trunks, a machine gun, and heavily armed fighters wearing red neckerchiefs and caps with the red crescent.

'Fuck!' said the driver. 'Sorry, sir. What am I to do?' Stones skittled under the wheels. The truck rolled to a halt and one by one the others slowed and stopped behind.

'Do nothing.' The Wehrmacht Lieutenant climbed down from the truck and with his hands in the air, walked firmly towards the partisans. He saluted and came to a stop a metre from the leader.

'Lieutenant Hans Fallmeyer,' he said in German, and clicked his heels. 'We have safe passage. There is an agreement. You know this.' He was unarmed.

The narrow verge was crammed with men, all armed with heavy weapons.

The brigade leader nodded to him. 'Do you speak Italian?' He barely came to the lieutenant's chest but his shoulders were much wider. His ebony beard was so thick and curly it almost hid the scarf, but there was no doubt of his affiliation. *Garibaldini*. Communists.

Fallmeyer nodded and replied in perfect cultivated Italian. 'Yes, I understand well. We have no desire to fight Italians.'

In clearly enunciated sentences, as if the lieutenant had said no, the partisan replied, 'You may pass, and your convoy. However, we will search every vehicle. Only Germans will proceed. No Italians. No *fascisti* will be permitted to leave the country.' He gestured with his *mitra*. 'You may lower your hands. Tell your troops. Tell the drivers to step down, tell the men to remain seated. All weapons to be laid down.' To his deputy, he said in an aside, 'No fucking SS or *fascisti* to pass through! Most of these look like Wehrmacht. I have to go and get orders.'

'Boss,' said another lieutenant, approaching him from the rear of the convoy, 'there are civilians in several cars at the back.'

The narrow lakeside road swelled with squeaking leather and sliding hobnails and clanking metal as the trucks opened, men climbed down, weapons were laid to the ground. Partisans strode the length of the cavalcade, throwing back the canvas drops at the rear of each truck. Confused exhausted faces peered out, most of them boys who understood only that they might be about to die. Some sullen, ready to do just that, some too dazed to care. The air was full of breath held.

One by one they searched the trucks, a partisan standing at the rear, machine gun trained on the occupants, as another mounted the ramp and inspected each soldier and his documents.

'Take care,' shouted one of the partisans, 'there is always bound to be at least one hero or martyr.'

No-one looked very heroic. Another man came from the rear of the convoy with the news that there were men, women and children in the civilian group, one claiming to be the Spanish Consul.

'I don't care if he is Jesus Christ, search every one of them.'

Time slowed, congealed about the occupants of the cars. At the roadside, trees dripped moisture and fog drifted in wispy trails about the passengers who alighted, shivering, and lounged against the vehicles and the tree trunks and stone walls, smoking, chatting and effecting nonchalance. Some wandered up and down for a view of the front of the convoy. More than twenty-eight trucks, all loaded to the chassis with heavy weapons and soldiers – it took an age to search them all, but if the Germans had known how few partisans there really were, it would have all taken much less time. 'Pedro' – Count Bellini delle Stelle, their leader – had gone for instructions and reinforcements. The local parish priest joined them, chatting to the Germans about large numbers of partisans in the area, so no-one felt inclined to act rashly. The search of the trucks ground on. Checking the documents of every single soldier took time.

In the fourth truck, Giuseppe Negri handed documents back to a soldier the age of an altar boy. He put out his hand to an older soldier who appeared to be asleep, slumped in a corner of the vehicle behind the driver's cabin, his greatcoat pulled up to his chin, helmet over his eyes.

'*Documenti!*' said Negri again, louder. He nudged the man, lifted the helmet and let it fall. The man still did not move.

'Drunk. Drunk,' said the boy seated beside him.

Negri shook the soldier one more time. He shrugged and put his hand out to the next soldier, checked the papers and flipped them back to their owner. His eyes flicked to the floor of the truck and he backed out. He climbed down and put his face beside his superior, Lazzaro.

'Boss, the Duce is in there,' he muttered.

'*Fesso.* Don't be an idiot,' he responded. 'I've heard three reports of Mussolini's death today already.'

'No, I am certain. I know him. He's got a coat too big for him, a helmet too big for him and he is wearing his own uniform boots. I tell you, it's the big man himself.'

The partisans fanned in a semicircle at the back of the truck, every gun trained on the entrance. The silence crisped with the sound of guns cocking. The seated soldiers tensed, ground jaws, gritted teeth. They shuffled along the seat-board away from the sleeping man. Negri climbed in again, his gun at the ready. He moved to the end of the row.

'Duce, you are required to come with me,' he said.

He leaned forward and removed the machine gun resting in the man's lap. He lifted the helmet. Mussolini nodded and clambered stiffly to his feet. One of the older soldiers put out a hand to steady him as he climbed over their feet. The partisans helped him down from the truck.

'Do you have any other weapons?'

Mussolini unbuttoned the German coat and, without a word, handed over a revolver from the waistband of his trousers. Beneath the ridiculous coat he wore a black shirt, militia trousers and his own highly polished, brown leather military boots. In the cold pale air his naked skull gleamed, clammy and grey. Goosebumps pimpled his neck. A flash of pity arced through his captor, but fleetingly. Perplexity spread across the face of each of the partisans. What the hell do we do now?

It spread further on their arrival in the village. Bellini delle Stelle was less surprised but just as perplexed. The prisoner appeared not to care.

'I arrest you in the name of the Italian people.'

'I shall not do anything,' Mussolini replied.

The Mayor approached and assured him of safe conduct.

'I am sure of it,' he responded calmly.

In the Town Hall, in the face of muttering, accusations and even abuse from the partisans, he remained impassive, unperturbed. He was once again the courteous compliant prisoner of the Gran Sasso.

With the German convoy disarmed and cleared to proceed, the partisans turned to the civilians in the cars. Lounging beside a yellow Alfa Romeo the tall, fair, moustachioed Spanish Consul awaited interviewing. In the car with him were two women and two children. The Consul handed Lazzaro his documents, irritated at the delay.

'You are the Spanish Consul?' asked Lazzaro.

'I have already told you this. I have already had my documents inspected.' His tone was peremptory, his Italian perfect. 'My wife and children and I must proceed at once.'

'And the other lady?' Lazzaro indicated the dark-haired woman in a heavy fur coat.

'I have nothing to do with this,' she answered for herself, with the same inflection as the Consul. 'These people were kind enough to offer me a lift from Como. No more.' She leaned against the car and examined her fingernails.

'Roman, all of them,' muttered the partisan to his comrade. He shifted his gaze from one to the other, slowly, running a thumb over the ridges of the stamp on the papers. 'These documents are forged. You are all under arrest.'

He pointed with his machine gun to the car, where one of the partisans was already in the driver's seat.

'The ladies and the children will travel in there. You will come with me,' he said to the Consul.

Mussolini was exhausted but the interrogation proceeded while Count Bellini delle Stelle awaited orders from the CLN. What were they to do with their prisoner? He was worried the Germans might try to free him again or local partisans would try to kill him. They had already executed several of the captured fascists. Shortly after the family from the motor car was brought in, great confusion and shouting in the piazza heralded the arrival of yet more fascists who had apparently escaped from the motorcade and been recaptured. Among them was Pavolini, who had been shot. Nothing stirred Mussolini's interest.

The Count returned to the inventory of the contents of Mussolini's briefcase and those of the other ministers. Each was filled with files intended to exonerate the holder for past misdeeds, and in the bottom of Mussolini's was a pile of gold sovereigns and several very large cheques on Italian banks.

'The documents are confidential and the cheques are for my trusted friends. The money is mine, from royalties for my book.' His tone said, 'It is of no interest to me'.

Unable to get more out of the prisoner, the Count handed him a paper to sign:

> *I was captured by the 52nd Garibaldi Brigade today, the 27th of April in Dongo. I have been treated correctly at all times.*

Bellini informed him he would be moved to a safehouse and he rose to leave. As he opened the door, Mussolini stirred and sat forward, his wattle quivering.

'There is a lady in the yellow Alfa,' he said.

The Count paused. 'Who is she?'

'She is the *Signora* Petacci. Will you tell her I am safe?'

The Count shrugged and said he would pass the message.

Marcello and his wife and children were taken to a hotel and Clara was closed into a room in the Town Hall. In the car, she had passed her last letter from Ben to her sister-in-law. An hour later she received a visit from Count Bellini delle Stelle. Clara was relaxed. She had removed the fur coat and was modestly dressed in a dark skirt, white blouse and soft cardigan. She wore little jewellery apart from a wedding ring, a fine gold bracelet and a watch. She crossed one stockinged leg over the other, dangling a very high-heeled shoe from her foot. As the Count entered she was examining her face in the oval mirror of a gold compact, which she snapped shut and placed on the table before her.

'I demand the Duce be handed to the Allies.' Her tone was imperious. 'He has been deserted and betrayed by traitors and cowards. I must go to him at once.'

'I am afraid, *Signora*, that he must be tried by Italians for his crimes. And you yourself must also answer many questions.'

'Then he might as well die now.' Tears brimmed and spilled and she mopped with an embroidered handkerchief. 'I want to die with him,' she sobbed. 'You cannot deny me the only thing I ask, to die with him.'

The Count barely restrained himself from patting her hand. 'I cannot promise anything, but I will have you taken to him.'

Surely they must be moved at once, the Count said. Why, oh why had they not received official instructions? What to do with them? Where to put them? The questions flitted about the room and no answers settled upon them. Finally, a message from the Allied Command to the CLNAI arrived:

A PLANE WILL ARRIVE TOMORROW AT 6 PM TO TAKE THE BIG
FISH STOP PREPARE LANDING SIGNALS STOP

The partisans would transfer the prisoners to Germasino, to a barracks where they could be easily guarded and await the handover to a representative of the CLNAI. At eleven thirty that night Bellini was informed plans had changed, yet again, and he was to transfer the prisoner, in haste, to another location and in great secrecy.

In a raging storm, he drove up the mountain. He ordered Mussolini's head bandaged, as a wounded partisan being taken to Como hospital. Clara was dressed as a Red Cross nurse. The vehicle bucked its way through the storm over washed-out roads, rocking and swaying through ditches until, at a bend, the sky lit up with rockets and flares and the radio blasted into life with the news the Allies had taken Como.

They could not get through. No further orders followed. The vehicle slewed and skittered off in another direction but Mussolini slept through it all, his head on Clara's shoulder. When he awoke, they were rolling and bumping up an unmade track into the yard of a large farmhouse, looming pale against the dark early hours of the morning.

The De Maria family was used to sheltering partisans. They asked no questions, made no comment, as the passengers clambered awkwardly down from the truck, lurching and staggering with exhaustion. The girl stumbled through the mire of the farmyard in high heels, steadied by the other prisoner and the guard, each with a hand under her arms. Beneath a full moon and scudding clouds, their shadows reared and pranced over mud, straw, ploughshares. Shadowy images of scythes and mattocks and rakes writhed against the rough wooden planks of a barn and from within, came the outraged hiss of geese disturbed by the intruders. The night air smelt of manure and rain.

The prisoners could sleep, Giacomo de Maria said, in his son's bed upstairs. He lit a kerosene lantern and ushered them through the darkened cow stalls to the cavernous kitchen on the first floor where his wife, Lia, dwarfed by a great hearth, fanned life and sparks into the embers of a log fire. Three hundred years of feet had worn runnels in the brick paving, an ancient track of habit and ritual, from fireplace to table to stone sink. Above, the tiles and beams were visible, the underside of the topmost floor. The prisoners, arm in arm, shivering, sagged to a seat at a long, scrubbed table.

'Can I get you something to eat?' she said. Poor things, they looked completely done in, she whispered to Giacomo.

'Coffee for me, please,' the girl replied, as if she were in a bar in the city.

Lia smiled. 'There is no coffee, only ersatz, my dear.'

She brewed the barley 'coffee' for everyone except the old man, who shook his head. The girl drank hers without comment.

When Lia returned from making up the bed, the girl helped the old man to his feet and assisted him to climb the steep stone stairs to the bedroom, where he slumped on one side of the bed. The girl straightened the cover a little, examined a pillowcase with a darn in it and swapped it from his side to her own, then gently lay the old man back and removed his boots. Beautiful boots. Not a partisan, then, Lia could see.

The girl began to tenderly unwind the bandages covering the old man's head. Her skin prickling as if she had touched a live wire, Lia recognised the famous face. Depleted, to be sure, but as recognisable as any portrait in any schoolroom. Lia had received bigger shocks in these years. Impassive, she handed the girl a linen towel.

'Where is the bathroom?' The girl checked the towel as if for darns there too, and turned to look about the room.

'You must excuse us, *Signora*, but this is the mountains, we have no bathroom.' Lia opened the door of the bedside cupboard, indicating the chamber pot. 'But you will have to bathe downstairs.'

The girl nodded and, still wearing the high heels, followed Lia back down the stairs, back through the kitchen, back across the mud, and through the drizzle to the outhouse attached to the barn, ignoring the partisan sent to guard her. In the rickety shed, she stripped naked and washed her body carefully with a cloth, from her face to her feet, unselfconscious and uninterested in the eye spying through a knothole.

'Didn't take my eye off her,' she heard the guard report to his companion, on their return. 'Great body, great tits.'

'The door is to remain ajar,' he called to the prisoners, and he and his comrade settled to sleep on the bare floor in the corridor. They had slept in worse places.

It would soon be dawn.

❧

'What a pity you cannot play for me.' Ben spoke for the first time. He lay rigid on his back, arms at his sides.

Her violin. Clara had not thought of it for so long. All through the time on the lake – 597 days, she had counted – it lay in its case. She was a good, solid violinist. Not inspired, she knew that, but still, not bad. She often played for Ben. It soothed him. He liked to vaunt her talent, liked people to know she had talents. Apart from Rachele, Ben always preferred women with talents.

Clara undressed and slid in next to him, taking his cold left hand between her warm ones. She squeezed his fingers. From outside, lightning flashed across the bare beams of the raked ceiling. They must be on the top floor, she noted. The room was not bad. At least the bed was large and comfortable, quite nice – walnut, with its high ornate head and foot. The clean linen smelled of laundry blue, starch and sunshine. It had the look of a trousseau – old but good quality, with handworked detail on the heavy sheets and pillowcases, a pale embroidered coverlet. Two cane chairs, a washstand – perhaps in the morning the woman might bring some water to wash their faces. Above the bed was a picture of the Sacred Heart, the golden gaze of a beatific, fair-haired Jesus as dazzling as the glittering rays of the mutilated heart. Ben would hate it. Her own heart thumped loudly in the silence, out of rhythm. She thought of her First Communion, her Confirmation. She would say a rosary later, or at least a couple of decades.

'We have spent so few nights together, my love.' She kept her voice to a murmur.

Ben turned his face to her, kissed the back of her hand and whispered, 'Can you ever forgive me? Look at what I have brought you to.'

She kissed his cheek and lay the length of her naked body along his own. For warmth, for reassurance, for love. 'I wish I had not lost the baby.'

Ben did not respond. Instead, he leaned up on an elbow and retrieved his wallet from the bedside table. In the back was a photograph, worn and creased. He passed it to her. 'This is how you will always be for me.'

Lying on her back, she held the photo before her. In the tenebrous light, she could just make it out. A young woman, eyes blazing, head thrown back, lithe body outlined by the wind in a light summer dress, before the mast of a sailing boat. The sail at her back, one arm raised to hold the stays, she laughed into the eyes of the photographer. Not a care in the world.

Clara pressed the photograph to her heart. 'We had what no-one else had. We had a great love. People will know that.'

Thirteen years together. Her entire adult life. Clara knew no other world but that of Ben. She had belonged to all the fascist children's groups – the *Piccole Italiane* and the *Giovani Italiani* – she loved it all, believed in everything, threw stones at communists and Jews. She wrote her first letter to Ben when she was fourteen. 'Duce,' it said, 'my life is for you.' She was a virgin. It felt like joining the Church, becoming a novitiate. After nearly six years of letters, they became lovers. The Duce was her destiny.

Ben's breathing was slow and regular. 'I tried, I really tried.' He sighed deeply. 'I did not want the war, you know that. It was the people who wanted the war, or their representatives at least.'

He had spent the past weeks mitigating the violence, commuting sentences and freeing prisoners, remonstrating with the RSI and the Germans over torture and persecutions. He had done his best. He could not be blamed. He really could not.

'I never authorised such methods. I feel no need to be justified or rehabilitated. I need no vindication. I have run my course.' He sighed again. 'But it is not how I would have wished to be remembered. Fascism is greater than a single man. It will survive.'

Hot tears dribbled down her cheeks onto the pillowcase. She made no attempt to staunch them, though she knew her mascara would run onto the white linen. She eased her aching left ankle, which had swollen, hoping she would be able to get her shoe on in the morning.

'I did not have Giacomo Matteotti killed, you know,' said Ben.

Matteotti. She had only been twelve then. Matteotti was history to her, but the name haunted Ben.

'I know. These things were not your fault, *amore*. You were betrayed by those around, you, by Graziani, by Pavolini.'

'By some. Others did their best. Pavolini has always been loyal to me. He will be there to the end. None of it matters anymore.'

Clara could just make out Ben's profile, the ashen stubble of his jaw, in the pallid light of approaching dawn. 'Sleep, my love. Sleep.'

'I am sure they will not kill me,' he said.

When his breathing deepened to a comforting snore, Clara pulled her rosary from her bag. She fingered the filigree chain and the pearls of its crucifix and sank into the liturgical familiarity of the beads. 'I believe in God, the Father Almighty, Creator of Heaven and Earth …'

Eleven o'clock. They woke together to clear light, a day of snowy mountains and dainty fluffy clouds. Perhaps it will be all right, Clara thought. She was in better spirits. Ben too seemed a little more animated. He leaned from the windows, his elbows on the sill, hands clasped, calling out for her the names of the nearby peaks.

'As if they were on holidays in the mountains,' Lia who had seen him from the garden, reported to Giacomo. 'What a strange world.' She went up to the room to offer them some breakfast.

'I will have polenta with a little milk,' said Clara.

'Yes, yes, me too,' said Ben in a low voice. 'Thank you.'

Downstairs, the hosts had made an effort to serve the meal with a little ceremony, on a white tablecloth. Milk fresh from their own goats, grilled polenta from the night before, and salami, said Giacomo, made by the De Maria men when they killed the pig in the winter. The guests ate without speaking, but they left nothing on their plates. Then they returned upstairs. No-one asked what was to happen next.

In the chilly bedroom Clara lay fully dressed on the bed, without worrying about flattening her hair. She pulled the covers over her and felt for the locket she had pinned securely into her brassiere, reassured by the warmth it drew from her breast. With her forefinger she traced round and round the fine etching, Ben's words engraved not only in the golden heart, but in her own.

He sat on the edge of the bed, staring at the floor. Occasionally, he lifted his head to gaze out the window. Clara prayed silently to Saint Rita, 'Deliver us from evil …'

'Will we go to hell?' she said.

'An invention of Saint Paul's, which Dante copied. They loved obscene violence,' said Ben. He did not believe in hell.

She wished she could be so sure. Romano was wrong about Ben not reading Greek, though. She smiled at the memory. Romano had said it in front of visitors and it made Ben quite angry. Romano was a very silly little boy at times. She herself had seen the copy of the *Apocalypse of St Paul* on Ben's shelf and it *was* in Greek. Clara found Dante – secretly, mind you – very boring.

For a long time neither spoke. The air carried the slightest scent of lilac.

Without turning to her, Ben said, 'There will be a spring day, but we will not be here to see it. We will not see the trees or the flowers. We will be underground. But where, oh where will that be?'

At 5 am on the twenty-eighth of April, Walter Audisio and his men of the Oltrepò Pavese Brigade set off from Milan, arriving at Dongo in the early afternoon. The meeting between Audisio and the Count was not a friendly one. Audisio claimed to have been sent from Milan to take charge and he was not to be denied. He would, he shouted, brook no disobedience and he would, if necessary, arrest everyone.

'I am here to execute my mission. It is the sentence of the Liberation Committee and of the General Command.'

Demanding a full list of all prisoners, he read down the list, ticking each name as he went. Beside Mussolini and Petacci he pencilled, 'Death'.

'Surely not the woman,' remonstrated the Count.

'She is as guilty as he. I have orders.'

One of Audisio's men, wearing two ammunition belts crossed on his chest, dragged Marcello in by a rope attached to manacles.

'So this is the Spanish Consul who speaks no Spanish.' Audisio's tone was derisory and he spoke in rapid-fire Spanish.

Still in Spanish, he hammered questions: where was Marcello born, where were his parents, why did he speak no Spanish, where was he going and where he had come from? Audisio's gestures became wilder, his voice louder and louder. Finally he lost control altogether and slapped the prisoner in the face.

'I know who you are,' he shouted in Italian now. 'You are Vittorio

Mussolini and you are a coward and a traitor.'

Marcello's knees buckled. He lurched forward, stuttering. His mouth opened and closed but he could barely speak, even in Italian. Still spluttering and protesting that he was not Vittorio, he was dragged to the door.

Audisio said to one of the men, 'Take him out and shoot him at once.'

Thrown in with other prisoners, Marcello was herded onto a covered truck to be transported to the town.

One of the prisoners asked glumly, 'I wonder what possessed Il Duce to bring us here? I always knew it was the wrong route to take.'

Pavolini, elegantly casual to the end, replied with a shrug and the old fascist mantra, '*Il Duce ha sempre ragione*. The Duce is always right.'

His boots noisy on the gritty limestone, Walter Audisio mounted the stairs of the farmhouse, two at a time. Without knocking, he pushed open the bedroom door. The prisoners were ready to go, though where, they had no idea. Mussolini wore a beret and his black uniform. Clara wore the dark skirt and white blouse of the day before. She lay on the bed with the cover thrown lightly over her. Mussolini paced.

'Are you armed?' Audisio asked him.

He replied, courteously, that he was not. He was tranquil. Clara, her breathing rackety and tremulous, gathered her things, moved wordlessly to the door and down the steep steps, holding to the wall so as not to fall. In the yard, she stumbled and tottered on the high heels, favouring the swollen ankle.

In the sunlight, the scene was one of great beauty. Great calm. The pretty house of white stone perched high on the side of the mountain. Far below a lake glimmered, aquamarine against the emerald of the forest. About the edge of the lake, a village formed a sparkling necklace and diminutive figures went, unconcerned, about their daily tasks. The prisoners were shepherded to the car and placed in the back seat, with men on the running boards and inside. As the car rolled out of the farmyard, tyres sucking at the mud and manure, Lia De Maria crossed herself.

The black Fiat travelled slowly down the mountain road, coming to a halt before the gates of a villa in the hamlet of Giulino di Mezzegra. If the prisoners wondered what they were doing at the villa, they gave no sign. Audisio ordered everyone out of the car and posted a man at either end of the bend in the road. The prisoners linked arms, stumbling against one another along the gravel road as directed, to a low stone wall.

'Stop! Stand there,' Audisio ordered.

They halted before the pillars of tall wrought-iron gates. 'Villa Belmonte' read Clara, from a brass plate, 'Beautiful Mountain'. She turned to Ben, looked into his face and said, 'I have followed you all the way.'

She was very pale. Her voice was soft and clear. She no longer trembled and her breath was even.

From the garden behind the gates, the voices of children at play were as light as the spring air. From the terrace of the villa, a woman called down to a man in the garden to bring some onions up when he came. Audisio shouted to the woman to take the children and everyone else indoors. In these times, no-one needed to be told more than once. Silence rolled down.

The shots should have come, should have shattered the silence. Before the pillar, the two figures leaned closer together, clutched each other tighter, facing the machine gun – the jammed machine gun, the useless machine gun. It was Walter Audisio who trembled now. In a frenzy, he threw the gun to the ground and grabbed a pistol but that too jammed. The two figures remained, as immobile as the garden statues of the Villa Belmonte behind them.

On the third attempt, with the last machine gun, Mussolini opened his shirt and called, 'Aim for the heart.'

The shots exploded. Ten rounds. A crimson flowering, too early for poppies. Startled starlings screeched out of the trees. Smoke rose from the gun barrel. The acrid smell of cordite hung on the air and settled on the clothes of the men, who did not move. High above, in a crystalline sky, a plane, pregnant with bombs, droned overhead. Below in the valley, dogs barked, but not at the gunfire. They were used to gunfire. Beyond the open door of the car, a butterfly – perhaps the first of the season, flitted heedlessly across the tips of buds not yet open to it. In the new grass, behind the iron gates, crocus and iris peeped through and on the verge, wildflowers poked their heads up cautiously.

The bodies crumpled, quivered, quieted. Stilled. Together.

Benito Amilcare Andrea Mussolini

Born 29th July 1883, Predappio

Died 28th April 1945, Mezzegra

Clara Petacci

Born 28th February 1912, Rome

Died 28th April 1945, Mezzegra

PART FIVE

CHAPTER 21

Florence, April 2008

'You know, people in Brisbane are just about drinking their own pee while we are nearly drowning!'

Delia shook out the sodden umbrella, flapped her dripping rain hat against the doorpost and flung them aside, where the water pooled on the stone threshold. Outside the windows, the autumn rain showed no mercy. She unwrapped the week-old *Sydney Morning Herald*, and theatrically intoned the headline announcing the official end of '... the worst drought in living memory. Or since the Pleistocene, or something.' The rest of the east coast, Brisbane especially, was still deep in drought.

Annabelle and Delia moved fluently and fluidly between English and Italian, but to each other, they spoke English, Delia's mother tongue.

'We should get them onto the shelves, Belle,' Delia said, nodding at the diaries.

'I'm not sure,' Delia had said to her mother on the phone that morning. Annabelle seemed to be bearing up well, but Enrico's death was always going to be a big one for her. On the surface, she told her mother, Annabelle was dealing with it as she dealt with everything. With calm. On the surface. 'She's hit a slump. It's only a few days since the election and she's still talking about leaving Italy.'

Delia began to shift stuff from the lower shelves above the desk, shunting aside a pile of folders and the last five days of *Il Corriere*. She picked up three of the foxed notebooks and held one out. Annabelle took it without comment, glanced through it for an opening date and placed it on the shelf towards the centre. The diaries had no markings on their covers and were in no particular order. They could only be sorted by the date of the first entry. She picked up three more. After a while, Delia pulled up a chair beside her, but she did not lift her head.

The notebooks were not all alike – some smaller than others. Annabelle, or at first, her father, when she was young, had bought them in lots of four or five at a time. A couple from early 1944 had loose leaves in the front, held closed with string. There were gaps, some missing here and there. Perhaps she found little to record in peaceful times, Annabelle said with a shrug, and it was not always easy to conserve them in the mountains; then later, the odd one got lost. The older notebooks had marbled endpapers with pink and blue mottling. The covers of stiff cardboard had a design of squares and many corners had thickened and split. The earliest pages, written in a perfect, copybook script, in freshly sharpened pencil, were decorated with childishly drawn fish and flowers and animals, in coloured pencils and crayons. Bit by bit the drawings gave way to quotes, aphorisms, adages and axioms. By the time Annabelle turned the pages of the book that opened with *'lunedì il 9 maggio, 1938'*, little of childhood remained.

> *Hitler came today. Papà says we will go to war. He is sending Umberto and Giacomo to Australia. I am afraid.*

Hours later, Annabelle sat back in her deep-buttoned revolving chair, with a shaky sigh. This was once her father's study and now it was hers. Little had changed. And everything had changed. The faded rose-coloured silk had covered the back wall for more than a hundred years – a replacement, her father once told her, for the deep green William Morris wallpaper imported from England, which had turned out to be poison and had nearly killed her grandfather from arsenic poisoning. The soft colours of the Persian rug had mellowed but not faded. The octagonal design of the tiled flooring, laid down in the Renaissance, was as clear as ever, despite soft hollows of wear in the doorways. Two of the ornate lampshades of tasselled silk had been there in her father's time, but the soaring lines of the Castiglioni floor lamp, flowing in a great arc from the corner into a cascade of light on the desk, was a more recent acquisition. Life moves on.

At the window, evening closed in. The random flitting through more than half a century of history, much of it in fuzzed lead-pencil, left her dizzy and distressed. Her hands were cold, with a slight tremor, as if from too much caffeine or the shifting of tectonic plates. Her mind was as fuzzy as the smudged writing. It was one thing to hold her memories in the storehouse of the past, at a controlled temperature, but quite another to live them again as they happened, in the pages of the notebooks. She had closed so many doors, made decisions about how to order her memories, rewrite her narrative. Was she, at this late stage, to begin studiously unpicking the seams of her past to make of it a more attractive, more modern, more acceptable garment? She would not do it.

In the crammed space of the Harold Acton Library, on a hard stackable chair, Delia shifted restlessly on her numbed buttocks. The lecture on 'Women in Renaissance Art' droned on at a great distance. A muscle twitched in her right eyelid. She was used to History. With a capital H. Family history, though, was not her field. Not live families. She preferred the comforting distance that came with the study of dysfunctional families long dead. It was a bit cloying, knowing each and every one of your ancestors for nearly a millennium. She was glad hers was a distant, cadet branch of the original family and glad of the rupture of her Australianness. For her, the searing events of Italy's modern civil war were only general knowledge. For Delia there had always been an invisible border between the present and the past. Suddenly, this was *her* past too.

The Guardian was open on the desk. Annabelle leaned over it, hair obscuring her face, as Delia entered with coffee on a tray. The headline blared:

> *2008 April 15.* BERLUSCONI SWEEPS BACK TO POWER AS LEFT CONCEDES DEFEAT IN ITALIAN ELECTIONS. *Government seems to be most right-wing in fourteen years.*

'April it seems, is indeed, the cruellest month.'

Annabelle was in the Qantas pyjamas she had taken to wearing in the house since she abandoned her principles and began to fly in Business – might as well get my money's worth out of them, she said. She wore Enrico's old leather slippers. She shook her head slowly from side to side as if seeing the results for the first time, although it was five days since the elections. Each day's issue of *Il Corriere della Sera*, with its grisly details of the polls and the aftermath, was piled to one side of the desk. Seen from the outside world, though, it was irrevocably real.

They had lived every moment of the ghastly lead-up to the elections – Annabelle choleric as Berlusconi, in another of his nine lives, campaigned throughout on essentially a fascist platform, to oust the decent Economist from Bologna, Romano Prodi. In the streets, especially in Rome where Casa Pound attracted young thugs wearing T-shirts with Mussolini's face on their chest, the resurgence of fascism was like the reappearance of an old, communicable disease. We were never vaccinated properly, said Annabelle. Antique shops advertised Mussolini memorabilia. Souvenir shops sold Mussolini busts, even anniversary wine bottles with the dictator's face on the label. It used to be just far-right maniacs, but since the nineties it had grown and now it was everywhere. Behind his cash register, Paolo, the butcher, hung a calendar with twelve photos of Il Duce. Why? Annabelle asked him, why? Because, he answered, when I was a child he was the only one to put food on our table. I am loyal to him.

Berlusconi had always modelled himself on Il Duce. How could he … how could he have actually given the Roman salute wearing a black shirt, in front of the world? 'We all saw it! He might as well have said *Eviva Il Duce.*' And no-one, *no-one* seemed to be outraged! Outrage was Annabelle's default position these days. What was wrong with Italians that they continued to tolerate this man? The Northern League and all its vicious racist policies had been returned with an increased majority and Berlusconi had their support.

'Italy's most right-wing government since Berlusconi came to power fourteen years ago,' she read aloud, stabbing the words with her finger. So, Berlusconi was back and Enrico was dead. 'There's nothing here for me any longer.' Annabelle folded the newspaper into a small thick wad and shoved it into a desk drawer, which she shut with a vicious slam.

'Do you want to talk?' said Delia.

'Not yet, *Tesoro*. Soon.' Annabelle smiled as if she were calm and eased her back as she turned away from the desk. She rubbed the ball of her forefinger round and round her thumbnail. She must stop. It was becoming a tic. She wanted to throw something. Instead, she poured the coffee and slumped into her creaky armchair.

Delia cleared the cups and left her to drink her coffee in silence. How could he be gone? Not there? Enrico was her past. The only person left who had known her, really known her, all her life. Now, he was not left. Knew her. Had known her. Might have known her. Should have known her. The many tenses of the past. She leaned down, scrabbling about in the bottom drawer of her desk, under paperclips and pens and glue and stamps and scraps of paper, and blew the dust off a cigarette lighter. Heavy and cool in her hand, the polished steel cylindrical Imco was battered and scarred. The intricate design within a small circle was hard to make out now. EFA. It had sat on his desk in Sydney until that last visit, when he left it behind in the restaurant in San Casciano.

Empty now, his study, faraway in the glary Sydney sunlight that bleached the colour from things. Empty now, that room, yet unchanged: the books and notes and pens and sharpened pencils, stern piles of research papers ranged with military precision along broad shelves behind his chair. One wall covered by three large maps of the world: a Mollweide projection from 1857, a Mercator projection from fifty years later, and his most treasured possession – an original 1559 Portolan map of the Mediterranean, inked onto vellum. He had many others, not originals but precious to him. Enrico did not care about provenance, he cared about adventure, about beauty. The Mollweide had miniscule black dots of texta on the glass, where he had traced a route, like a trail of insect droppings across the globe.

On his high cedar desk, Post-it notes – blue and pink, never yellow – formed a paper-chain in a row across the balcony shelf at the back, each with a sentence to be inserted somewhere, at some time. Photos pinned to the corkboard, some curling, had been there for years. Scraps of poems or jokes or aphorisms overheard, and recorded with the habit of a lifetime, awaited retelling in the moments of high laughter and repartee for which he was known. Everyone loved Enrico's stories; a great raconteur, whose candid and self-deprecating tales always concealed more than they revealed.

A jacket would be slung over the back of the armchair where he read late into each night, sitting upright, never in bed. Enrico was never on good terms with sleep. From the walls, the mordant gaze of his paintings would find only the empty chair: the Boyds – all of them – Blackman, Whitely, Brack, Preston; a long list of Australian painters or the photographs of Cazneaux or Dupain. No sculpture. He could not see the point of sculpture, even modern sculpture. Too much of it in the house as he grew up, he said, shadowy figures watching over his every move. Enrico was fascinated, absorbed by the modernity of the new world, uncorrupted for him by a continuous past or a recent one. He wanted nothing to do with old Europe. His vinyl records and collection of CDs were almost all jazz, with the exception of Monteverdi, Telemann. No classical composer made it past the Baroque. Objects become hieroglyphs, no longer decipherable, when their owner is gone.

In a long life in forensic medicine, Annabelle had seen so many dead people. She was thankful Enrico had been cremated. Australians believed in cremation; Italians did not. With macabre consequences – bodies exhumed after ten years, the bones placed in an ossuary to make room for the next cadaver. It hurt like a paper-cut to the heart to think of those beautiful brown hands, the body she knew so well, being devoured by the flames, yet it was so much cleaner. To lie awake at night, imagine him decomposing, melting back into the earth, would be torture. Decomposition and putrefaction may have been a normal part of her working life, and God knows she saw enough of it during the war, but not now. Not Enrico. How was it possible the sun would still come up every day and the stars still come out at night? The stars, the moon and the sun, unwanted now. She could not remember who said that. When life is gone, the lights are out.

Tears crept up behind her – unfamiliar for so long – but she shook them off, though the effort hurt her throat. Once, when her tears spilled, Enrico wiped them slowly with his forefinger and licked them dry. He would not admit fear but like Ulysses, he was never ashamed to weep. There *were* tears coming but not yet. If she allowed them now she might drown in them. She swallowed the stone in her throat and took some deep, shuddery breaths. There was a biography half-written by some academic from the university. What would become of that? She had said no last year, when asked to be interviewed for it. She turned her chair full circle, taking in the cosy jumble of books and music and lamps and rugs and pictures. Odd to imagine all this without her. At least posterity had no prurient interest in her.

When Delia had phoned from London to say she was coming, Annabelle had thought, thank God. She needed to see her, needed to talk to her, needed the only person left who really loved her. Delia had been her sounding board for most of her life, but Annabelle was not quite ready yet. Just a little longer to think about things. Talking about 'things' was not her strong point. Nor, for that matter, Enrico's. 'The War' was part of the weft and warp of Italian society and of their lives – unavoidable. Italians were not like Australians who fought on someone else's land and then went back and turned their minds as much as they could from the horror. For Italians who stayed, it was still their land and every day was lived in those same streets and fields and landscape. It took an acrobatic feat of forgetting to be able to go on, a conscious decision to close off those rooms in the mind and the memory. To close them off and seal them tight. Enrico and Annabelle had once understood that. But forgetting was not always as easy as all that.

February 1944

It is still very cold. We have had word of Leone's death in Regina Coeli. They had him for four months. I do not know how he held out that long. It began when they killed the Rossellis. Seven years of murder. Leone Ginsburg was a hero. Who will be next? I think of Anna all the time. Will I be strong enough if it is me?

Delia snapped the diary shut and rose creakily from Annabelle's desk. Who was Anna? she wondered. She yawned, stretched and shook herself, casting off the spell of the diaries. It was four hours since, unable to sleep, she had taken herself into the study to read the diaries. She was becoming obsessed by them: the long fingers of that world beckoning into hers.

At the window, the sun climbed over the edge of another April Florence morning where things were all right – where news of murder was distant, and turned mostly on the convoluted internal worlds of domestic violence or the doings of Mafia dons whose deaths disturbed few. Outside, beneath the tall windows, the shutters of the shops clanged up and the tumbrel-roll of trolley wheels heralded the day's plentiful deliveries of fruit and vegetables and meat and fish. Shopkeepers shouted greetings and ribaldry to each other, in a world where few people asked themselves if they would be strong enough to face the day. It was still dark in the street; Summer Time, *l'ora legale,* started three weeks ago, robbing her of the mornings before they even got started. Delia hated daylight saving. It was the same in Sydney – the mornings were dark and the hot evenings endless. Annabelle too was depressed by the dark mornings. There – Delia had said the word. Annabelle was depressed. Enrico's death came at a bad time for her, right at that moment when the bleak situation in Italy made a mockery of all the things they had both lived for, fought for.

Enrico, she thought. A force of nature. Hard to love. Too domineering, too charming, too single-minded. He used up all the oxygen in the room. Enrico did not care for the good opinion of others. He made you laugh and he made you like him because it pissed him off if someone failed to fall beneath his spell, but he did not really care. 'Opinions,' he said, 'are like arseholes. Everyone has one.' In argument, he was vicious. It was the Italian in him. Italians, Delia had learned, did not understand the rules of fair play or debating – like cricket, an English affectation. Theirs was an older, darker, winner-takes-all mindset, harking back to the times of Homer or Herodotus or Sallust. For Enrico, there was no room for second place or pity for the loser. When she was small and timid, Delia kept out of his boisterous way as much as possible, but as she grew older she enjoyed engaging him, courting danger: bear-baiting. He could be fun. He was certainly brilliant, but he formed his own opinions early on, imbibed from voracious reading of the classics of every language and honed by life and death in the mountains, and he saw no need to recast them as time went by.

Enrico's fallings-out with friends and colleagues were regular and spectacular. He had no gift for sustained friendship – too combative, too contrarian, he regarded friendship as a competitive sport. In fact, thought Delia, Enrico regarded life as a competitive sport – not for him the gentle bobbing around on Sydney Harbour of the day sailors. From the moment he learned to sail, he raced to win. He loved the Sydney to Hobart. His likes and dislikes were violent. He loathed history in its modern forms. Marxist history, Subaltern history – what in the name of Christ was that, he thundered. Nothing but revisionism! Yet in music and art he rejected the traditional, loved the modern. A volatile mix, Enrico, best handled with care. Delia kept a safe distance.

All her life Delia knew, even as child, that Annabelle and Enrico were a pair. The older they got, the more they looked alike but the more different they became in character and personality. Whenever Annabelle visited Sydney, Enrico was much more in evidence and much nicer. More jokes, less sarcasm. It was the same when he came to Florence. There was a softening about the edges of both of them, a harmony. But then they would part and each would retreat into a world of their own again. Delia belonged to Annabelle's private world but not to Enrico's. Her parents never discussed relations between Annabelle and Enrico but as Delia grew older, she knew instinctively they were lovers. Once she was admitted to the world of adults, the two women spent many evenings over many bottles of good red, dissecting the lover of the moment. Have you ever slept with someone out of good manners? Delia once asked, but she knew her aunt never would have. Annabelle was made of sterner stuff. She had Enrico's lack of compulsion to please. They often discussed Enrico. Annabelle was not reticent about their relations.

'Did you still ... well, you know ... ? Delia asked.

'What, screw like rabbits?' laughed Annabelle. 'Well, there's not as much hanging from chandeliers, perhaps, but sex does not stop when oestrogen runs out, you know, my dear.'

Delia's first visit to Florence without her parents was in 1964. Annabelle travelled to Sydney from Genoa on the maiden voyage of the MV *Guglielmo Marconi* and after Christmas, she took Delia back with her on the return voyage through the Suez Canal. In the long weeks on the ocean, Delia left behind her Australian life. Once they began to travel by air, via London in a trip taking more than four or five days, the colours of Cairo and Manila were imprinted indelibly on her retinas. She was already in love with the idea of her aunt, and in Florence she fell in love with the place that had once been the capital city of Italy.

Two years later in 1966, when she was twelve, the Arno reared up, a vengeful griffin obliterating the city. The Arno had done what the Germans could not, said Enrico. He wept. Annabelle did not. Delia had never seen her aunt cry. Enrico, so harsh in so much, was easily moved to tears, which perplexed people. Delia's memories of the flood were of being treated as an adult for the first time. Annabelle enrolled her with the 'Mud Angels' flocking in from all over the world to help with the clean-up, to help save the art that gave the city its soul. Even Maddie came to help, returning each evening, resembling a photo of a New Guinea mud man Delia had seen in a magazine. Bert stayed at home – someone had to keep things going here, he said.

A memory: a long-ago visit to Bondi with her two brothers, and her two adult cousins. She must have been about five years old. She closed her eyes and every detail glowed in the colours no photo of the time could have shown. The sunlight was molten silver. She wore yellow, elasticised, smocked-cotton bathers – the wet sand gathered into the saggy crotch. The red rubber bathing cap pulled her hair and hurt as it was stretched on. The boys and Enrico wore dark woollen trunks with a white belt. Annabelle was in a green and pink and white floral two-piece with square legs and a scanty top tied in a bow between her breasts. Annabelle and Enrico sat side by side, knees drawn up, watching the children at the edge of the water. Delia was afraid of those giant waves. She played behind Annabelle and Enrico, decorating her sandcastle with twigs and shells. Enrico's hand rested lightly on the back of Annabelle's neck, beneath tendrils of her hair, which was loosely pinned up. Their shoulders touched, their voices a companionable murmur in the sleepy glare. Delia wanted to stay there forever. As they nattered, Enrico gently massaged the nape of Annabelle's neck. Delia was fascinated by the missing tips of two of his fingers and by their slow circular movement beneath the escaped curls, by the swan-like curve of their slender, tanned spines, the broad shoulders and narrow waists, as they leaned together into the shape of a heart.

❧

'I heard you up at some ungodly hour.' Annabelle entered with two cups of chromatic black coffee and placed one before Delia. Her hair was a tangle, her eyes were puffy. It was already 8.30 am.

Delia stretched and yawned again and drank the coffee gratefully. 'Who was Anna?' She waved a diary, which opened at a page marked with a scrap of paper.

'I never knew Anna. She died before I was truly involved. But I never forgot her.'

'Yet you've never mentioned her. So much you never mentioned.'

'There's too much talk, too much empty talk in the name of telling the truth.'

Annabelle put her cup down with a thump, slopping blips of coffee onto the diary and the papers on her desk. 'There is a place for silence too. It is what we do not talk about, that's how we survive. There is far too much talking about things these days. Truth is a highly overrated commodity. At my age, I know I will be dead soon. My lease is almost up. But I don't say it and you don't say it. That's the convention.'

Delia's weariness evaporated. 'And the truth? The truth doesn't matter? If not, why did you keep the diaries all these years?' There was a quiver to her voice.

'Truth.' Annabelle's tone was acerbic. 'Truth can kill. Don't historians know what an ephemeral commodity the truth is?' Then viciously, 'You people all think things are so simple. Have you never read Ibsen? Truths kill.'

You people. Delia's eyes smarted.

Annabelle turned away to the window where the sun was fully risen, demanding admittance. Enrico had bent the truth to his will, as he bent everything and everybody. His was 'the truth of the moment'. Annabelle's truth was hers alone, not of the moment, not as mutable as that. She owed no-one her truth. She hoarded her truth. She did not tell lies but she was secretive by nature.

'The more talk about truth,' she said, less violently, 'the less of it there is. One man's truth ...! There is nothing more cowardly than confessing your secrets. Unloading them onto someone else.' She loathed people who felt they had to give you their truth, a piece of their mind, a piece they could usually ill do without. 'I loathe this modern, self-help confessional crap.'

'Ooh! The list of things you do not loathe is getting shorter.' Delia recovered herself. 'You're certainly getting more like Enrico. You know you two sound ...' – Delia did not alter the tense – '... exactly alike? Same diction, same cadence.'

'Did *you* know, Kafka ordered Max Brod to burn all his diaries and papers after his death?'

'Bullshit, Belle. If he really wanted that, what was stopping him from doing it himself? Henry James did.'

The spell of the diaries held them fast in its grip.

If you have died my love, ... if you have died.

Annabelle snapped the diary shut. Neruda's lament was the only entry for the terrible day that brought the news of Enrico's death. But Enrico did not die then. Elsa died instead. Now Enrico was irrevocably dead. She knew Delia had been walking around her on eggshells, waiting for the explosion. There was a storm coming. She was surprised by the anger welling in her. Floods of anger. Scalding waves of anger. There was a lot of anger in grieving.

She flipped the pages forward to Elsa. *Now I am an orphan.* Elsa's funeral. She had chosen clothes from Elsa's wardrobe to dress her. While Eleanora wore her hair in a tidy roll, Elsa's hair flowed. Everything about Elsa flowed, was fluid, riparian, exotic. Not for her Eleanora's pastel-grey wool frock with a modest crossover bodice and pearls at the throat. No. Elsa was garbed in the softest, floatiest silk skirt and fringed shawls that Annabelle could find in her wardrobe.

Enrico left immediately after the interment – his only words: We will find out who betrayed her.

There had been a memorial service in Sydney for Enrico. Annabelle was glad she'd not been there. She could not have sat in a draughty university hall listening to people who thought they knew him, extolling his virtues. Colleagues to whom he had been inexcusably rude, telling hearty stories about what a character he was. Much would have been made of his ready jokes and his classical allusions. Maddie would have cried. Dear Maddie, she always had the right tears for the occasion. Bert would have been stoic, phlegmatic. Enrico and Bert had formed an unlikely but fond friendship. Great bloke he was, according to Bert. Elisa did not go – she had not travelled much in recent years. After all this time, she told Maddie, I am hardly his widow.

Delia would be back soon. She had gone to some sort of memorial service at Mt Pratomagno for Bert Hinkler. Delia was part of a rich weave of Australians in Florence, each there for different reasons, each bringing something of the new world into the old, old world of shadows and images that was Florence. Annabelle remembered the State funeral held by Mussolini for Hinkler. She was seven and she loved the solemnity of the cortege in all its colourful glory and pomp – the ornate gilded hearse drawn by magnificent black horses, with a coachman in breeches, more like images of the English royal ceremonies than the drab fascist entertainment she had seen up to then. Aviation was an obsession for Mussolini and Italo Balbo and others, with an almost totemic significance for the Regime and all its followers, and all children were steeped in images and stories of flight. When the Australian aviator's plane crashed onto the slopes of the mountain there was widespread consternation, and weeks later, when his body appeared as the snows melted, it seemed natural that much would be made of it. For both children it set forever the idea of themselves as having foreign, exotic roots in that strange land. How could they ever have imagined that one far-off day, Enrico would die there?

Florence 2008

Tired and ready for bed, Annabelle surveyed her diaries neatly ranged along the shelves she and Delia had cleared for them, directly under a shelf holding framed family photographs. Behind her, the TV droned with the turgid analysis of the elections, which by now she knew by heart. On her desk was a loose pile of old photos from the bottom of the diary boxes. She put down the novel she was not reading, shuffled the loose photos a bit and then, from the shelf, reached down a heavy silver-framed photograph of her father, gazing off slightly to his left, his expression serious, a little self-conscious. Not a family snap but a portrait of an important man.

Achille was a patrician who had not properly come to terms with the twentieth century. The code of honour and manners he lived by had shrivelled around him, but he had turned away and tried not to see. He held an aristocratic affection for the peasantry and a slight disdain for the bourgeoisie. He despised Mussolini and consist-ently underestimated him. With most of his land-owning class, he had once thought Mussolini might be useful, firmly agreeing with Giolitti in 1921 that the fascists were like fireworks and after the noise had subsided, only the smoke would remain. All through 1922, Mussolini's writings and ravings included statements such as 'the era of democracy is over', but hardly any Italian believed in democracy, such as it was. Few had ever had the vote anyway.

'Oh, Papà.' Annabelle's eyes prickled.

All through 1923, he and his friends looked on as socialists, com-munists, unionists, liberals, and anyone at all opposing the fascists was beaten, exiled, jailed, political parties abolished. When Matteotti was murdered a year later, they were beginning to think they might have been wrong, but by then it was too late. At any time, he said, the government, or certainly the King, could have stopped the fascist excesses, but it didn't suit them – the King was flattered into wel-coming the rag-tag army and its vain little leader to Rome. Queen Margherita even had them for lunch! When Achille read in *Il Corriere della Sera* on the thirty-first of October 1922, that women threw flowers at the 'man of destiny' on his unimpeded procession through Rome, he knew things were serious. 'March on Rome! What a farce!'

Annabelle's mother recalled him throwing the newspaper to the table, knocking crockery and cutlery in every direction, but the crashing of domestic accoutrements was no impediment to Mussolini. From farce it turned to tragedy. Their mistake, Achille admitted, had been to think 'the little clown' and 'puffed-up baboon' could ever be taken seriously.

Now it was happening again with Berlusconi. Just as a youthful Annabelle had known no politics but that of Mussolini, for the young today there had been no other politics but that of Berlusconi. A generation ruined and perverted by a clown and a buffoon who had set back the cause of all Italians, and women in particular, by half a century. Neither Mussolini nor Berlusconi came from the moon. They were no foreign invaders. They sprang from the same soil as all Italians. Mussolini was appointed by the King, dismissed by the King.

'I do not think I can live in this country any longer.' She spoke aloud.

The bang of the door below echoed in the narrow street and Delia's key scraped in their front door. Annabelle willingly gave up any idea of an early night. Delia had been staying with her now, on and off, since she was ten. Maddie would not let her go alone before that, though they had all travelled back and forth often, more often to London than to Florence. Annabelle usually met them in London. In 1954, Delia was born early, in St Barts in London while Maddie and Bert were spending the year there. Annabelle travelled back to Australia with them, to help Maddie with the children. It felt redemptive, she said – one pure thing in all our lives.

She fell in love with Sydney on that trip, for much the same reason. It was free of the ancient woes of the old continent. Sydney had a past all its own: a racy, tough past. She was taken by surprise at the kindness and the openness, the willingness to try anything. Most of all, she loved the rough egalitarianism and the tall walk of Australians. She thought she might stay forever. She rented a honey-coloured house built of soft sandstone, and from its lacy veranda she watched the boxy, green and cream ferries plying the choppy waters of that turbulent city. But she did not stay. The verdant decadence of the harbour city at the bottom of the world would always have a claim on her but the umber and ochre, the stone and tile, the medieval mazes of Florence were home. After a time, she went home to her ghosts.

The pastel frescoes far above on the vaulted ceiling, vaguely illuminated at night by the street lamps through the open shutters, had been Delia's company after lights-out during school holidays in Florence. Like the forms of clouds, she made them into anything she wanted them to be. She still adored her room in the vast apartment covering the whole of the first floor of the building in Borgo Pinti. Although the floor above belonged to Enrico, he rarely used it. Many of her cousins came and went, providing company for her as a child, and later as an adult. The building had been in the family for eight hundred years, but the ground floor had been let as offices for forty years or more. Who can afford the upkeep on these buildings otherwise, said Annabelle. Like half the properties in Tuscany, the castle in the countryside had passed to the trust set up by Francesco, run as holiday rental apartments by one of Enrico's granddaughters.

Annabelle turned at the clink of a bottle and glasses. She did not speak. Delia threw her coat over a chair, carrying wine and glasses in one hand. She kissed the top of Annabelle's head and sat in the armchair directly before her. Delia poured two glasses of wine, very full.

'When we were young, women and children had their wine cut with water.' Annabelle took a deep draught. The memory of the homemade wine from the farm was not a fond one. 'Tasted as if it had been strained through old underpants!'

Neither suggested they should be eating rather than drinking without food. They raised their glasses and Annabelle nodded and said, 'So!'

Delia kicked off her stilettos and put her feet up on the sofa. 'Let's start with Enrico,' she said. 'As a child, I thought he was a grumpy, impatient old bastard. He didn't like children. As an adult, of course

I fell beneath his spell. Everyone did. He made sure of that. Hard to like him though, too prickly. I could never understand why you put up with him, but chemistry is a strange thing. And let's not go into my own choices in men!'

Annabelle smiled. Enrico and Delia had a lot in common. Patience was not Delia's chief virtue. Annabelle too had her bare feet up on the footstool. It was still too cold to go barefoot in the house, but in the summer she loved to go barefoot indoors – a secret vice contracted in Sydney, not respectable to Italians who think bare feet, *piedi nudi*, are either a careless risk of kidney damage or an invitation to sex.

Annabelle was ready to talk. She was comfortable and she knew it would be a long night. She sipped her wine.

'I did not like children either, you know.'

'You liked me.'

'I love you. That is different. Love is not the same as liking. I did not always like Enrico – he was an impossible man – but I always loved him.' She took a deep breath. 'I have loved him all my life. He was three when I was born and he held me on his lap that first day. Concordance. It is the blood: sharing the same blood and the same genes and the same memories. I have lost a twin.'

'Ah, the blood, the soil, *gli avi*, the ancestors,' said Delia. 'I've never been all that interested in the ancestors.' Nor, she went on, were Clare and Diana, who were more likely to ski in the Dolomites than spend time in Florence. Her brothers showed more interest in the bloodlines of their stallions and bulls than their Italian relatives.

When, after the war, Bert inherited Achille's title, he was horrified. That stuff was The Past, he said. Give it to Enrico. As if Enrico would ever have used a title.

'I know,' said Annabelle. 'Australians are not tied to their soil the way we are.'

'Well, Aboriginal Australians are,' replied Delia, 'but *we* have not spilled enough of our own blood on our own soil to have that. Thank God. Why didn't you marry him? Why have I never asked you before?'

'I don't think we could have married,' replied Annabelle. 'Wouldn't it have been incest – wasn't it against the law? Though we had broken so many laws that there was no meaning left in laws for us.'

It was not the law. She knew that. Enrico did not believe in marriage but no-one would have known or cared whether they were married, in Australia.

'It was not for those reasons. It was because we did not believe in marriage and we did not believe enough in us,' she said. 'Certainly, Enrico married and had children, but men do that, don't they? Some atavistic drive to reproduce. He needed someone to keep the home fires burning, I imagine.'

'Were they ever happy, Enrico and Elisa?' asked Delia.

'Who knows?' She shrugged. 'They stayed together a long time. He did not believe in monogamy. Marriage was a purely contractual arrangement for society's ends, he said.'

Every time he came back, or Annabelle went to Australia, or they met elsewhere in the world, they made love. 'I always said I would never do it again and then I did. He thought I didn't marry because of him, but it was not true. Or perhaps it was and I have deluded myself all these years.'

Annabelle had hardly been celibate. Delia had observed the constant parade of lovers, none of whom ever lasted until Christmas. It saved on gifts, said Annabelle.

'Anyway, I did not – do not – believe in marriage. I read somewhere: a husband is what is left of a lover once the nerve has been extracted.' Annabelle smiled.

She leaned across and ejected the CD of Beethoven's 2nd Romance, which had been playing on a loop, and replaced it with John Coltrane's 'Blue Train', to please Delia.

'We thought the war had changed things forever. We thought things would be better. But no. Women were expected to go back into the kitchen as if nothing had happened. And they did.'

She leaned forward as Delia refilled her glass.

'We expected utopia. There was nothing civil about our war. There was nothing civil about the aftermath. I do not blame him for leaving. To see the old men back in control was more than he could bear. I did not like the idea of the frontier but it suited him. The Australia you inhabit now was not the Australia he went to. I could not have gone. Too arid, too dusty, too empty, too far.'

A new bottle was opened.

'Australia – in the '50s and '60s, outside of Sydney or Melbourne – it was not habitable. The very harshness of life there appealed to the Spartan in him, the Stoic. And your father was there.'

Enrico renounced his Italian citizenship and became an Australian as soon as he could. When dual citizenship became available, he rejected it.

'He was always good at cutting off his nose to spite his face.' Enrico, Annabelle said, was fortunate in his early life. The times suited him. He was made for war and passion and hardship and frontiers and to die young. In his later years, he ran out of windmills.

She wished, for the first time in twenty years, that she still smoked. 'The War. The Post-war. We did not speak about those times,' she continued. 'Not in all the years. He never forgave me for not going with him to Australia and I never forgave him for leaving me. *Move on*, you say these days. *Closure*. That ridiculous English word. Everyone today wants closure. You lie awake at night remembering the smells, the screams, the betrayal, the sheer awfulness of it all. And yet we were so alive then.'

Annabelle was having those dreams again. Delia sat very still, lest she break the spell.

'I could never trust that we might not return to the nightmare,' Annabelle continued, 'that I might not wake up one day and find us under the yoke again. I felt I had to remain here, try to do something useful. It weighed upon me. He became so Australian. You Australians do not seem to bear that weight. You are all so very cheerful. So optimistic. We are not optimists. Now I am afraid. Again. I see what has happened to women in this country after twenty years of Berlusconi and I despair. Twenty years of Berlusconi,' she repeated. 'We had twenty years of Mussolini.' She expelled a long breath.

With the wine and the late hour and the lightness of the confessional, the mood lifted.

'Belle, you two could never have been right for each other, you know,' said Delia. 'Enrico was a classic Leo and you are the classic Virgo.'

Annabelle laughed. 'What nonsense.'

'QED! Exactly what a Virgo would say!'

CHAPTER 22

FLORENCE April 2008

Annabelle stirs, feels the mattress shift as Enrico slides quietly out of his side. He pulls the covers high against her back and tucks them tight, in case the cold air sneaks in. She hears him pad to the kitchen and the raucous grinding of the beans, and she drifts off again on the soft morning, to the rich aroma of coffee brewing. When he brings her caffe latte she is on her side and he rolls her knees away and sits on the bed, one hand on her thigh. She pushes herself up on the pillows to take the cup and he brushes her hair back with his free hand, smiling into her eyes. When her cup is empty, he traces her upper lip with a forefinger, licks the froth off his finger as he once did with her tears. Then he takes the cup and stands for a moment, smiling down at her.

She reaches for his hand. 'Don't go just yet.'

He smiles again and walks to the door.

Awake now, her heart racketing, Annabelle could not breathe. She was having a heart attack. Not the kind a cardiologist could deal with. A gigantic wave reared on the horizon, moving closer. A tidal wave, a tsunami, which she had held off forever and was here for her now. The trembling began from deep, deep within, and finally she let it come. She flopped back on her pillows and seventy years of tears broke free. Convulsive, salty, clamorous tears rolled down her cheeks, flooded the folds and creases of her neck, soaked into the pleats of her nightgown, and still they came. Across her bed, across the tiles and out into a dawn the colour of pewter: a raging flood of tears. It was the loneliest moment of her life. *I am a widow*, she thought.

Dragging herself out of bed, she went to make her own coffee. Delia would be out walking by now. Annabelle brought the coffee back to bed and sank against the sodden pillows. After a while, she rose heavily – an old lady – and crossed to the tall *armadio*, where the linen and blankets were stored. On her knees on the cold tiles, she ratted deep into the bottom drawer, throwing aside rugs and covers, until she found the cashmere pullover Enrico had left on the back of the chair at Omero's. He looked to her that day, like Aslan. She knew he was ready to leave. She sank back onto the mat and buried her face in the soft grey wool that still carried his scent. She felt winter at the gate.

'We shared the same memories of our childhood. Or our youth, rather – we did not have a childhood,' Annabelle said, slicing *melanzana* for their *Parmigiana*. Beside her on the kitchen bench, her wine glass was half empty. Her eyes were still puffy from the morning.

'Probably not, you know,' said Delia. Her job was to make the sauce and her glass was already empty. She leaned across and refilled both glasses. 'Did you ever compare or did you just assume you had the same memories? This whole family runs on silence.'

'The fuel all families run on is silence and secrets,' Annabelle replied.

'I've decided I can't trust my memories.' Delia had thought she knew Annabelle's history, she said, but she now realised no-one is known. The more talk there is, the more easily the secrets can hide.

'I've cannibalised memories so often for good stories that I don't know any more what's real and what's not,' said Delia. 'What's a memory and what is several of them knitted into one, and what's a memory of someone else's I've appropriated? I can't understand how anyone can go into a witness box and testify to a memory of some day or event in the past and be even mildly reliable.' We elide memories, she went on, licking the spoon. Sometimes more than two, several. We shape them to help us rewrite our past into a version that suits us better.

'I thought I had mine under control.' Annabelle waved the large knife.

'Huh! You're such a control freak! We all use our memories to rewrite the bits about the past that didn't suit us. Some of us just don't like to admit it.' Delia warmed to her topic.

The oil was smoking in the pan. Annabelle turned the stove off. Dinner could wait. 'Me too. We all do it. For many of us, our memories are not bearable. We do bear them. We go on living.'

Some of us, she continued, try to make up for the things we did, the things we witnessed. Others excise them from their memory. Others adjust their memories to sanitise them, arrange them in a tidier order. She often wondered about the others – the Germans who committed atrocities, how did they live their lives afterwards? Did they go home and make love, have babies, get jobs, live normal lives? Or did they beat their wives, abuse their children, torture small animals, get into drunken brawls? Kill themselves? How many of them went on to murder again? In the endless trials after the war, few were found guilty, and even fewer paid any real penalty. And that was only the Germans. The militia were as bad, often worse.

'And they grew old among us.' She picked up the bottle and Delia followed her through to the sitting room.

On the television, the *telegiornale* droned silently, images of *Forza Italia* politicians mouthing platitudes. And Berlusconi, always Berlusconi. In a meeting with Putin, to the great amusement of both men, he mimed shooting a journalist with a machine gun.

'They deserve each other,' Annabelle muttered.

Now, apparently, he was off to Libya to sign an accord with Muammar Gaddafi, and his team, AC Milan, had won some stupid soccer game. Annabelle was not a football fan.

'Mussolini invented modern *Calcio*, so Berlusconi bought himself a team and named his political party after a soccer slogan.'

She flicked the TV off and put on a Miles Davis CD. She poured more wine and sank into her chair, legs curled beneath her.

'Sant'Anna di Stazzema.'

It was an answer to Delia's earlier question. Her tone was level, inexorable. Three hundred *ReichsFührer*-SS, under a general named Max Simon, surrounded the village and closed off every pathway in

336

or out. They executed every last person. They killed the priest, they killed the children – with bayonets, they killed the pregnant women, they cut a baby from the womb and killed her too. These people all have names. One was a baby, not even three weeks old. They did that in every village. There was a monument now, in each of the villages. Of course there was a monument. The country was filled with monuments. The dead are many.

'It's not in the diaries because I did not know enough at the time – it was only afterwards as the evidence was discovered. I could not bear to write it. We all did things we can only just live with. You find a way of justifying the unthinkable.' She picked at a loose thread of the tapestry chair-cover.

'And that was only the Germans,' she said again. 'What about the fascists, what about the true believers? Then there was the vendetta of the Jewish Brigades in contact with the Allies, as they tracked down Nazis in retreat and strangled them with their bare hands. Could you blame them? How many hands had strangled the life out of other humans? How do we wash that off? Then what about us, the partisans themselves?

'The Allies couldn't stand us, you know. They thought we were an undisciplined rabble. They were right, in many cases. More importantly, they thought we were all communists and they were more afraid of the communists gaining power after the war than they were of the Germans. Risible, when you think that it was fear of the communists that gave us Mussolini in the first place.

'Some were worse than others,' she continued. 'We all did terrible things, but the orgiastic violence of people like Mario Carità and Pietro Koch, or Walter Reder and Max Simon, *that* was matchless, except perhaps in the extermination camps.'

No evidence had ever suggested that the Allies or the partisans, or for that matter, most Italians or most Germans, did things like that.

'Carità and Koch were the Laurel and Hardy of horror and tragedy – the one short, pudgy, gross, the other, tall, lean, avid. People like them always exist. They are always there, like those insects that can live through the summer, dormant, in the desert, awaiting the right conditions, the rain, to spawn and thrive.' By now, the loose yellow thread of the tapestry had become a long skein.

'We stepped across a line,' she went on, 'a line in the dirt, like children playing hopscotch. We decided killing was justified. We were Freedom Fighters! After that, nothing was taboo, nothing unthinkable. Then much later, we turned back into citizens: suburban green-grocers, newsagents, doctors, parents. We embraced the drudgery of houses, mortgages, bills to pay, dull lives, boring marriages.

'But beneath it all, we are still killers. We stand on the other side of that line.' She drained her glass.

Delia had not spoken. Her eyes and the tip of her nose were red. She pulled out a used tissue from the sleeve of her cardigan and blew her nose loudly. Her hands were a little unsteady. The creamy petal of an orchid let go and drifted lightly to the long table behind the sofa.

She got up and went to get another bottle of wine. The *Parmigiana* was not going to get made tonight. Better eat something, she thought. She hung on the door of the fridge, as she always did in her mother's house or Annabelle's, thinking that no matter how old you get, you never lose this habit. There was a big hunk of *Grana Padano* – that would do, and some olives. Towards the back, there was a large jar of plump black olives from the farm at Impruneta, marinated in lemon rind and olive oil – just the thing. She spooned out a big dishful and arranged them on a *tagliere*, with a sliced pear, the cheese and a big piece of ciabatta. She tucked some paper napkins under her arm and, balancing the whole thing like a good waiter, sailed back to Annabelle.

'I could never understand how Italians allowed themselves to be tricked by Mussolini,' said Delia. 'Now here's this fuckwit Berlusconi, and it's just as hard to fathom.'

'Ahhh. Hindsight. So many reasons. The war, the depression, the revolution in Russia ...' Annabelle was calmer now. 'It's hard for you to get it, seeing things from a distance, from a county that had never had a nationwide war of any sort, civil or otherwise, on its soil.' She had managed to unravel the yellow embroidered lily, which had withstood the ravages of two hundred years. She looked at the bits of thread with surprise, as if someone else had unpicked it.

'Fear of communism,' she went on. 'Literacy was less than twenty-five per cent, it's not hard to see why people were gullible and responded easily to rhetoric and imagery. It's the Church to blame. And the Pope. All the Catholic countries had low literacy. Education is the death of religion. And of dictatorship.'

Delia climbed out of her chair to change the CD to John Coltrane. 'Why on earth don't you buy a new CD player, one that takes more than a single CD?'

She was amazed Annabelle did not still use cassettes! She had a horror of extravagance or ostentation. She would happily drink wine out of a jam jar, but her wild extravagance was flowers – fresh flowers. Her study and sitting room always held deceptively casual bunches of flowers, which she spent ages arranging after each week's visit to the flower market beneath the colonnades of Piazza Repubblica. From the side table close to the sofa, the rich perfume of lily-of-the valley saturated the room, and in the study, on a small table at the very centre, the butter and cream of freesias and the ultramarine of delphiniums drew the light.

Delia liked modernity and a bit of extravagance. Especially when it came to sound equipment. She loved music. She wished she had some musical gift. Music did not seem to be a big thing in her family. Annabelle too regretted not learning music. In the cloistered world of her childhood, she grumbled, wouldn't you think, if they were going to keep her locked up, they might at least have provided a music tutor! She had tried to insist with Delia's parents, so Delia could not blame her, but Maddie and Bert saw no point whatever in learning to play an instrument when one could perfectly well listen to others who did it better.

Delia laughed. 'I know. Roger, you know, the pianist, reckons my passion for jazz and chamber music is only because my tastes and appreciation are too untutored for full orchestral pieces!'

Still, Annabelle had given her a passion for reading, the most important thing of all. As a reader, you could rise to a challenge, be the very equal of the great. Do battle in your own mind with or against Shakespeare, Boccaccio, Kundera, Dostoevsky. They came straight to you, unmediated. Though concerts had their place. Inside the translucent bubble of a concert was where Delia did some of her best and clearest thinking. She hit the play button and refilled their glasses.

'Go on. You can't stop now.'
'I'll tell you Carla's story.'

'Carla Capponi died in 2000, after decades of disgraceful right-wing revisionism, which sought to besmirch her name and culminated in a trial for war crimes. In the end, she was exonerated; all her group were, but it tarnished her life. While Walter Reder and so many others went free.' Annabelle rummaged about in a deep bottom drawer of her desk, emerging with a copy of *L'Espresso*. The title shouted: *Resistenza: 1945-1995.*

'This is what it is all about,' she said, waving it. 'What happened then made us what we are today. In so many ways. Now we are sliding back, back into the mud. Look at the women here,' – she shook the journal again – 'look at what women like Carla fought for, then look at where women are in this country today, the image Berlusconi promotes. Dancing girls and escorts, in parliament.'

She threw the magazine to the desk and trailed back to her chair, talking over her shoulder.

'Democracy is a fragile flower, growing in shallow soil in this country. You,' meaning you Australians, 'through no merit of your own, have been the recipients of parliamentary democracy for centuries. Your civil war took place thousands of kilometres away, over four hundred years ago. We were handed democracy on a platter in '46. We are still learning what to do with it. It is not only Berlusconi who does not understand the democratic process.'

Delia's face showed she had noted the 'You Australians' again.

Annabelle flung herself into her chair and reopened her assault on the tapestry lily. She stopped for breath. Delia breathed out too.

'We just wanted to be free,' said Annabelle, and yawned. 'Free of all of them.' She stretched out in her chair. She'd had enough for the time being.

Both heaved companionable sighs and relaxed. For a long while, they were silent, relieved: convalescent. After a time, Annabelle rose and pulled out a shoe-box of photos from under a side table. She drew out one taken in the late summer, nearly four months after the end of the war. August 1945 was scribbled on the bottom, close to the deckled edge. A huge, happy group – Enrico in a white open-necked shirt, the centre of attention. Roberto had his arm draped about Annabelle's floral shoulders but she was looking pouty – Elisa was seated between Enrico and Marco.

'Poor Elisa, she didn't get a bargain in the end,' said Annabelle with a smile. She threw the photo back in the box and pulled out another.

In this one, more recent, Enrico was seated behind his own desk, the one upstairs in his study. It was from that last visit. Behind him, in the dark mahogany shadows of the shelves, thousands of books and thousands of writers looked over his shoulder. He was spare, refined away to his essence. Only his mane of white hair was still abundant. His eyes, free of the round bottle-thick glasses held in his left hand, burned like the cigarette in the ashtray beside him. The spiral of smoke wreathed his head in a halo, giving him the look of an ancient god. Annabelle reached for a heavy silver-filigree frame with a photograph of Nonna Annabelle. With the letter opener, she pried back the clips at the top and bottom and replaced Nonna with Enrico. She carried it to her desk in the study and placed it with care beside her father's pipe rack on the upper shelf, at eye level.

It was late. Outside, the city noise had settled, turned to night sounds – the occasional burr of a distant *motorino*, the rattle of a bicycle, a lone voice calling *buona notte*, the melancholy cry of an owl. Delia closed the windows on the chilly April air. There was still some cheese left. No wine, no olives, no pear, only a nub of the bread. Annabelle carried the wooden platter through to the kitchen and stood at the sink, as if she had forgotten why she was there.

'Go on,' urged Delia, 'throw it away. I'll bet you can't do it.'

The bread, she meant. No Italian of that age could throw away bread. *Panus angelicus* – bread was sacred. Bread was a cult. *Rompere il pane insieme*, they said, break bread together. Ciabatta, it was, not the flat dry, salt-less Tuscan *schiacciata*.

'Obsessed with bread, you all are, obsessed! Go on, I dare you!' Delia leaned back against the counter, a little wobbly. 'Go on. Do it. Cut loose!'

Annabelle too was a little unsteady. Throw away bread! The war is over, she thought. Sixty-three years. The war is over. There was a *forno* on every corner now. She placed her slippered foot on the pedal of the kitchen tidy. The lid yawned. Fuck it, she thought, and tipped the entire contents of the *tagliere* into the bin. Fuck you too, Enrico.

The second coming

The door to Delia's room was open. Australians always left bedroom doors open. Carrying a pile of clean linen just delivered from the laundry, Annabelle poked her head through, smiling at the usual disarray. How anyone of Delia's age could happily leave her bed unmade, she would never understand. The bedside table was a litter of nail polish bottles, emery boards, a butterfly hairclip, a glittering chocolate wrapper with half a rejected soft-centre strawberry chocolate, scrunched tissues, two hard-cover books interleaved so as to mark the page in each. Silver headphones dangled rakishly, still docked to their iPod. In the midst of it, a water glass held a handful of the lily-of-the-valley pinched from the big vase in the sitting room. Annabelle enjoyed the abandon of Delia's disorder, a freedom, an ease she envied but could never emulate.

She picked up a spiky-heeled shoe and tossed it out of the doorway. The perfume of the flowers mingled with the Chanel No 5 that accompanied Delia everywhere. She was comforted by Delia's confidence that came from the easygoing clan in Sydney. Perhaps it was because Sydney was a city that allowed for that. Florence was not. Her family was not. Her times were not. If only she had Delia's easy empathy. That must be Maddie's influence. It was all she could want for her, to glide through life feeling confident of meeting the challenges. She stepped over the lacy bra and knickers on the floor, dropped the linen onto the rumpled bed and went back to work.

'You haven't written in your diary for quite a while.' Delia glanced up to the high shelf holding rows of diaries. Tan, leather-covered volumes, each cover decorated with a rectangular miniature oil on enamel, the work of a famous artist friend, filled a whole shelf. Twenty of them, from 1988 to the present. Above the leather diaries was another shelf of twenty volumes, unmatched, from 1968.

'Not for a bit,' replied Annabelle without glancing up from her desk. In the pool of light from the great arc lamp, her heavy hair was thinning at the crown.

No, thought Delia, not since 2005, because she had climbed up to have a look, feeling deliciously guilty, just as she had as a child when she climbed right to the highest shelves to look at *Nonno's* naughty books. Only a little more shamefaced at fifty-five.

'You were always scribbling in your diaries. It's how I think of you. You know I used to peek.'

'You don't say!' Annabelle put down her pen and turned in her chair with a smile.

'Is that why all the earlier ones were put away? Because I was such a stickybeak?'

'Could be. *Ficanaso*. A real sticky beak. You used to go through my underwear drawers and all my wardrobes too.'

Delia laughed. True. She could not wait for her parents and her aunt to go out so she could be deliciously, terrifyingly, alone. Many rooms on the upper floors were closed off and even she did not venture into the haunted-house part. The first floor with Annabelle's apartment, and all the arches, stairways and entrances leading to it, however, was her domain. Her skin prickled and her tummy squirmed in the shadows of the empty rooms as she explored the hidden nooks and crannies. Most of all she loved the solitary possession of her aunt's life, through the scents and sensations of shoe-racks and stocking drawers, hat cupboard and glove boxes. Who wears hats and gloves today, except in winter, she wondered.

She picked up *La Nazione* from an armchair. The front page carried a story about a football player who, frustrated at roadworks for the planned light rail to Scandicci, parked his four-wheel drive across a roundabout and left it there while he went to Mass. Seventeen blocked buses brought city traffic to a complete halt. Delia loved these stories and *La Nazione* provided endless amusement. She waved the paper at Annabelle and left to read it with a coffee and a grappa in the bar downstairs.

How could anyone drink coffee at this hour? Annabelle shook her head. If she did that she would be up all night. She flicked across the TV channels and settled on *Porta a Porta*. Silvio Berlusconi was debating Walter Veltroni. Not that you could call it debate.

'I don't need to go into politics,' Berlusconi boasted. 'I am making a sacrifice.'

Walter Veltroni, the highly respected Mayor of Rome, a man who had collaborated with Obama in the writing of his book, a man of decency who would have made a good Prime Minister, was also a man of good manners and he kept his expression neutral. Berlusconi gathered momentum, expounding the cost of the great sacrifice he was willing to make, his botoxed forehead unworried, impassive, his ageing voice querulous: 'I am the Jesus Christ of politics.'

The second coming now! We have come to this. Annabelle had a powerful urge to spit. She did not throw the TV remote. It had taken Delia ages to fix it with sellotape after election night. Instead, she rose and walked slowly to her desk. For some time she sat quietly, hands still. Then she pushed back in her chair, closed the file before her, closed down the computer. She rolled the walnut library ladder from a shadowy corner, and climbed to the diaries. With the 2008 diary before her on the desk, Annabelle splayed her hands into her hair and closed her eyes. After some time, she took up her pen, opened the stiff pages and began to write.

> *The war dribbled to an end. Not in a nice tidy, conclusive way that you could believe in, but in a ragged, piecemeal sort of way people found hard to trust. Peace, it was called, whatever that meant. It was hard to know what peace might look like …*

It took three months for the epidemic of peace to make its way around the greater world. First in Italy, then in France. Not until August in far-off Japan, where, according to the headlines in the papers, whole cities were incinerated with everyone in them. There was some new weapon, a bomb, which would change things forever and mean there would never be another war. 'We heard that last time,' said the carter who delivered Annabelle's firewood. 'The war to end all wars. And then we had this one.'

On the second of June 1946, Italians voted to reject the wizened little King who had so resoundingly rejected them. In another time and another place he might have lost his head, but Italians were weary of death, so they sent him and the son for whom he had abdicated, and the whole reviled family, to France instead. French was his first language anyway, they said. Send the Savoys back where they came from. Let the French keep them, as long as they never set foot on our soil again.

Italians had never really liked killing. The Grand Duchy of Tuscany was the first state in Europe to abolish capital punishment, the only European country to forgo state-sanctioned murder. Until 1931, when Mussolini brought it back. Even then, the appetite for it was poor and only nine or ten executions took place under the criminal code. The Regime, now that was another matter.

Italians were weary of foreign rulers: Celts from Gaul, with their wild ways; Alaric, the heathen king of the Visigoths and his romantic successor, Ataulf, who kidnapped and married the beautiful Empress Galla Placidia; the exotic, turbanned Moors and Saracens in the South; the long-bearded Lombards, who invaded on an Easter Monday and found it propitious; Charlemagne, King of the Franks, who dreamed the first dream of a united Europe; the French Bourbons and the Spanish Aragons in Naples and Sicily – called, oddly, the Kingdom of the Two Sicilies. In an endless procession of conquest, they traipsed throughout the land leaving their imprint, for better, for worse, forever, on every aspect of Italian life. Then there were the Germans. Italian history was bookended by the Germans, from the Vandals to the Nazis.

The twenty years of fascism seemed like an aberration. Italians needed something to be proud of and they voted for a new constitution, for a nascent democratic republic. They *all* voted in 1946 and 1948 – women too cast their ballot, had their say. Universal suffrage to expunge the memory of universal suffering. In 1946, Annabelle wore a new hat – straw with a wide brim and a jaunty emerald-green satin ribbon fluttering in the hot breeze. It put her in mind of the fluttering of pennants in one of Lorenzo the Magnificent's famous jousting tournaments, when bejewelled damsels thronged at every window onto Piazza Santa Croce, waving embroidered handkerchiefs at their handsome knights. In 1948 she chose a sober wool cloche. Euphoria was less called for.

As the appetite for revenge diminished, the streets filled with dark green octagonal newspaper kiosks, the heady perfume and vivid joy of flower stalls, the pungent smell of chestnuts roasting, instead of dead bodies. People lingered outdoors, sat over coffees, chatted and smoked in the piazza standing astride bicycles, without looking over their shoulders. It was still hard not to duck when you heard a bang. Dread took a long time to dissipate. Faith was in short supply, a commodity the generous funds of the Marshall Plan could not offer. It could supply everything else, however, and within not much more than a decade, Federico Fellini offered not just Italians but the whole world a new image for Italy. It arrived with Marcello Mastroiani on a Vespa, the hedonistic carefree blueprint for the good life, *La Dolce Vita*.

'Enrico could be a dickhead, you know, but still ...' Delia basked in the mild sun.

'Charming!'

'I saw him in a dream last night. We were on a street together somewhere, and he was wearing a blue shirt, and he was young and strong in a middle-aged way and talking a lot. It was nice to hear his voice,' Delia said.

The day was warm and they were seated on the parapet of the Ponte Santa Trinità. Beneath them the Arno boiled and tumbled in a rage of melting snow but the sun was gentle on their shoulders. Delia would have to leave for Sydney soon. Her book on medieval food was coming out and the publishers wanted her back.

'I did not marry him,' Annabelle said, 'because I would not have been good at it, no better than Enrico, in fact.'

The difference was that she'd always known that. Her view of marriage was formed by her family, by her parents, as it was for most people. She saw it as form of servitude for women: benevolent servitude if you were lucky, but servitude all the same. There was never a time when she had been tempted to marry.

'I have never seen a marriage yet that I thought was a fair and equal exchange. Heinrich Heine said wedding music reminded him of soldiers going into battle.'

Delia stretched lazily. 'Mum and Dad aren't like that, though. They're happy, in their own way. Funny old things.'

In 1978, after divorce in Italy was finally recognised, Elisa applied for one. No hard feelings, she told Annabelle. Enrico was not cut from husband cloth.

'He was never really housebroken, was Dad,' Clare said. 'He was like Socrates, a pain in the neck. At home and abroad. Always offending someone. No wonder he chose the Greeks and Romans as his life's work. Dad was a Pagan, better suited to the times when the gods roamed the earth than the tameness of domesticity, or even academe.'

When Enrico came to Florence for the *decree nisi*, he asked Annabelle to marry him.

'I told him he was mad,' she said. 'Why would anyone, least of all Enrico, wish to marry!'

Annabelle had had two abortions. Abortion and birth control were prohibited in 1931 when capital punishment was brought back.

'You could breed for the Regime, but execute people,' she said. Not that it stopped people having abortions; it just made it more dangerous. It was officially legalised in 1972. 'Too late for me but good for young women.'

'Wasn't it Gloria Steinem,' said Delia, nodding, 'who said that if men could get pregnant, abortion would be a sacrament?'

'Did you never want children?' Delia asked the question after dinner, in much the same way she might have thrown a bomb into the room. 'Have you ever regretted it?'

A long silence. 'I've got you. That's enough.' Annabelle nodded at the shelves of photos of Delia in every stage and at every age.

'Yes, but you had the easy parts. You don't have to put up with the messy bits with someone else's child. The sleepless, nights, the dirty nappies, the tantrums, of which,' Delia laughed, 'in my case there were lots.'

'You were not that bad. But you're right. I didn't have the messy bits.' Annabelle turned to face her from the desk. 'So what about you, if we're having show and tell. Do you regret it?'

'No … No. I hadn't really asked myself until lately, but no I don't.' She was not cut out for family life, she said. She too was happy to have missed out on the messy bits. 'We are two of a kind.'

Annabelle nodded and turned back to her desk. Family life. What would she know about family life? Nothing in her upbringing had prepared her for the rambunctious disorder of Bert and Maddie's household where nothing seemed to be out of bounds. The three children ran wild, their needs and desires paramount. They invaded every room; not even the bathroom was sacrosanct. It was rather appealing, especially the way they all ran to burrow into their parents' bed at first daylight. If Annabelle was there, Delia would run to her bed. She would curl her soft little body into the curve of Annabelle's stomach, place her aunt's arms about herself like a little koala and go back to sleep, her regular breathing soft and sweet.

For long after each visit, the imprint of that tiny body and the sweet morning breath remained with Annabelle. So different from the reserved, respectful atmosphere of Borgo Pinti. In so many ways it was another century. She had long given up her image of her own childhood as Leopardian, but the scar tissue from the loneliness of it still gave her pain at night, causing her to toss and turn in search of relief.

She had her work and she loved it. She had been involved in the examination of the bodies, long, long after the war – ten years after Mussolini's cadaver, which had been hidden, stolen, hidden, recovered, reburied and exhumed, was finally reinterred, or what was left of it, in Predappio. She had also worked on the project to exhume the early Medici corpses, a fascinating study of diseases of the early Renaissance, and equally absorbing, the research for the body of Richard III. More touching than any of those was the sight of the mummified corpse of the Ice Man of Bolzano, Otzi. In 1991, his body re-emerged from the ice after thousands of years. To have his life recreated and honoured made her think of Ettore Castiglioni and the *sentiero* in the Dolomites, named for him, two years after his death. But for the young, it was different.

In this country they still had no better prospects now than they had had in the years after the war, when a tidal wave of them washed up onto the shores of any country that could offer work. Mostly southerners, but many professionals like Enrico who could not see hope here. Everyone was on the take and everyone had what is now called an agenda: fascists, communists, socialists – riddled with nepotism and clientelism resurgent from the Renaissance, the 'years of lead' and death. It could come again. *Povera Italia*! She sighed and pushed back from her desk, the rollers of her chair crumping over the *cotto* of the ancient floor.

'Dad has never talked much about being interned,' Delia said. She put a glass of Vin Santo and some *biscotti* beside Annabelle and poured a glass for herself. She hesitated, then took two of the *biscotti*, thinking, bugger it! 'That's when he met Mum, isn't it?'

She had a little twinge of missing them. Poor old dears. Maddie was very vague last week when they spoke. She must phone them tonight.

'Yes,' replied Annabelle. 'He was deeply offended, and Giacomo much more so, but then so were the English and other foreigners here. Or the Italians and Germans in England. At least he was safe. It happened everywhere.'

The Anglo-Florentines were outraged at their treatment by the fascists, by Mussolini. Most of them thought highly of Il Duce; he certainly had his followers – Mosely and the British Union in England, Ezra Pound in Europe. You could find a thousand quotes extolling his virtues. Churchill once thought he was a fine fellow.

'Pound's ranting had a terrible effect on the Jews and the whole population. Now, Casa Pound is the rock that most of the Neo-Fascists crawl out from under.' Annabelle's tone could have etched glass. 'Or the young violent ones, that is. The old paunchy ones make pilgrimages to Predappio!' Mussolini's birthplace and final resting place.

Annabelle paced in a circle, hands in her hair. Predappio, undistinguished by anything but the reliquary of the slivers of bone left of Mussolini's body after its years of misadventure.

'You can buy aprons, mugs, plates, all the paraphernalia of celebration,' said Annabelle, 'like souvenirs of David, or the English royals. Obscene! Christ I wish I still smoked!'

'To change the subject,' said Delia, 'there's someone I would like you to meet.' Her eyes flicked to the diary lying on the desk.

'A man?' Annabelle smiled at her.

'No.' Delia smiled too. 'I'm having a go at celibacy for the moment. No, Flavia is a doctor at the university. She read a paper of yours on decomposition. She is an immunologist or something. I think you'll like her.'

'I'll be happy to meet her. Why don't we have a bite to eat at the market next week?'

PART SIX

CHAPTER 23

Florence 1945

... the blood of Piazzale Loreto

The war is over! The war is over! The great bass of the Bargello's bell pealed out, followed by the baritone of Palazzo Vecchio. Next, the grandfather boom of the Duomo, then one after the other, every bell in the city joined the chorus, the peals rolling in joyous thunder across the ancient buildings, reverberating in the stones of Florence. Then came the smaller, tinnier bells of the suburbs and towns and villages, bells pealing from Venice to Palermo, from Turin to Bari, an earthquake of campanology roiling the length and breadth of Italy, a boundless carillon. Across the hills, the valleys, the towns, the villages, the rocky pathways and the shattered buildings, the bells – finally pealing, not tolling. Mad joy was everywhere. All over Italy, people shouted, wept, screamed, hugged friends and complete strangers. In Florence, men, women and children hugged every Allied serviceman in their vicinity, proffered flowers, wine, kisses, dashing about the streets in a frenzy of release.

Buffeted by the swirling hordes, Annabelle was not the only one to stand silent, swaying. Jubilation eluded her. In their dining room, pictures of Florence in the 1800s, painted by Borbottoni, covered the wall above the walnut curlicues of the sideboard. A Florence vanished, a Florence of once-upon-a-time. A Florence razed to the ground and rebuilt. The old market, the ghetto, all gone to make way for the strident triumphalism of Piazza Repubblica and Piazza Signoria. The Duomo and Santa Croce naked in their stern stone, before their icing-sugar raiment. So many wars. Tribal wars, internecine wars.

How many times had Florence arisen, a phoenix, a griffin, from the ashes of her past?

We did it before, we can do it again, she resolved. Before, the dead were history, but the dead must always have been real to someone. Now they were real to her. And the bells pealed on. *When will you pay me / Say the bells of Old Bailey.* What now, what now?

April 30, 1945
Milano

> *Carissima Belle*
>
> *There is much to do here. I cannot tell when I will be back. Milan is a charnel house. Cristo! I thought I had seen the worst but I was wrong. We lack only cannibalism to complete the picture ...*

It was not dawn, though light enough to make out the truck as it clanked into Piazzale Loreto. Enrico awoke instantly. They had slept where they fell after digging out the survivors from a crumpled building. Aboard were bodies and some *Garibaldini*, who dropped the back of the truck and tipped the bodies onto the stones as if delivering meat. Mussolini and Clara Petacci. There were several others, all tipped out on top of each other into a heap. Within minutes a crowd gathered, murmuring, and by daylight the crowd turned to a milling mass. Kicking, hissing, pissing, spitting and screaming, they set upon the bodies. They kicked Mussolini's face to a pulp. A woman fired a revolver into his body, screaming he had killed her sons. Someone took a whip to him. I hope, wrote Enrico, never to see such depravity again. Some of the partisans tried to hold them off, others did not bother. Someone dragged the girl's body onto Mussolini's and placed her head on his shoulder. A woman screamed insults about her stockings.

They began to chant names – Pavolini, Mussolini, Farinacci, Buffarini, Bombacci. One of the men held up each body in turn for the crowd, but it was impossible to see and they screamed for more, as if in the Colosseum. Someone found wire and rope, and to the sound of cheering and jeering, one by one the carcasses were strung upside down from the girders of a garage. People poked at them with sticks and gun barrels. There is more, wrote Enrico, much more I cannot stomach to repeat. In a grotesque parody of modesty in that Catholic country, a priest had the woman's skirt held in place with a rope between her legs.

Sunday morning and the church bells were ringing for Mass. The sun was out and girls wore summer dresses and sat astride bicycles, chatting and laughing as if at a fair. The crowd bristled with gun barrels and hats of every description – fedoras, borsalini, berets and military caps, all bobbing back and forth to get a better view of the spectacle. Brave men and women captured young girls, shaved their heads and dragged them through the streets. I struggle for comparisons, Enrico said – surely the death of Caesar was not this vulgar? More the carnival atmosphere of the guillotines?

Another truck arrived with the fascist leader, Achille Starace. He saluted and shouted, *Viva Il Duce.* They shot him there and then and strung him up with the others, after taunting him for his loyalty to Mussolini. A few stalwarts stayed with him to the end. Eventually the rope broke and Mussolini's body dropped to the stones. His head exploded like a melon. I left, Enrico's letter concluded, Montanelli was there and other journalists too, enough to record our shame.

> *I wept for what we have become. Have we learned nothing? Many wore the party badge yesterday. Many of these were Mussolini's people who lost faith in him. Hope and trust betrayed turns to rage. We will never know who ordered this obscenity. The Allies are outraged. No-one wanted him captured alive, for so many reasons, and his death, all their deaths, seem fitting to me. But not this theatre of the degenerate. Cardinal Schuster ordered them cut down or he would do it himself. We have all been debased, dishonoured. We will carry the stain forever. I did not fight for this.*

Annabelle sat quietly, Enrico's letter in her lap. The autumn light slanted through the bottle-glass windows, throwing dancing colours across his elegant script. It was the first real letter she had received, written on good paper with a fountain pen, in an unhurried hand. Tainted, we are all tainted, she thought. We rush to exculpate, mitigate, justify. Beside her, lay the newspaper of the twenty-ninth.

Allied troops receive a triumphant welcome to a free Milan.
The bodies of Mussolini and his henchmen displayed
before a crowd in the piazza where fifteen martyrs died.

Claretta. The past couple of days had rushed her to the forefront of Annabelle's mind, like a relative she had once known slightly, but had lost contact with. Clara. The tragic end of a great love affair, or the tawdry death of a deluded woman? Rumours, once let loose, infected, festered and burst: Clara had been a spy for Churchill; Clara was murdered on the instructions of Rachele; Clara was murdered because she knew too much; Clara was murdered for her diaries.

Diaries. How important diaries would be as they all tried to understand what had happened to them. Annabelle must take great care of her own. For the first time she saw herself as a cipher in an historical event. Marcello Petacci had been shot dead trying to escape. It seemed he had been mistaken for Vittorio Mussolini. Poetic justice! Vittorio had escaped. The radio had just announced the suicides of Hitler and Eva Braun. Whole families of the Nazi hierarchy had committed suicide. They were certainly all part of history.

In Rome there was a new national government. Ferruccio Parri was Prime Minister. Surely they should celebrate that? For a moment, for the first time in their lives, they could see their ideals expressed and put into action. How strange and fragile. Annabelle had not met Parri but Enrico had – brave, but limited, he said. The Action Party in government. A dream long held, but never for a moment truly imagined. How long would it last?

After what some newspapers referred to as 'the tragic end of the ex-Duce', it was more than a week before the final German surrender.

Partisans and the populace yesterday celebrated the
glorious end to the insurrection.

Glorious! Like faith, glory was in short supply. The eighth of

May was VE Day, Churchill announced. Tito tried to annexe Trieste. Japan was extinguished by a bomb the likes of which they had never heard. Conferences and more conferences. In Padua, Mario Carità and his band of degenerate torturers went on trial. Among the twelve defendants were his two young daughters, Franca and Elisa, willing spectators to rape, humiliation, persecution, and medieval torture. Few saints, many sinners, and sometimes, pure evil. So many gone. How would it look in the ledger? Elsa, Giacomo, Achille. Enrico, Annabelle. Elisa. Roberto had survived, Falco too, with one leg.

Optimism was not foremost in Annabelle's nature. She wondered if it ever had been? Was that a character flaw or a result of the war? She must try harder.

Florence 1945
Outbreak of peace

'Haven't you got anything better to do?' Enrico leaned against the kitchen doorjamb. Alive. Real.

All her life, Enrico had appeared as if by magic. He did not enter a room but materialised, as if he had always been there. Now he inclined his head to one side, watching her, hands in his pockets. His mouth belied the casual pose. His hair was nearly shoulder-length, his face and throat deeply bronzed against the white of the open-necked shirt. His grey pleated trousers were too loose on him and, unbelievably, he wore black loafers. No boots.

From the garden the zizz of cicadas climbed on the June heatwave, and for an instant Annabelle thought the sound was in her head. She swayed and steadied herself with soapy hands, up to her elbows in the sudsy water of the stone sink. Then he was behind her, his arms about her waist, his lips at her ear and on her throat. The scent of him dizzied her further and only his solid form held her upright. In the immediate flooding joy, the release, the relief, the liberation ... just for a moment everything seemed possible.

It was a week since General Wolff signed the surrender at Caserta. Officially war was at an end. Officially. The country was crawling with spies and agents from America and Britain, and Russia – insects on a decaying corpse. All searching for documents, testimonies, treasures, money, evidence of all sorts, principally for the forthcoming trials. There would be lots of trials. Then there was the art. Half the art treasures of the western world seemed to have found their way onto transports to Germany.

The towns and villages and countryside teemed with hordes of the displaced: prisoners of war from England, India, Australia, South Africa, Brazil, Poland, and smaller countries whose names did not mean a thing, all trying to find their way back to their regiments or anyone who could help them. There were ravenous, roaming, disbanded soldiers from the Italian Army and from the partisan units, many of whom tramped hundreds of kilometres back to the city or village they had left more than a year before, only to find in some cases they had been declared dead. German prisoners, justifiably anxious, shuffled in dejected procession from one jail to another, guarded by tired, tight-lipped GIs, who were known to be very fast on the trigger. Women with despairing eyes trailed from office to office in search of news of missing sons or husbands or fathers or brothers. Fascists burned uniforms and party badges and buried evidence but, especially in small towns, could not burn their past. The cloying smell of vendetta was heavy on the air. No-one had ever been a fascist, yet their bodies turned up everywhere.

When would they know how many had died? How many more would die? Would they ever know? Mussolini's vast mausoleum – the Redipuglia War Memorial outside Trieste – held the bodies of over a hundred thousand Italians murdered by the Germans in 1917. The massive monument reared backwards up a hill crowned by three crosses, like the pyramids of Egypt – graves too, those. The shape of a hundred thousand bodies. *Presente presente presente* – so many who answered the rollcall then. Who could have thought so many more would die?

But still, the irises and lilacs were in full flower, the fields full of crimson poppies; it was summer and Annabelle and Enrico were alive and, to their amazement, they were still young.

July 10, 1945

Today we pedalled our bicycles to the lake for lunch. The sun tried to make us sweat. We revelled in it. We pedalled and puffed and laughed and talked and arrived ready to eat everything in sight. We wanted this day to last for a month. We planned a journey to Spain and lolled in the warmth and gave thanks for our lives together and pretended, just for a while, that happiness was possible.

The two men leaned on their shovels, sweat rolling in shimmering beads down the sides of their faces and into the collars of their shirts. There were no green *fazzoletti* at their throats to soak it up now. Three months since they changed back into civilian clothes. The war is over, people said, again and again. They had been digging for more than half an hour in the parched earth. All over the country, others were doing the same. Above them, the cobalt sky rolled on like the deep ocean and the zinging of cicadas made them dizzy. Below in the valley, the fields of crimson poppies were ponds of blood. Even beneath the sheltering chestnut trees, the August heat was unbearable. Nothing was bearable here.

The hole was a metre deep now and they knew they were very close. Enrico pushed his smudged glasses up, rubbed the bridge of his nose and with a deep sigh, nodded at his companion. They plunged the shovels carefully into the resistant soil. It only took a few more piles of dirt before the stench assailed them. To tell the truth, they had been able to smell it for a while now but this was different. Different and so very much the same. Soon the ragged bits of cloth began to appear. Then a buckle, then a boot. They dropped down into the excavation. Slowly, very gently now, with small trowels like archaeologists, they eased the soil away from the outline of the body.

They no longer noticed the smell. There was little flesh left. When the tall body lay uncovered in bas-relief, they stood back, gazing down at the boy whose hair still matted in clumps about the bullet hole in his skull. The heavy jacket with its etched buckle and sheepskin lining looked senseless in the August heat.

"He did not have a plausible story,' said Enrico, 'so he had to be a spy. Fucking communists!'

It had happened just after the massacre on Monte Morello. Enrico knew they would have done the same thing, had done the same thing. Pointless to wonder now. *Acqua passata.* You did not get a second chance in those times.

From deep in his chest, a great ache welled. 'Let's get him down.'

They drew the body onto a canvas stretcher, as carefully as they handled the living wounded. Then without words, they decided to leave the hole as it was. Leave it all. They hefted the stretcher and began the long descent to take Lorenzo home.

September: fig trees with tortured trunks bent beneath their purple, globular crop; the grapes were ready to be gathered; the hunting season opened – for animals, this time, and the university semester started again. As if it were the most natural thing in the world, as if the past five years had not happened. At school, they would have divided into *Liceo Classico* for Enrico, and for Annabelle, the *Liceo scientifico*. Now, Enrico enrolled in Classics at the University of Bologna and Annabelle, inspired by Rita Levi-Montalcini, was accepted into Medicine in the University of Turin. All around her, women who had taken their place alongside men in the mountains traipsed back into the kitchen.

The past five years *had* happened and the aftershocks rumbled along fault lines laid down well before. The Communist Party was in the ascendency, pressing its causes urgently. The peasants were in turmoil: not quite the Peasant's Revolt, but a social upheaval with similar consequences. The *contadini* and other farm workers wanted land, better wages, the vote: rights in a modern world. Many walked off the land, disappeared to the cities to find better paid work, or emigrated in hordes.

Eleanora fretted aloud – she could not find anyone to help in the house since Anna Maria and Sesto had left without so much as a goodbye. Ungrateful, they were, all the *contadini*. After all we did for them. The farm was going to wrack and ruin and she could do nothing about it.

'If only your father were here. And you show no interest, nor your uncle.' Eleanora had the face of an intelligent five-year-old who had grown old but never grown up, her petulant little mouth constantly pursed.

'Our slaves have bolted,' Enrico said. The Roman Empire could not have existed without slavery and nor could their family, their patrons, the Medici, nor most of the wealthy families of the fourteenth century. The *mezzadria* share-cropping might not be slavery on that scale, but it still left the peasants tied to earth they could never own. When Carlo Levi wrote about his time in exile in Lucania before the war, it was a disquieting picture of poverty and deprivation, the like of which they had never seen. Naturally people wanted change. Who could blame them?

After Elsa's death, Francesco retreated into a world of his own devising, much as Eleanora had done. He did not understand the new world ushered in by the end of the war. Perhaps he had always misunderstood, he said. He took little further interest in the their affairs and spent his time concentrating on the foundation he intended to set up in Elsa's name, to care for the children left orphaned by the carnage.

When Ferruccio Parri became Prime Minister, Italy was almost ungovernable. Enrico was right, Parri was brave and honourable but it was beyond him. He and his government did their best to guide the country into the new world order, but he only lasted six months. Fascism was once supposed to be the solution to communism, then communism was supposed to be the antidote to fascism, then the Christian Democrats once again employed the rhetoric of anti-communism. The communists wanted power, not just in Italy, but everywhere. Totalitarianism – Mussolini's new word – was going to be around for quite a while it seemed.

Coming in to SM Novella took forever. The train slowed with hissing of steam, grinding of brakes and the acrid odour of coal and excitement. Annabelle could taste soot on her tongue and her gloves were black with it, but she did not mind. She loved train travel and stations.

Bouncing up and down like a child, she wanted to jump down from the train before it came properly to a halt. Where was Enrico?

Pulling the cherry wool of her coat closer about her with one gloved hand, she held onto her hat with the other and leaned dangerously out the open door as far as she dared. The air was icy. Christmas – her first visit home since leaving for Torino for the start of the university term.

These weeks had been hard. It was not easy to concentrate on her introductory studies. The tranquil interior of the University of Turin was a mirage, a bubble. Outside, tension trembled on the air. The war was over but the fighting continued, with ongoing battles of attrition and reprisal between fascists and non-fascists and partisans and civilians. Too many old scores to settle. Too much power to fight for. Too many dead to avenge. The odour of guilt permeated their clothes like cigarette smoke. She had tried to put her head down and bury herself in Medicine, in the study of something she thought would be worthwhile. And tried not to think too much about Enrico.

On his return at war's end, Florence had changed and so had Enrico. In his letters from Bologna he was restless, unsettled. They all were. Around them, the rebuilding had started but it was the rebuilding of towns and cities and bridges and railway lines: of things. The detritus of ruined lives was harder to tidy away. Meaning was not easy to come by. Peace was dull. A heavy grey smog of order descended upon them. After the heady and colourful mantle of battle, it did not suit Enrico.

There was also the problem of the family. It was clear to everyone that Annabelle and Enrico were in love. They would 'come to their senses' was the general view. It was the war. The war turned everything topsy turvy. The war made people do things ... Well, that was certainly true, the lovers said, but they had no intention of coming to their senses. The future was a chimera and they did not poke or prod it.

Enrico was waiting for her. For now, that was enough. Through the noise and hissing steam, she saw him striding the length of the platform. She loved to watch him: his big walk, head thrown back, hands deep in his pockets. He walked like a god. A full head taller than anyone else on the platform, or in the world, for that matter. Her breathing was erratic and she was already wet to her knees. Please let him have found somewhere to go to make love. It was easy in Torino

362

but not easy here. Their home was haunted by the living ghosts of his father upstairs and her mother downstairs. She was jolted against the clattery door of the halting train and then she was tumbling into his arms.

'*Buon natale,*' he said. 'Happy Christmas.'

1946

The trip from Milan to Paris and on to London was thrilling – Annabelle's first journey outside Italy since the war. Since childhood. Leaving Paris at 9.45 pm from the Gare du Nord, she luxuriated in the new, glossy, royal-blue carriages of the Night Ferry, the overnight sleeper train to Victoria station, thanks to the Marshall Plan. She did not sleep; it seemed such a waste. She thought she would sleep in forever when the war was over. Yet, she did not. Nights were often filled with terrors, and if not, then with the simple joy of being alive. The night train sped through the dark, France unspooling at the windows. There were fewer lights than she expected, but in France especially, so many towns and villages simply no longer existed. Her head was bursting with dreams and hopes and plans.

Enrico had already gone, riding his old *Moto Guzzi* through Switzerland. The plan was to ride the huge wartime bike to London, sell it, and collect his new passion – a Triumph of some sort, the very latest thing. It was, he explained in excruciating detail, the most powerful motorbike ever made, with telescopic forks and rear suspension. Umm, she said. It was also amaranth red, with gold pinstripes. Imagine! she replied. She had wanted to go too; she loved riding pillion with him, but he was set on making the journey alone. She was angry at being left behind. She was angry about a lot of things these days.

Arriving at exactly 9.10 am the next morning in her *wagon-lit*, she took a taxi to the Kensington hotel to await Enrico, registering as Mr and Mrs Albizzi. Londoners were rather stuffy about such things but having the same name on their passports made it easy.

She was standing on the footpath outside the hotel when he turned into the street up the hill. With a final roar, the great beast of a bike pulled into the curb. Enrico did not so much dismount as fling himself off. He strode with giant steps towards her, pulling his leather helmet off and shaking out his hair, which had grown even longer. In his great boots, heavy canvas trousers and leather flying jacket, he was like a medieval knight clanking towards her in armour. Sir Lancelot. She thought she might swoon. Swoon seemed the only word. She would forgive him for not taking her, then!

The break in England should have improved Annabelle's humour, but back in Italy she was angrier than ever. As the country heaved a sigh and attempted to settle back on its pillows like a convalescent, people were expected to forgive and forget. Annabelle found it harder and harder to be magnanimous. The story of the war was being rewritten all around her and in particular, the story of women. Especially the women who had fought in the Resistance. The new versions grated on her. Few of the women who participated had actually fought side-by-side with the men, but thousands fought and died. The *staffette* who ran risks day and night were often caught and tortured and executed as examples – more than five thousand, like Elsa. More than six hundred died in battle. You could know these things now; it had all become statistics.

In the corner shop of the village, she heard three women, farmers' wives, talking about the death from illness of a local woman who had been a brave fighter and *staffetta*. *Partigiana*, they said. Huh! *Puttana* more like. Whore! Women were not meant to behave like the men.

Would this country never change? Never grow up? Annabelle did not care about being called a whore – country habits and mores died hard, but the world had changed and *she* was not going back to the dark ages.

Florence, May 1951
Coming up. Arriving Wed train 3 pm. Must talk. All well. Enrico.

Annabelle's stomach churned. It was too soon, too close to the war for telegrams to have lost their power. Enrico's visits to Turin were normally preceded by a letter or a telephone call, not the peremptory announcement of a telegram.

Annabelle met him at the station, her pulse a little too fast, in the familiar noise and excitement of steam and jangling iron wheels. She had taken greater care than usual with her dress, spending a long time deciding on a claret cloche hat with matching gloves. He was not hanging out the window as usual, but standing at the door with his hat in his hand. He lifted it to her as the train crawled past and she stood where she was as he descended the stairs and turned back towards her. His face was grave.

'Why so serious?'

'There is nothing wrong,' he assured her as he tilted her face to his and kissed her long and firmly.

So why the telegram? She linked her arm through his and kept pace as they made their way through the station to the street. They turned into a bar just outside the entrance and he ordered a coffee with a shot of grappa.

Dear God, she thought, her hands suddenly cold, he has come to tell me there is someone else. It was a thought she had never entertained. In the hours, or the minute or so it took for their coffees to arrive, she gave free rein to her imagination and had almost prepared a calm response. If he wanted to be free, she would not beg or entreat, she would be dignified; she would not try to hold him. She felt like a child playing charades: toying with emotions and attitudes and sensations as if they might be real, as if an adult might behave that way.

There was a ringing in her ears. She sipped her coffee and sat back, observing him as he spooned sugar into the coffee and trickled grappa from the bottle. He was very beautiful. He had slowly gained weight since the mountains and it suited him. He still wore his hair long. His restlessness had increased; he fidgeted and fumed at any small wait or delay or impediment to the instant satisfaction of his plans and enthusiasms, but he had always been that way. It was harder to find windmills now. She remembered a time when watching him approach used to make her feel faint with anticipation. She thought she might faint now, but there was no pleasure. Let us get this over with.

'Please tell me now. I think we should discuss whatever is on your mind at once.' She was surprised at how level her voice was.

'Don't be so tragic,' he said. 'It is not the end of the world, you know, *amore*. I want to go to Australia, that is all. Us. I mean, I want us to go to Australia.'

'Australia? What has Australia … got to do with … with us?' She stuttered and stumbled like someone who had fumbled a ball or walked into the wrong room.

He leaned in, his face close to hers, persuasive, tender. He took her hands and played with her numb fingers.

'This country is stuffed. You know it. We all know it. We cannot do anything more here and there is no opportunity for any of us. I have decided to emigrate. To Sydney.'

He had decided! 'But … I … I cannot go to, to Sydney … to …'

'Of course you can.' Briskly. 'Anyway, you have got family there. *We* have got family there.' Then placatingly, he added, 'I love you. I want us to go.'

Family there! As if he wanted anything to do with family. 'Papà sent them out there when we were so young,' she replied. 'We hardly know them.'

That was not true; she was very fond of Bert and Maddie. She had met them and their boys that year when they holidayed in London and Enrico knew it.

She sucked in a deep, raggedy breath. 'That is not the point. I still have years of study and then at least another three for research.'

'*E allora?*' His face said, give that up, it is not important.

'It *is* important! Education is everything, the only way forward for women. I. will. Not. Be. My. Mother!' Her voice rose.

She did not say, think of Elsa. She could not be that cruel. It was the first time in her life they had quarrelled. She felt tears behind her eyes and a tremor began in the centre of her body. Enrico's face was set.

They did not make love, but lay side by side all night, rigid, unyielding. It was two o'clock in the morning for hours and hours. From time to time she moved against him but he was as ungiving as a rock. Enrico was good at anger.

When a grey dawn found them out, he was still angry.

'I thought you believed in Italy,' she said.

'There is no hope in this country. For the country or for us to be together. You know it. *Veritas odit moras*. The truth will take too long in this country. A country run by fucking priests and communists.'

Twenty thousand fascists murdered since the war. Reprisals. No-one felt like a winner.

'We have not just lost the war, we have lost our way,' he said, his voice a little unsteady. 'Everyone wants to close the ledger, go back to normal life.'

'What is a normal life?' Her eyes were puffy, her brain fogged.

'There has been no attempt to come to terms with what happened in this country,' he said, louder, 'either before or during the war – which, God forbid, we should call a civil war. Now it is 'The Resistance', as if we only fought against the Germans, instead of our own people. Or worse, it is a revolution, as if we were all communists.' He was shouting now.

Neither suggested going down for breakfast. Annabelle had a ringing in her ears, which she put down to shock. With all her newly acquired learning, she knew it now as acute stress reaction, but it was still shock to her. Her legs were heavy and numb, her mind oddly detached, exactly as it had been in the mountains after trauma.

'Australia. What on earth will you do there?' Her own voice wobbled.

'If I have to, I'll clean lavatories. It is a new country. They need men there.'

She should not have been surprised, or shocked. Enrico could not accept the peace. Peace did not suit him. War suited him. Danger suited him. He was a conquistador, a *condottiero*, a Soldier of Fortune. He needed a frontier.

But Annabelle had found a place for herself. 'I must stay. We must learn to live this democracy we have been handed.'

'I can't see ... I can't see why ... why you cannot be what you want to be in Australia. I ... I cannot imagine being without you.' Quieter now, he waved a hand vaguely, as if grasping for a stronger argument, and let it fall.

At the station, ready to board his train, he held her and murmured into her hair. 'Come with me.'

The warm scent of him was overwhelming and he held her close, putting his hand inside her coat, with the ball of his thumb gently against her nipple. Through the thin silk of her blouse, the current scorched her. She thought she might die of it.

'Come! We can be everything we ever thought we could be. We can be together. We can leave behind this old country of old men and old lies and live as we lived before.'

Before when? Too much had gone before. Too many things he refused even to talk about. 'I am needed here. I must finish my studies. There is too much to do here.'

They all had blood on their hands, sins on their souls, guilt to expiate, all witting participants. He was running away.

'And me? What about me? I need you.' His bottom lip dropped. 'You know I can make you happy. I love you.'

He rotated his thumb, so very gently, knowing he could almost make her faint. Annabelle pushed back from his chest and looked up into his eyes behind the rimless glasses.

'You are asking too much of me. I will not leave Italy. *We* are needed here.'

There was no pleading in her tone. Whose voice was this? Please do not say this. Do not do this. Yet it was said. It was done.

'Right!' He let her go and stepped back. 'Just remember, you won't be young and beautiful forever.' He wanted to cut now, draw blood, leave wounds.

A spurt of fury singed the skin of her chest. Her voice was hoarse and uneven. '*We* won't be young and beautiful forever. But I will not abandon the country we supposedly fought for.' She wanted to hurt too.

'*E vaffanculo*! Well fuck you!'

With a shove, he turned and walked away towards via Nizza. His neck above the stiff collar was scarlet. The steam hissed about him and he was gone.

Annabelle stood gazing after him until she could see only his fedora above the ghostly vapours, swallowed by the vastness of *Torino Porta Nuova*. He did not turn. She had said nothing about being pregnant.

Florence 1952

Annabelle was home for a week to rest. Another harsh winter had taken its toll on everyone and even she, usually so robust, had succumbed to a bad cold. Hearing the post lady buzz at the door below, she roused herself to collect the mail. She descended the stairs heavily, trailing her hand along the smooth icy iron of the railing. From the last landing, she could see letters protruding from the basket at the bottom of the stairs where Lina the maid had put them.

The top envelope struck her like an emetic. She approached with caution. A cream parchment envelope with deckled edges and Enrico's considered copperplate on the front. She sat on the freezing stone of the bottom step, holding the envelope before her – gingerly, as if it had bacteria on it. No. Not here. She pulled herself back up the stairs, which had grown much steeper.

Annabelle turned up the heating and sat carefully at her desk again, smoothing the envelope with the palm of her hand, then slit the seal.

'I have been offered a job at Sydney University. I am returning to Florence next month. Elisa and I are to be married.'

Elisa … Elisa … Elisa. The words swam together, colours flashed as if she were having a migraine. Her heart swelled and cut off her air supply. He had only been gone twelve months. Elisa. How was that possible? *Now* she was not well. She walked calmly, so very calmly, to the kitchen, wishing she liked grappa or whiskey, or anything at all that was more than twelve per cent alcohol. But the Sangiovese would have to do. She reached down a wineglass, regarded it for a moment, pushed it aside in favour of a large white breakfast cup, which she filled to the brim.

Her mother wandered into the kitchen. Well, said Annabelle, it is nearly lunchtime, isn't it? What times we live in, muttered Eleanora. She waved her hand vaguely at her daughter, obviously thought better of saying more and wandered off again. Annabelle leaned against the counter and sipped the wine slowly then drained the cup and refilled it, slopping ruby droplets as she carried it to the pantry to get another bottle. Back in the kitchen, scrabbling in the drawer for the corkscrew, she knocked the clean wine glass on its side and a shard chipped out.

She was finding it hard to breathe. She opened a window over the sink but it did not help. Carefully, so as not to cut herself – she was pleased with that care – she used the side of her hand to sweep the wineglass from the counter to the floor and watched with satisfaction as it shattered into a thousand sparkling diamonds. She drained the cup, then held it on high and let it fall – that was not as satisfactory. Now she would have to get another.

Florence 1954

Toiling up to the final landing of the stone staircase, laden with the daily shopping, Annabelle could hear her telephone ringing. She made it a rule never to run for the telephone. It stopped just as she entered. The food from Sant'Ambrogio market was still strewn across the kitchen counter when the ringing started again – imperious now. It almost shrilled off the wall and she caught an onion as it rolled from the bench and ran to answer the telephone anyway.

'*Pronto?*'

'*Sono io.* It's me.'

Annabelle prickled all over her body. She held the earpiece away from her face as if it were live. Enrico's voice was tinny through the brass earpiece.

'Where are you?' She knew the answer. She knew.

'I am here. I arrived this morning.'

Several months after Enrico had left for Australia, Annabelle too made the arduous journey to Sydney, in the company of Bert and Maddie whom she had been to meet in London. Come with us, they said, it will do you good, be an adventure. Feeling shaken by the abortion and by events around her, she took time off from the university for the northern summer and travelled to the other end of the earth for the first time. She made the voyage – on the luxurious *Flotta Lauro* vessel, TN *Roma* – in a fug of nausea, swearing she would never get on a ship again as long as she lived.

Enrico had gone to Australia with the intention of remaining there.

Annabelle went as a visitor in the year of the UN Refugee Convention. Australia was in a ferment of immigration and reinvention. Migrants from every strife-torn corner of the earth vied for a place in the sun, in a country with sunshine and work and hope to spare. Britons flooded into the country on assisted passages. Europeans abounded, fleeing the desolation of the continent: Italians, Greeks, Poles, Estonians, Latvians, Balts, Croats, Serbs. Many had survived the concentration camps. Optimism fizzed in the air.

Annabelle loved Sydney and the clean slate it offered. She had never heard an Australian accent. All her Australian relatives called England 'Home' and they all sounded like the King. She was shocked by the Australian idiom in the streets and markets – did these people never open their mouths?

She refused to see or speak to Enrico. She simply had nothing to say to him. It was easy not to take his telephone calls as they all had to be filtered through Maddie and Bert, who understood perfectly why she did not want to communicate with him and so fended him off.

The following year, he and Elisa were married in the Red Room of Palazzo Vecchio. Annabelle stayed in Turin until they departed for Australia.

Now, after two years, there was no-one to defend her, no drawbridge to pull up.

'I want to see you,' he said.

'No,' she replied. Or did she speak? She could not hear her own voice. 'I cannot see you, Enrico. I do not wish to see you.'

He was having none of it. She had not answered his letters, nor taken his long-distance phone calls.

'Enough of this hysterical silence,' he replied brutally. 'I am coming down now. Right now.' He broke off the connection.

Some time later, Annabelle replaced the receiver very gently on its hook, as if great care were now indicated. She sat down, one hand flat on the desk, giving minute attention to the pale squares of her fingernails. She thought of nothing. After a second or two she pushed the chair back like an old woman and shambled into the kitchen where she poked about under the vegetables for the keys she had thrown down with the shopping. The confusion of celery and fennel and capsicums on the pale marble had the look of a still life from another epoch – a time before the phone call.

She unlocked the front door, left it ajar and returned to the study where she sat like an invalid, listening for the footsteps on the stairs.

In a gust of energy through the door, he was there before her. As he had been so many times. She felt a wave of nausea at the familiarity of him.

He paused inside the door and studied her from afar. The man so used to having his own way, so confident, was, she realised, afraid of her reaction. She thought of Françoise Sagan's description of men as strong and childish. Against all her good sense, she was moved. She did not stand though; she was afraid of tottering.

He came to her and knelt at her side, one hand against her cheek. 'Do not say no, my love,' he said. 'Let us not waste another day.'

'You are married,' she said dully. Knowing that was of no importance here.

He said nothing. He remained on his knees on the rug, took her hands and gently drew her forward. Falling, falling, falling.

Enrico wanted to see Fangio race in the Italian Grand Prix. After the tragedy of Le Mans, tensions were high. There were still two weeks left before the university term re-commenced and he swept her along on holiday. Come on, relax, he urged. Always study and research. You work too hard. She said yes, and yes and yes and so he packed a tent and the side-saddlebags of his growling motorbike and they headed for Lago di Garda. Italy was dressed in festive, high summer garb and Annabelle felt silly and young again. She hardly ever did foolish things. Her mother was sulkily disapproving, which only added to the excitement. She was surprised Eleanora even noticed.

They lay in long waving grass and wild perfumed flowers and made love by clear lakes and fields and foraged for *rucola* in the pastures and gorged on bread and cheese and rough wine in the mountain *rifugi* and forgot to be sad. And she was never sorry. At night, tears welled but did not spill.

Annabelle decided then never, ever to be sorry again.

✣

The Dolomites 2005

The last fifty metres were the hardest. They both breathed with difficulty in the thin air and the muscles in Enrico's calves burned and stung. His heart was swollen in his chest but he was exultant. They had followed the razorback ridgeline along the spine of the mountain, a rocky pathway at times no wider than their boots. If you tripped and stumbled up here, you could fall into either Italy or Austria. Now they stood side by side on the highest peak, arms about each other's shoulders, gazing into Austria.

'We are old, my friend, but we can still do it.' He gave Roberto's shoulder a squeeze. He lowered his stick and his *zaino* to the grass and turned slowly, enjoying the sun on his back and the crisp September air and the green of the lower pastures. Cowbells clanged softly from just below them. There was something timeless and reassuring about the seasonal migration of the animals. *La transumanza.* Enrico loved the wait on dirt roads for the animals and their cowherds to pass as they were driven to the high pasture in the spring, then down again to the protection of the lower fields, and then the stall as the cold came on. Soon it would be time to drive the beasts down as autumn drew in, but for now, the last of the summer heat rose in shimmers from the valley floor below.

How different it was here now. Sixty years. A lifetime, many lifetimes. They could stand in the sun, no need to crouch behind machine guns, no longer any need to guard this pass. From deep in the zigzag valley came the echoing rumble and roar of motors. A small column of motorbikes appeared, a trail of growling, whining black insects making a racket out of all proportion to their size as the sound rose on the light air.

'*Tedeschi*,' said Roberto, nodding towards the cavalcade. 'Germans.'
'*Sì*,' replied Enrico. 'But today they're only coming for lunch.'
The two old men sat stiffly and unwrapped their own lunch.

CHAPTER 24

Florence 2008

> *One generation vanishing into another*
> *gone as utterly as we ourselves shall shortly be gone.*
> G M Trevelyan

You could not get a simpler place than Da Rocco – just benches like a canteen or school *mensa*, really. Annabelle was waiting for Delia and her friend. The bustle of Sant'Ambrogio soothed her. Her favourite market. Outside, fruit and vegetable stalls ringed the covered section in an artful seasonal cornucopia reminiscent of Renaissance images of harvest plenty, in Arcimboldo's faces composed of fruit, vegetables, fish and flowers. Inside, mountains of cheese towered over trays of handmade pasta, whole fowl dangled from the ceiling, whole rabbits gazed sightlessly from glass cases, and blankets of tripe and other intestines sagged on vast trays. Annabelle was a hypocrite – she loved meat but turned her face from the spectacle of whole animals with eyes and ears and feet.

'Thank God you aren't eating tripe!' *La trippa fiorentina.* 'Ugh!' Delia shoved her along and sat beside her.

'With you here, there would be no pleasure in it,' Annabelle answered. 'A bowl of *Ribollita* and a glass of wine – what could be better?' She sat back contentedly.

'Ah, here she is,' Delia said. 'Flavia! Here we are.'

Annabelle turned to see a young woman threading her way through the lunchtime crowd and her heart turned right over in her chest.

'*Scusate.*' Flavia was breathless and her flurried arrival gave

Annabelle time to regain her own breath.

Elsa. Elsa. Flavia's delicate features and soft, unruly aureole of chestnut hair, her air of a Waterhouse painting, her penetrating amber eyes. Elsa. Even the long swinging skirt and slightly hippy style was reminiscent of Elsa's floaty clothing, could have *been* Elsa's, bought from some 'vintage' shop. Flavia kissed Delia on both cheeks and held out her hand to Annabelle, who had recovered just enough to respond as if she had not been dealt a blow to her stomach.

'Delia said you are an immunologist,' said Annabelle. In the bustle of ordering food – no wine for Flavia, she was *astemio* – a non-drinker, Annabelle had time to settle. But she needed wine.

'Yes, I trained in Torino but I am working here in Florence now, on a research project. I have read several of your papers on parasites. You have certainly examined some famous dead Italians.'

Annabelle nodded. Yes. Most of her work had centred, though, on rates of larval decomposition and putrefaction in early cadavers. What, she wondered, was the connection with immunology?

'Ah,' replied Flavia, 'not much at all. That is not why I asked Delia to introduce us.'

No. What was of interest to Flavia was Annabelle's time as a partisan, her engagement in the post-war period with liberal causes – divorce, women's rights, abortion and the contraceptive pill, her activities with groups opposed to violence and corruption.

Flavia Levi came from Turin, but her husband was Sicilian. She was born in 1960 and her father and grandfather fought as partisans in Alba. Her grandfather died there. She had two children. They wanted their children to grow up in a country with a fair chance, without *raccomandazione, nepotismo, clientilismo*, and shame. They were involved in campaigns such as *addiopizzo*, the anti-bribery movement in the south, and a group called *RENA* – thousands of young professionals already working together throughout the country for equality, advancement, social change.

'We did not all vote for Berlusconi. We cannot all leave. There are so many of us. Do you know of *Addiopizzo* or *Adesso Ammazzateci Tutti*?'

Addiopizzo – 'Goodbye Bribes', or *Adesso Ammazzateci Tutti* – 'Now Kill us All', the bravery, the courage, the deaths. Of course,

Annabelle knew of these groups. The latter was the first one to use the internet to go after the criminals, a modern-day version of what they themselves did during the war with the clandestine press.

There was, said Flavia, a nationwide tide of people like her. 'We are young. We need your help. There are kids today who do not even know who Mussolini really was. We need your generation. We cannot do this alone.'

'So tell me, what was it that threw you off balance?' Delia asked that evening. Even she knew about *Addiopizzo*, but it was not that, she said, that had discombobulated Annabelle. 'There was something else. You went pale when you saw her.'

For a moment Annabelle hesitated then she leaned across with her elbows on the table. 'Elsa. She is the image of Elsa. It was as if the past sixty-three years had never been.' Her voice trembled and she cleared her throat. 'Elsa, Enrico's mother. She was my ... my adored aunt. They killed her.' The blessed tears that came so much more easily now, brimmed and spilled.

Delia sat still, her hands tightly clasped in her lap.

'For a whole day after Elsa's funeral I could not walk.' Annabelle's knee jumped as if at the memory. 'I was paralysed. I thought if I sat very still, the pain might stop.'

Annabelle massaged her swollen fingers. The hands she used to be so vain about now reminded her of Anna Maria's knobbly knuckles. She shivered.

Elsa was awarded a Gold Medal for Military Valour. There were nineteen women awarded the medal, mostly posthumous. More than a thousand died in combat, nearly five thousand of them were arrested and tortured, nearly three thousand were deported to Germany. So many disappeared.

'You cannot imagine,' Annabelle said, 'what it was like not to hear, to have no idea whether someone was alive or dead. Today it is unthinkable – communication is around us every minute of every day. But then, days, weeks, in some cases months, passed without news. The only safe form of communication was in person. From the moment you parted from someone you would never know their fate until the next time a message came through. By then they could have been dead for a week. Or longer. Or you might never hear again, never know.'

Annabelle snorted. 'And people bang on about the sanctity of human life! No-one truly holds human life sacred. Everyone has their exceptions. Some believe in capital punishment. Look at America and Japan, so called enlightened liberal democracies. Others believe in suicide. Others in euthanasia. Everyone except a few conscientious objectors – pacifists we used to call them – believes in a national army, killing enemies. Many believe in abortion. Most of us would kill for our children or in self-defence. Human life is only sacred to some people at some times in some circumstances.'

'Would you have died for Enrico?'

'Yes. No. I don't know. I suppose so.' Annabelle paused. 'For that brief intense time. It is obsessive, you get caught up in it, so maybe. At the time, but not afterwards.'

They both leaned in, tense and a little anxious.

'History books are full of women who wanted to die beside their man,' Annabelle continued. 'Think of Anita and Garibaldi, Eva Braun, Goebbels' wife and children, and Clara Petacci – they were very similar. It's a pathology.'

Clara. So long since she had thought of Claretta.

The war gave Annabelle a distinct outlook on the human body, she said. The body itself was just a carapace. Once human consciousness – call it what you will: mind, spirit, soul – once that is gone, there is nothing left but the shell. Snakes, molluscs and crabs shed their skin or shell, their outer casing, while they are alive. Once we leave ours, there is nothing left but the memory of us in the hearts of others. But the casing itself can teach us a great deal about humans. Fascinating, that gossamer line between a living being and a cadaver. That was why she chose forensic medicine. It was how she came face to face with Clara for the first time, when she examined the file on her ruined corpse, years later. The photos of Clara's body showed a bullet wound to the throat, just below the jawline, exactly where Elsa's had been. Clara too was brave in her own way, at the end.

'It's all hindsight now, but today we would call Mussolini's relationship with Clara co-dependent, from the moment they became lovers. In a way, people were right that she was the cause of his madness, but he was already losing control. His spiral into madness began earlier.'

Clara was not alone in her obsession with Mussolini. A cult, Elsa had called it – they were all in love with him. There was a bizarre sensual element to the adoration. Ciano once called him 'The sun of my life'. Hitler idolised him to the point of embarrassment; women he had never met sent him their underwear; his ministers described their love for him in carnal terms. Love and war. Eros and Thanatos, who can explain these things? He was not beautiful but he was charismatic.

'There was absolutely nothing wrong with him, you know,' said Annabelle. 'Apart from being shot. As healthy as a bull. He was just a hypochondriac, it seems.' At the autopsy, his corpse measured only 5 foot 3. Not unusual for the times. Silvio Berlusconi could not be much taller. He had his own, inexplicable charisma.

When the corpses of Ben and Clara were cut down from the scaffolding in Piazzale Loreto, Mussolini's adventures continued. Photographs of both their bodies and of his beaten and disfigured face circulated freely, ghoulish confirmation the monster was dead.

Delia shivered. Outside the windows, the air was redolent of the tripe stand and the 'Eau de Firenze' of the drains.

'I'm off to bed.' She kissed Annabelle gently on her head.

Annabelle drifted to her desk and took up the diary she had begun writing a few days before.

> *We went out of fashion. No longer 'di moda'. We were heroes there for a few minutes but we did not feel like heroes. I want people to know that partisan does not equal communist. I saw a photo of a group taken on the day Florence was abandoned by the Germans: they all wore their star proudly and I wish them well. Now the pendulum swings and there is even talk of a medal for Mario. He has been dead since 1938! I did understand why Enrico could not stomach it.*
>
> *I can see why Communism was appealing, to women.*

We all had to fill men's shoes during the war and then at its end, we were expected to return to the kitchen. So many did. I have always marvelled at that. But not in Russia. There were women fighter pilots during the war there, then after, they had free education, religion removed from the centre of life, child minding. By the time they realised the price, it was too late.

1980s mani pulite. With the Clean Hands campaign we hoped then too for a big change, a turning point but instead …

Whining. Repetitive. Old people do this, whine about the past. Why had she not thought that other young people would take up the baton? Why would there be less courage today? Some of those she had agreed to meet through Flavia were inspirational, their courage every bit as great as their own had been. Where had hers gone to in recent times? Many people had continued the struggle. The communists were not the bogeymen. For many, it was the only meaningful way of opposing fascism. They sheared away from Stalinism in the post-war period and Berlinguer was a decent person. They did not mean to steal our Resistance, there were just more of them and they had a clearer objective. She herself, as Flavia had reminded her, still believed in struggle, or did until not long ago.

Outside, the city slept, undisturbed by the occasional whine of a Vespa. Delia was not undisturbed, did not sleep. Italy was not just food and wine and *la dolce vita*. Of course Italy had its dark side. But Annabelle had always known that, always known the right course to take, too. She was always more sure of herself. Like Enrico. Maybe it was their generation, what they went through, that made them less inclined to worry about being right or wrong. They simply pushed ahead. Sometimes though, they could be wrong, and this was one of those times. This wanting to leave seems to have come out of nowhere. She could not see Annabelle leaving forever and being happy. Not the right move. Italians couldn't just up and leave, not without too much loss, too much pain. Annabelle was used to her life of coming and going, but she was deeply Italian, more perhaps than she herself realised, and Italy was not the black hole she presently saw. Italy could be wonderful. Two years earlier, they watched on TV as a ship loaded with Libyan refugees limped its way into the port of Lampedusa. The *Carabinieri* waiting on the docks, armed like riot police with helmets, shields and machine guns, had instructions from the government to prevent the refugees landing. The leaky ship came on, lowering, lumbering, unstoppable. As it shuddered against the dock and pitiable people threw themselves over the rails and down the gangplanks, the *Carabinieri* were at first hesitant, nonplussed. Then they simply laid down their weapons, took up the scabrous, malnourished children with eyes too big for their heads; the stumbling, women clutching babies their empty breasts could not feed; the frail men with vacant eyes, and carried them to the sheds.

'Well, what do they expect us to do?' said one stocky officer to the swarming journalists. 'Shoot them?' His eyes glittered and one young corporal wept openly.

Italy was a more compassionate society than Australia.

Delia was not a complete outsider. She took out Italian citizenship as soon as dual citizenship became available in the April of 2002. For purely pragmatic reasons – to have EU citizenship. Who wouldn't? Someone once wrote that Australia has no history; that is at once its disadvantage and its great benefit. She agreed. She loved her attachment to the unwinding skein of the past in Florence, but even more, she loved the absence of the weight of what had gone before, in Australia. The inclination to innovate, to 'give it a go', to do things differently. To experiment with food. To go barefoot. To never use the formal 'lei'. To feel affronted at inequalities. To sit in the front seat in a taxi. She loved the light and the landscape. White Australians *could* have a visceral attachment to the place of their birth, but never the mystical umbilical cord of the original inhabitants, nor the *campanilismo* and links to the soil of Italians. To Delia, that was a relief, a freedom.

Over the years, she had read Berlusconi's egregious comments as comedy instead of tragedy. Just another B-grade actor in a pornographic film. There were long internet lists of his gaffes and outrages:

The worst thing Mussolini did was the racial laws,

but apart from that, he did well ... If, in taking care
of everyone's interests, I take care of my own, you can't
call that a conflict of interest ... Today we have fewer
communists and those who are here deny having been
one ... And we have beautiful secretaries.

It no longer felt funny.

'Italians,' Roberto once said, 'do not learn from the past. They live in the continuous present.'

Italy was a difficult love, but Delia did love it, despite being permanently perplexed at dealing with the daily anxieties. How much should she tip the man who helped her when the wheel fell off her suitcase? Should she leave a tip in a bar where the staff had been surly? Should she buy tissues and umbrellas from the African street hawkers? If not, how were they to survive? What about being constantly accosted by young people to sign petitions 'against drugs', petitions they knew were invalid? Were they in some way being exploited and if so, by whom? Even the beggars in Florence worried her – should she give something to the man who plays the accordion? Or what about the heap of rags on the footpath with a cardboard cup before it, which stirs nothing but revulsion in her and that she knows to be an old woman? Or the shuffling gnome in SM Novella who sidles up, every single time, with a confiding 'How about a coffee for an old friend?' Real Italians knew how to get it right. For Delia it was still hard to know how to respond. In Sydney, you just voted Green and bought *The Big Issue*. Much easier.

She was shocked by the lacunae in her knowledge of Annabelle's life – so many things she did not know about her aunt. In some odd way she had assumed, as children do, that Annabelle's life was on pause when Delia was not in it. She conceived of Annabelle's life as a series of scenes – scenes featuring herself. She remembered being taken to mass in the Duomo as a child. They still went. Not for the mass itself, Annabelle told her, but for the awe and wonder to be found in that soaring edifice after it closed for the day to the flocks of earnest tourists. For reflection, she said. Annabelle loved ecclesiastical music and architecture, therefore so did Delia.

Annabelle taught her to row. She took her down deep into

the cavern beneath the Uffizi, to the seat of the *Società Canottieri Fiorentini*, the Florence Rowing Club, with its room of polished mahogany and burnished silver trophies, its racks and racks of sleek rowing shells and sculls, some fibreglass and others of gleaming wood dating back to the 1880s. She was terrified on the soupy water of the Arno, the fishing weirs and swirling eddies, but if Annabelle was not afraid, then she would not be afraid. All her life she had watched Annabelle writing in her diaries. She had snooped and spied too, at times confused, at times worried by their contents, but only really interested when her own name jumped out, her exploits lauded, her stories retold, her misdeeds recast in a softer, more indulgent light. Now they had tilted her world sideways.

Delia knew well the power and the limitations of diaries. She had worked from letters and diaries for most of her professional life. Diaries could be dangerous for many reasons. Annabelle admitted she more often wrote in her diary when she was angry or sad or nostalgic, but rarely of the mundane and quotidian. Her diaries presented a heightened emotional picture of a life with many, many calm, uneventful periods that went unrecorded. Some people, Annabelle said, only write when they are in love, or others when they are heart-broken. Some write to explicate, some to obfuscate. They are not the truth, but what we felt at the time. Others write to skew the story, to have the last word – what we wanted to leave as our version.

Now this sudden talk of leaving, destroying her diaries. Primary sources – those precious documents no historian could bear to see destroyed. Much of the contents of the diaries was disturbing, even now. Did Annabelle have the right to destroy them? Did she really want to? Did anyone really want their diaries destroyed? Enrico's favourite book, Marcus Aurelius' *Meditations*, was really called, *To Myself* – a diary, or journal. What if that had been destroyed? Truth was important, even if it made for personal discomfort. That was why Delia had introduced her to Flavia. Annabelle was not afraid of danger. Why was she afraid of the truth?

Delia knew Italy's murderous history, but in an abstract, detached way. She could not actually feel the fear. There was a time when she found the uncertainty of life in Europe exhilarating. When contingency polished the edge of each day to a fine, sharp clarity. But she was getting tired of living at altitude. She had fallen in and out of love with Italy a hundred times over the years. Just when she decided to leave forever, Italy would charm her back again, like a lover who mistreats you and then begs and pleads until you take him back. Maybe Annabelle *should* come back to Oz? She gave herself a mental shaking and turned back to her present – a present knocked askew by the past.

'Mum and Dad worried about the conditions here, but they were happy to send me to you to soften the teenage rebellion. I *was* a very naughty child. Granny was horrified by my behaviour.' Granny was Maddie's mother. Delia had not known Eleanora.

'Well, there was a lot to be worried about here,' replied Annabelle. 'Mothers do worry.'

'What was your mother like? You always sound a little dismissive of her.'

'She was lovely, I think, but … I hardly knew her and I did not give her much of a chance to know me. I was not very kind.' Annabelle chewed her bottom lip. 'She was subsumed by my father, and the times, and the war. The war took everything and everyone from her.'

Achille died, Giacomo died without ever seeing her again, Umberto did not return and Eleanora refused to travel to Australia. Annabelle returned as another person. For the years remaining to her, Eleanora polished teaspoons, snipped roses and meandered through memories of happier times. She was one of many. Delia only knew one grandparent. In the 1950s there were fewer men left than women. Her grandfather, Sir Michael Morton, died the year she was born. The Mortons were not as illustrious as the Albizzi, or the Drummonds who were descended from one of the great recusant families of England, but Granny Morton had more pretensions. She was very much the Grand Dame, quite imperious, but kindly. She left little mark on Delia.

Annabelle paused, with a heavy white plate ready for the dishwasher. She had splashed tomato sauce on her pyjama top.

'Nothing Napisan won't get out.' Delia said.

'Another wonderful modern invention. The thing I appreciate most about today is comfort. Comfort is a modern concept. You lot have only ever known comfort.'

There was, she said, no comfort in the mountains, only pain and discomfort. 'If you had a wound or dysentery you could very easily die ... and in the mountains we soon learned not to be coy about bodily functions. Dysentery and vomiting and rotting corpses. Every time I use a clean white porcelain lavatory, I am grateful.'

Later, closing up before bed, Delia said, 'Australia's not Nirvana, you know. Italians might think *furbo,* cunning, is an attribute instead of a fault, but they are kind, not bitter and angry.'

Italians in the post-war period were not bitterly anti-German in the way many Australians were anti-Japanese. Today, she continued, Italians are not as angry. Italians are a gentler, kinder people in so many ways. Their treatment of refugees, their lower rates of rape and violence, of alcohol abuse. Kinder than Australians. They do not have a term for road rage. Delia once saw a hand-written sign, on brown paper, taped to the windscreen of a car parked at a crazy angle, blocking the doorway to a house.

'If you fuck like you park,' it read, 'don't be surprised to find yourself cuckolded.'

Outside in the street, tourists threw themselves daily under the spell of Florence, willing victims of Stendhal Syndrome. Who was to say they were wrong?

'Who said Italy has always conducted its whole life and politics in the piazza instead of at the ballot box? Berlusconi, too, will pass.' Delia stretched and yawned.

The dawn sky was the colour of the lapis in a Fra Angelico painting.

April limped to a close, not yet warm. Annabelle trailed about the house, assailed by a deep melancholy, by wistfulness, nostalgia, remembrance, *bramare* – to yearn. The word drew her back to her childhood. She shivered and prayed for a warm May. Not the heat of July or August. A gentle warmth, a healing warmth, a balm. In his later years, Enrico never, ever came to Italy in the summertime. He hated the heat and he hated the beach, in Italy or in Australia. The sight of glistening mahogany bodies stretched out side by side on the baking sands of Riccione or Bondi made him fulminate. Fulminate was the word for Enrico. He held no moderate opinions: either he could not care less or he fulminated.

He understood tenderness, though. He would tuck a strand of hair behind Annabelle's ear with the softest touch, take her hand to help with the sleeve of a cardigan, sing her to sleep, recount stories. She was spellbound. No-one ever made her so angry, no-one ever gave her such joy. There was no middle ground for Enrico. He lived on the heights and he could take you there with him.

All their lives she vibrated with the sense of him. When he was close by, the chemistry of the body told her, without turning her head, he was in the room. At night, watching him breathe, watching him sleep. Enrico too. Never for a moment was he unaware of her presence. The heat of his knowing warmed her, scorched her. Even if they were not speaking, even if he was flirting with another woman, he would reach behind him in a crowd, find her hand, draw her to his side. Now he had left her.

It was not his fault. Annabelle had invented Enrico. A lonely, enclosed, romantic child, she invented him because she needed him. He could never have been the character she drew for him. He was busy drawing his own character, just as difficult to inhabit. His too, was a childhood lived through books, but where Annabelle sighed with Leopardi, Enrico greedily consumed heroes, or Dickens' characters – 'reading as if for life'. He shared 'an undisciplined heart' with David Copperfield, and his fascination with Australia, which stood for freedom to him. She should always have known he would go there.

Sometimes she felt Enrico would walk up to her on the street and say, 'Where have you been, I've been searching for you.' Often, her heart skittered at a familiar walk, a turn of the head, a hat, a coat, or a glimpse in a mirror or a shop window. She listened over and over to his last message on her phone.

His death catapulted her into old age. She was in shock, not that he was dead but that she was old and it was all over. Her run was up. She knew she might not die yet for ages, but she was shocked to realise that her lease, too, was nearly up. She felt like Rip Van Winkle, awakened after a long sleep to find herself old and the world changed. So we are mortal after all. Damn! She did not feel old: her hearing was perfect, her sight excellent, her knees worked fairly well, she had no arthritis of which to complain, only the knobbly hands. She was in perfect, rude good health. She was just surprised. Having evaded Death in all His terrible force, so many times, it amused her to think she had forgotten that sooner or later, He would find her.

It was like a dream. Or a dream of a dream.

'I could wait another few days …' Delia had to go. To London, then to Sydney. Her voice wobbled.

'I … No. We both need to take up life again.' Annabelle's voice was firm but gravelly. 'You have a book to sell.'

'I have a lot of gaps to fill, thinking to do.' Delia's eyes glittered, her chin quivered.

They both badly needed to step back. Had a lot of pondering to do, a lot to mull over. Nothing was the same as before.

'I will be there next month,' Annabelle said, 'and you will be back in October.'

It was time. They were tired, claustrophobic – characters on a stage too small for them. For three weeks they had barely left the house, talked themselves to a standstill, picked at scabs, skirted too many dangers, buried more than they had uncovered. It was time to stop. Annabelle had a ticket for Sydney in a couple of weeks, but sooner or later, she would be back. For all its faults, Florence was where she belonged, and where she would probably stay. That lush, brash city at the other end of the world was not her city. Not really. Lucky she had come to her senses – she would never be able to close up this house anyway. It was not even possible to remove the furniture from a building as old as this without a crane to take the stuff out by the windows, and what would she do with it anyway? It was only stuff to her now, and it would all be Delia's. It was time to think about her legacy. She would leave no letters, no diaries, no documents, no problems. She would be methodical, she would search through drawers and cupboards and hidey holes. No love letters in the back of *her* drawers. Nothing for posterity.

Annabelle dragged out the little toolbox she used for household tasks and took out a screwdriver. She tugged a stepladder into a back bedroom, never used, inhabited by the largest *armadio* of the whole house, which came apart into four pieces. It had a false back – one of the very few secret places Dellie had not discovered. While Delia was in Prato for the day, it was time to start. She tossed out old wellington boots and galoshes, prised off the back with surprising difficulty, slid out a cardboard box and carried it to her study. She knelt on the floor beside her desk.

A yellowed folder sat on top of the box. She blew off the dust and opened it. Sepia images from the time in the mountains – a happy shot of Enrico reclining in the sun in a moment of repose, his bare chest burnished, gleaming with sweat; sickening images of hanging bodies – evidence never used; handwritten notes stained with sweat, mud, rusty flecks of blood. Last century. The room smelled of mould. She shifted uncomfortably on her knees, pulled a dusty cushion from the bed, sat cross-legged and began to sift. Diaries first.

August 1945, just a month before they went off to university as if they were innocent. They had managed seventy years without a word.

March of 1954. They would have been better off without a word.

Truth. Confession was for cowards. Despicable. She loved Delia more than any living creature. She could never have imagined the power of such a love and would never tear away her past. *You do not know, my dear*, she thought, *what you ask when you say you want the truth.* Delia was happy, her life was rich and full. The past was dead people. The present was for the living. Delia's life, Flavia's life, the continuum. She sat back on her cushion, easing her stiffening legs. We Italians must resolve our own problems. We must all go on. Things go on. People go on. Piazza Tasso now hosts a festival of food. Despite all, Carla Capponi married Rosario Bentivegna, had children, lived in Rome, died of old age. Even Rachele lived out her life in Predappio and ran a restaurant with Vittorio, who came back from Argentina. People go on.

We must talk, she had said to Enrico on her birthday. Yes, he said, we must talk. So they sat at the table in Omero's and talked, but the words missed each other. The time for talking, it turned out, was past.

Florence 1945

> *We cross a line. We decide killing is justified. We have no choice, do we? After that, nothing is taboo. Nothing is unthinkable. We are Freedom Fighters. We are heroes. We have right on our side. Then wars end. We sleep and try to forget. But beneath it all we are still killers. We stand on the other side of that line. They were seated on hard kitchen chairs ...*

August 1945

They were seated on hard kitchen chairs, against the wall. Annabelle carried a coiled rope on her belt, but they were not tied up.

'It was you. We know it was you.' Say no. Say no.

Annabelle looked the old woman directly in the eyes, averting her gaze from the sagging stockings, the pink scalp visible through straggly grey hair. She wished they had never known. She closed her mind to the old-woman smell. She would not allow pity – it was not as hard as she had expected.

Anna Maria was defiant. In her lap her hands moved, telling the beads of her rosary. She knew they would not shoot her.

'It was all her fault. Her own son, she sent him off. She sent you off too. She made you all do it. You think I am stupid. Deaf. I am not. I knew it was her doing.'

They had given her a choice, the militia, between her own daughter and Elsa. Paolo, the sergeant, had said to her, what are these people to you, anyway? He was right. What had Elsa's class ever done for her? What had they ever done but use them? Pass you in the street half the time, they would, without giving you the time of day. Did they care when her babies died? Where were they when Sesto nearly died in the accident in the mountains? If you cut us, do we not bleed like them? Are we not all God's creatures? Although *Il Signore* seems to have gone missing lately. She hurriedly crossed herself and turned to be sure he had missed that. She was beginning to sound like those communists, she was. She never thought for a minute they would have killed the *Signora* Elsa. Who could have thought it? Now she was damned. Damned. She crossed herself again.

'Lorenzo gone, *povero ragazzo*.' Anna Maria sniffled. 'You all gone. Gino gone, they had him. They told me if I did not tell them, they would kill Gino and my daughter and the children. They said they deserved to die for betraying the country but I could save them if I told them about all of you – I had no idea where you were. I only knew about the *Signora* Elsa. And they killed him anyway, those *fascisti*, they killed Gino after I told them what they wanted to know.' Then aggressively, 'Sesto had nothing to do with it.'

Sesto shook his head at her. He was as pale as his wife was florid. 'No. I knew. We agreed. We did not think they would kill her.'

He caved inwards upon himself, collapsing into his own frame. 'So now you are doing to us what was done to her.'

He gazed intently at some point in the far corner of the room, some small object visible only to him.

'No. Not what was done to her.'

Annabelle heard a ringing in her ears as she lifted the pistol to his head. She thought her eardrums would explode with the shot. Her hand did not tremble. Enrico's shot followed as closely as an echo. Sesto's body slumped forward but Enrico held the back of his arm across Anna Maria, who looked strangely alive. Enrico's shot had taken only the back of her head. He rested her against the mess on the wall, put his head out the window and whistled to Roberto to bring the tarpaulins. They were not worried about witnesses. They had not been able to get silencers for the Berettas but the shots evaporated into the dark cotton-wool night. No-one ventured out to investigate shots in those times of retribution. Eyes shut tight, ears stopped right. That was how people managed to live – little different from the years of fascism, really. Would it ever be different? They were all truly murderers now.

❦

Florence 2008

One foot on the threshold, an arm tensed to hold back the great studded *portone*, Annabelle waved one last time as Delia's taxi disappeared, then she turned back into the courtyard. Her eyes brimmed. She might as well collect the mail since she was down there. The elegant, intricately worked brass letterbox engraved with *posta*, set into the front wall of the building, once held all the mail for the household. Now it gaped empty, a toothless gargoyle. The letters and glossy brochures advertising takeaway pizza and bicycle tours and washing machines were shoved into an ugly modern bank of letterboxes in the foyer serving the little shops and restaurants whose owners rented the ground floor premises. For a moment, she saw the bobbing heads of fractious families crowded into that space during the war, heard the hubbub, smelled the sweat, the oil, the cooking fires. She tugged her mail out, sorting the junk mail into the bin under the mailboxes. Among the medical journals and bills was a large buff envelope from Maddie. Must be stuff to do with Enrico's estate, she thought, taking the back stairway up to her study.

Annabelle made herself a coffee and carried it to the little terrace giving onto the old courtyard. It was barely warm enough to sit outside yet, but the sun was out, the apricot trees were in bud, crocus peeped through and irises spread in a carpet of purple in the garden below. The iris – symbol of Florence, symbol of spring. Her favourite flower. Her favourite word.

She slit the top of Maddie's envelope to find an A4 sheet folded in two and stapled. In Maddie's scatty writing, sloping airily up towards a corner, it said:

> *Darling Belle. Inside is a letter for you from Enrico. It*
> *was sealed and addressed and we found it on his desk.*
> *No stamp, so he hadn't got around to posting it. I am*
> *thinking of you. All my love. Maddie*

With her fingernail, Annabelle prised the staple out, and sat for long moments, her heart drumming. She pressed on the staple until it bit into her finger. Stopped just short of drawing blood. What if

I do not open it, she wondered. Slowly, she drew the envelope from its sheath. Enrico's writing did not slope, but ran straight and true. She tore one end roughly and drew out the single sheet. The heavy parchment, filled with Enrico's looping ornate hand, had the look of Dickens.

> *Amore mio. My time is up. You are my love. You have always been my love. I have been angry with you and with myself. Now it is too late. You should have told me. Why did you not tell me? You said it would have made no difference. Perhaps you were right.*
>
> *You wanted to talk. You wanted absolution. There is none. We carry our sins within us. We did what we did. We were who we were. The times were what they were. Punto e basta. We wrote our own story. More words would not have helped. Nor all thy tears wash out a word of it. You always worried too much.*
>
> *We were young. We were full of romance and rebellion. We had the courage you only have when you have no idea what will be asked of you. The other sort of courage comes later when you no longer have a choice. When your innocence has been burnt to a cinder and you have grown old in the space of twenty months. In those days when we said Viva l'Italia we did not have to be ashamed of saying it. We still thought it was an idea worth fighting for. They were the last words of so many of our friends.*
>
> *Why did you not tell me sooner about Delia? I could not forgive you for not telling me. I have known Delia all her life and I cannot understand how I did not know. Perhaps the fact that I did not realise explains everything. I have been wilfully blind. I was not a bad father, in the end. A bad husband, a bad lover, but not a bad father. Things could have been different.*
>
> *Why did you care about us being cousins? Now none of it matters. Remember this. I have always loved you. I love you still. I have loved you all my life. The only promise I ever kept.*
>
> *Sempre tuo Enrico*

It was still cool enough for a fire. Annabelle huffed and puffed, lugging and lurching a heavy brass bucket of kindling up the iron stairway from the courtyard – the dried cuttings of olive trees and grapevines from Impruneta. In her study, she laid the fire with ceremony. She screwed spills of *Il Corriere della Sera* from the fifteenth, piled coals over the starter bricks, arranged the kindling in a cross-hatch, arrayed logs in a pleasing teepee. She flicked the Imco lighter until it flared, and lit a corner of the newspaper. The flames licked along the paper and up through the intricate little edifice and she wiped her blackened fingers on her trousers. She drew the curtains and lit the lamps – only the old ones, not the Castiglioni – and the shadows danced and the timber gleamed and the colours glowed, as they did when it was her father's *studiolo*. On the Persian rug before the fire, she sat back on her heels. If she screwed up her eyes just so, she could make out the pea-sized burn from a cinder long spent, the ebony centre of a faded dusky rose medallion. The smell of scorched silk and her father's dismay. She felt for its rough edge with her forefinger.

When the flames played high enough and embers glowed, she placed another log in a glitter of sparks, then rose with a creaky groan and fetched the folder and the box. On the way, she collected her phone from the desk, tore the page from the other day from her diary and dragged a cushion onto the carpet – her knees could only take so much. She had already pulled the covers off the two diaries, and slowly, with patience, she fed them, a page at a time, to the flames. Then the photos. She had all the time in the world. She laid Enrico's letter on the top. The heat scorched her cheeks. The parchment curled at the corners, writhed and twisted, the letters contorting, cavorting, as the words, Enrico's words, flew upwards on the sparks – like transubstantiation.

While the diaries burned steadily in flames of azure, pink and gold, drifting in silvered tissue to the bottom of the grate, she rose again and returned with the Qantas ticket for Sydney, laid it onto the pyre. In the rainbow blaze from the glossy cover, she scanned through her phone messages, listened once more, pushed delete. She believed in Italy, in Europe – beautiful, ugly, resilient Europe. She belonged to the world of Nonna Lucrezia, not the shiny world of faraway Nonna Annabelle. Australia was Delia's country. It was not hers.

Tomorrow she would telephone Flavia. All she had was a voice and she would raise her voice. In the end, roots are important. Italy is not a bad county. It is a mad country. Sometimes a sad country. Often dangerous to know. But it is a great country. It is her country. The only place she can forgive and be forgiven.

> *Dead my old fine hopes*
> *And dry my dreaming but still ...*
> *Iris, blue each spring*

ACKNOWLEDGEMENTS

This is a work of fiction, not of history. Although I have tried to be faithful to historic events, I have elided timelines where I felt the narrative required it. Annabelle, Enrico, Delia and their family members are entirely fictional characters, bearing no relation to real people. For many of their experiences I drew on the works listed here. Ben and Clara are also fictionalised characters constructed from my interpretation of diaries, reports and histories.

This book was inspired, firstly, by the works of Beppe Fenoglio and in particular, *Il Partigiano Johnny*, from where the heading within Chapter 3, 'The wrong sector of the right side', is drawn. Aspects of Enrico's character were influenced by the writings of Fenoglio, and of course, by Primo Levi. The life and words of Renata Viganò and Rosetta Solari Knox were the inspiration for much of Annabelle's story. Carla Capponi, Gino Bartali, Ettore Castiglione and the heroes of Radio CORA were real. I owe a huge debt to these people, without whose stories I could not have written this book. I want to acknowledge the courage and the memory of all the women and the men, so very many of them, who fought this battle – all those whose memories I have incorporated into this work. I only hope I have been faithful to them.

My thanks to Sandy McCutcheon who told me many years ago that I could do this; to Lisa Clifford, whose encouragement early on, was pivotal; to Di Blacklock, without whose severity this book would have been unreadable; and to Joel Naoum for his support and guidance. I would also like to thank Kathryn Heyman for advice, and the NSWWC for providing writing space when things got too hectic in my own study. One section of this book was written at Varuna, the beautiful writers' retreat in the Blue Mountains, and another in the wonderful Harold Acton Library of the British Institute of Florence. I am grateful to Tara Wynne for her generosity and clear-sighted appraisal of the manuscript in its early form and to Anna Rosner Blay and Louis de Vries for having faith in it at the end.

And to John, Andrew, Phillip and Trish, whose support never wavers.

For much of the Florence history, I am indebted to the files of ANPI (National Association of Italian Partisans) and, particularly, sections on the women partisans, the *donne partigiane*; also to the *Archivio storico della Città* (The Florence City Archives) and to the archives of the ISRT (The Institute for the Study of the Tuscan Resistance). I was thankful for the opportunity to read the works of Paolo Monelli in the library of The British Institute of Florence.

For the broader history, I am grateful to writers such as Italo Calvino, Ignazio Silone and Cesare Pavese; to journalists Enzo Biagi and Giorgio Bocca; and historians Richard Bosworth and Ray Mosely whose work is fundamental to an understanding of Mussolini. The work of writers such as James Holland, Robert M Edsel, Christopher Duggan, Thomas R Brooks and many others gave me the background and setting to World War II in Italy and Florence. Each of them inspired elements of the story.

GLOSSARY

acqua passata: water under the bridge

addiopizzo: no more bribes

alea iacta est (Latin): the die is cast

amore mio: my love

armadio: large wardrobe

asino: donkey

babbo: Tuscan term for dad

baita: log or stone mountain hut; also see *capann*a

Balilla Giovani Italiani: Fascist Boys Brigade

baracca: hut or shack or even hovel

bici: bike

bosco: woods, forest

brigata: brigade

Calcio: football/soccer

campanilismo: parochialism

cancello: gate

capo squadra: leader

Carabinieri: military police

carità: charity

Caserma: military barracks

caspita: good heavens!

chi c'è: who is there?

chiasso/chiassi: noisy, narrow little laneways in Florence

ciabatte: slippers

ciccia: endearment/sweetie

cinghiale: wild boar

clientilismo: patronage, or the granting of political favours to supporters

CLN: Committee of National Liberation. It was comprised mainly of Communist Garibaldi brigades, Justice and Liberty Brigades and the Socialist Matteotti Brigades

come un corpo morto cadde: Dante – like a dead body

contadino/contadini: rural peasants

cortile: internal courtyard

cotto: terra cotta tiles

deficiente: idiot

Dio infame: curse – God Almighty!

dopolavoro: after work

e allora?: So? Now what?

Eviva Il Duce: Long live the Duce

fattore: farm manager

fattoria: farm

fazzoletti: the neck scarves worn by the partisans, red, green, blue. Red for the communist Garibaldi brigades, green for the Justice and Liberty brigades (GL). The various groups distinguished themselves by their *fazzoletti* and their insignia – the red star for the communists and the red flame for the GL

Ferragosto: August 15 – the start of the summer holidays; Holiday of Augustus *fesso*: fool

forno: oven

GAP: 'Patriotic Action Group' of the communist Garibaldi brigades

Gapisti: fighters of the GAP

Garibaldini: communist partisans

Giellisti: members of the GL, *Brigate Giustizia e Libertà*, Justice and Liberty Brigades

Giustizia e Libertà: Justice and Liberty

Il Cenacolo: The Last Supper

il dado e tratto: the die is cast

inglesi: the English

l'eminenza grigia: the power behind the throne

Le Murate: the city prison

Lenci doll: a brand of children's doll

Liceo classico: classical studies

Liceo scientifico: scientific studies

lunedi il 9 maggio: Monday 9 March

lupo: wolf

Mantovano fu: this is a reference to Virgil – 'He came from Mantova'

maresciallo: marshall

mezzadria: share-farming

mitra: machine-gun

motorino: scooter

nepotismo: nepotism, the favouring of friends and family in business and politics

Oddio!: My God!

OVRA: *Organizzazione per la Vigilanza e la Repressione dell'Antifascismo*

– Mussolini's secret police, founded in 1927

partigiani: partisans

Partito D'Azione: Action Party

piano nobile: first floor/formal rooms

Piccole Italiane: Italian Girls Brigade

porci fascisti: fascist pigs

portone: the heavy wooden external doors to the street. They usually have a smaller door cut into them for pedestrian entry

posta: mail

poverini: poor things

pozzo: a well

raccolta: olive harvest

raccomandazione: nepotism; the favouring of those who come recommended by friends and allies

ragazzi/ragazzo: boys/girls

ribelli: rebels

ribollita: a thick, heavy Tuscan soup of bread and beans

rifugi: plural mountain hut/refuge

RSI: Republican National Army formed by Mussolini in 1943

salotto: sitting room

SAP: Patriotic Action Squad of the GAP

schiacciata: saltless Tuscan bread

sempre: always

senti amico: listen, my friend

senti bello: listen, my friend

sentiero: track, pathway

staffetta: women and boys who carried the news and information and supported the partisans

stalla: stable

stella: star

studiolo: study

tagliere: wooden board

tenente: lieutenant

tesoro: endearment /treasure

'Tu scendi dalle stelle': Italian Christmas carol

Va bene: okay

vendemmia: wine harvest

Veritas odit moras (Latin): Seneca – Truth hates delay

vicoli: allies/laneways

zaino: rucksack

Zia: Aunt

Zio: Uncle

zoccoli: wooden clogs

Printed in June 2023
by Rotomail Italia S.p.A., Vignate (MI) - Italy